# JOHN UPDIKE

## RABBIT IS RICH

Penguin Books

Penguin Books Ltd., Harmondsworth, Middlesex, England
Penguin Books, 625 Madison Avenue, New York, New York 10022, U.S.A.
Penguin Books Australia Ltd, Ringwood, Victoria, Australia
Penguin Books Canada Ltd, 2801 John Street, Markham, Ontario, Canada L3R 1B4
Penguin Books (N.Z.) Ltd, 182–190 Wairau Road, Auckland 10, New Zealand

First published by André Deutsch Limited 1982
Published in Penguin Books 1982
Reprinted 1983

All characters, localities, and business establishments represented in this
book are fictional, and any resemblance to actual places or to persons living
or dead is purely coincidental. No actual Toyota agency in southeastern
Pennsylvania is known to the author or in any way depicted herein.

Grateful acknowledgement is made to the following for permission to
reprint from previously published material:
Alfred A. Knopf, Inc.: Excerpt from 'A Rabbit as King of the Ghosts'
by Wallace Stevens. From *The Collected Poems of Wallace Stevens*.
Copyright 1942 by Wallace Stevens, copyright renewed 1970 by Holly
Stevens. Used by permission.
Rightsong Music, Inc.: Excerpts from 'Hot Stuff' by Pete Bellotte,
Harold Faltermeyer, and Keith Forsey. Copyright © 1979 by Rick's
Music, Inc. Excerpt from 'One Night in a Lifetime' by Pete Bellotte and
Harold Faltermeyer. Copyright © 1979 by Rick's Music, Inc., and
Revelation Music/Ed. Intro. Published in the U.S.A. by Rightsong Music,
Inc. Excerpt from 'Can't Get to Sleep at Night' by Bob Conti and Bruce
Sudano. Copyright © 1979 by Rick's Music, Inc., Earborn Music, Inc.,
throughout the world. International Copyright Secured. All Rights
Reserved. Used by permission.

Made and printed in Great Britain by
Richard Clay (The Chaucer Press) Ltd, Bungay, Suffolk
Filmset in Monophoto Plantin by
Northumberland Press Ltd, Gateshead, Tyne and Wear

*'At night he lights up a good cigar, and climbs into the
little old 'bus, and maybe cusses the carburetor, and shoots
out home. He mows the lawn, or sneaks in some practice
putting, and then he's ready for dinner.'*

GEORGE BABBITT of the 'Ideal Citizen'

*The difficulty to think at the end of day,
When the shapeless shadow covers the sun
And nothing is left except light on your fur ...*

WALLACE STEVENS
'A Rabbit as King of the Ghosts'

# I

Running out of gas, Rabbit Angstrom thinks as he stands behind the summer-dusty windows of the Springer Motors display room watching the traffic go by on Route 111, traffic somehow thin and scared compared to what it used to be. The fucking world is running out of gas. But they won't catch him, not yet, because there isn't a piece of junk on the road gets better mileage than his Toyotas, with lower service costs. Read *Consumer Reports*, April issue. That's all he has to tell the people when they come in. And come in they do, the people out there are getting frantic, they know the great American ride is ending. Gas lines at ninety-nine point nine cents a gallon and ninety per cent of the stations to be closed for the weekend. The governor of the Commonwealth of Pennsylvania calling for five-dollar minimum sales to stop the panicky topping-up. And truckers who can't get diesel shooting at their own trucks, there was an incident right in Diamond County, along the Pottsville Pike. People are going wild, their dollars are going rotten, they shell out like there's no tomorrow. He tells them, when they buy a Toyota, they're turning their dollars into yen. And they believe them. A hundred twelve units new and used moved in the first five months of 1979, with eight Corollas, five Coronas including a Luxury Edition Wagon, and that Celica that Charlie said looked like a Pimpmobile unloaded in these first three weeks of June already, at an average gross mark-up of eight hundred dollars per sale. Rabbit is rich.

He owns Springer Motors, one of the two Toyota agencies in the Brewer area. Or rather he co-owns a half-interest with his wife Janice, her mother Bessie sitting on the other half inherited when old man Springer died five years back. But Rabbit feels as though

7

he owns it all, showing up at the showroom day after day, riding herd on the paperwork and the payroll, swinging in his clean suit in and out of Service and Parts where the men work filmed with oil and look up white-eyed from the bulb-lit engines as in a kind of underworld while he makes contact with the public, the community, the star and spearpoint of all these two dozen employers and hundred thousand square feet of working space, which seem a wide shadow behind him as he stands there up front. The wall of imitation boards, really sheets of random-grooved Masonite, around the door into his office is hung with framed old clippings and team portraits, including two all-county tens, from his days as a basketball hero twenty years ago – no, more than twenty years now. Even under glass, the clippings keep yellowing, something in the chemistry of the paper apart from the air, something like the deepening taint of sin people used to try to scare you with. ANGSTROM HITS FOR 42. *'Rabbit' Leads Mt Judge Into Semi-Finals.* Resurrected from the attic where his dead parents had long kept them, in scrapbooks whose mucilage had dried so they came loose like snakeskins, these clippings thus displayed were Fred Springer's idea, along with that phrase about an agency's reputation being the shadow of the man up front. Knowing he was dying long before he did, Fred was getting Harry ready to be the man up front. When you think of the dead, you got to be grateful.

Ten years ago when Rabbit got laid off as a Linotyper and reconciled with Janice, her father took him on as salesman and when the time was ripe five years later had the kindness to die. Who would have thought such a little tense busy bird of a man could get it up for a massive coronary? Hypertense: his diastolic had been up around one-twenty for years. Loved salt. Loved to talk Republican, too, and when Nixon left him nothing to say he had kind of burst. Actually, he had lasted a year into Ford, but the skin of his face was getting tighter and the red spots where the cheek and jaw bones pressed from underneath redder. When Harry looked down at him rouged in the coffin he saw it had been coming, Fred hadn't much changed. From the way Janice and her mother carried on you would have thought a mixture of Prince Valiant and Moses had bit the dust. Maybe having already buried both his own parents made Harry hard. He looked down, noticed that Fred's hair had been parted wrong, and felt nothing. The great thing about the dead, they make space.

While old man Springer was still prancing around life at the lot was hard. He kept long hours, held the showroom open on winter nights when there wasn't a snowplow moving along Route 111, was always grinding away in that little high-pitched grinder of a voice about performance guidelines and washout profits and customer servicing and whether or not a mechanic had left a thumbprint on some heap's steering wheel or a cigarette butt in the ashtray. When he was around the lot it was like they were all trying to fill some big skin that Springer spent all his time and energy imagining, the ideal Springer Motors. When he died that skin became Harry's own, to stand around in loosely. Now that he is king of the lot he likes it here, the acre of asphalt, the new-car smell present even in the pamphlets and pep talks Toyota mails from California, the shampooed carpet wall to wall, the yellowing basketball feats up on the walls along with the plaques saying Kiwanis and Rotary and C of C and the trophies on a high shelf won by the Little League teams the company sponsors, the ample square peace of this masculine place spiced by the girls in billing and reception that come and go under old Mildred Kroust, and the little cards printed with HAROLD C. ANGSTROM on them and CHIEF SALES REPRESENTATIVE. The man up front. A center of sorts, where he had been a forward. There is an airiness to it for Harry, standing there in his own skin, casting a shadow. The cars sell themselves, is his philosophy. The Toyota commercials on television are out there all the time, preying on people's minds. He likes being part of all that; he likes the nod he gets from the community, that had overlooked him like dirt ever since high school. The other men in Rotary and Chamber turn out to be the guys he played ball with back then, or their ugly younger brothers. He likes having money to float in, a big bland good guy is how he sees himself, six three and around two ten by now, with a forty-two waist the suit salesman at Kroll's tried to tell him until he sucked his gut in and the man's thumb grudgingly inched the tape tighter. He avoids mirrors, when he used to love them. The face far behind him, crew-cut and thin-jawed with sleepy predatory teen-age eyes in the glossy team portraits, exists in his present face like the chrome bones of a grille within the full front view of a car and its fenders. His nose is still small and straight, his eyes maybe less sleepy. An amply blown-dry-looking businessman's haircut masks his eartips and fills in where his temples are receding. He didn't much like the counterculture with all its drugs and draft-dodging but he does like being allowed within limits to let your hair grow longer than those old Marine cuts and to have it naturally fluff out. In the shaving mirror a chaos of wattles and slack cords blooms beneath his chin in a way that doesn't bear study. Still, life is sweet. That's what old people used to say and when he was young he wondered how they could mean it.

Last night it hailed in Brewer and its suburbs. Stones the size of marbles leaped up from the slant little front yards and drummed on the tin signs supporting flickering neon downtown; then came a downpour whose puddles reflected a dawn gray as stone. But the day has turned breezy and golden and the patched and white-striped asphalt of the lot is dry, late in the afternoon of this long last Saturday in June and the first of calendar summer. Usually on a Saturday Route 111 is buzzing with shoppers pillaging the malls hacked from the former fields of corn, rye, tomatoes, cabbages, and strawberries. Across the highway, the four concrete lanes and the median divider of aluminum battered by many forgotten accidents, stands a low building faced in dark clinker brick that in the years since Harry watched its shell being slapped together of plywood has been a succession of unsuccessful restaurants and now serves as the Chuck Wagon, specializing in barbecued take-outs. The Chuck Wagon too seems quiet today. Beyond its lot littered with flattened take-out cartons a lone tree, a dusty maple, drinks from a stream that has become a mere ditch. Beneath its branches a picnic table rots unused, too close to the overflowing dumpster the restaurant keeps by its kitchen door. The ditch marks the bound of a piece of farmland sold off but still awaiting its development. This shapely old maple from its distance seems always to be making to Harry an appeal he must ignore.

He turns from the dusty window and says to Charlie Stavros, 'They're running scared out there.'

Charlie looks up from the desk where he is doing paperwork, the bill of sale and NV-1 on a '74 Barracuda 8 they finally moved for twenty-eight hundred yesterday. Nobody wants these old guzzlers, though you got to take them on trade-in. Charlie handles the used cars. Though he has been with Springer Motors twice as long as Harry, his desk is in a corner of the showroom, out in the open, and the title on his card is SENIOR SALES REPRESENTATIVE. Yet he bears no grudge. He sets down his pen even with the edge of his papers and in response to his boss asks, 'Did you see in the paper the other day where some station owner and his wife somewhere in the middle of the state were pumping gas for a line and one of the cars slips its clutch and crushes the wife against the car next in line, broke her hip I think I read, and while the husband was holding her and begging for help the people in the cars instead of giving him any help took over the pumps and gave themselves free gas?'

'Yeah,' Harry says, 'I guess I heard that on the radio, though it's hard to believe. Also about some guy in Pittsburgh who takes a couple of two-by-fours with him and drives his back wheels up on them so as to get a few more cents' worth of gas in his tank. That's fanatical.'

Charlie emits a sardonic, single-syllabled laugh, and explains, 'The little man is acting like the oil companies now. I'll get mine, and screw you.'

'I don't blame the oil companies,' Harry says tranquilly. 'It's too big for them too. Mother Earth is drying up, is all.'

'Shit, champ, you never blame anybody,' Stavros tells the taller man. 'Skylab could fall on your head right now and you'd go down saying the government had done its best.'

Harry tries to picture this happening and agrees, 'Maybe so. They're strapped these days like everybody else. About all the feds can do these days is meet their own payroll.'

'That they're guaranteed to do, the greedy bastards. Listen, Harry. You know damn well Carter and the oil companies have rigged this whole mess. What does Big Oil want? Bigger profits. What does Carter want? Less oil imports, less depreciation of the dollar. He's too chicken to ration, so he's hoping higher prices will do it for him. We'll have dollar-fifty no-lead before the year is out.'

'And people'll pay it,' Harry says, serene in his middle years. The two men fall silent, as if arrived at a truce, while the scared traffic kicks up dust along the business strip of Route 111 and the unbought Toyotas in the showroom exude new-car smell. Ten years ago Stavros had had an affair with Harry's wife Janice. Harry thinks of Charlie's prick inside Janice and his feeling is hostile and cozy in almost equal proportions, coziness getting the edge. At the time he took his son-in-law on, old man Springer asked him if he could stomach working with him, Charlie. Rabbit didn't see why not. Sensing he was being asked to bargain, he said he'd work with him, not under him. *No question of that, you'd be under me only, as long as I'm among the living,* Springer had promised: *you two'll work side by side.* Side by side they had waited for customers in all weathers and bemoaned their boss's finickiness and considered monthly which of the used cars on inventory would never move and should be wholesaled to cut carrying costs. Side by side they had suffered with Springer Motors as the Datsun franchise came into the Brewer area, and then those years when everyone was buying VWs and Volvos, and now the Hondas and Le Car presenting themselves as the newest thing in cute economy. In these nine years Harry added thirty pounds to his frame while Charlie went from being a chunky Greek who when he put on his shades and a checked suit looked like an enforcer for the local numbers racket to a shrivelled little tipster-type. Stavros had always had a tricky ticker, from rheumatic fever when he was a boy. Janice had been moved by this, this weakness hidden within him, his squarish chest. Now like a flaw ramifying to the surface of a crystal his infirmity has given him that de-hydrated prissy look of a reformed rummy, of a body preserved day to day by taking thought. His eyebrows that used to go straight across like an iron bar have dwindled in to be two dark clumps, disconnected, almost like the charcoal dabs clowns wear. His sideburns have gone white but the top of his hair looks dyed in a broad stripe. Each morning at work Charlie changes his lavender-tinted black hornrims for ones with amber lenses the instant he's indoors, and walks through the day's business like a grizzled old delicate ram who doesn't want to slip on a crag and fall. *Side by side, I promise you.* When old man Springer promised that, when he turned his full earnestness on anything, the pink patches in his face glowed red and his lips tightened back from his teeth so you thought all the more of his skull. Dirty yellow teeth loaded with gum-line fillings, and his mustache never looked quite even, or quite clean.

The dead, Jesus. They were multiplying, and they look up begging you to join them, promising it is all right, it is very soft down here. Pop, Mom, old man Springer, Jill, the baby called Becky for her little time, Tothero. Even John Wayne, the other day. The obituary page every day shows another stalk of a harvest endlessly rich, the faces of old teachers, customers, local celebrities like himself flashing for a moment and then going down. For the first time since childhood Rabbit is happy, simply, to be alive. He tells Charlie, 'I figure the oil's going to run out about the same time I do, the year two thousand. Seems funny to say it, but I'm glad I lived when I did. These kids coming up, they'll be living on table scraps. We had the meal.'

'You've been sold a bill of goods,' Charlie tells him. 'You and a lot of others. Big Oil has enough reserves located right now to last five hundred years, but they want to ooze it out. In the Delaware Bay right now I heard there's seventeen supertankers, seventeen, at anchor waiting for the prices to go up enough for them to come into the South Philly refineries and unload. Meanwhile you get murdered in gas lines.'

'Stop driving. Run,' Rabbit tells him. 'I've begun this jogging thing and it feels great. I want to lose thirty pounds.' Actually his resolve to run before breakfast every day, in the dew of the dawn, lasted less than a week. Now he contents himself with trotting around the block after supper sometimes to get away from his wife and her mother while they crab at each other.

He has touched a sore point. Charlie confides as if to the NV-1 form, 'Doctor tells me if I try any exercise he washes his hands.'

Rabbit is abashed, slightly. 'Really? That's not what that Doctor Whatsisname used to say. White. Paul Dudley White.'

'He died. Exercise freaks are dropping down dead in the parks like flies. It doesn't get into the papers because the fitness industry has become big bucks. Remember all those little health-food stores hippies used to run? You know who runs 'em now? General Mills.'

Harry doesn't always know how seriously to take Charlie. He does know, in relation to his old rival, that he is hearty and huge, indisputably preferred by God in this chance matter of animal health. If Janice had run off with Charlie like she wanted to she'd be nothing but a nursemaid now. As is, she plays tennis three, four times a week and has never looked sharper. Harry keeps wanting to soften himself above Charlie, protect the more fragile man from the weight of his good fortune. He keeps silent, while Charlie's mind works its way back from the shame and shadow of his doctor washing his hands, back into memory's reserves of energy. 'Gasoline,' he suddenly says, giving it that Greek cackle, almost a wheeze. 'Didn't we used to burn it up? I had an Imperial once with twin carburetors and when you took off the filter and looked down through the inlet valve when the thing was idling it looked like a toilet being flushed.'

Harry laughs, wanting to ride along. 'Cruising,' he says, 'after high school got out, there was nothing to do but cruise. Back and forth along Central, back and forth. Those old V-8s, what do you think they got to the gallon? Ten, twelve miles? Nobody ever thought to keep track.'

'My uncles still won't drive a little car. Say they don't want to get crumpled if they meet a truck.'

'Remember Chicken? Funny more kids weren't killed than were.'

'Cadillacs. If one of his brothers got a Buick with fins, my father had to have a Cadillac with bigger fins. You couldn't count the taillights, it looked like a carton of red eggs.'

'There was one guy at Mt Judge High, Don Eberhardt, 'd get out on the running board of his Dad's Dodge when it was going down the hill behind the box factory and steer from out there. All the way down the hill.'

'First car I bought for myself, it was a '48 Studebaker, with that nose that looked like an airplane. Had about sixty-five thousand miles on it, it was the summer of '53. The dig-out on that thing! After a stoplight you could feel the front wheels start to lift, just like an airplane.'

14

'Here's a story. One time when we were pretty newly married I got sore at Janice for something, just being herself probably, and drove to West Virginia and back in one night. Crazy. You couldn't do that now without going to the savings bank first.'

'Yeah,' Charlie says slowly, saddened. Rabbit hadn't wanted to sadden him. He could never figure out, exactly, how much the man had loved Janice. 'She described that. You did a lot of roaming around then.'

'A little. I brought the car back though. When she left me, she took the car and kept it. As you remember.'

'Do I?'

He has never married, and that says something flattering, to Janice and therefore to Harry, the way it's worked out. A man fucks your wife, it puts a new value on her, within limits. Harry wants to restore the conversation to the cheerful plane of dwindling energy. He tells Stavros, 'Saw a kind of funny joke in the paper the other day. It said, You can't beat Christopher Columbus for mileage. Look how far he got on three galleons.' He pronounces the crucial word carefully, in three syllables; but Charlie doesn't act as if he gets it, only smiles a one-sided twitch of a smile that could be in response to pain.

'The oil companies made us do it,' Charlie says. 'They said, Go ahead, burn it up like madmen, all these highways, the shopping malls, everything. People won't believe it in a hundred years, the sloppy way we lived.'

'It's like wood,' Harry says, groping back through history, which is a tinted fog to him, marked off in centuries like a football field, with a few dates – 1066, 1776 – pinpointed and a few faces – George Washington, Hitler – hanging along the sidelines, not cheering. 'Or coal. As a kid I can remember the anthracite rattling down the old coal chute, with these red dots they used to put on it. I couldn't imagine how they did it, I thought it was something that happened in the ground. Little elves with red brushes. Now there isn't any anthracite. That stuff they strip-mine now just crumbles in your hand.' It gives him pleasure, makes Rabbit feel rich, to contemplate the world's wasting, to know that the earth is mortal too.

15

'Well,' Charlie sighs. 'At least it's going to keep those chinks and jigaboos from ever having an industrial revolution.'

That seems to wrap it up, though Harry feels they have let something momentous, something alive under the heading of energy, escape. But a lot of topics, he has noticed lately, in private conversation and even on television where they're paid to talk it up, run dry, exhaust themselves, as if everything's been said in this hemisphere. In his inner life too Rabbit dodges among more blanks than there used to be, patches of burnt-out gray cells where there used to be lust and keen dreaming and wide-eyed dread; he falls asleep, for instance, at the drop of a hat. He never used to understand the phrase. But then he never used to wear a hat and now, at the first breath of cold weather, he does. His roof wearing thin, starlight showing through.

YOU ASKED FOR IT, WE GOT IT, the big paper banner on the showroom window cries, in tune with the current Toyota television campaign. The sign cuts a slice from the afternoon sun and gives the showroom a muted aquarium air, or that of a wide sunken ship wherein the two Coronas and the acid-green Corolla SR-5 liftback wait to be bought and hoisted into the air on the other side of the glass and set down safe on the surface of the lot and Route 111 and the world of asphalt beyond.

A car swings in from this world: a fat tired '71 or '2 Country Squire wagon soft on its shocks, with one dented fender hammered out semi-smooth but the ruddy rustproofing underpaint left to do for a finish. A young couple steps out, the girl milky-pale and bare-legged and blinking in the sunshine but the boy roughened and reddened by the sun, his jeans dirt-stiffened by actual work done in the red mud of the county. A kind of crate of rough green boards has been built into the Squire's chrome roof rack and from where Rabbit is standing, a soft wedge shot away, he can see how the upholstery and inner padding have been mangled by the station wagon's use as a farm truck. 'Hicks,' Charlie says from his desk. The pair comes in shyly, like elongated animals, sniffing the air-conditioned air.

Feeling protective, God knows why, Charlie's snipe ringing in his ears, Harry walks towards them, glancing at the girl's hand to see if she wears a wedding ring. She does not, but such things

16

mean less than they used to. Kids shack up. Her age he puts at nineteen or twenty, the boy a bit older – the age of his own son. 'Can I help you folks?'

The boy brushes back his hair, showing a low white forehead. His broad baked face gives him a look of smiling even when he isn't. 'We chust came in for some information.' His accent bespeaks the south of the county, less aggressively Dutch than the north, where the brick churches get spiky and the houses and barns are built of limestone instead of sandstone. Harry figures them for leaving some farm to come into the city, with no more need to haul fenceposts and hay bales and pumpkins and whatever else this poor heap was made to haul. Shack up, get city jobs, and spin around in a little Corolla. We got it. But the boy could be just scouting out prices for his father, and the girlfriend be riding along, or not even be a girlfriend, but a sister, or a hitchhiker. A little touch of the hooker about her looks. The way her soft body wants to spill from these small clothes, the faded denim shorts and purple Paisley halter. The shining faintly freckled flesh of her shoulders and top arms and the bushy wanton abundance of her browny-red many-colored hair, carelessly bundled. A buried bell rings. She has blue eyes in deep sockets and the silence of a girl from the country used to letting men talk while she holds a sweet-and-sour secret in her mouth, sucking it. An incongruous disco touch in her shoes, with their high cork heels and ankle straps. Pink toes, painted nails. This girl will not stick with this boy. Rabbit wants this to be so; he imagines he feels an unwitting swimming of her spirit upward toward his, while her manner is all stillness. He feels she wants to hide from him, but is too big and white, too suddenly womanly, too nearly naked. Her shoes accent the length of her legs; she is taller than average, and not quite fat, though tending toward chunky, especially around the chest. Her upper lip closes over the lower with a puffy bruised look. She is bruisable, he wants to protect her; he relieves her of the pressure of his gaze, too long by a second, and turns to the boy.

'This is a Corolla,' Harry says, slapping orange tin. 'The two-door model begins at thirty-nine hundred and will give you highway mileage up to forty a gallon and twenty to twenty-five city driving. I know some other makes advertise more but believe me you can't get a better buy in America today than this jalopy right here. Read *Consumer Reports*, April issue. Much better than average on maintenance and repairs through the first four years. Who in this day and age keeps a car much longer than four years? In four years we may all be pushing bicycles the way things are going. This particular car has four-speed synchromesh transmission, fully transistorized ignition system, power-assisted front disc brakes, vinyl reclining bucket seats, a locking gas cap. That last feature's getting to be pretty important. Have you noticed lately how all the auto-supply stores are selling out of their siphons? You can't buy a siphon in Brewer today for love nor money, guess why. My mother-in-law's old Chrysler over in Mt Judge was drained dry the other day in front of the hairdresser's, she hardly ever takes the buggy out except to go to church. People are getting rough. Did you notice in the paper this morning where Carter is taking gas from the farmers and going to give it to the truckers? Shows the power of a gun, doesn't it?'

'I didn't see the paper,' the boy says.

He is standing there so stolidly Harry has to move around him with a quick shuffle-step, dodging a cardboard cutout of a happy customer with her dog and packages, to slap acid-green. 'Now if you want to replace your big old wagon, that's some antique, with another wagon that gives you almost just as much space for half the running expense, this SR-5 has some beautiful features – a *five*-speed transmission with an overdrive that really saves fuel on a long trip, and a fold-down split rear seat that enables you to carry one passenger back there and still have the long space on the other side for golf clubs or fenceposts or whatever. I don't know why Detroit never thought it, that split seat. Here we're supposed to be Automobile Heaven and the foreigners come up with all the ideas. If you ask me Detroit's let us all down, two hundred million of us. I'd much rather handle native American cars but between the three of us they're junk. They're cardboard. They're pretend.'

'Now what are those over there?' the boy asks.

'That's the Corona, if you want to move toward the top of the line. Bigger engine – twenty-two hundred ccs. instead of sixteen. More of a European look. I drive one and love it. I get about thirty miles to the gallon on the highway, eighteen or so in Brewer.

Depends on how you drive, of course. How heavy a foot you have. Those testers for *Consumer Reports*, they must really give it the gun, their mileage figures are the one place they seem off to me. This liftback here is priced at sixty-eight five, but remember you're buying yen for dollars, and when trade-in time comes you get your yen back.'

The girl smiles at 'yen.' The boy, gaining confidence, says, 'And this one here now.' The young farmer has touched the Celica's suave black hood. Harry is running out of enthusiasm. Interested in that, the kid wasn't very interested in buying.

'You've just put your hand on one super machine,' Harry tells him. 'The Celica GT Sport Coupe, a car that'll ride with a Porsche or an MG any day. Steel-belted radials, quartz crystal clock, AM/FM stereo – all standard. *Standard.* You can imagine what the extras are. This one has power steering and a sun roof. Frankly, it's pricey, pretty near five figures, but like I say, it's an investment. That's how people buy cars now, more and more. That old Kleenex mentality of trade it in every two years is gone with the wind. Buy a good solid car now, you'll have something for a long while, while the dollars if you keep 'em will go straight to Hell. Buy good goods, that's my advice to any young man starting up right now.'

He must be getting too impassioned, for the boy says, 'We're chust looking around, more or less.'

'I understand that,' Rabbit says quickly, pivoting to face the silent girl. 'You're under absolutely no pressure from me. Picking a car is like picking a mate – you want to take your time.' The girl blushes and looks away. Generous paternal talkativeness keeps bubbling up in Harry. 'It's still a free country, the Commies haven't gotten any further than Cambodia. No way I can make you folks buy until you're good and ready. It's all the same to me, this product sells itself. Actually you're lucky there's such a selection on the floor, a shipment came in two weeks ago and we won't have another until August. Japan can't make enough of these cars to keep the world happy, Toyota is number one import all over the globe.' He can't take his eyes off this girl. Those chunky eyesockets reminding him of somebody. The milky flecked shoulders, the dent of flesh where the halter strap digs.

Squeeze her and you'd leave thumbprints, she's that fresh from the oven. 'Tell me,' he says, 'which size're you thinking of? You planning to cart a family around, or just yourselves?'

The girl's blush deepens. Don't marry this chump, Harry thinks. His brats will drag you down. The boy says, 'We don't need another wagon. My dad has a Chevy pick-up, and he let me take the Squire over when I got out of high school.'

'A great junk car,' Rabbit concedes. 'You can hurt it but you can't kill it. Even in '71 they were putting more metal in than they do now. Detroit is giving up the ghost.' He feels he is floating – on their youth, on his money, on the brightness of this June afternoon and its promise that tomorrow, a Sunday, will be fair for his golf game. 'But for people planning to tie the knot and get serious you need something more than a nostalgia item, you need something more like this.' He slaps orange tin again and reads irritation in the cool pallor of the girl's eyes as they lift to his. Forgive me, baby, you get so fucking bored standing around in here, when the time comes you tend to run off at the mouth.

Stavros, forgotten, calls from his desk, across the showroom space awash in sun shafts slowly approaching the horizontal, 'Maybe they'd like to take a spin.' He wants peace and quiet for his paperwork.

'Want to test drive?' Harry asks the couple.

'It's pretty late,' the boy points out.

'It'll take a minute. You only pass this way once. Live it up. I'll get some keys and a plate. Charlie, are the keys to the blue Corolla outside hanging on the pegboard or in your desk?'

'I'll get 'em,' Charlie grunts. He pushes up from his desk and, still bent, goes into the corridor behind the waist-high partition of frosted glass – a tacky improvement ordered by Fred Springer toward the end of his life. Behind it, three hollow flush doors in a wall of fake-walnut pressboard open into the offices of Mildred Kroust and the billing girl, whoever she is that month, with the office of the Chief Sales Representative between them. The doors are usually ajar and the girl and Mildred keep crossing back and forth to consult. Harry prefers to stand out here on the floor. In the old days there were just three steel desks and a strip of carpet; the one closed door marked the company toilet with its dispenser of powdered soap you turned upside down to get any out. Reception now is off in another separate cubicle, adjoining the waiting room where few customers ever wait. The keys Charlie needs hang, among many others, some no longer unlocking anything in this world, on a pegboard darkened by the touch of greasy fingertips beside the door on the way to Parts: Parts, that tunnel of loaded steel shelves whose sliding window overlooks the clangorous cavern of Service. No reason for Charlie to go except he knows where things are and you don't want to leave customers alone for a moment and feeling foolish, they're apt to sneak away. More timid than deer, customers. With nothing to say between them, the boy, the girl, and Harry can hear the faint strained wheeze of Charlie's breathing as he comes back with the demonstrator Corolla keys and the dealer's plate on its rusty spring clip. 'Want me to take these youngsters out?' he asks.

'No, you sit and rest,' Harry tells him, adding, 'You might start locking up in back.' Their sign claims they are open Saturdays to six but on this ominous June day of gas drought quarter of should be close enough. 'Back in a minute.'

The boy asks the girl, 'Want to come or stay here?'

'Oh, *come*,' she says, impatience lighting up her mild face as she turns and names him. 'Jamie, Mother expects me *back*.'

Harry reassures her, 'It'll just take a minute.' Mother. He wishes he could ask her to describe Mother.

Out on the lot, bright wind is bringing summer in. The spots of grass around the asphalt sport buttery dabs of dandelion. He clips the plate to the back of the Corolla and hands the boy the keys. He holds the seat on the passenger side forward so the girl can get into the rear; as she does so the denim of her shorts permits a peek of cheek of ass. Rabbit squeezes into the death seat and explains to Jamie the trinkets of the dashboard, including the space where a tape deck could go. They are, all three passengers, on the tall side, and the small car feels stuffed. Yet with imported spunk the Toyota tugs them into rapid motion and finds its place in the passing lane of Route 111. Like riding on the back of a big bumblebee; you feel *on top* of the buzzing engine. 'Peppy,' Jamie acknowledges.

'And smooth, considering,' Harry adds, trying not to brake on the bare floor. To the girl he calls backwards, 'You O.K.? Shall I slide my seat forward to give more room?' The way the shorts are so short now you wonder if the crotches don't hurt. The stitching, pinching up.

'No I'm all right, I'll sit sideways.'

He wants to turn and look at her but at his age turning his head is not so easy and indeed some days he wakes with pains all through the neck and shoulders from no more cause than his dead weight on the bed all night. He tells Jamie, 'This is the sixteen hundred cc., they make a twelve hundred base model but we don't like to handle it, I'd hate to have it on my conscience that somebody was killed because he didn't have enough pick-up to get around a truck or something on these American roads. Also we believe in carrying a pretty full complement of options; without 'em you'll find yourself short-changed on the trade-in when the time comes.' He manages to work his body around to look at the girl. 'These Japanese for all their virtues have pretty short legs,' he tells her. The way she has to sit, her ass is nearly on the floor and her knees are up in the air, these young luminous knees inches from his face.

Unself-consciously she is pulling a few long hairs away from her mouth where they have blown and gazing through the side window at this commercial stretch of greater Brewer. Fast-food huts in eye-catching shapes and retail outlets of everything from bridal outfits to plaster birdbaths have widened the aspect of this, the old Weisertown Pike, with their parking lots, leaving the odd surviving house and its stump of a front lawn sticking out painfully. Competitors – Pike Porsche and Renault, Diefendorfer Volkswagen, Old Red Barn Mazda and BMW, Diamond County Automotive Imports – flicker their FUEL ECONOMY banners while the gasoline stations intermixed with their beckoning have shrouded pumps and tow trucks parked across the lanes where automobiles once glided in, were filled, and glided on. An effect of hostile barricade, late in the day. Where did the shrouds come from? Some of them quite smartly tailored, in squared-off crimson canvas. A new industry, gas pump shrouds. Among vacant lakes of asphalt a few small stands offer strawberries and early peas. A tall sign gestures to a cement-block building well off the road; Rabbit can remember when this was a giant Mister Peanut pointing toward a low shop where salted nuts were arrayed in glass cases, Brazil nuts and hazelnuts and whole cashews and for a lesser price broken ones, Diamond County a great area for nuts but not that great, the shop failed. Its shell was broken and doubled in size and made into a nightclub and the sign repainted, keeping the top hat but Mister Peanut becoming a human reveller in white tie and tails. Now after many mutilations this sign has been turned into an ill-fitted female figure, a black silhouette with no bumps indicating clothing, her head thrown back and the large letters DISCO falling in bubbles as if plucked one by one from her cut throat. Beyond such advertisements the worn green hills hold a haze of vapor and pale fields bake as their rows of corn thicken. The inside of the Corolla is warming with a mingled human smell. Harry thinks of the girl's long thigh as she stretched her way into the back seat and imagines he smells vanilla. Cunt would be a good flavor of ice cream, Sealtest ought to work on it.

The silence from the young people troubles him. He prods it. He says, 'Some storm last night. I heard on the radio this morning the underpass at Eisenhower and Seventh was flooded for over an hour.'

Then he says, 'You know it seems gruesome to me, all these gas stations closed up like somebody has died.'

Then he says, 'Did you see in the paper where the Hershey company has had to lay off nine hundred people because of the trucker's strike? Next thing we'll be in lines for Hershey bars.'

The boy is intently passing a Freihofer's Bakery truck and Harry answers for him: 'The downtown stores are all pulling out. Nothing left in the middle of the city now but the banks and the post office. They put that crazy stand of trees in to make a mall but it won't do any good, the people are still scared to go downtown.'

The boy is staying in the fast lane, and in third gear, either for the pep or because he's forgotten there is a fourth. Harry asks him, 'Getting the feel of it, Jamie? If you want to turn around, there's an intersection coming up.'

The girl understands. 'Jamie, we better turn around. The man wants to get home for supper.'

As Jamie slows to ease right at the intersection, a Pacer – silliest car on the road, looks like a glass bathtub upside-down – swings left without looking. The driver is a fat spic in a Hawaiian shirt. The boy slaps the steering wheel in vain search for the horn. Toyota indeed has put the horn in a funny place, on two little arcs a thumb's reach inside the steering-wheel rim; Harry reaches over quick and toots for him. The Pacer swerves back into its lane, with a dark look back above the Hawaiian shirt. Harry directs, 'Jamie, I want you to take a left at the next light and go across the highway and take the next left you can and that'll bring us back.' To the girl he explains, 'Prettier this way.' He thinks aloud, 'What can I tell you about the car I haven't? It has a lot of locks. Those Japanese, they live on top of each other and are crazy about locks. Don't kid yourselves, we're coming to it, I won't be here to see it, but you will. When I was a kid nobody ever thought to lock their house and now everybody does, except my crazy wife. If she locked the door she'd lose the key. One of the reasons I'd like to go to Japan, Toyota asks some of their dealers but you got to have a bigger gross than I do, is to see how you lock up a paper house. At any rate. You can't get the key out of the ignition without releasing this catch down here. The trunk in back releases from this lever. The locking gas cap you already know about. Did either of you hear about the woman somewhere around Ardmore this week who cut into a gas line and the guy behind her got so mad he sneaked his own locking gas cap onto her tank so when she got to the pump the attendant couldn't remove it? They had to tow her away. Serve the bitch right, if you ask me.'

They have taken their two lefts and are winding along a road where fields come to the edge so you can see the clumps of red earth still shiny from where the plow turned them, and where what businesses there are – LAWNMOWERS SHARPENED, PA. DUTCH QUILTS – seem to stem from an earlier decade than those along Route 111, which runs parallel. On the banks of the road, between mailboxes some of which are painted with a heart or hex design, crown vetch is in violet flower. At a crest the elephant-colored gas tanks of Brewer lift into view, and the brick-red rows as they climb Mt Judge and smudge its side. Rabbit dares ask the girl, 'You from around here?'

'More toward Galilee. My mother has a farm.'

*And is your mother's name Ruth?* Harry wants to ask, but doesn't, lest he frighten her, and destroy for himself the vibration of excitement, of possibility untested. He tries to steal another peek at her, to see if her white skin is a mirror, and if the innocent blue in her eyes is his, but his bulk restrains him, and the tightness of the car. He asks the boy, 'You follow the Phillies, Jamie? How about that seven-zip loss last night? You don't see Bowa commit an error that often.'

'Is Bowa the one with the big salary?'

Harry will feel better when he gets the Toyota out of this moron's hands. Every turn, he can feel the tires pull and the sudden secret widen within him, circle upon circle, it's like seed: seed that goes into the ground invisible and if it takes hold cannot be stopped, it fulfills the shape it was programmed for, its destiny, sure as our death, and shapely. 'I think you mean Rose,' he answers. 'He's not been that much help, either. They're not going anywhere this year, Pittsburgh's the team. Pirates or Steelers, they always win. Take this left, at the yellow blinker. That'll take you right across One Eleven and then you swing into the lot from the back. What's your verdict?'

From the side the boy has an Oriental look – a big stretch of skin between his red ear and red nose, puffy eyes whose glitter gives away nothing. People who gouge a living out of the dirt are just naturally mean, Harry has always thought. Jamie says, 'Like I said we were looking around. This car seems pretty small but maybe that's chust what you're used to.'

'Want to give the Corona a whirl? That interior feels like a palace after you've been in one of these, you wouldn't think it would, it's only about two centimeters wider and five longer.' He marvels at himself, how centimeters trip off his tongue. Another five years with these cars and he'll be talking Japanese. 'But you better get used,' he tells Jamie, 'to a little scaling down. The big old boats have had it. People trade 'em in and we can't give 'em away. Wholesale half of 'em, and the wholesalers turn 'em into windowboxes. The five hundred trade-in I'd allow you on yours is just a courtesy, believe me. We like to help young people out. I think it's a helluva world we're coming to, where a young couple like yourselves can't afford to buy a car or own a home. If you can't get your foot on even the bottom rung of a society geared like this, people are going to lose faith in the system. The Sixties were a lark in the park compared to what we're going to see if things don't straighten out.'

Loose stones in the back section of the lot crackle. They pull into the space the Corolla came from and the boy can't find the button to release the key until Harry shows him again. The girl leans forward, anxious to escape, and her breath stirs the colorless hairs on Harry's wrist. His shirt is stuck to his shoulder blades, he discovers standing to his height in the air. All three of them straighten slowly. The sun is still bright but horsetails high in the sky cast doubt upon the weather for tomorrow's golf game after all. 'Good driving,' he says to Jamie, having given up on any sale. 'Come back in for a minute and I'll give you some literature.' Inside the showroom the sun strikes the paper banner and makes the letters TI TOƆ ƎW show through. Stavros is nowhere to be seen. Harry hands the boy his CHIEF card and asks him to sign the customer register.

'Like I said –' the boy begins.

Harry has lost patience with this escapade. 'It doesn't commit you to a blessed thing,' he says. 'Toyota'll send you a Christmas card is all it means. I'll do it for you. First name James –?'

'Nunemacher,' the boy says warily, and spells it. 'R. D. number two, Galilee.'

Harry's handwriting has deteriorated over the years, gained a twitch at the end of his long arm, which yet is not long enough for him to see clearly what he writes. He owns reading glasses but it is his vanity never to wear them in public. 'Done,' he says, and all too casually turns to the girl. 'O.K. young lady, how about you? Same name?'

'No way,' she says, and giggles. 'You don't want me.'

A boldness sparks in the cool flat eyes. In that way of women she has gone all circles, silly, elusive. When her gaze levels there is something sexy in the fit of her lower lids, and the shadow of insufficient sleep below them. Her nose is slightly snub. 'Jamie's our neighbor, I just came along for the ride. I was going to look for a sundress at Kroll's if there was time.'

Something buried far back glints toward the light. Today's slant of sun has reached the shelf where the trophies Springer Motors sponsors wait to be awarded; oval embossments on their weightless white-metal surfaces shine. Keep your name, you little cunt, it's still a free country. But he has given her his. She has taken his card from Jamie's broad red hand and her eyes, childishly alight, slip from its lettering to his face to the section of far wall where his old headlines hang yellowing, toasted brown by time. She asks him, 'Were you ever a famous basketball player?'

The question is not so easy to answer, it was so long ago. He tells her, 'In the dark ages. Why do you ask, you've heard the name?'

'Oh no,' this visitant from lost time gaily lies. 'You just have that look.'

When they have gone, the Country Squire swaying off on its soupy shocks, Harry uses the toilet down past Mildred Kroust's door along the corridor half of frosted glass and meets Charlie coming back from locking up. Still, there is pilferage, mysterious discrepancies eating into the percentages. Money is like water in a leaky bucket: no sooner there, it begins to drip. 'Whajja think of the girl?' Harry asks the other man, back in the showroom.

'With these eyes, I don't see the girls anymore. If I saw 'em, with my condition I couldn't do anything about it. She looked big and dumb. A lot of leg.'

'Not so dumb as that hick she was with,' Harry says. 'God when you see what some girls are getting into it makes you want to cry.'

Stavros's dark dabs of eyebrows lift. 'Yeah? Some could say it was the other way around.' He sits down to business at his desk. 'Manny get to talk to you about that Torino you took on trade?'

Manny is head of Service, a short stooping man with black pores on his nose, as if with that nose he burrows through each day's dirty work. Of course he resents Harry, who thanks to his marriage to Springer's daughter skates around in the sun of the showroom and accepts clunky Torinos trade-in. 'He told me the front end's out of alignment.'

'Now he thinks in good conscience it should have a valve job. He also thinks the owner turned back the odometer.'

'What could I do, the guy had the book right in his hand, I couldn't give him less than book value. If I don't give 'em book value Diefendorfer or Pike Porsche sure as hell will.'

'You should have let Manny check it out, he could have told at a glance it had been in a collision. And if he spotted the odometer business put the jerk on the defensive.'

'Can't he weight the front wheels enough to hide the shimmy?'

Stavros squares his hands patiently on the olive-green top of his desk. 'It's a question of good will. The customer you unload that Torino on will never be back, I promise you.'

'Then what's your advice?'

Charlie says, 'Discount it over to Ford in Pottsville. You had a cushion of nine hundred on that sale and can afford to give away two rather than get Manny's back up. He has to mark up his parts to protect his own department and when they're Ford parts you're carrying a mark-up already. Pottsville'll put a coat of wax on it and make some kid happy for a week.'

'Sounds good.' Rabbit wants to be outdoors, moving through the evening air, dreaming of his daughter. 'If I had my way,' he tells Charlie, 'we'd wholesale the American makes out of here as fast as they come in. Nobody wants 'em except the blacks and the spics, and even they got to wake up some day.'

Charlie doesn't agree. 'You can still do well in used, if you pick your spots. Fred used to say every car has a buyer somewhere, but you shouldn't allow more on any trade-in than you'd pay cash for that car. It *is* cash, you know. Numbers are cash, even if you don't handle any lettuce.' He tips back his chair, letting his palms screech with friction on the desktop. 'When I first went to work for Springer in '63 we sold nothing but second-hand American models, you never saw a foreign car this far in from the coast. The cars would come in off the street and we'd paint 'em and give 'em a tune-up and no manufacturer told us what price to attach, we'd put the price on the windshield in shaving cream and wipe it off and try another if it didn't move inside a week. No import duty, no currency devaluation; it was good clean dog eat dog.'

Reminiscence. Sad to see it rotting Charlie's brain. Harry waits respectfully for the mood to subside, then asks as if out of the blue, 'Charlie, if I had a daughter, what d'you think she'd look like?'

'Ugly,' Stavros says. 'She'd look like Bugs Bunny.'

'It'd be fun to have a daughter, wouldn't it?'

'Doubt it.' Charlie lifts his palms so the legs of his chair slap to the floor. 'What d'you hear from Nelson?'

Harry turns vehement. 'Nothing much, thank God,' he says. 'The kid never writes. Last we heard he was spending the summer out in Colorado with this girl he's picked up.' Nelson attends college at Kent State, in Ohio, off and on, and has a year's worth of credits still to go before he graduates, though the boy was twenty-two last November.

'What kind of girl?'

'Lordy knows, I can't keep track. Each one is weirder than the last. One had been a teen-age alcoholic. Another told fortunes from playing cards. I think that same one was a vegetarian, but it may have been somebody else. I think he picks 'em to frustrate me.'

'Don't give up on the kid. He's all you've got.'

'Jesus, what a thought.'

'You just go ahead. I want to finish up here. I'll lock up.'

'O.K., I'll go see what Janice has burned for supper. Want to come take pot luck? She'd be tickled to see you.'

'Thanks, but *Manna mou* expects me.' His mother, getting decrepit herself, lives with Charlie now, in his place on Eisenhower Avenue, and this is another bond between them, since Harry lives with his mother-in-law.

'O.K. Take care, Charlie. See you in Monday's wash.'

'Take care, champ.'

The day is still golden outside, old gold now in Harry's lengthening life. He has seen summer come and go until its fading is one in his heart with its coming, though he cannot yet name the weeds that flower each in its turn through the season, or the insects that also in ordained sequence appear, eat, and perish. He knows that in June school ends and the playgrounds open, and the grass needs cutting again and again if one is a man, and if one is a child games can be played outdoors while the supper dishes tinkle in the mellow parental kitchens, and the moon is discovered looking over your shoulder out of a sky still blue, and a silver blob of milkweed spittle has appeared mysteriously on your knee. Good luck. Car sales peak in June: for a three-hundred-car-a-year dealer like Harry this means upwards of twenty-five units, with twenty-one accounted for already and six selling days to go. Average eight hundred gross profit times twenty-five equals twenty grand minus the twenty-five per cent they estimate for salesmen's compensation both salary and incentives leaves fifteen grand minus between eight and ten for other salaries those cute little cunts come and go in billing one called Cissy a Polack a few years ago they got as far as rubbing fannies easing by in that corridor and the rent that Springer Motors pays itself old man Springer didn't believe in owing anything the banks could own but even he had to pay off the mortgage eventually boy the rates now must kill anybody starting up and the financing double-digit interest Brewer Trust been doing it for years and against the twelve per cent you got to figure the two or three per cent that comes back as loss reserves nobody likes to call it kick-back and the I R S calls it taxable earnings and the upkeep the electricity that Sun 2001 Diagnostic Computer Manny wants would use a lot of juice and the power tools they can't even turn a nut on a wheel anymore it has to be pneumatic *rrrrrrt* and the heat thank God a few months reprieve from that the fucking Arabs are killing us and the men won't wear sweaters under the coveralls the young mechanics are the worst they say they lose feeling in their finger tips and health insurance there's another killer up and up the hospitals keeping people alive that are really dead like some game they're playing at Medicaid's expense and the advertising he often wonders how much good it does a rule of thumb he read some-where is one and a half per cent of gross sales but if you look at the Auto Sales page of the Sunday paper you never saw such a jumble just the quiet listing of the prices and the shadow of the dealer like old man Springer said the man he gets known to be at Rotary and in the downtown restaurants and the country club really he should be allowed to take all that off as business expenses the four seventy-five a week he pays himself doesn't take into account the suits to make himself presentable he has to buy three or four a year and not at Kroll's anymore he doesn't like that salesman who measured his fat waist Webb Murkett knows of a little shop on Pine Street that's as good as hand tailoring and then the property taxes and the kids keep throwing stones or shooting BBs at the glass signs outside we ought to go back to wood grouted wood but national Toyota has its specifications, where was he, let's say nine total monthly expenses variable and invariable that leaves four net profit and deduct another thousand from that for inflation and pilferage and the unpredictable that's always there you still have three, fifteen hundred for Ma Springer and fifteen hundred for Janice and him plus the two thousand salary when his poor dead dad used to go off to the print shop at quarter after seven every morning for forty dollars a week and that wasn't considered bad money then. Harry wonders what his father would think if he could only see him now, rich.

His 1978 Luxury Edition liftback five-door Corona is parked in its space. Called Red Metallic, it is a color more toward brown, like tired tomato soup. If the Japanese have a weakness it is their color sense: their Copper Metallic to Harry's eyes is a creosote brown, the Mint Green Metallic something like what he imagines cyanide to be, and what they called Beige a plain lemon yellow. In the war there used to be all these cartoons showing the Japanese wearing thick glasses and he wonders if it can be true, they don't see too well, all their colors falling in between the stripes of the rainbow. Still, his Corona is a snug machine. Solid big-car feel, padded tilt steering wheel, lumbar support lever for adjustable driver comfort, factory-installed AM/FM/MPX four-speaker radio. The radio is what he enjoys, gliding through Brewer with the windows up and locked and the power-boosted ventilation flowing through and the four corners of the car dinging out disco music as from the four corners of the mind's ballroom. Peppy and gentle, the music reminds Rabbit of the music played on radios when he was in high school, 'How High the Moon' with the clarinet breaking away, the licorice stick they used to call it, 'Puttin' on the Ritz': city music, not like that country music of the Sixties that tried to take us back and make us better than we are. Black girls with tinny chiming voices chant nonsense words above a throbbing electrified beat and he likes that, the thought of those black girls out of Detroit probably, their boyfriends goofing off on the assembly line, in shimmery tinsel dresses throbbing one color after another as the disco lights spin. He and Janice ought to visit at least the place down Route 111 DISCO he noticed today for the hundredth time, never dared to go in. In his mind he tries to put Janice and the coloured girls and the spinning lights all together and they fly apart. He thinks of Skeeter. Ten years ago this small black man came and lived with him and Nelson for a crazy time. Now Skeeter is dead, he learned just this April. Someone anonymous sent him, in a long stamped envelope such as anybody can buy at the post office, addressed in neat block ballpoint printing such as an accountant or a schoolteacher might use, a clipping in the familiar type of the Brewer *Vat*, where Harry had been a Linotyper until Linotyping became obsolete:

## FORMER RESIDENT
## SLAIN IN PHILLY

Hubert Johnson, formerly of Brewer, died of gunshot wounds in General Municipal Hospital, Philadelphia, after an alleged shoot-out with police officers.

Johnson was purported to have fired the first shots without provocation upon officers investigating re ported violations of sanitation and housing laws in a religious commune supposedly headed by Johnson, whose Messiah Now Freedom Family included a number of black families and young persons.

Numerous complaints had been occasioned among neighbors by their late singing and abrasive behavior. The Messiah Now Freedom Family was located on Columbia Avenue.

### Johnson Wanted

Johnson, last of Plum Street, city, was remembered locally as 'Skeeter' and also went under the name of Farnsworth. He was wanted here under several complaints, local officials confirmed.

Philadelphia police lieutenant Roman Surpitski informed reporters that he and his men had no choice but to return fire upon Johnson. Fortunately, no officers and no other 'commune' members suffered wounds in the exchange.

The office of outgoing Mayor Frank Rizzo declined to comment upon the incident. 'We don't
come up against as many of these crazies as we used
to,' Lieutenant Surpitski volunteered.

The clipping had been accompanied by no note. Yet the sender
must have known him, known something of his past, and be
watching him, as the dead supposedly do. Creepy. Skeeter dead,
a certain light was withdrawn from the world, a daring, a promise
that all would be overturned. Skeeter had foretold this, his death
young. Harry last had seen him heading across a field of corn
stubble, among crows gleaning. But that had been so long ago the
paper in his hand this last April felt little different from any other
news item or from those sports clippings hanging framed in his
showroom, about himself. Your selves die too. That part of him
subject to Skeeter's spell had shrivelled and been overlaid. In his
life he had known up close no other black people and in truth had
been beyond all fear and discomfort flattered by the attentions of
this hostile stranger descended like an angel; Harry felt he was
seen by this furious man anew, as with X-rays. Yet he was surely
a madman and his demands inordinate and endless and with him
dead Rabbit feels safer.

As he sits snug in his sealed and well-assembled car the venerable city of Brewer unrolls like a silent sideways movie past his
closed windows. He follows 111 along the river to West Brewer,
where once he lived with Skeeter, and then cuts over the Weiser
Street Bridge renamed after some dead mayor whose name
nobody ever uses and then, to avoid the pedestrian mall with
fountains and birch trees the city planners put in the broadest two
blocks of Weiser to renew the downtown supposedly (the joke
was, they planted twice as many trees as they needed, figuring half
would die, but in fact almost all of them thrived, so they have a
kind of forest in the center of town, where a number of muggings
have taken place and the winos and junkies sleep it off), Harry cuts
left on Third Street and through some semi-residential blocks of
mostly ophthalmologists' offices to the diagonal main drag called
Eisenhower, through the sector of old factories and railroad yards.
Railroads and coal made Brewer. Everywhere in this city, once the
fourth largest in Pennsylvania but now slipped to seventh,

structures speak of expended energy. Great shapely stacks that have not issued smoke for half a century. Scrolling cast-iron light stanchions not lit since World War II. The lower blocks of Weiser given over to the sale of the cut-rate and the X-rated and the only new emporium a big windowless enlargement in white brick of Schoenbaum Funeral Directors. The old textile plants given over to discount clothing outlets teeming with a gimcrack cheer of banners FACTORY FAIR and slogans *Where the Dollar Is Still a Dollar*. These acres of dead railroad track and car shops and stockpiled wheels and empty boxcars stick in the heart of the city like a great rusting dagger. All this had been cast up in the last century by what now seem giants, in an explosion of iron and brick still preserved intact in this city where the sole new buildings are funeral parlors and government offices, Unemployment and Join the Army.

Beyond the car yards and the underpass at Seventh that had been flooded last night, Eisenhower Avenue climbs steeply through tight-built neighborhoods of row houses built solid by German workingmen's savings and loans associations, only the fanlights of stained glass immune to the later layers of aluminum awning and Permastone siding, the Polacks and Italians being squeezed out by the blacks and Hispanics that in Harry's youth were held to the low blocks down by the river. Dark youths thinking in languages of their own stare from the triangular stone porches of the old corner grocery stores.

The vanished white giants as they filled Brewer into its grid named these higher streets that Eisenhower crosses for fruits and the seasons of the year: Winter, Spring, Summer, but no Fall Street. For three months twenty years ago Rabbit lived on Summer with a woman, Ruth Leonard. There he fathered the girl he saw today, if that was his daughter. There is no getting away; our sins, our seed, coil back. The disco music shifts to the Bee Gees, white men who have done this wonderful thing of making themselves sound like black women. 'Stayin' Alive' comes on with all that amplified throbbleo and a strange nasal whining underneath: the John Travolta theme song. Rabbit still thinks of him as one of the Sweathogs from Mr Kotter's class but for a while back there last summer the U.S.A. was one hundred per cent his, every

34

twat under fifteen wanting to be humped by a former Sweathog in the back seat of a car parked in Brooklyn. He thinks of his own daughter getting into the back seat of the Corolla, bare leg up to her ass. He wonders if her pubic hair is ginger in color like her mother's was. That curve where a tender entire woman seems an inch away around a kind of corner, where no ugly penis hangs like sausage on the rack, blue-veined. Her eyes his blue: wonderful to think that he has been turned into cunt, a secret message carried by genes all that way through all these comings and goings all these years, the bloody tunnel of growing and living, of staying alive. He better stop thinking about it, it fills him too full of pointless excitement. Some music does that.

Some car with double headlights, a yellow LeMans with that big vertical bar in the middle of the grille, is riding his tail so close he eases over behind a parked car and lets the bastard by: a young blonde with a tipped-up tiny profile is driving, how often that seems to be the case these days, some pushy road-hog you hate turns out to have a little girl at the wheel, who must be somebody's daughter and from the lackadaisical glassy look on her face has no idea of being rude, just wants to get there. When Rabbit first began to drive the road was full of old fogeys going too slow and now it seems nothing but kids in a hell of a hurry, pushing. Let 'em by, is his motto. Maybe they'll kill themselves on a telephone pole in the next mile. He hopes so.

His route takes him up into the area of the stately Brewer High School, called the Castle, built in 1933, the year of his birth is how he remembers. They wouldn't build it now, no faith in education, indeed they say with zero growth rate approaching there aren't enough students to fill the schools now, they are closing a lot of the elementary schools down. Up this high the city builders had run out of seasons and went to tree names. Locust Boulevard east of the Castle is lined with houses with lawns all around, though the strips between are narrow and dark and rhododendrons die for lack of sun. The better-off live up here, the bone surgeons and legal eagles and middle management of the plants that never had the wit to go south or have come in since. When Locust begins to curve through the municipal park its name changes to Cityview Drive, though with all the trees that have grown up in time there isn't much view left, Brewer can be seen all spread out really only from the Pinnacle Hotel, now a site of vandalism and terror where once there had been dancing and necking. Something about spics they don't like to see white kids making out, they surround the car and smash the windshield with rocks and slit the clothes off the girl while roughing up the boy. What a world to grow up in, especially for a girl. He and Ruth walked up to the Pinnacle once or twice. The railroad tie steps probably rotted now. She took off her shoes because the high heels dug into the gravel between the railroad ties, he remembers her city-pale feet lifting ahead of him under his eyes, naked for him as it seemed. People satisfied with less then. In the park a World War II tank, made into a monument, points its guns at tennis courts where the nets, even the ones made of playground fencing, keep getting ripped away. The strength these kids use, just to destroy. Was he that way at that age? You want to make a mark. The world seems indestructible and won't let you out. Let 'em by.

There is a stoplight and, turning left, Harry passes between houses gabled and turreted the way they did early in the century when men wore straw hats and made ice cream by hand and rode bicycles, and then there is a shopping center, where a four-theatre movie complex advertises on its sign high up where vandals can't reach it to steal letters ALIEN MOONRAKER MAIN EVENT ESCAPE FROM ALCATRAZ. None of them does he want to see though he likes the way Streisand's hair frizzes up and that Jewish nose, not just the nose, there is Jewishness in the thrust of her voice that thrills him, must have to do with being the chosen people, they do seem more at home here on Earth, the few he knows, more full of bounce. Funny about Streisand, if she isn't matched up with an Egyptian like Sharif it's with a superWaspy-looking type like Ryan O'Neal; same thing with Woody Allen, nothing Jewish about Diane Keaton, though her hair does frizz come to think of it.

The music stops, the news comes on. A young female voice reads it, with a twang like she knows she's wasting our time. Fuel, truckers. Three-Mile Island investigations continue. Date for Skylab fall has been revised. Somoza in trouble too. Stay of execution of convicted Florida killer denied. Former leader of

36

Great Britain's Liberal Party acquitted of charges of conspiring to murder his former homosexual lover. This annoys Rabbit, but his indignation at this pompous pansy's getting off scot-free dissolves in his curiosity about the next criminal case on the news, this is of a Baltimore physician who was charged with murdering a Canada goose with a golf club. The defendant claims, the disinterested female voice twangs on, that he had accidentally struck the goose with a golf ball and then had dispatched the wounded creature with a club to end its misery. The voice concludes, 'A mercy killing, or murder most foul?' He laughs aloud, in the car, alone. He'll have to try to remember that, to tell the gang at the club tomorrow. Tomorrow will be a sunny day, the woman reassures him, giving the weather. 'And now, the Number One Hit coast to coast, "Hot Stuff," by the Queen of Disco, Donna Summer!'

Sittin' here eatin' my heart out waitin'
Waitin' for some lover to call . . .

Rabbit likes the chorus where the girls in the background chime in, you can picture them standing around some steamy city corner chewing gum and who knows what else:

Hot stuff
I need hot stuff
I want some hot stuff
I need hot stuuuuuff!

Still he liked Donna Summer best in the days when she was doing those records of a woman breathing and panting and sighing like she was coming. Maybe it wasn't her, just some other slim black chick. But he thinks it was her.

The road takes on a number, 422, and curves around the shoulders of Mt Judge, with a steep drop on the right side and a view of the viaduct that once brought water to the city from the north of the country across the black breadth of the Running Horse River. Two gas stations mark the beginning of the borough of Mt Judge; instead of keeping on 422 toward Philadelphia Harry steers his Corona off the highway onto Central by the granite Baptist church and then obliquely up Jackson Street and after three blocks right onto Joseph, If he stays on Jackson two more blocks he will pass his old house, one number in from the corner of Maple, but since Pop passed on, after holding on without Mom for a number of years, doing all the yardwork and vacuuming and meals by himself until his emphysema just got too bad and you'd find him sitting in a chair all curled over like a hand sheltering a guttering candleflame from the wind, Rabbit rarely drives by: the people he and Mim had sold it to had painted the wood trim an awful apple green and hung an ultraviolet plant light in the big front window. Like these young couples in Brewer who think anything goes on a row house, however cute, and they're doing the world a favor by taking it on. Harry hadn't liked the guy's accent, haircut, or leisure suit; he had liked the price he had paid, though: fifty-eight thousand for a place that had cost Mom and Pop forty-two hundred in 1935. Even with Mim taking her half with her back out to Nevada the capital gains had hurt, nearly half of a half of a half or seven thousand dollars, not to mention the estate taxes and the lawyers' fees, they just step in everywhere where money's changing hands; to avoid capital gains he had begged Janice at the time to buy a new house, just for them, maybe over in Penn Park in West Brewer, five minutes from the lot. But no, Janice didn't think they should desert Mother: the Springers had taken them in when they had no house, their own house had burned, and their marriage had hit rock bottom and what with Harry starting as Associate Sales Representative at about the time Pop died and Nelson having had so many shocks already in his life and so many bad aftereffects still smoldering at that end of Brewer, the inquest for Jill and a police investigation and her parents thinking of suing all the way from Connecticut and the insurance company taking forever to come through with the claim because there were suspicious circumstances and poor Peggy Fosnacht having to swear Harry had been with her and so couldn't have set it himself, what with all this it seemed better to lie low, to hide behind the Springer name in the big stucco house, and the weeks had become months and the months years without the young Angstroms going into another place of their own, and then with Fred dying so suddenly and Nelson going off to college there seemed more room and less reason than ever to move. The house,

89 Joseph, always reminds Harry under its spreading trees with its thready lawn all around of the witch's house made out of candy, vanilla fudge for walls and licorice Necco wafers for the thick slate roof. Though the place looked big outside the downstairs is crammed with furniture come down through Ma Springer's people the Koerners and the shades are always half drawn; except for the screened-in back porch and the little upstairs room that had been Janice's when she was a girl and then Nelson's for those five years before he went away to Kent, there isn't a corner of the Springer house where Harry feels able to breathe absolutely his own air, feels the light can get to him easily.

He circles around into the alley of bluestone grit and puts the Corona into the garage beside the '74 navy-blue Chrysler Newport that Fred got the old lady for her birthday the year before he died and that she drives around with both hands tight on the wheel, with the look on her face as if a bomb might go off under the hood. Janice always keeps her Maverick convertible parked out front by the curb, where the maple drippings can ruin the top faster. When the weather gets warm she leaves the top down for nights at a time so the seats are always sticky. Rabbit swings down the overhead garage door and carries up the cement walk through the back yard like twin car headlights into a tunnel his strange consciousness of having not one child now but two.

Janice greets him in the kitchen. Something's up. She is wearing a crisp frock with pepperminty stripes but her hair is still scraggly and damp from an afternoon of swimming at the club pool. Nearly every day she has a tennis date with some of her girlfriends at the club they belong to, the Flying Eagle Tee and Racquet, a newish organization laid out on the lower slopes of Mt Judge's woodsy brother mountain with the Indian name, Mt Pemaquid, and then kills the rest of the afternoon lying at poolside gossiping or playing cards and getting slowly spaced on Spritzers or vodka-and-tonics. Harry likes having a wife who can be at the club so much. Janice is thickening through the middle at the age of forty-four but her legs are still hard and neat. And brown. She was always dark-complected and with July not even here she has the tan of a savage, legs and arms almost black like some little

39

Polynesian in an old Jon Hall movie. Her lower lip bears a trace of zinc oxide, which is sexy, even though he never loved that stubborn slotlike set her mouth gets. Her still-wet hair pulled back reveals a high forehead somewhat mottled, like brown paper where water has been dropped and dried. He can tell by the kind of heat she is giving off that she and her mother have been fighting. 'What's up now?' he asks.

'It's been wild,' Janice says. 'She's in her room and says we should eat without her.'

'Yeah well, she'll be down. But what's to eat? I don't see anything cooking.' The digital clock built into the stove says 6:32.

'Harry. Honest to God I was going to shop as soon as I came back and changed out of tennis things but then this postcard was here and Mother and I have been at it ever since. Anyway it's summer, you don't want to eat too much. Doris Kaufmann, I'd give anything to have her serve, she says she never has more than a glass of iced tea for lunch, even in the middle of winter. I thought maybe soup and those cold cuts I bought that you and Mother refuse to touch, they have to be eaten sometime. And the lettuce is coming on in the garden now so fast we must start having salads before it gets all leggy.' She had planted a little vegetable garden in the part of the back yard where Nelson's swing set used to be, getting a man from down the block to turn the earth with his Rototiller, the earth miraculously soft and pungent beneath the crust of winter and Janice out there enthusiastic with her string and rake in the gauzy shadows of the budding trees; but now that summer is here and the leafed-out trees keep the garden in the shade and the games at the club have begun she has let the plot go to weeds.

Still, he cannot dislike this brown-eyed woman who has been his indifferent wife for twenty-three years just this May. He is rich because of her inheritance and this mutual knowledge rests adhesively between them like a form of sex, comfortable and sly. 'Salad and baloney, my favorite meal,' he says, resigned. 'Lemme have a drink first. Some bastards came in to the lot today just as I was leaving. Tell me what postcard.'

As he stands by the refrigerator making a gin-and-bitter-lemon, knowing these sugary mixers add to the calories in the alcohol and help to keep him overweight but figuring that this Saturday evening meal in its skimpiness will compensate and maybe he'll jog a little afterwards, Janice goes in through the dark dining room into the musty front parlor where the shades are drawn and Ma Springer's sulking spirit reigns, and brings back a postcard. It shows a white slope of snow under a stark blue wedge of sky; two small dark hunched figures are tracing linked S's on the slanted snow, skiing. GREETINGS FROM COLORADO red cartoon letters say across the sky that looks like blue paint. On the opposite side a familiar scrawled hand, scrunched as if something in the boy had squeezed too tight while his handwriting was coming to birth, spells out:

> Hi Mom & Dad & Grandmom:
>    These mts make Mt Judge
> look sick! No snow tho,
> just plenty of grass (joke).
> Been learning to hang glide.
> Job didn't work out, guy was
> a bum. Penna. beckons.
> O K if I bring Melanie
> home too? She could get
> job and be no troble. Love,
>                         Nelson

'Melanie?' Harry asks.

'That's what Mother and I have been fighting about. She doesn't want the girl staying here.'

'Is this the same girl he went out there with two weeks ago?'

'I was wondering,' Janice says. 'She had a name more like Sue or Jo or something.'

'Where would she sleep?'

'Well, either in that front sewing room or Nelson's room.'

'*With* the kid?'

'Well really, Harry, I wouldn't be utterly surprised. He is twenty-two. When have you gotten so Puritanical?'

'I'm not being Puritanical, just practical. It's one thing to have these kids go off into the blue and go hang gliding or whatever else and another to have them bring all their dope and little tootsies back to the nest. This house is awkward upstairs, you

41

know that. There's too much hall space and you can't sneeze or fart or fuck without everybody else hearing; it's been bliss, frankly, with just us and Ma. Remember the kid's radio all through high school to two in the morning, how he'd fall asleep to it? That bed of his is a little single, what are we supposed to do, buy him and Melody a double bed?'

'Melanie. I don't know, she can sleep on the floor. They all have sleeping bags. You can try putting her in the sewing room but I know she won't stay there. We wouldn't have.' Her blurred dark eyes gaze beyond him into time. 'We spent all our energy sneaking down hallways and squirming around in the back seats of cars and I thought we could spare our children that.'

'We have a child, not children,' he says coldly, as the gin expands his inner space. They had children once, but the infant daughter Becky died. It was his wife's fault. The entire squeezed and cut-down shape of his life is her fault; at every turn she has been a wall to his freedom. 'Listen,' he says to her, 'I've been trying to get out of this fucking depressing house for years and I don't want this shiftless arrogant goof-off we've raised coming back and pinning me in. These kids seem to think the world exists to serve them but I'm sick of just standing around waiting to be of service.'

Janıce stands up to him scarcely flinching, armored in her country-club tan. 'He is our son, Harry, and we're not going to turn away a guest of his because she is female in sex. If it was a boyfriend of Nelson's you wouldn't be at all this excited, it's the fact that it's a *girl*friend of Nelson's that's upsetting you, a girl-friend of *Nel*son's. If it was a girlfriend of *yours*, the upstairs wouldn't be too crowded for you to fart in. This is my son and I want him here if he wants to be here.'

'I don't have any girlfriends,' he protests. It sounds pitiful. Is Janice saying he should have? Women, once sex gets out in the open, they become monsters. You're a creep if you fuck them and a creep if you don't. Harry strides into the dining room, making the glass panes of the antique breakfront shudder, and calls up the dark stained stairs that are opposite the breakfront, 'Hey Bessie, come on down! I'm on your side!'

There is a silence as from God above and then the creak of a bed being relieved of a weight, and reluctant footsteps slither across the ceiling toward the head of the stairs. Mrs Springer on her painful dropsical legs comes down talking: 'This house is legally mine and that girl is not spending one night under a roof Janice's father slaved all his days to keep over our heads.'

The breakfront quivers again; Janice has come into the dining room. She says in a voice turned tight to match her mother's, 'Mother you wouldn't be keeping this enormous roof over your head if it weren't for Harry and me sharing the upkeep. It's a great sacrifice on Harry's part, a man of his income not having a house he can call his own, and you have no right to forbid Nelson to come home when he wants to, *no* right, Mother.'

The plump old lady groans her way down to the landing three steps shy of the dining-room floor and hesitates there saying, in a voice tears have stained, 'Nellie I'm happy to see whenever he deems fit, I love that boy with all my heart even though he hasn't turned out the way his grandfather and I had hoped.'

Janice says, angrier in proportion as the old lady makes herself look pathetic, 'You're always bringing Daddy in when he can't speak for himself but as long as he was alive he was *very* hospitable and tolerant of Nelson and his friends. I remember that cookout Nelson had in the back yard for his high school graduation when Daddy had had his first stroke already, I went upstairs to see if it was getting too rowdy for him and he said with his wry little smile' – tears now stain her own voice too – ' "The sound of young voices does my old heart good." '

That slippery-quick salesman's smile of his, Rabbit can see it still. Like a switchblade without the click.

'A cookout in the back yard is one thing,' Mrs Springer says, thumping herself in her dirty aqua sneakers down the last three steps of the stairs and looking her daughter level in the eye. 'A slut in the boy's bed is another.'

Harry thinks this is pretty jazzy for an old lady and laughs aloud. Janice and her mother are both short women; like two doll's heads mounted on the same set of levers they turn identically chocolate-eyed, slot-mouthed faces to glare at his laugh. 'We don't know the girl is a slut,' Harry apologizes. 'All we know is her name is Melanie instead of Sue.'

'You said you were on my side,' Mrs Springer says.

'I am, Ma, I am. I don't see why the kid has to come storming home; we gave him enough money to get him started out there, I'd like to see him get some kind of grip on the world. He's not going to get it hanging around here all summer.'

'Oh, money,' Janice says. 'That's all you ever think about. And what have *you* ever done except hang around here? Your father got you one job and my father got you another, I don't call that any great adventure.'

'That's not all I think about,' he begins lamely, of money, before his mother-in-law interrupts.

'Harry doesn't want a home of his own,' Ma Springer tells her daughter. When she gets excited and fearful of not making herself understood her face puffs up and goes mottled. 'He had such disagreeable associations from the last time you two went out on your own.'

Janice is firm, younger, in control. 'Mother, you know nothing about it. You know nothing about life period. You sit in this house and watch idiotic game shows and talk on the phone to what friends you have that haven't died off yet and then sit in judgment on Harry and me. You know *nothing* of life now. You have no *idea*.'

'As if playing games at a country club with the nickel rich and coming home tiddled every night is enough to make you wise,' the old lady comes back, holding on with one hand to the knob of the newel post as if to ease the pain in her ankles. 'You come home,' she goes on, 'too silly to make your husband a decent supper and then want to bring this tramp into a house where I do all the housekeeping, even if I can scarcely stand to stand. I'm the one that would be here with them, you'd be off in that convertible. What will the neighbors make of it? What about the people in the church?'

'I don't care even if they care, which I dare say they won't,' Janice says. 'And to bring the church into it is ridiculous. The last minister at St John's ran off with Mrs Eckenroth and this one now is so gay I wouldn't let my boy go to his Sunday school, if I had a boy that age.'

'Nellie didn't go that much anyway,' Harry recalls. 'He said it gave him headaches.' He wants to lower the heat between the two women before it boils over into grief. He sees he must break this up, get a house of his own, before he runs out of gas. Stone outside, exposed beams inside, and a sunken living room: that is his dream.

'Melanie,' his mother-in-law is saying, 'what kind of name is that? It sounds colored.'

'Oh Mother, don't drag out all your prejudices. You sit and giggle at the Jeffersons as if you're one of them and Harry and Charlie unload all their old gas-hogs on the blacks and if we take their money we can take what else they have to offer too.'

Can she actually be black? Harry is asking himself, thrilled. Little cocoa babies. Skeeter would be so pleased.

'Anyway,' Janice is going on, looking frazzled suddenly, 'nobody's said the girl is black, all we know is she hang glides.'

'Or is that the other one?' Harry asks.

'If she comes, I go,' Bessie Springer says. 'Grace Stuhl has all those empty rooms now that Ralph's passed on and she's more than once said we should team up.'

'Mother, I find that hum*il*iating, that you've been begging Grace Stuhl to take you in.'

'I haven't been begging, the thought just naturally occurred to the both of us. I'd expect to be bought out here, though, and the values in the neighborhood have been going way up since they banned the through truck traffic.'

'Mother. Harry *hates* this house.'

He says, still hoping to calm these waters, 'I don't hate it, exactly; I just think the space upstairs –'

'Harry,' Janice says. 'Why don't you go out and pick some lettuce from the garden like we said? Then we'll eat.'

Gladly. He is glad to escape the house, the pinch of the women, their heat. Crazy the way they flog at each other with these ghosts of men, Daddy dead, Nelson gone, and even Harry himself a kind of ghost in the way they talk of him as if he wasn't standing right there. Day after day, mother and daughter sharing that same house, it's not natural. Like water blood must run or grow a scum. Old lady Springer always plump with that sausage look to her wrists and ankles but now her face puffy as well like those movie stars whose cheeks they stuff cotton up into to show them getting older. Her face not just plumper but wider as if a screw turning inside is spreading the sides of her skull apart, her eyes getting smaller, Janice heading the same way though she tried to keep trim, there's no stopping heredity. Rabbit notices now his own father talking in his own brain sometimes when he gets tired.

Bitter lemon fading in his mouth, an aluminum colander pleasantly light in his hand, he goes down the brick back steps into grateful space. He feels the neighborhood filter through to him and the voices in his brain grow still. Dark green around him is damp with coming evening, though this long day's lingering brightness surprises his eye above the shadowy masses of the trees. Rooftops and dormers notch the blue beginning to blush brown; here also electric wires and television aerials mar with their scratches the soft beyond, a few swallows dipping as they do at day's end in the middle range of air above the merged back yards, where little more than a wire fence or a line of hollyhocks marks the divisions of property. When he listens he can hear the sounds of cooking clatter or late play, alive in this common realm with a dog's bark, a bird's *weep weep*, the rhythmic far tapping of a hammer. A crew of butch women has moved in a few houses down and they're always out in steel-toed boots and overalls with ladders and hammers fixing things, they can do it all, from rain gutters to cellar doors: terrific. He sometimes waves to them when he jogs by in twilight but they don't have much to say to him, a creature of another kind.

Rabbit swings open the imperfect little gate he constructed two springs ago and enters the fenced rectangle of silent vegetable presences. The lettuce flourishes between a row of bean plants whose leaves are badly bug-eaten and whose stems collapse at a touch and a row of feathery carrot tops all but lost in an invasion of plantain and chickweed and purselane and a pulpy weed with white-and-yellow flowers that grows inches every night. It is easy to pull, its roots let go docilely, but there are so many he wearies within minutes of pulling and shaking the moist earth free from the roots and laying bundles of the weed along the chicken-wire fence as mulch and as barrier to the invading grasses. Grass that won't grow in the lawn where you plant it comes in here wild to multiply. Seed, so disgustingly much of it, Nature such a cruel smotherer. He thinks again of the dead he has known, the growingly many, and of the live child, if not his then some other father's, who visited him today with her long white legs propped up on cork heels, and of the other child, undoubtedly his, the genes show even in that quick scared way he looks at you, who has threatened to return. Rabbit pinches off the bigger lettuce leaves (but not the ones at the base so big as to be tough and bitter) and looks into his heart for welcome, welcoming love for his son. He finds instead a rumple of apprehensiveness in form and texture like a towel tumbled too soon from the dryer. He finds a hundred memories, some vivid as photographs and meaningless, snapped by the mind for reasons of its own, and others mere facts, things he knows are true but has no snapshot for. Our lives fade behind us before we die. He changed the boy's diapers in the sad apartment high on Wilbur Street, he lived with him for some wild months in an apple-green ranch house called 26 Vista Crescent in Penn Villas, and here at 89 Joseph he watched him become a high-school student with a wispy mustache that showed when he stood in the light, and a headband like an Indian's instead of getting a haircut, and a fortune in rock records kept in the sunny room whose drawn shades are above Harry's head now. He and Nelson have been through enough years together to turn a cedar post to rot and yet his son is less real to Harry than these crinkled leaves of lettuce he touches and plucks. Sad. Who says? The calm eyes of the girl who showed up at the lot today haunt the growing shadows, a mystery arrived at this time of his own numb life, death taking his measure with the invisible tapping of that neighborhood hammer: each day he is a little less afraid to die. He spots a Japanese beetle on a bean plant leaf and with a snap of his fingernail – big fingernails, with conspicuous cuticle moons – snaps the iridescent creature off. Die.

Back in the house, Janice exclaims, 'You've picked enough for six of us!'

'Where'd Ma go?'

'She's in the front hall, on the telephone to Grace Stuhl. Really, she's impossible. I really think senility is setting in. Harry, what shall we *do*?'

'Ride with the punches?'

'Oh, great.'

'Well honey it *is* her house, not ours and Nelson's.'

'Oh, drop dead. You're no help.' An illumination rises sluggishly within her sable, gin-blurred eyes. 'You don't want to be any help,' she announces. 'You just like to see us fight.'

The evening passes in a stale crackle of television and suppressed resentment. *Waitin' for some lover to call* ... Ma Springer, having condescended to share with them at the kitchen table some lumpy mushroom soup Janice has warmed and the cold cuts slightly sweaty from waiting too long in the refrigerator and all that salad he picked, stalks upstairs to her own room and shuts the door with a firmness that must carry out into the neighborhood as far as the butch women's house. A few cars, looking for hot stuff, prowl by on Joseph Street, with that wet tire sound that makes Harry and Janice feel alone as on an island. For supper they opened a half-gallon of Gallo Chablis and Janice keeps drifting into the kitchen to top herself up, so that by ten o'clock she is lurching in that way he hates. He doesn't blame people for many sins but he does hate uncoordination, the root of all evil as he feels it, for without coordination there can be no order, no connecting. In this state she bumps against doorframes coming through and sets her glass on the sofa arm so a big translucent lip of contents slops up and over into the fuzzy gray fabric. Together they sit through *Battlestar Galactica* and enough of *The Love Boat* to know it's not one of the good cruises. When she gets up to fill her glass yet again he switches to the Phillies game. The Phillies are being held to one hit by the Expos, he can't believe it, all that power. On the news, there is rioting in Levittown over gasoline, people are throwing beer bottles full of gasoline; they explode, it looks like old films of Vietnam or Budapest but it is Levittown right down the road, north of Philadelphia. A striking trucker is shown holding up a sign saying TO HELL WITH SHELL. And Three-Mile Island leaking radioactive neutrons just down the road in the other direction. The weather for tomorrow looks good, as a massive high continues to dominate from the Rocky Mountain region eastward all the way to Maine. Time for bed.

48

Harry knows in his bones, it has been borne in on him over the years, that on the nights of the days when Janice has fought with her mother and drunk too much she will want to make love. The first decade of their marriage, it was hard to get her to put out, there were a lot of things she wouldn't do and didn't even know were done and these seemed to be the things most on Rabbit's mind, but then since the affair with Charlie Stavros opened her up at about the time of the moon shot, and the style of the times proclaiming no holds barred, and for that matter death eating enough into her body for her to realize it wasn't such a precious vessel and there wasn't any superman to keep saving it for, Harry has no complaints. Indeed what complaints there might be in this line would come from her about him. Somewhere early in the Carter administration his interest, that had been pretty faithful, began to wobble and by now there is a real crisis of confidence. He blames it on money, on having enough at last, which has made him satisfied all over; also the money itself, relaxed in the bank, gets smaller all the time, and this is on his mind, what to do about it, along with everything else: the Phils, and the dead, and golf. He has taken the game up with a passion since they joined the Flying Eagle, without getting much better at it, or at least without giving himself any happier impression of an absolute purity and power hidden within the coiling of his muscles than some lucky shots in those first casual games he played once did. It is like life itself in that its performance cannot be forced and its underlying principle shies from being permanently named. *Arms like ropes*, he tells himself sometimes, with considerable success, and then, when that goes bad, *Shift the weight*. Or, *Don't chicken-wing it*, or, *Keep the angle*, meaning the angle between club and arms when wrists are cocked. Sometimes he thinks it's all in the hands, and then in the shoulders, and even in the knees. When it's in the knees he can't control it. Basketball was somehow more instinct-ive. If you thought about merely walking down the street the way you think about golf you'd wind up falling off the curb. Yet a good straight drive or a soft chip stiff to the pin gives him the bliss that used to come thinking of women, imagining if only you and she were alone on some island.

Naked, Janice bumps against the doorframe from their bathroom back into their bedroom. Naked, she lurches onto the bed where he is trying to read the July issue of *Consumer Reports* and thrusts her tongue into his mouth. He tastes Gallo, baloney, and toothpaste while his mind is still trying to sort out the virtues and failings of the great range of can openers put to the test over five close pages of print. The Sunbeam units were most successful at opening rectangular and dented cans and yet pierced coffee cans with such force that grains of coffee spewed out onto the counter. Elsewhere, slivers of metal were dangerously produced, magnets gripped so strongly that the contents of the cans tended to spatter, blades failed to reach deep lips, and one small plastic insert so quickly wore away that the model (Ekco C865K) was judged Not Acceptable. Amid these fine discriminations Janice's tongue like an eyeless eager eel intrudes and angers him. Ever since in her late thirties she had her tubes burned to avoid any more bad side effects from the Pill, a demon of loss (never any more children never ever) has given her sexuality a false animation, a thrust somehow awry. Her eyes as her face backs off from the kiss he has resisted, squirming, have in them no essential recognition of him, only a glaze of liquor and blank unfriendly wanting. By the light by which he had been trying to read he sees the hateful aged flesh at the base of her throat, reddish and tense as if healed from a burn. He wouldn't see it so clearly if he didn't have his reading glasses on. 'Jesus,' he says, 'at least let's wait till I turn out the light.'

'I like it on.' Her insistence is slurred. 'I like to see all the gray hair on your chest.'

This interests him. 'Is there much?' He tries to see, past his chin. 'It's not gray, it's just blond, isn't it?'

Janice pulls the bedsheet down to his waist and crouches to examine him hair by hair. Her breasts hang down so her nipples, bumply in texture like hamburger, sway an inch above his belly. 'You do here, and here.' She pulls each gray hair.

'Ouch. Damn you, Janice. *Stop*.' He pushes his stomach up so her nipples vanish and her breasts are squashed against her own frail ribs. Gripping the hair of her head in one fist in his rage at being invaded, the other hand still holding the magazine in which he was trying to read about magnets gripping, he arches his spine so she is thrown from his body to her side of the bed. In her boozy haze mistaking this for love play, Janice tugs the sheets down still lower on him and takes his prick in a fumbling, twittering grip. Her touch is cold from having just washed her hands in the bathroom. The next page of *Consumer Reports* is printed on blue and asks, *Summer cooling, 1979: Air-conditioner or fan?* He tries to skim the list of advantages and disadvantages peculiar to each (*Bulky and heavy to install* as opposed to *Light and portable*, *Expensive to run* as against *Inexpensive to run*, the fan seems to be scoring all the points) but can't quite disassociate himself from the commotion below his waist, where Janice's anxious fingers seem to be asking the same question over and over, without getting the answer they want. Furious, he throws the magazine against the wall behind which Ma Springer sleeps. More carefully, he removes his reading glasses and puts them in his bedside table drawer and switches off the bedside lamp.

His wife's importunate flesh must then compete with the sudden call to sleep that darkness brings. It has been a long day. He was awake at six-thirty and got up at seven. His eyelids have grown too thin to tolerate the early light. Even now near midnight he feels tomorrow's early dawn rotating toward him. He recalls again the blue-eyed apparition who seemed to be his and Ruth's genes mixed; he is reminded then from so long ago of that Ruth whom he fucked upwards the first time, saying 'Hey' in his surprise at her beauty, her body one long underbelly erect in light from the streetlamp outside on Summer, his prick erect in her loveliness above him, *Hey*, it seems a melancholy falling that an act so glorious has been dwindled to this blurred burrowing of two old bodies, one drowsy and one drunk. Janice's rummaging at his prick has become hostile now as it fails to rise; her attention burns upon it like sun's rays focused by a magnifying glass upon a scrap of silk, kids used to kill ants that way, Harry watched but never participated. We are cruel enough without meaning to be. He resents that in her eagerness for some dilution of her sense of being forsaken, having quarrelled with her mother, and perhaps also afraid of their son's return, Janice gives him no space of secrecy in which blood can gather as it did behind his fly in ninth-grade algebra sitting beside Lotty Bingaman who in raising her hand to show she had the answers showed him wisps of armpit hair and pressed the thin cotton of her blouse tighter against the elastic trusswork of her bra, so its salmon color strained through. Then the fear was the bell would ring and he would have to stand with this hard-on.

He resolves to suck Janice's tits, to give himself a chance to pull himself together, this is embarrassing. A pause at the top, you need a pause at the top to generate momentum. His spit glimmers within her dark shape above him; the headboard of their bed is placed between two windows shaded from the light of sun and moon alike by a great copper beech whose leaves yet allow a little streetlight through.

'That feels nice.' He wishes she wouldn't say this. Nice isn't enough. Without some shadow of assault or outrage it becomes another task, another duty. To think, all along, that Lotty was sitting there itching to be fucked. It wasn't just him. She was holding a dirty yearning between her legs just like the lavatory walls said, those drawings and words put there by the same kids who magnified the ants to death, that little sticky pop they died with, you could hear it, did girls too make a little sticky noise when they opened up? The thought of her *knowing* when she raised her hand that her blouse was tugged into wrinkles all pointing to the tip of her tit and that an edge of bra peeped out through the cotton armhole with those little curly virgin hairs and that he was watching for it all to happen does make blood gather. In the fumbly worried dark, with Ma Springer sleeping off her sulk a thickness of plaster away, Harry as if casually presents his stiffened prick to Janice's hand. *Hot stuuuuff*.

But wanderings within her own brain have blunted her ardor and her touch conveys this, it is too heavy, so in a desperate mood of self-rescue he hisses 'Suck' in her ear, 'Suck.' Which she does, turning her back, her head heavy on his belly. Diagonal on the bed he stretches one arm as if preparing to fly and caresses her ass, these lower globes of hers less spherical than once they were, and the fur between more findable by his fingers. She learned to blow when she went away with Stavros but doesn't really get her head into it, nibbles more, the top inch or two. To keep himself excited he tries to remember Ruth, that exalted 'Hey' and the way she swallowed it once, but the effort brings back with such details the guilt of their months together and, betrayal betrayed, his desertion and the final sour sorrow of it all.

Janice lets him slide from her mouth and asks, 'What are you thinking about?'

'Work,' he lies. 'Charlie worries me. He's taking such good care of himself you hate to ask him to do anything. I seem to handle most of the customers now.'

'Well why not? You give yourself twice the salary he gets and he's been there forever.'

'Yeah, but I married the boss's daughter. He could have, but didn't.'

'Marriage wasn't our thing,' Janice says.

'What was?'

'Never mind.'

Absent-mindedly he strokes her long hair, soft from all that swimming, as it flows on his abdomen. 'Pair of kids came into the lot late today,' he begins to tell her, then thinks better of it. Now that her sexual push is past, his prick has hardened, the competing muscles of anxiety having at last relaxed. But she, she is relaxed all over, asleep with his prick in her face. 'Want me inside?' he asks softly, getting no answer. He moves her off his chest and works her inert body around so they lie side by side and he can fuck her from behind. She wakes enough to cry 'Oh' when he penetrates. Slickly admitted, he pumps slowly, pulling the sheet up over them both. Not hot enough yet for the fan *versus* air-conditioner decision, both are tucked around the attic somewhere, back under the dusty eaves, strain your back lifting it out, he has never liked the chill of air-conditioning even when it was only to be had at the movies and thought to be a great treat drawing you in right off the hot sidewalk, the word COOL in blue-green with icicles on the marquee, always seemed to him healthier to live in the air God gave however lousy and let your body adjust, Nature can adjust to anything. Still, some of these nights, sticky, and the cars passing below with that wet-tire sound, the kids with their windows open or tops down and radios blaring just at the moment of dropping off to sleep, your skin prickling wherever it touched cloth and a single mosquito alive in the room. His prick is stiff as stone inside a sleeping woman. He strokes her ass, the crease where it nestles against his belly, must start jogging again, the crease between its halves and that place within the crease, opposite of a nipple, dawned on him gradually over these years that she had no objection to being touched there, seemed to like it when she was under him his hand beneath her bottom. He touches himself too now and then to test if he is holding hard, he is, thick as a tree where it comes up out of the grass, the ridges of the roots, her twin dark moons swallowing and letting go, a little sticky sound. The long slack oily curve of her side, ribs to hip bone, floats under his fingertips idle as a gull's glide. Love has lulled her, liquor has carried her off. Bless that dope. 'Jan?' he whispers. 'You awake?' He is not displeased to be thus stranded, another consciousness in bed is a responsibility, a snag in the flow of his thoughts. Further on in that issue an article *How to shop for a car loan* he ought to look at for professional reasons though it's not the sort of thing that interests him, he can't get it out of his head how they noticed those coffee grounds that jump out of the can when punctured. Janice snores: a single rasp of breath taken underwater, at some deep level where her nose becomes a harp. Big as the night her ass unconscious wraps him all around in this room where dabs of streetlight sifted by the beech shuffle on the ceiling. He decides to fuck her, the stiffness in his cock is killing him. His hard-on was her idea anyway. The Japanese beetle he flicked away comes into his mind as a model of delicacy. Hold tight, dream girl. He sets three fingers on her flank, the pinky lifted as in a counting game. He is stealthy so as not to wake her but single in his purpose, quick, and pure. The climax freezes his scalp and stops his heart, all stealthy; he hasn't come with such a thump in months. So who says he is running out of gas?

'I hit the ball O.K.,' Rabbit says next afternoon, 'but damned if I could score.' He is sitting in green bathing trunks at a white outdoor table at the Flying Eagle Tee and Racquet Club with the partners of his round and their wives and, in the case of Buddy Inglefinger, girlfriend. Buddy had once had a wife too but she left him for a telephone lineman down near West Chester. You could see how that might happen because Buddy's girlfriends are sure a sorry lot.

'When did you *ever* score?' Ronnie Harrison asks him so loudly heads in the swimming pool turn around. Rabbit has known Ronnie for thirty years and never liked him, one of those locker-room show-offs always soaping himself for everybody to see and giving the J Vs redbellies and out on the basketball court barging around all sweat and elbows trying to make up in muscle what he lacked in style. Yet when Harry and Janice joined Flying Eagle there old Ronnie was, with a respectable job at Schuylkill Mutual and this nice proper wife who taught third grade for years and must be great in bed, because that's all Ronnie ever used to talk about, he was like frantic on the subject, in the locker room. His kinky brass-colored hair, that began to thin right after school, is pretty thoroughly worn through on top now, and the years and respectability have drained some pink out of him; the skin from his temples to the corners of his eyes is papery and bluish, and Rabbit doesn't remember that his eyelashes were white. He likes playing golf with Ronnie because he loves beating him, which isn't too hard: he has one of those herky-jerky punch swings short stocky guys gravitate toward and when he gets excited he tends to roundhouse a big banana right into the woods.

'I heard Harry was a big scorer,' Ronnie's wife Thelma says softly. She has a narrow forgettable face and still wears that quaint old-fashioned kind of one-piece bathing suit with a little pleated skirt. Often she has a towel across her shoulders or around her ankles as if to protect her skin from the sun; except for her sunburnt nose she is the same sallow color all over. Her wavy mousy hair is going gray strand by strand. Rabbit can never look at her without wondering what she must do to keep Harrison happy. He senses intelligence in her but intelligence in women has never much interested him.

'I set the B-league county scoring record in 1951,' he says, to defend himself, and to defend himself further adds, 'Big deal.'

'It's been broken long since,' Ronnie feels he has to explain. 'By blacks.'

'Every record has,' Webb Murkett interposes, being tactful. 'I don't know, it seems like the miles these kids run now have

shrunk. In swimming they can't keep the record books up to date.'
Webb is the oldest man of their regular foursome, fifty and then
some – a lean thoughtful gentleman in roofing and siding con-
tracting and supply with a calming gravel voice, his long face
broken into longitudinal strips by creases and his hazel eyes
almost lost under an amber tangle of eyebrows. He is the steadiest
golfer, too. The one unsteady thing about him, he is on his third
wife; this is Cindy, a plump brown-backed honey still smelling of
high school, though they have two little ones, a boy and a girl, ages
five and three. Her hair is cut short and lies wet in one direction,
as if surfacing from a dive, and when she smiles her teeth look
unnaturally even and white in her tan face, with pink spots of
peeling on the roundest part of her cheeks; she has an exciting
sexually neutral look, though her boobs slosh and shiver in the
triangular little hammocks of her bra. The suit is one of those
minimal black ones with only a string or two between the nape of
her neck and where her ass begins to divide, a cleft more or less
visible depending on the sag of her black diaper. Harry admires
Webb. Webb always swings within himself, and gets good roll.

'Better nutrition, don't you think that's it?' Buddy Inglefinger's girl pipes up, in a little-girl reedy voice that doesn't go
with her pushed-in face. She is some kind of physical therapist,
though her own shape isn't too great. The girls Buddy brings
around are a good lesson to Harry in the limits of being single –
hard little secretaries and restaurant hostesses, witchy-looking
former flower children with grizzled ponytails and flat chests full
of Navajo jewelry, overweight assistant heads of personnel in one
of those grim new windowless office buildings a block back from
Weiser where they spend all day putting computer print-outs in
the wastebasket. Women pickled in limbo, their legs chalky and
their faces slightly twisted, as if they had been knocked into their
thirties by a sideways blow. They remind Harry somehow of
pirates, jaunty and maimed, though without the eye patches.
What the hell was this one's name? She had been introduced
around not a half hour ago, but when everybody was still drunk
on golf.

Buddy brought her, so he can't let her two cents hang up there
while the silence gets painful. He fills in, 'My guess is it's mostly

in the training. Coaches at even the secondary level have all these techniques that in the old days only the outstanding athlete would discover, you know, pragmatically. Nowadays the outstanding isn't that outstanding, there's a dozen right behind him. Or her.' He glances at each of the women in a kind of dutiful tag. Feminism won't catch him off guard, he's traded jabs in too many singles bars. 'And in countries like East Germany or China they're pumping these athletes full of steroids, like beef cattle, they're hardly human.' Buddy wears steel-rimmed glasses of a style that only lathe operators used to employ, to keep shavings out of their eyes. Buddy does something with electronics and has a mind like that, too precise. He goes on, to bring it home, 'Even golf. Palmer and now Nicklaus have been trampled out of sight by these kids nobody has heard of, the colleges down south clone 'em, you can't keep their names straight from one tournament to the next.'

Harry always tries to take an overview. 'The records fall because they're there,' he says. 'Aaron shouldn't have been playing, they kept him in there just so he could break Ruth's record. I can remember when a five-minute mile in high school was a miracle. Now girls are doing it.'

'It is amazing,' Buddy's girl puts in, this being her conversation, 'what the human body can do. Any one of us women here could go out now and pick up a car by the front bumper, if we were motivated. If say there was a child of ours under the tires. You read about incidents like that all the time, and at the hospital where I trained the doctors could lay the statistics of it right out on paper. We don't use half the muscle-power we have.'

Webb Murkett kids, 'Hear that, Cin? Gas stations all closed down, you can carry the Audi home. Seriously, though. I've always marvelled at these men who know a dozen languages. If the brain is a computer think of all the gray cells this entails. There seems to be lots more room in there, though.'

His young wife silently lifts her hands to twist some water from her hair, that is almost too short to grab. This action gently lifts her tits in their sopping black small slings and reveals the shape of each erect nipple. A white towel is laid across her lap as if to relieve Harry from having to think about her crotch. What turns him off about Buddy's girl, he realizes, is not only does she have pimples on her chin and forehead but on her thighs, high on the inside, like something venereal. Georgene? Geraldine? She is going on in that reedy too-eager voice, 'Or the way these yogas can lift themselves off the ground or go back in time for thousands of years. Edgar Cayce has example after example. It's nothing supernatural, I can't believe in God, there's too much suffering, they're just human powers we all have and never develop. You should all read the Tibetan Book of the Dead.'

'Really?' Thelma Harrison says dryly.

Now silence does invade their group. A greenish reflective wobble from the pool washes ghostly and uneasy across their faces and a child gasping as he swims can be heard. Then Webb kindly says, 'Closer to home now, we've had a spooky experience lately. I bought one of these Polaroid SX-70 Land Cameras as kind of a novelty, to give the kids a charge, and all of us can't stop being fascinated, it is super*natural*, to watch that image develop right under your eyes.'

'The kind,' Cindy says, 'that spits it out at you like this.' She makes a cross-eyed face and thrusts out her tongue with a *thrrupp*-ing noise. All the men laugh, and laugh.

'*Consumer Reports* had something on it,' Harry says.

'It's magical,' Cindy tells them. 'Webb gets really turned on.' When she grins her teeth look stubby, the healthy gums come so babyishly low.

'Why is my glass empty?' Janice asks.

'Losers buy,' Harry virtually shouts. Such loudness years ago would have been special to male groups but now both sexes have watched enough beer commercials on television to know that this is how to act, jolly and loud, on weekends, in the bar, beside the barbecue grill, on beaches and sundecks and mountainsides. 'Winners bought the first round,' he calls needlessly, as if among strangers or men without memories, while several arms flail for the waitress.

Harry's team lost the Nassau, but he feels it was his partner's fault. Buddy is such a flub artist, even when he hits two good shots he skulls the chip and takes three putts to get down. Whereas Harry as he has said hit the ball well, if not always straight: arms like ropes, start down slow, and *look at the ball* until it seems to

58

swell. He ended with a birdie, on the long par-five that winds in around the brook with its watercress and sandy orange bottom almost to the clubhouse lawn, and that triumph (the wooden gobbling sound the cup makes when a long putt falls) eclipses many double bogeys and suffuses with limpid certainty of his own omnipotence and immortality the sight of the scintillating chlorinated water, the sunstruck faces and torsos of his companions, and the undulant shadow-pitted flank of Mt Pemaquid where its forest begins above the shaven bright stripes of the fairways. He feels brother to this mountain in the day's declining sunlight. Mt Pemaquid has only been recently tamed; for the two centuries while Mt Judge presided above the metropolitan burgeoning of Brewer, the mountain nearby yet remained if not quite a wilderness a strange and forbidding place, where resort hotels failed and burned down and only hikers and lovers and escaping criminals ventured. The developers of the Flying Eagle (its name plucked from a bird, probably a sparrow hawk, the first surveyor spotted and took as an omen) bought three hundred acres of the lower slopes cheap; as the bulldozers ground the second-growth ash, poplar, hickory, and dogwood into muddy troughs that would become fairways and terraced tennis courts, people said the club would fail, the county already had the Brewer Country Club south of the city for the doctors and the Jews and ten miles north the Tulpehocken Club behind its fieldstone walls and tall wrought-iron fencing for the old mill-owning families and their lawyers and for the peasantry several nine-hole public courses tucked around in the farmland. But there was a class of the young middle-aged that had arisen in the retail businesses and service industries and software end of the new technology and that did not expect liveried barmen and secluded cardrooms, that did not mind the pre-fab clubhouse and sweep-it-yourself tennis courts of the Flying Eagle; to them the polyester wall-to-wall carpeting of the locker rooms seemed a luxury, and a Coke machine in a cement corridor a friendly sight. They were happy to play winter rules all summer long on the immature, patchy fairways and to pay for all their privileges the five hundred, now risen to six-fifty, in annual dues, plus a small fortune in chits. Fred Springer for years had angled for admission to the Brewer C.C. – the Tulpehocken was as out of reach as the College of Cardinals, he knew that – and failed; now his daughter Janice wears whites and signs chits just like the heiresses of Sunflower Beer and Frankhauser Steel. Just like a Du Pont. At the Flying Eagle Harry feels exercised, cleansed, cherished; the biggest man at the table, he lifts his hand and a girl in the restaurant uniform of solid green blouse and checked skirt of white and green comes and takes his order for more drinks on this Sunday of widespread gas dearth. She doesn't ask his name; the people here know it. Her own name is stitched Sandra on her blouse pocket; she has milky skin like his daughter but is shorter, and the weary woman she will be has already crowded into her face.

'Do you believe in astrology?' Buddy's girl abruptly asks Cindy Murkett. Maybe she's a Lesbian, is why Harry can't remember her name. It was a name soft around the edges, not Gertrude.

'I don't know,' Cindy says, the widened eyes of her surprise showing very white in her mask of tan. 'I look at the horoscope in the papers sometimes. Some of the things they say ring so true, but isn't there a trick to that?'

'It's no trick, it's ancient science. It's the most ancient science there is.'

This assault on Cindy's repose agitates Harry so he turns to Webb and asks if he watched the Phillies game last night.

'The Phillies are dead,' Ronnie Harrison butts in.

Buddy comes up with the statistic that they've lost twenty-three of their last thirty-four games.

'I was brought up a Catholic,' Cindy is saying to Buddy's girl in a voice so lowered Harry has to strain to hear. 'And the priests said such things are the work of the Devil.' She fingers as she confides this the small crucifix she wears about her throat on a chain so fine it has left no trace in her tan.

'Bowa's being out has hurt them quite a lot,' Webb says judiciously, and pokes another cigarette into his creased face, lifting his rubbery upper lip automatically like a camel. He shot an 84 this afternoon, with a number of three-putt greens.

Janice is asking Thelma where she bought that lovely bathing suit. She must be drunk. 'You can't find that kind at all in Kroll's anymore,' Rabbit hears her say. Janice is wearing an old sort of

Op-pattern blue two-piece, with a white cardigan bought to go with her tennis whites hung capelike over her shoulders. She holds a cigarette in her hand and Webb Murkett leans over to light it with his turquoise propane lighter. She's not so bad, Harry thinks, remembering how he fucked her in her sleep. Or was it, for she seemed to moan and stop snoring afterwards. Compared to Thelma's boneless sallow body Janice's figure has energy, edge, the bones of the knees pressing their shape against the skin as she leans forward to accept his light. She does this with a certain accustomed grace. Webb respects her, as Fred Springer's daughter.

Harry wonders where his own daughter is this afternoon, out in the country. Doing some supper chore, having come back from feeding cattle or whatever. Sundays in the sticks aren't so different, animals don't know about holidays. Would she have gone to church this morning? Ruth had no use for that. He can't picture Ruth in the country at all. For him, she was city, those solid red brick rows of Brewer that take what comes. The drinks come. Grateful cries, like on the beer commercials, and Cindy Murkett decides to earn hers by going for another swim. When she stands, the backs of her thighs are printed in squares and her skimpy black bathing suit bottom, still soaked, clings in two arcs a width of skin below two dimples symmetrically set in her fat like little whirl-pools; the sight dizzies Harry. Didn't he used to take Ruth to the public pool in West Brewer? Memorial Day. The smell of grass pressed under your damp towel spread out in the shade of the trees away from the tile pool. Now you sit in chairs of enamelled wire that unless you have a cushion print a waffle pattern on the backs of your thighs. The mountain is drawing closer. Sun reddening beyond the city dusts with gold the tips of trees high like a mane on the crest of Pemaquid and deepens the pockets of dark between each tree in the undulating forest that covers like deep-piled carpet the acreage between crest and course. Along the far eleventh fairway men are still picking their way, insect-sized. As his eyes are given to these distances Cindy flat-dives and a few drops of the splash prick Harry's naked chest, that feels broad as the basking mountain. He frames in his mind the words, *I heard a funny story on the radio yesterday driving home . . .*

'. . . if I had your nice legs,' Ronnie's plain wife is concluding to Janice.

'Oh but you still have a waist. Creeping middle-itis, that's what I've got. Harry says I'm shaped like a pickle.' Giggle. First she giggles, then she begins to lurch.

'He looks asleep.'

He opens his eyes and announces to the air, 'I heard a funny story on the radio yesterday driving home.'

'Fire Ozark,' Ronnie is insisting loudly. 'He's lost their respect, he's demoralizing. Until they can Ozark and trade Rose away, the Phillies are d-e-a-d, dead.'

'I'm listening,' Buddy's awful girlfriend tells Harry, so he has to go on.

'Oh just some doctor down in Baltimore, the radio announcer said he was hauled into court for killing a goose on the course with a golf club.'

'Course on the golf with a goose club,' Janice giggles. Some day what would give him great pleasure would be to take a large round rock and crush her skull in with it.

'Where'd you hear this, Harry?' Webb Murkett asks him, coming in late but politely tilting his long head, one eye shut against the smoke of his cigarette.

'On the radio yesterday, driving home,' Harry answers, sorry he has begun.

'Speaking of yesterday,' Buddy has to interrupt, 'I saw a gas line five blocks long. That Sunoco at the corner of Ash and Fourth, it went down Fourth to Buttonwood, Buttonwood to Fifth, Fifth back to Ash, and then a new line beginning the other side of Ash. They had guys directing and everything. I couldn't believe it, and cars were still getting into it. Five fucking blocks long.'

'Big heating-oil dealer who's one of our clients,' Ronnie says, 'says they have plenty of crude, it's just they've decided to put the squeeze on gasoline and make more heating oil out of it. The crude. In their books winter's already here. I asked the guy what was going to happen to the average motorist and he looked at me funny and said, "He can go screw himself instead of driving every weekend to the Jersey Shore."'

'Ronnie, Harry's trying to tell a story,' Thelma says.

'It hardly seems worth it,' he says, enjoying now the prolonged focus on him, the comedy of delay. Sunshine on the mountain. The second gin is percolating through his system and elevating his spirits. He loves this crowd, his crowd, and the crowds at the other tables too, that are free to send delegates over and mingle with theirs, everybody knowing everybody else, and the kids in the pool, that somebody would save even if that caramel-colored lifeguard-girl popping bubble gum weren't on duty, and loves the fact that this is all on credit, the club not taking its bite until the tenth of every month.

Now they coax him. 'Come on, Harry, don't be a prick,' Buddy's girl says. She's using his name now, he has to find hers. Gretchen. Ginger. Maybe those aren't actually pimples on her thighs, just a rash from chocolate or poison oak. She looks allergic, that pushed-in face, like she'd have trouble breathing. Defects come in clumps.

'So this doctor,' he concludes, 'is hauled into court for killing a goose on the course with a golf club.'

'What club?' Ronnie asks.

'I knew you'd ask that,' Harry says. 'If not you, some other jerk.'

'I'd think a sand wedge,' Buddy says, 'right at the throat. 'D clip the head right off.'

'Too short in the handle, you couldn't get close enough,' Ronnie argues. He squints as if to judge a distance. 'I'd say a five or even an easy four would be the right stick. Hey Harry, how about that five-iron I put within a gimme on the fifteenth from way out on the other side of the sand trap? In deep rough yet.'

'You nudged it,' Harry says.

'Heh?'

'I saw you nudge the ball up to give yourself a lie.'

'Let's get this straight. You're saying I cheated.'

'Something like that.'

'Let's hear the story, Harry,' Webb Murkett says, lighting another cigarette to dramatize his patience.

Ginger was in the ballpark. Thelma Harrison is staring at him with her big brown sunglasses and that is distracting too. 'So the doctor's defense evidently was that he had hit the goose with a golf ball and injured it badly enough he had to put it out of its misery. Then this announcer said, it seemed cute at the time, she was a female announcer –'

'Wait a minute sweetie, I don't understand,' Janice says. 'You mean he threw a golf ball at this goose?'

'Oh my God,' Rabbit says, 'am I ever sorry I got started on this. Let's go home.'

'No *tell* me,' Janice says, looking panicked.

'He didn't *throw* the ball, the goose was on the fairway probably by some pond and the guy's drive or whatever it was –'

'Could have been his second shot and he shanked it,' Buddy offers.

His nameless girl friend looks around and in that fake little-girl voice asks, 'Are geese allowed on golf courses? I mean, that may be stupid, Buddy's the first golfer I've gone out with –'

'You call *that* a golfer?' Ronnie interrupts.

Buddy tells them, 'I've read somewhere about a course in Alaska where these caribou wander. Maybe it's Sweden.'

'I've heard of moose on courses in Maine,' Webb Murkett says. Lowering sun flames in his twisted eyebrows. He seems sad. Maybe he's feeling the liquor too, for he rambles on, 'Wonder why you never hear of a Swedish golfer. You hear of Bjorn Borg, and this skier Stenmark.'

Rabbit decides to ride it through. 'So the announcer says, "A mercy killing, or murder most foul?"'

'Ouch,' someone says.

Ronnie is pretending to ruminate, 'Maybe you'd be better off with a four-wood, and play the goose off your left foot.'

'Nobody heard the punch line,' Harry protests.

'I heard it,' Thelma Harrison says.

'We all heard it,' Buddy says. 'It's just very distressing to me,' he goes on, and looks very severe in his steel-rimmed glasses, so the women at first take him seriously, 'that nobody here, I mean *no*body, has shown any sympathy for the goose.'

'Somebody sympathized enough to bring the man to court,' Webb Murkett points out.

'I discover myself,' Buddy complains sternly, 'in the midst of a crowd of people who while pretending to be liberal and tolerant are really anti-goose.'

'Who, me?' Ronnie says, making his voice high as if goosed. Rabbit hates this kind of humour, but the others seem to enjoy it, including the women.

Cindy has returned glistening from her swim. Standing there with her bathing suit slightly awry, she tugs it straight and blushes in the face of their laughter. 'Are you talking about me?' The little cross glints beneath the hollow of her throat. Her feet look pale on the poolside flagstones. Funny, how pale the tops of feet stay.

Webb gives his wife's wide hips a sideways hug. 'No, honey. Harry was telling us a shaggy goose story.'

'Tell me, Harry.'

'Not now. Nobody liked it. Webb will tell you.'

Little Sandra in her green and white uniform comes up to them. 'Mrs Angstrom.'

The words shock Harry, as if his mother has been resurrected.

'Yes,' Janice answers matter-of-factly.

'Your mother is on the phone.'

'Oh, Lordie, what now?' Janice stands, lurches slightly, composes herself. She takes her beach towel from the back of her chair and wraps it around her hips rather than walk in mere bathing suit past dozens of people into the clubhouse. 'What do you think it is?' she asks Harry.

He shrugs. 'Maybe she wants to know what kind of baloney we're having tonight.'

A dig in that, delivered openly. The awful girlfriend titters. Harry is ashamed of himself, thinking in contrast of Webb's sideways hug of Cindy's hips. This kind of crowd will do a marriage in if you let it. He doesn't want to get sloppy.

In defiance Janice asks, 'Honey, could you order me another vod-and-ton while I'm gone?'

'No.' He softens this to, 'I'll think about it,' but the chill has been put on the party.

The Murketts consult and conclude it may be time to go, they have a thirteen-year-old babysitter, a neighbor's child. The same sunlight that ignited Webb's eyebrows lights the halo of fine hairs standing up from the goosebumps on Cindy's thighs. Not bothering with any towel around her she saunters to the ladies' locker room to change, her pale feet leaving black prints on the gray flagstones. Wait, wait, the Sunday, the weekend cannot be by, a golden sip remains in the glass. On the transparent tabletop among the wire chairs drinks have left a ghostly clockwork of rings refracted into visibility by the declining light. What can Janice's mother want? She has called out to them from a darker older world he remembers but wants to stay buried, a world of constant clothing and airless front parlors, of coal bins and narrow houses with spitefully drawn shades, where the farmer's drudgery and the millworker's lowered like twin clouds over land and city. Here, clean children shivering with their sudden emergence into the thinner element are handed towels by their mothers. Cindy's towel hangs on her empty chair. To be Cindy's towel and to be sat upon by her: the thought dries Harry's mouth. To stick your tongue in just as far as it would go while her pussy tickles your nose. No acne in that crotch. Heaven. He looks up and sees the shaggy mountain shouldering into the sun still, though the chairs are making long shadows, lozenge checkerboards. Buddy Inglefinger is saying to Webb Murkett in a low voice whose vehemence is not ironical, 'Ask yourself sometime who benefits from inflation. The people in debt benefit, society's losers. The government benefits because it collects more in taxes without raising the rates. Who doesn't benefit? The man with money in his pocket, the man who's paid his bills. That's why' – Buddy's voice drops to a conspiratorial hiss – 'that man is vanishing like the red Indian. Why should I work,' he asks Webb, 'when the money is taken right out of my pocket for the benefit of those who don't?'

Harry is thinking his way along the mountain ridge, where clouds are lifting like a form of steam. As if in motion Mt Pemaquid cleaves the summer sky and sun, though poolside is in shadow now. Thelma is saying cheerfully to the girlfriend, 'Astrology, palm-reading, psychiatry – I'm all for it. Anything that helps get you through.' Harry is thinking of his own parents. They should have belonged to a club. Living embattled, Mom feuding with the neighbors, Pop and his union hating the men who owned the printing plant where he worked his life away, both of them scorning the few kin that tried to keep in touch, the four of them, Pop and Mom and Hassy and Mim, against the world and a certain guilt attaching to any reaching up and outside for a friend. *Don't trust anybody: Andy Mellon doesn't, and I don't.* Dear Pop. He never got out from under. Rabbit basks above that old remembered world, rich, at rest.

Buddy's voice nags on, aggrieved. 'Money that goes out of one pocket goes into somebody else's, it doesn't just evaporate. The big boys are getting rich out of this.'

A chair scrapes and Rabbit feels Webb stand. His voice comes from a height, gravelly, humorously placating. 'Become a big boy yourself I guess is the only answer.'

'Oh sure,' Buddy says, knowing he is being put off.

A tiny speck, a bird, the fabled eagle it might be, no, from the motionlessness of its wings a buzzard, is flirting in flight with the ragged golden-green edge of the mountain, now above it like a speck on a Kodak slide, now below it out of sight, while a blue-bellied cloud unscrolls, endlessly, endlessly. Another chair is scraped on the flagstones. His name, 'Harry,' is sharply called, in Janice's voice.

He lowers his gaze at last out of glory and as his eyes adjust his forehead momentarily hurts, a small arterial pain; perhaps with such a negligible unexplained ache do men begin their deaths, some slow as being tumbled by a cat and some fast as being struck by a hawk. Cancer, coronary. 'What did Bessie want?'

Janice's tone is breathless, faintly stricken. 'She says Nelson's come. With this girl.'

'Melanie,' Harry says, pleased to have remembered. And his remembering brings along with it Buddy's girlfriend's name. Joanne. 'It was nice to have met you, Joanne,' he says in parting, shaking her hand. Making a good impression. Casting his shadow.

As Harry drives them home in Janice's Maverick convertible with the top down, air pours over them and lends an illusion of urgent and dangerous speed. Their words are snatched from their mouths. 'What the fuck are we going to do with the kid?' he asks her.

'How do you mean?' With her dark hair being blown back, Janice looks like a different person. Eyes asquint against the rush of wind and her upper lip lifted, a hand held near her ear to keep her rippling silk head scarf from flying away. Liz Taylor in *A Place in the Sun*. Even the little crow's-feet at the corner of her eye look glamorous. She is wearing her tennis dress and the white cashmere cardigan.

'I mean is he going to get a job or what?'

'Well, Harry. He's still in college.'

'He doesn't act it.' He feels he has to shout. 'I wasn't so fucking fortunate as to get to college and the guys that did didn't goof off in Colorado hang gliding and God knows what until their father's money ran out.'

'You don't know what they did. Anyway times are different. Now you be nice to Nelson. After the things you put him through –'

'Not just me.'

'– after what he went through you should be grateful he *wants* to come home. Ever.'

'I don't know.'

'You don't know *what*?'

'This doesn't feel good to me. I've been too happy lately.'

'Don't be irrational,' Janice says.

She is not, this implies. But one of their bonds has always been that her confusion keeps pace with his. As the wind pours past he feels a scared swift love for something that has no name. Her? His life? The world? Coming from the Mt Pemaquid direction, you see the hillside borough of Mt Judge from a spread-out angle altogether different from what you see coming home from the Brewer direction: the old box factory a long lean-windowed slab down low by the dried-up falls, sent underground to make electricity, and the new supertall Exxon and Mobil signs on their tapered aluminum poles along Route 422 as eerie as antennae arrived out of space. The town's stacked windows burn orange in the sun that streams level up the valley, and from this angle great prominence gathers to the sandstone spire of the Lutheran church where Rabbit went to Sunday school under crusty old Fritz Kruppenbach, who pounded in the lesson that life has no terrors for those with faith but for those without faith there can be no salvation and no peace. *No* peace. A sign says THICKLY SETTLED.

As the Maverick slows, Harry is moved to confess to Janice, 'I started to tell you last night, this young couple came into the lot yesterday and the girl reminded me of Ruth. She would be about the right age too. Slimmer, and not much like her in her way of talking, but there was, I don't know, something.'

'Your imagination is what it was. Did you get the girl's name?'

'I asked, but she wouldn't give it. She was cute about it, too. Kind of flirty, without anything you could put your finger on.'

'And you think that girl was your daughter.'

From her tone he knows he shouldn't have confessed. 'I didn't say that exactly.'

'Then what did you say? You're telling me you're still thinking of this bag you fucked twenty years ago and now you and she have a darling little *baby*.' He glances over and Janice no longer suggests Elizabeth Taylor, her lips all hard and crinkled as if baked in her fury. Ida Lupino. Where did they go, all the great Hollywood bitches? In town for years there had been just a Stop sign at the corner where Jackson slants down into Central but the other year after the burgess's own son smashed up a car running the sign the borough put in a light, that is mostly on blink, yellow this way and red the other. He touches the brake and takes the left turn. Janice leans with the turn to keep her mouth close to his ear. 'You are crazy,' she shouts. 'You *al*ways want what you don't have instead of what you *do*. Getting all cute and smiley in the face thinking about this *girl* that doesn't exist while your *real* son, that you had with your *wife*, is waiting at home right now and you saying you wished he'd stay in Colo*r*ado.'

'I do wish that,' Harry says – anything to change the subject even slightly. 'You're wrong about my wanting what I don't have. I pretty much like what I have. The trouble with that is, then you get afraid somebody will take it from you.'

'Well it's not going to be Nelson, he wants nothing from you except a little love and he doesn't get that. I don't know *why* you're such an unnatural father.'

So they can finish their argument before they reach Ma Springer's he has slowed their speed up Jackson, under the shady interlock of maples and horsechestnuts, that makes the hour feel later than it is. 'The kid has it in for me,' he says mildly, to see what this will bring on.

It re-excites her. 'You keep saying that but it's not *true*. He *loves* you. Or did.' Where the sky shows through the mingled tree tops there is still a difference of light, a flickering that beats upon their faces and hands mothlike. In a sullen semi-mollified tone she says, 'One thing definite, I don't want to hear any more about your darling illegitimate daughter. It's a disgusting idea.'

'I know. I don't know why I mentioned it.' He had mistaken the two of them for one and entrusted to her this ghost of his alone. A mistake married people make.

'Dis*gu*sting!' Janice cries.

'I'll never mention it again,' he promises.

They ease into Joseph, at the corner where the fire hydrant still wears, faded, the red-white-and-blue clown outfit that school-children three Junes ago painted on for the Bicentennial. Polite in his fresh dislike of her, he asks, 'Shall I put the car in the garage?'

'Leave it out front, Nelson may want it.'

As they walk up the front steps his feet feel heavy, as if the world has taken on new gravity. He and the kid years ago went through something for which Rabbit has forgiven himself but which he knows the kid never has. A girl called Jill died when Harry's house burned down, a girl Nelson had come to love like a sister. At least like a sister. But the years have piled on, the surviving have patched things up, and so many more have joined the dead, undone by diseases for which only God is to blame, that it no longer seems so bad, it seems more as if Jill just moved to another town, where the population is growing. Jill would be twenty-eight now. Nelson is twenty-two. Think of all the blame God has to shoulder.

Ma's front door sticks and yields with a shove. The living room is dark and duffel bags have been added to its clutter of padded furniture. A shabby plaid suitcase, not Nelson's, sits on the stair landing. The voices come from the sunporch. These voices lessen Harry's gravity, seem to refute the world's rumors of universal death. He moves toward the voices, through the dining room and then the kitchen, into the porch area conscious of himself as slightly too drunk to be cautious enough, overweight and soft and a broad target.

Copper beech leaves crowd at the porch screen. Faces and bodies rise from the aluminum and nylon furniture like the cloud of an explosion with the sound turned down on TV. More and more in middle age the world comes upon him like images on a set with one thing wrong with it, like those images the mind entertains before we go to sleep, that make sense until we look at them closely, which wakes us up with a shock. It is the girl who has risen most promptly, a curly-headed rather sturdy girl with shining brown eyes halfway out of her head and a ruby-red dimpling smile lifted from a turn-of-the-century valentine. She has on jeans that have been through everything and a Hindu sort of embroidered shirt that has lost some sequins. Her handshake surprises him by being damp, nervous.

Nelson slouches to his feet. His usual troubled expression wears a mountaineer's tan, and he seems thinner, broader in the shoulders. Less of a puppy, more of a mean dog. At some point in Colorado or at Kent he has had his hair, which in high school used to fall to his shoulders, cut short, to give a punk look. 'Dad, this is my friend Melanie. My father. And my mother. Mom, this is Melanie.'

'Pleased to meet you both,' the girl says, keeping the merry red smile as if even these plain words are prelude to a joke, to a little circus act. That is what she reminds Harry of, those somehow unreal but visible brave women who hang by their teeth in circuses, or ride one-footed the velvet rope up to fly through the spangled air, though she is dressed in that raggy look girls hide in now. A strange wall or glare has instantly fallen between himself and this girl, a disinterest that he takes to be a gesture toward his son.

Nelson and Janice are embracing. *Those little Springer hands,* Harry remembers his mother saying, as he sees them press into the back of Janice's tennis dress. Tricky little paws, something about the curve of the stubby curved fingers that hints of sneaky strength. No visible moons to the fingernails and the ends look nibbled. A habit of sullen grievance and blank stubbornness has descended to him from Janice. The poor in spirit.

Yet when Janice steps aside to greet Melanie, and father and son are face to face, and Nelson says, 'Hey, Dad,' and like his father wonders whether to shake hands or hug or touch in any way, love floods clumsily the hesitant space.

'You look fit,' Harry says.

'I feel beat.'

'How'd you get here so soon?'

'Hitched, except for a stretch after Kansas City where we took a bus as far as Indianapolis.' Places where Rabbit has never been – his blood has travelled for him, along the tracks of his dreams. The boy tells him, 'The night before last we spent in some field in western Ohio, I don't know, after Toledo. It was weird. We'd gotten stoned with the guy who picked us up in this van all painted with designs, and when he dumped us off Melanie and I were really disoriented, we had to keep talking to each other so we wouldn't panic. The ground was colder than you'd think, too. We woke up frozen but at least the trees didn't look like octopuses.'

'Nelson,' Janice cries, 'something dreadful could have happened to you! To the two of you.'

'Who cares?' the boy asks. To his grandmother, Bessie, sitting in her private cloud in the darkest corner of the porch, he says, 'You wouldn't care, would you Mom-mom, if I dropped out of the picture?'

'Indeed I would,' is her stout response. 'You were the apple of your granddad's eye.'

Melanie reassures Janice, 'People are basically very nice.' Her voice is strange, gurgling as if she has just recovered from a fit of laughter, with a suspended singing undertone. Her mind seems focused on some faraway cause for joy. 'You only meet the difficult ones now and then, and they're usually all right as long as you don't show fear.'

'What does your mother think of your hitchhiking?' Janice asks her.

'She hates it,' Melanie says, and laughs outright, her curls shaking. 'But she lives in California.' She turns serious, her eyes shining on Janice steadily as lamps. 'Really though, it's ecologically sound, it saves all that gas. More people should do it, but everybody's afraid.'

A gorgeous frog, is what she looks like to Harry, though her body from what you can tell in those flopsy-mopsy clothes is human enough, and even exemplary. He tells Nelson, 'If you'd budgeted your allowance better you'd've been able to take the bus all the way.'

'Buses are boring, Dad, and full of creeps. You don't *learn* anything on a bus.'

'It's true,' Melanie chimes in. 'I've heard terrible stories from girlfriends of mine, that happened to them on buses. The drivers can't do anything, they just drive, and if you look at all, you know, what they think of as hippie, they egg the guys on it seems.'

'The world is no longer a safe place,' Ma Springer announces from her dark corner.

Harry decides to act the father. 'I'm glad you made it,' he tells Nelson. 'I'm proud of you, getting around the way you do. If I'd seen a little more of the United States when I was your age, I'd be a better citizen now. The only free ride I ever got was when Uncle sent me to Texas. They'd let us out,' he tells Melanie, 'Saturday nights, in the middle of a tremendous cow pasture. Fort Hood, it was called.' He is overacting, talking too much.

'Dad,' Nelson says impatiently, 'the country's the same now wherever you go. The same supermarkets, the same plastic shit for sale. There's nothing to see.'

'Colorado was a disappointment to Nelson,' Melanie tells them, with her merry undertone.

'I liked the state, I just didn't care for the skunks who live in it.' That aggrieved stunted look on his face. Harry knows he will never find out what happened in Colorado, to drive the kid back to him. Like those stories kids bring back from school where it was never them who started the fight.

'Have these children had any supper?' Janice asks, working up her mother act. You get out of practice quickly.

Ma Springer with unexpected complacence announces, 'Melanie made the most delicious salad out of what she could find in the refrigerator and outside.'

'I love your garden,' Melanie tells Harry. 'The little gate. Things grow so beautifully around here.' He can't get over the way she warbles everything, all the while staring at his face as if fearful he will miss some point.

'Yeah,' he says. 'It's depressing, in a way. Was there any baloney left?'

Nelson says, 'Melanie's a veggy, Dad.'

'Veggy?'

'Vegetarian,' the boy explains in his put-on whine.

'Oh. Well, no law against that.'

The boy yawns. 'Maybe we should hit the hay. Melanie and I got about an hour's sleep last night.'

Janice and Harry go tense, and eye Melanie and Ma Springer.

Janice says, 'I better make up Nellie's bed.'

'I've already done it,' her mother tells her. 'And the bed in the old sewing room too. I've had a lot of time by myself today, it seems you two are at the club more and more.'

'How was church?' Harry asks her.

Ma Springer says unwillingly, 'It was not very inspiring. For the collection music they had brought out from St Mary's in Brewer one of those men who can sing in a high voice like a woman.'

Melanie smiles. 'A countertenor. My brother was once a countertenor.'

'Then what happened?' Harry asks, yawning himself. He suggests, 'His voice changed.'

Her eyes are solemn. 'Oh no. He took up polo playing.'

'He sounds like a real sport.'

'He's really my half-brother. My father was married before.'

Nelson tells Harry, 'Mom-mom and I ate what was left of the baloney, Dad. We ain't no veggies.'

Harry asks Janice, 'What's there left for me? Night after night, I starve around here.'

Janice waves away his complaint with a queenly gesture she wouldn't have possessed ten years ago. 'I don't know, I was thinking we'd get a bite at the club, then Mother called.'

'I'm not sleepy,' Melanie tells Nelson.

'Maybe she ought to see a little of the area,' Harry offers. 'And you could pick up a pizza while you're out.'

'In the West,' Nelson says, 'they hardly have pizzas, everything is this awful Mexican crap, tacos and chili. Yuk.'

'I'll phone up Giordano's, remember where that is? A block beyond the courthouse, on Seventh?'

'Dad, I've lived my whole life in this lousy county.'

'You and me both. How does everybody feel about pepperoni? Let's get a couple, I bet Melanie's still hungry. One pepperoni and one combination.'

'Jesus, Dad. We keep telling you, Melanie's a vegetarian.'

'Oops. I'll order one plain. You don't have any bad feelings about cheese, do you Melanie? Or mushrooms. How about with mushrooms?'

'I'm full,' the girl beams, her voice slowed it seems by its very burden of delight. 'But I'd love to go with Nelson for the ride, I really like this area. It's so lush, and the houses are all kept so neat.'

Janice takes this opening, touching the girl's arm, another gesture she might not have dared in the past. 'Have you seen the upstairs?' she asks. 'What we normally use for a guest room is across the hall from Mother's room, you'd share a bathroom with her.'

'Oh, I didn't expect a room at all. I had thought just a sleeping bag on the sofa. Wasn't there a nice big sofa in the room where we first came in?'

Harry assures her, 'You don't want to sleep on that sofa, it's so full of dust you'll sneeze to death. The room upstairs is nice, honest; if you don't mind sharing with a dressmaker's dummy.'

'Oh no,' the girl responds. 'I really just want a tiny corner where I won't be in the way, I want to go out and get a job as a waitress.'

The old lady fidgets, moving her coffee cup from her lap to the folding tray table beside her chair. 'I made all my dresses for years but once I had to go to the bifocals I couldn't even sew Fred's buttons on,' she says.

'By that time you were rich anyway,' Harry tells her, jocular in his relief at the bed business seeming to work out so smoothly. Old lady Springer, when you cross her there's no end to it, she never forgets. Harry was a little hard on Janice early in the marriage and you can still see resentment in the set of Bessie's mouth. He dodges out of the sunporch to the phone in the kitchen. While

Giordano's is ringing, Nelson comes up behind him and rummages in his pockets. 'Hey,' Harry says, 'what're ya robbing me for?'

'Car keys. Mom says take the car out front.'

Harry braces the receiver between his shoulder and ear and fishes the keys from his left pocket and, handing them over, for the first time looks Nelson squarely in the face. He sees nothing of himself there except the small straight nose and a cowlick in one eyebrow that sends a little fan of hairs the wrong way and seems to express a doubt. Amazing, genes. So precise in all that coiled coding they can pick up a tiny cowlick like that. That girl had had Ruth's tilt, exactly: a little forward push of the upper lip and thighs, soft-tough, comforting.

'Thanks, Pops.'

'Don't dawdle. Nothing worse than cold pizza.'

'What was that?' a tough voice at the other end of the line asks, having at last picked up the phone.

'Nothing, sorry,' Harrys says, and orders three pizzas – one pepperoni, one combination, and one plain in case Melanie changes her mind. He gives Nelson a ten-dollar bill. 'We ought to talk sometime, Nellie, when you get some rest.' The remark goes with the money, somehow. Nelson makes no answer, taking the bill.

When the young people are gone, Harry returns to the sunporch and says to the women, 'Now that wasn't so bad, was it? She seemed happy to sleep in the sewing room.'

'Seems isn't being,' Ma Springer darkly says.

'Hey that's right,' Harry says. 'Whaddid you think of her anyway? The girlfriend.'

'Does she feel like a girlfriend to you?' Janice asks him. She has at last sat down, and has a small glass in her hand. The liquid in the glass he can't identify by its color, a sickly but intense red like old-fashioned cream soda or the fluid in thermometers.

'Whaddeya mean? They spent last night in a field together. God knows how they shacked up in Colorado. Maybe in a cave.'

'I'm not sure that follows anymore. They try to be friends in a way we couldn't when we were young. Boys and girls.'

'Nelson does not look contented,' Ma Springer announces heavily.

'When did he ever?' Harry asks.

'As a little boy he seemed very hopeful,' his grandmother says.

'Bessie, what's your analysis of what brought him back here?'

The old lady sighs. 'Some disappointment. Some thing that got too big for him. I'll tell you this though. If that girl doesn't behave herself under our roof, I'm moving out. I talked to Grace Stuhl about it after church and she's more than willing, poor soul, to have me move in. She thinks it might prolong her life.'

'Mother,' Janice asks, 'aren't you missing *All in the Family*?'

'It was to be a show I've seen before, the one where this old girlfriend of Archie's comes back to ask for money. Now that it's summer it's all reruns. I did hope to look at *The Jeffersons* though, at nine-thirty, before this hour on Moses, if I can stay awake. Maybe I'll go upstairs to rest my legs. When I was making up Nellie's little bed, a corner hit a vein and it won't stop throbbing.' She stands, wincing.

'Mother,' Janice says impatiently, 'I would have made up those beds if you'd just waited. Let me go up with you and look at the guest room.'

Harry follows them out of the sunporch (it's getting too tragic in there, the copper beech black as ink, captive moths beating their wings to a frazzle on the screens) and into the dining room. He likes the upward glimpse of Janice's legs in the tennis dress as she goes upstairs to help her mother make things fit and proper. Ought to try fucking her some night when they're both awake. He could go upstairs and give her a hand now but he is attracted instead to the exotic white face of the woman on the cover of the July *Consumer Reports*, that he brought downstairs this morning to read in the pleasant hour between when Ma went off to church and he and Janice went off to the club. The magazine still rests on the arm of the Barcalounger, that used to be old man Springer's evening throne. You couldn't dislodge him, and when he went off to the bathroom or into the kitchen for his Diet Pepsi the chair stayed empty. Harry settles into it. The girl on the cover is wearing a white bowler hat on her white-painted face above the lapels of a fully white tuxedo; she is made up in red, white, and blue like a clown and in her uplifted hand has a dab of gooey white face cleaner. Jism, models are prostitutes, the girls in blue movies rub their faces in jism. *Broadway tests face cleansers* it says beneath her, for face cleansers are one of the commodities this month's issue is testing, along with cottage cheese (how unclean is it? rather), air-conditioners, compact stereos, and can openers (why do people make rectangular cans anyway?). He turns to finish with the air-conditioners and reads that if you live in a high-humidity area (and he supposes he does, at least compared to Arizona) almost all models tend to drip, some enough *to make them doubtful choices for installation over a patio or walkway*. It would be nice to have a patio, along with a sunken living room like Webb Murkett does. Webb and that cute little cunt Cindy, always looking hosed down. Still, Rabbit is content. This is what he likes, domestic peace. Women circling with dutiful footsteps above him and the summer night like a lake lapping at the windows. He has time to read about compact stereos and even try the piece on car loans before Nelson and Melanie come back out of this night with three stained boxes of pizza. Quickly Harry snatches off his reading glasses, for he feels strangely naked in them.

The boy's face has brightened and might even be called cheerful. 'Boy,' he tells his father, 'Mom's Maverick really can dig when you ask it to. Some jungle bunny in about a '69 Caddy kept racing his motor and I left him standing. Then he tailgated me all the way to the Running Horse Bridge. It was scarey.'

'You came around that way? Jesus, no wonder it took so long.'

'Nelson was showing me the city,' Melanie explains, with her musical smile, that leaves the trace of a hum in the air as she moves with the flat cardboard boxes toward the kitchen. Already she has that nice upright walk of a waitress.

He calls after her, 'It's a city that's seen better days.'

'I think it's beauti-ful,' her answer floats back. 'The people paint their houses in these different colors, like something you'd see in the Mediterranean.'

'The spics do that,' Harry says. 'The spics and the wops.'

'Dad, you're really prejudiced. You should travel more.'

'Naa, it's all in fun. I love everybody, especially with my car windows locked.' He adds, 'Toyota was going to pay for me and your mother to go to Atlanta, but then some agency toward Harrisburg beat our sales total and they got the trip instead. It was a regional thing. It bothered me because I've always been curious about the South: love hot weather.'

'Don't be so chintzy, Dad. Go for your vacation and pay your way.'

'Vacations, we're pretty well stuck with that camp up in the Poconos.' Old man Springer's pride and joy.

'I took this course in sociology at Kent. The reason you're so tight with your money, you got the habit of poverty when you were a child, in the Depression. You were traumatized.'

'We weren't that bad off. Pop got decent money, printers were never laid off like some of the professions. Anyway who says I'm tight with my money?'

'You owe Melanie three dollars already. I had to borrow from her.'

'You mean those three pizzas cost thirteen dollars?'

'We got a couple of sixpacks to go with them.'

'You and Melanie can pay for your own beer. We never drink it around here. Too fattening.'

'Where's Mom?'

'Upstairs. And another thing. Don't leave your mother's car out front with the top down. Even if it doesn't rain, the maples drop something sticky on the seats.'

'I thought we might go out again.'

'You're kidding. I thought you said you got only an hour's sleep last night.'

'Dad, lay off the crap. I'm going on twenty-three.'

'Twenty-three, and no sense. Give me the keys. I'll put the Maverick out back in the garage.'

'*Mo-om*,' the boy shouts upwards. 'Dad won't let me drive your car!'

Janice is coming down. She has put on her peppermint dress and looks tired. Harry tells her, 'All I asked was for him to put it in the garage. The maple sap gets the seats sticky. He says he wants to go out again. Christ, it's nearly ten o'clock.'

'The maples are through dripping for the year,' Janice says. To

Nelson she merely says, 'If you don't want to go out again maybe you should put the top up. We had a terrible thunderstorm two nights ago. It hailed, even.'

'Why do you think,' Rabbit asks her, 'your top is all black and spotty? The sap or whatever it is drips down on the canvas and can't be cleaned off.'

'Harry, it's not your car,' Janice tells him.

'Pizza,' Melanie calls from the kitchen, her tone bright and pearly. '*Mangiamo, prego!*'

'Dad's really into cars, isn't he?' Nelson asks his mother. 'Like they're magical, now that he sells them.'

Harry asks her, 'How about Ma? She want to eat again?'

'Mother says she feels sick.'

'Oh great. One of her spells.'

'Today was an exciting day for her.'

'Today was an exciting day for me too. I was told I'm a tight wad and think cars are magical.' This is no way to be, spiteful. 'Also, Nelson, I birdied the eighteenth, you know that long dog-leg? A drive that just cleared the creek and kept bending right, and then I hit an easy five-iron and then wedged it up to about twelve feet and sank the damn putt! Still have your clubs? We ought to play.' He puts his hand on the boy's back.

'I sold them to a guy at Kent.' Nelson takes an extra-fast step, to get out from under his father's touch. 'I think it's the stupidest game ever invented.'

'You must tell us about hang gliding,' his mother says.

'It's neat. It's very quiet. You're in the wind and don't feel a thing. Some of the people get stoned beforehand but then there's the danger you'll think you can really fly.'

Melanie has sweetly set out plates and transferred the pizzas from their boxes to cookie sheets. Janice asks, 'Melanie, do you hang glide?'

'Oh no,' says the girl. 'I'd be terrified.' Her giggling does not somehow interrupt her lustrous, caramel-colored stare. 'Pru used to do it with Nelson. I never would.'

'Who's Pru?' Harry asks.

'You don't know her,' Nelson calls him.

'I know I don't. I know I don't know her. If I knew her I wouldn't have to ask.'

'I think we're all cross and irritable,' Janice says, lifting a piece of pepperoni loose and laying it on a plate.

Nelson assumes that plate is for him. 'Tell Dad to quit leaning on me,' he complains, settling to the table as if he has tumbled from a motorcycle and is sore all over.

In bed, Harry asks Janice, 'What's eating the kid, do you think?'

'I don't know.'

'Something is.'

'Yes.'

As they think this over they can hear Ma Springer's television going, chewing away at Moses from the Biblical sound of the voices, shouting, rumbling, with crescendos of music between. The old lady falls asleep with it on and sometimes it crackles all night, if Janice doesn't tiptoe in and turn it off. Melanie had gone to bed in her room with the dressmaker's dummy. Nelson came upstairs to watch *The Jeffersons* with his grandmother and by the time his parents came upstairs had gone to bed in his old room, without saying goodnight. Sore all over. Rabbit wonders if the young couple from the country will come into the lot tomorrow. The girl's pale round face and the television screen floating unwatched in Ma Springer's mind become confused in his mind as the exalted music soars. Janice is asking, 'How do you like the girl?'

'Melanie baby. Spooky. Are they all that way, of that generation, like a rock just fell on their heads and it was the nicest experience in the world?'

'I think she's trying to ingratiate herself. It must be a difficult thing, to go into a boyfriend's home and make a place for yourself. I wouldn't have lasted ten minutes with your mother.'

Little she knows, the poison Mom talked about her. 'Mom was like me,' Harry says. 'She didn't like being crowded.' New people at either end of the house and old man Springer's ghost sitting downstairs on his Barcalounger. 'They don't act very lovey,' he says. 'Or is that how people are now? Cool.'

'I think they don't want to shock us. They know they must get around Mother.'

'Join the crowd.'

Janice ponders this. The bed creaks and heavy footsteps slither on the other side of the wall, and the excited cries of the television set are silenced with a click. Burt Lancaster just getting warmed up. Those teeth: can they be his own? All the stars have them crowned. Even Harry, he used to have a lot of trouble with his molars and now they're snug, safe and painless, in little jackets of gold alloy costing four hundred fifty each.

'She's still up,' Janice says. 'She won't sleep. She's stewing.' In the positive way she pronounces her *s*'s she sounds more and more like her mother. We carry our heredity concealed for a while and then it pushes through. Out of those narrow coils.

In a stir of wind as before a sudden rain the shadows of the copper-beech leaves surge and fling their ragged interstices of streetlight back and forth across the surfaces where the ceiling meets the far wall. Three cars pass, one after the other, and Harry's sense of the active world outside sliding by as he lies here safe wells up within him to merge with the bed's nebulous ease. He is in his bed, his molars are in their crowns. 'She's a pretty good old sport,' he says. 'She rolls with the punches.'

'She's waiting and watching,' Janice says in an ominous voice that shows she is more awake than he. She asks, 'When do I get my turn?'

'Turn?' the bed is gently turning, Stavros is waiting for him by the great display window that brims with dusty morning light. *You asked for it.*

'You came last night, from the state I was in this morning. Me and the sheet.'

The wind stirs again. Damn. The convertible is still out there with the top down. 'Honey, it's been a long day.' Running out of gas. 'Sorry.'

'You're forgiven,' Janice says. 'Just.' She has to add, 'I might think I don't turn you on much anymore.'

'No, actually, over at the club today I was thinking how much sassier you look than most of those broads, old Thelma in her little skirt and the awful girlfriend of Buddy's.'

'And Cindy?'

'Not my type. Too pudgy.'

'Liar.'

*You got it.* He is dead tired yet something holds him from the black surface of sleep, and in that half-state just before or after he sinks he imagines he hears lighter, younger footsteps slither outside in the hall, going somewhere in a hurry.

Melanie is as good as her word, she gets a job waitressing at a new restaurant downtown right on Weiser Street, an old restaurant with a new name, the Crêpe House. Before that it was the Café Barcelona, painted tiles and paella, iron grillwork and gazpacho; Harry ate lunch there once in a while but in the evening it had attracted the wrong element, hippies and Hispanic families from the south side instead of the white-collar types from West Brewer and the heights along Locust Boulevard, that you need to make a restaurant go in this city. Brewer never has been much for Latin touches, not since Carmen Miranda and all those Walt Disney Saludos Amigos movies. Rabbit remembers there used to be a Club Castanet over on Warren Avenue but the only thing Spanish had been the name and the frills on the waitresses' uniforms, which had been orange. Before the Crêpe House had been the Barcelona it had been for many years Johnny Frye's Chophouse, good solid food day and night for the big old-fashioned German eaters, who have eaten themselves pretty well into the grave by now, taking with them tons of pork chops and sauerkraut and a river of Sunflower Beer. Under its newest name Johnny Frye's is a success; the lean new race of downtown office workers comes out of the banks and the federal offices and the deserted department stores and makes its way at noon through the woods the city planners have inflicted on Weiser Square and sits at the little tile tables left over from the Café Barcelona and dabbles at glorified pancakes wrapped around minced whatever. Even driving through after a movie at one of the malls you can see them in there by candlelight, two by two, bending toward each other over the crêpes earnest as hell, on the make, the guys in leisure suits with flared open collars and the girls in slinky dresses that cling to their bodies as if by static electricity, and a dozen more just like them standing in the foyer waiting to be seated. It has to do with diet, Harry figures – people now want to feel they're

83

eating less, and a crêpe sounds like hardly a snack whereas if they called it a pancake they would have scared everybody away but kids and two-ton Katrinkas. Harry marvels that this new tribe of customers exists, on the make, and with money. The world keeps ending but new people too dumb to know it keep showing up as if the fun's just started. The Crêpe House is such a hit they've bought the venerable brick building next door and expanded into the storerooms, leaving the old cigar store, that still has a little gas pilot to light up by by the cash register, intact and doing business. To staff their new space the Crêpe House needed more waitresses. Melanie works some days the lunch shift from ten to six and other days she goes from five to near one in the morning. One day Harry took Charlie over to lunch for him to see this new woman in the Angstrom life, but it didn't work out very well: having Nelson's father show up as a customer with a strange man put roses of embarrassment in Melanie's cheeks as she served them in the midst of the lunchtime mob.

'Not a bad looker,' Charlie said on that awkward occasion, gazing after the young woman as she flounced away. The Crêpe House dresses its waitresses in a kind of purple colonial mini, with a big bow in back that switches as they walk.

'You can see that?' Harry said. 'I can't. It bothers me, actually. That I'm not turned on. The kid's been living with us two weeks now and I should be climbing the walls.'

'A little old for wall-climbing, aren't you, chief? Anyway there are some women that don't do it for some men. That's why they turn out so many models.'

'As you say she has all the equipment. Big knockers, if you look.'

'I looked.'

'The funny thing is, she doesn't seem to turn Nelson on either, that I can see. They're buddies all right; when she's home they spend hours in his room together playing his old records and talking about God knows what, sometimes they come out of there it looks like he's been crying, but as far as Jan and I can tell she sleeps in the front room, where we put her as a sop to old lady Springer that first night, never thinking it would stick. Actually Bessie's kind of taken with her by now, she helps with the housework more than Janice does for one thing, so at this point wherever Melanie sleeps I think she'd look the other way.'

'They've *got* to be fucking,' Stavros insisted, setting his hand on the table in that defining, faintly menacing way he has: palms facing, thumbs up.

'You'd think so,' Rabbit agreed. 'But these kids now are spooky. These letters in long white envelopes keep arriving from Colorado and they spend a lot of time answering. The postmark's Colorado but the return address printed on is some dean's office at Kent. Maybe he's flunked out.'

Charlie scarcely listened. 'Maybe I should give her a buzz, if Nelson's not ringing her bell.'

'Come on, Charlie. I didn't say he's not, I just don't get that vibe around the house. I don't think they do it in the back of the Maverick, the seats are vinyl and these kids today are too spoiled.' He sipped his Margarita and wiped the salt from his lips. The bartender here was left over from the Barcelona days, they must have a cellarful of tequila. 'To tell you the truth I can't imagine Nelson screwing anybody, he's such a sourpussed little punk.'

'Got his grandfather's frame. Fred was sexy, don't kid yourself. Couldn't keep his hands off the clerical help, that's why so many of them left. Where'd you say she's from?'

'California. Her father sounds like a bum, he lives in Oregon after being a lawyer. Her parents split a time ago.'

'So she's a long way from home. Probably needs a friend, along more mature lines.'

'Well I'm right there across the hall from her.'

'You're family, champ. That doesn't count. Also you don't appreciate this chick and no doubt she twigs to that. Women do.'

'Charlie, you're old enough to be her father.'

'Aah. These Mediterranean types, they like to see a little gray hair on the chest. The old *mastoras*.'

'What about your lousy ticker?'

Charlie smiled and put his spoon into the cold spinach soup that Melanie had brought. 'Good a way to go as any.'

'Charlie, you're crazy,' Rabbit said admiringly, admiring yet once again in their long relationship what he fancies as the other

85

man's superior grip upon the basic elements of life, elements that Harry can never settle in his mind.

'Being crazy's what keeps us alive,' Charlie said, and sipped, closing his eyes behind his tinted glasses to taste the soup better. 'Too much nutmeg. Maybe Janice'd like to have me over, it's been a while. So I can feel things out.'

'Listen, I can't have you over so you can seduce my son's girlfriend.'

'You said she wasn't a girlfriend.'

'I said they didn't act like it, but then what do I know?'

'You have a pretty good nose. I trust you, champ.' He changed the subject slightly. 'How come Nelson keeps showing up at the lot?'

'I don't know, with Melanie off at work he doesn't have much to do, hanging around the house with Bessie, going over to the club with Janice swimming till his eyes get pink from the chlorine. He shopped around town a little for a job but no luck. I don't think he tried too hard.'

'Maybe we could fit him in at the lot.'

'I don't want that. Things are cozy enough around here for him already.'

'He going back to college?'

'I don't know. I'm scared to ask.'

Stavros put down his soup spoon carefully. 'Scared to ask,' he repeated. 'And you're paying the bills. If my father had ever said to anybody he was scared of anything to do with me, I think the roof would have come off the house.'

'Maybe scared isn't the word.'

'Scared is the word you used.' He looked up squinting in what seemed to be pain through his thick glasses to perceive Melanie more clearly as, in a flurry of purple colonial flounces, she set before Harry a *Crêpe con Zucchini* and before Charlie a *Crêpe à la Champignons et Oignons*. The scent of their vegetable steam remained like a cloud of perfume she had released from the frills of her costume before flying away. 'Nice,' Charlie said, not of the food. 'Very nice.' Rabbit still couldn't see it. He thought of her body without the frills and got nothing in the way of feeling except a certain fear, as if seeing a weapon unsheathed, or gazing upon an inflexible machine with which his soft body should not become involved.

But he feels obliged to say to Janice, 'We haven't had Charlie over for a while.'

She looks at him curiously. 'You want to? Don't you see enough of him at the lot?'

'Yeah, but you don't see him there.'

'Charlie and I had our time, of seeing each other.'

'Look, the guy lives with his mother who's getting to be more and more of a drag, he's never married, he's always talking about his nieces and nephews but I don't think they give him shit actually –'

'All right, you don't have to sell it. I *like* seeing Charlie. I must say I think it's creepy that you encourage it.'

'Why shouldn't I? Because of that old business? I don't hold a grudge. It made you a niftier person.'

'Thanks,' Janice said drily. Guiltily he tries to count up how many nights since he's given her an orgasm. These July nights, you get thirsty for one more beer as the Phillies struggle and then in bed feel a terrific weariness, a bliss of inactivity that leads you to see how men can die willingly, gladly, into eternal release from the hell of having to perform. When Janice hasn't been fucked for a while, her gestures speed up, and the thought of Charlie's coming intensifies this agitation. 'What night?' she asks.

'Whenever. What's Melanie's schedule this week?'

'What does that have to do with it?'

'He might as well meet her properly. I took him over to the crêpe place for lunch and though she tried to be pleasant she was rushed and it didn't really work out.'

'What would "work out" mean, if it did?'

'Don't give me a hard time, it's too fucking humid. I've been thinking of asking Ma to go halves with us on a new air-conditioner, I read where a make called Friedrich is best. I mean "work out" just as ordinary human interchange. He kept asking me embarrassing questions about Nelson.'

'Like what? What's so embarrassing about Nelson?'

'Like whether or not he was going to go back to college and why he kept showing up at the lot.'

'Why shouldn't he show up at the lot? It was his grandfather's. And Nelson's always loved cars.'

'Loved to bounce 'em around, at least. The Maverick has a whole new set of rattles, have you noticed?'

'I hadn't noticed,' Janice says primly, pouring herself more Campari. In an attempt to cut down her alcohol intake, to slow down creeping middle-itis, she has appointed Campari-and-soda her summer drink; but keeps forgetting to put in the soda. She adds, 'He's used to those flat Ohio roads.'

Out at Kent Nelson had bought some graduating senior's old Thunderbird and then when he decided to go to Colorado sold it for half what he paid. Remembering this adds to Rabbit's suffocating sensation of being put upon. He tells her, 'They have the fifty-five-mile-an-hour speed limit out there too. The poor country is trying to save gas before the Arabs turn our dollars into zinc pennies and that baby boy of yours does fifty-five in second gear.'

Janice knows he is trying to get her goat now, and turns her back with that electric swiftness, as of speeded-up film, and heads toward the dining-room phone. 'I'll ask him for next week,' she says. 'If that'll make you less bitchy.'

Charlie always brings flowers, in a stapled green cone of paper, that he hands to Ma Springer. After all those years of kissing Springer's ass he knows his way around the widow. Bessie takes them without much of a smile; her maiden name was Koerner and she never wholly approved of Fred's taking on a Greek, and then her foreboding came true when Charlie had an affair with Janice with such disastrous consequences, around the time of the moon landing. Well, nobody was going to the moon much these days.

The flowers, unwrapped, are roses the color of a palomino horse. Janice puts them in a vase, cooing. She has dolled up in a perky daisy-patterned sundress for the occasion, that shows off her brown shoulders, and wears her long hair up in the heat, to remind them all of her slender neck and to display the gold necklace of tiny overlapping fish scales that Harry gave her for their twentieth wedding anniversary three years ago. Paid nine hundred dollars for it then, and it must be worth fifteen hundred now, gold going crazy the way it is. She leans forward to give Charlie a kiss, on the mouth and not the cheek, thus effortlessly reminding those who watch of how these two bodies have travelled within one another. 'Charlie, you look too thin,' Janice says. 'Don't you know how to feed yourself?'

'I pack it in, Jan, but it doesn't stick to the ribs anymore. You look terrific, on the other hand.'

'Melanie's got us all on a health kick. Isn't that right, Mother? Wheat germ and alfalfa sprouts and I don't know what all. Yogurt.'

'I feel better, honest to God,' Bessie pronounces. 'I don't know though if it's the diet or just having a little more life around the house.'

Charlie's square fingertips are still resting on Janice's brown arm. Rabbit sees the phenomenon as he would something else in Nature – a Japanese beetle on a leaf, or two limbs of a tree rubbing together in the wind. Then he remembers, descending into the molecules, what love feels like, huge, skin on skin, planets imping-ing.

'We all eat too much sugar and sodium,' Melanie says, in that happy uplifted voice of hers, that seems unconnected to what is below, like a blessing no one has asked for. Charlie's hand has snapped off Janice's skin; he is all warrior attention; his profile in the gloom of this front room through which all visitors to this household must pass shines, low-browed and jut-jawed, the muscles around the hollow of his jaw pulsing. He looks younger than at the lot, maybe because the light is poorer.

'Melanie,' Harry says, 'you remember Charlie from lunch the other day, doncha?'

'Of course. He had the mushrooms and capers.'

'Onions,' Charlie says, his hand still poised to take hers.

'Charlie's my right-hand man over there, or I'm his is I guess how he'd put it. He's been moving cars for Springer Motors since –' He can't think of a joke.

'Since they were called horseless buggies,' Charlie says, and takes her hand in his. Watching, Harry marvels at her young hand's narrowness. We broaden all over. Old ladies' feet: they look like little veiny loaves of bread, rising. Away from her spacey stare Melanie is knit as tight together as a new sock. Charlie is moving in on her. 'How are you, Melanie? How're you liking these parts?'

'They're nice,' she smiles. 'Quaint, almost.'

'Harry tells me you're a West Coast baby.'

Her eyes lift, so the whites beneath the irises show, as she looks toward her distant origins. 'Oh yes. I was born in Marin County. My mother lives now in a place called Carmel. That's to the south.'

'I've heard of it,' Charlie says. 'You've got some rock stars there.'

'Not really, I don't think ... Joan Baez, but she's more what you'd call traditional. We live in what used to be our summer place.'

'How'd that happen?'

Startled, she tells him. 'My father used to work in San Francisco as a corporation lawyer. Then he and my mother broke up and we had to sell the house on Pacific Avenue. Now he's in Oregon learning to be a forester.'

'That's a sad story, you could say,' Harry says.

'Daddy doesn't think so,' Melanie tells him. 'He's living with a lovely girl who's part Yakima Indian.'

'Back to Nature,' Charlie says.

'It's the only way to go,' Rabbit says. 'Have some soybeans.'

'This is a joke, for he is passing them Planter's freeze-dried cashews in a breakfast bowl, nuts that he bought on impulse at the grocery next to the state liquor store fifteen minutes ago, running out in the rattling Maverick to stoke up for tonight's company. He had been almost scared off by the price on the jar, $2.89, up 30¢ from the last time he'd noticed, and reached for the freeze-dried peanuts instead. Even these, though, were over a dollar, $1.09, peanuts that you used to buy a big sack of unshelled for a quarter when he was a boy, so he thought, What the hell's the point of being rich, and took the cashews after all.

He is offended when Charlie glances down and holds up a fastidious palm, not taking any. 'No salt,' Harry urges. 'Loaded with protein.'

'Never touch junk,' Charlie says. 'Doc says it's a no-no.'

'Junk!' he begins to argue.

But Charlie is keeping the pressure on Melanie. 'Every winter, I head down to Florida for a month. Sarasota, on the Gulf side.'

'What's that got to do with California?' Janice asks, cutting in.

'Same type of paradise,' Charlie says, turning a shoulder so as to keep speaking directly to Melanie. 'It's my meat. Sand in your shoes, that's the feeling, wearing the same ragged cut-offs day after day. This is over on the Gulf side. I hate the Miami side. The only way you'd get me over on the Miami side would be inside an alligator. They have 'em, too: come up out of these canals right onto your lawn and eat your pet dog. It happens a lot.'

'I've never been to Florida,' Melanie says, looking a little glazed, even for her.

'You should give it a try,' Charlie says. 'It's where the real people are.'

'You mean we're *not* real people?' Rabbit asks, egging him on, helping Janice out. This must hurt her. He takes a cashew between his molars and delicately cracks it, prolonging the bliss. That first fracture, in there with tongue and spit and teeth. He loves nuts. Clean eating, not like meat. In the Garden of Eden they ate nuts and fruit. Freeze-dried, the cashew burns a little. He prefers them salted, soaked in sodium, but got this kind in deference to Melanie, he's being brainwashed about chemicals. Still, some chemical must have entered into this freeze-drying too, there's nothing you can eat won't hurt you down here on Earth. Janice must hate this.

'It's not just all old people either,' Charlie is telling Melanie. 'You see plenty of young people down there too, just living in their skins. Gorgeous.'

'Janice,' Mrs Springer says, pronouncing it *Channis*. 'We should go on the porch and you should offer people drinks.' To Charlie she says, 'Melanie made a lovely fruit punch.'

'How much gin can it absorb?' Charlie asks.

Harry loves this guy, even if he is putting the make on Melanie in front of Janice, and on the porch, when they've settled on the aluminum furniture with their drinks and Janice is in the kitchen stirring at the dinner, asks him, to show him off, 'How'd you like Carter's energy speech?'

Charlie cocks his head toward the rosy-cheeked girl and says, 'I thought it was pathetic. The man was right. I'm suffering from a crisis in confidence. In him.'

Nobody laughs, except Harry. Charlie passes the ball. 'What did you think of it, Mrs Springer?'

The old lady, called onto the stage, smooths the cloth of her lap and looks down as if for crumbs. 'He seems a well-intentioned Christian man, though Fred always used to say the Democrats were just a tool for the unions. Still and all. Some businessman in there might have a better idea what to do with the inflation.'

'He *is* a businessman, Bessie,' Harry says. 'He grows peanuts. His warehouse down there grosses more than we do.'

'I thought it was sad,' Melanie unexpectedly says, leaning forward so her loose gypsyish blouse reveals cleavage, a tube of air between her braless breasts, 'the way he said people for the first time think things are going to get worse instead of better.'

'Sad if you're a chick like you,' Charlie says. 'For old crocks like us, things are going to get worse in any case.'

'You believe that?' Harry asks, genuinely surprised. He sees his life as just beginning, on clear ground at last, now that he has a margin of resources, and the stifled terror that always made him restless has dulled down. He wants less. Freedom, that he always thought was outward motion, turns out to be this inner dwindling.

'I believe it, sure,' Charlie says, 'but what does this nice girl here believe? That the show's over? How *can* she?'

'I believe,' Melanie begins. 'Oh, I don't know – Bessie, help me.'

Harry didn't know she calls the old lady by her first name. Took him years of living with her to work up to feeling easy about that, and it wasn't really until after one day he had accidentally walked in on her in her bathroom, Janice hogging theirs.

'Say what's on your mind,' the old woman advises the younger. 'Everybody else is.'

The luminous orbs of Melanie's eyes scout their faces in a sweep that ends in an upward roll such as you see in images of saints. 'I believe the things we're running out of we can learn to do without. I don't need electric carving knives and all that. I'm more upset about the snail darters and the whales than about iron ore and oil.' She lingers on this last word, giving it two syllables, and stares at Harry. As if he's especially into oil. He decides what he resents about her is she seems always to be trying to hypnotize him. 'I mean,' she goes on, 'as long as there are growing things, there's still a world with endless possibilities.'

The hum beneath her words hangs in the darkening space of the porch. Alien. Moonraker.

'One big weed patch,' Harry says. 'Where the hell is Nelson, anyway?' He is irked, he figures, because this girl is out of this world and that makes his world feel small. He feels sexier even toward fat old Bessie. At least her voice has a lot of the county, a lot of his life, in it. That time he blundered into the bathroom he didn't see much; she shouted, sitting on the toilet with her skirt around her knees, and he heard her shout and hardly saw a thing, just a patch of flank as white as a butcher's marble counter.

Bessie answers him dolefully, 'I believe he went out for a reason. Janice would know.'

Janice comes to the doorway of the porch, looking snappy in her daisies and an orange apron. 'He went off around six with Billy Fosnacht. They should have been back by now.'

'Which car'd they take?'

'They had to take the Corona. You were at the liquor store with the Maverick.'

'Oh great. What's Billy Fosnacht doing around anyway? Why isn't he in the volunteer army?' He feels like making a show, for Charlie and Melanie, of authority.

There is authority, too, in the way Janice is holding a wooden stirring spoon. She says, to the company in general, 'They say he's doing very well. He's in his first year of dental school up somewhere in New England. He wants to be a, what do they call it –?'

'Ophthalmologist,' Rabbit says.

'Endodontist.'

'My God,' is all Harry can say. Ten years ago, the night his house had burned, Billy had called his mother a bitch. He had seen Billy often since, all the years Nelson was at Mt Judge High, but had never forgotten that, how Peggy had then slapped him, this little boy twelve or maybe thirteen, the marks of her fingers leaping up pink on the child's delicate cheek. Then he had called her a whore, Harry's jism warm inside her. Later that night Nelson had vowed to kill his father. *You fucking asshole, you've let her die. I'll kill you. I'll kill YOU.* Harry had put up his hands to fight. The misery of life, it has carried him away from the faces on the porch; in the silence he hears from afar a neighbor woman's hammer knocking. 'How are Ollie and Peggy?' he asks, his voice rough even after clearing it. Billy's parents have dropped from his sight, as the Toyota business lifted him higher in the county.

'About the same,' Janice says. 'Ollie's still at the music store. They say Peggy's gotten into causes.' She turns back to her stirring.

Charlie tells Melanie, 'You should book yourself on a flight to Florida when you get fed up around here.'

'What's with you and Florida?' Harry asks him loudly. 'She says she comes from California and you keep pushing Florida at her. There's no connection.'

Charlie pulls at his spiked pink punch and looks like a pathetic old guy, the skin pegged even tighter to the planes of his skull. 'We can make a connection.'

Melanie calls toward the kitchen, 'Janice, can I be of any help?'

'No dear, thanks; it's all but done. Is everybody starving? Does anybody else want their drink freshened?'

'Why not?' Harry asks, feeling reckless. This bunch isn't going to be fun, he'll have to make his fun inside. 'How about you, Charlie?'

'Forget it, champ. One's my limit. The doctors tell me even that should be a no-no, in my condition.' Of Melanie he asks, 'How's your Kool-Aid holding up?'

'Don't call it Kool-Aid, that's rude,' Harry says, pretending to joust. 'I admire anybody of this generation who isn't polluting their system with pills and booze. Ever since Nelson got back, the sixpacks come and go in the fridge like, like coal down a chute.' He feels he has said this before, recently.

'I'll get you some more,' Melanie sings, and takes Charlie's glass, and Harry's too. She has no name for him, he notices. Nelson's father. Over the hill. Out of this world.

'Make mine weak,' he tells her. 'A g-and-t.'

94

Ma Springer has been sitting there with thoughts of her own. She says to Stavros, 'Nelson has been asking me all these questions about how the lot works, how much sales help there is, and how the salesmen are paid, and so on.'

Charlie shifts his weight in his chair. 'This gas crunch's got to affect car sales. People won't buy cows they can't feed. Even if so far Toyota's come along smelling pretty good.'

Harry intervenes. 'Bessie, there's no way we can make room for Nelson on sales without hurting Jake and Rudy. They're married men trying to feed babies on their commissions. If you want I could talk to Manny and see if he can use another kid on clean-up –'

'He doesn't want to work on clean-up,' Janice calls sharply from the kitchen.

Ma Springer confirms, 'Yes, he told me he'd like to see what he could do with sales, you know he always admired Fred so, idolized him you might say –'

'Oh come *on*,' Harry says. 'He never gave a damn about either of his grandfathers once he hit about tenth grade. Once he got onto girls and rock he thought everybody over twenty was a sap. All he wanted was to get the hell out of Brewer, and I said, O.K., here's the ticket, go to it. So what's he pussy-footing around whispering to his mother and grandmother now for?'

Melanie brings in the two men's drinks. Waitressly erect, she holds a triangulated napkin around the dewy base of each. Rabbit sips his and finds it strong when he asked for it weak. A love message, of sorts?

Ma Springer puts one hand on each of her thighs and points her elbows out, elbows all in folds like little pug dog faces. 'Now Harry –'

'I know what you're going to say. You own half the company. Good for you, Bessie, I'm glad. If it'd been me instead of Fred I'd've left it all to you.' He quickly turns to Melanie and says, 'What they really should do with this gas crisis is bring back the trolley cars. You're too young to remember. They ran on tracks but the power came from electric wires overhead. Very clean. They went everywhere when I was a kid.'

'Oh, I know. They still have them in San Francisco.'

'Harry, what I wanted to say –'

'But you're *not* running it,' he continues to his mother-in-law, 'and never have, and as long as I am, Nelson, if he wants a start there, can hose down cars for Manny. I don't want him in the sales room. He has none of the right attitudes. He can't even straighten up and smile.'

'I thought those were cable cars,' Charlie says to Melanie.

'Oh they just have those on a few hills. Everybody keeps saying how dangerous they are, the cables snap. But the tourists expect them.'

'Harry. Dinner,' Janice says. She is stern. 'We won't wait for Nelson any more, it's after eight.'

'Sorry if I sound hard,' he says to the group as they rise to go eat. 'But look, even now, the kid's too rude to come home in time for dinner.'

'Your own son,' Janice says.

'Melanie, what do you think? What's his plan? Isn't he heading back to finish college?'

Her smile remains fixed but seems flaky, painted-on. 'Nelson may feel,' she says carefully, 'that he's spent enough time at college.'

'But where's his degree?' He hears his own voice in his head as shrill, sounding trapped. 'Where's his degree?' Harry repeats, hearing no answer.

Janice has lit candles on the dining table, though the July day is still so light they look wan. She had wanted this to be nice for Charlie. Dear old Jan. As Harry walks to the table behind her he rests his eyes on what he rarely sees, the pale bared nape of her neck. In the shuffle as they take places he brushes Melanie's arm, bare also, and darts a look down the ripe slopes loosely concealed by the gypsy blouse. Firm. He mutters to her, 'Sorry, didn't mean to put you on the spot just now. I just can't figure out what Nelson's game is.'

'Oh you didn't,' she answers crooningly. Ringlets fall and tremble; her cheeks flame within. As Ma Springer plods to her place at the head of the table, the girl peeks up at Harry with a glint he reads as sly and adds, 'I think one factor, you know, is Nelson's becoming more security-minded.'

He can't quite follow. Sounds like the kid is going to enter the Secret Service.

Chairs scrape. They wait while a ghost of grace flies overhead. Then Janice dips her spoon into her soup, tomato, the color of Harry's Corona. Where is it? Out in the night. They rarely sit in this room, even with the five of them now they eat around the kitchen table, and Harry is newly aware of, propped on the sideboard where the family silver is stored, tinted photos of Janice as a high-school senior with her hair brushed and rolled under in a page-boy to her shoulders, of Nelson as an infant propped with his favorite teddy bear (that had one eye) on a stagy sunbathed window seat of this very house, and then Nelson as himself a high-school senior, his hair almost as long as Janice's, but less brushed, looking greasy, and his grin for the cameraman lopsided, half-defiant. In a gold frame broader than his daughter and grandson got, Fred Springer, misty-eyed and wrinkle-free courtesy of the portrait studio's darkroom magic, stares in studied three-quarters view at whatever it is the dead see.

Charlie asks the table, 'Did you see where Nixon gave a big party at San Clemente in honor of the moon-landing anniversary? They should keep that guy around forever, as an example of what sheer gall can do.'

'He did some good things,' Ma Springer says, in that voice of hers that shows hurt, tight and dried-out, somehow. Harry is sensitive to it after all these years.

He tries to help her, to apologize if he had been rough with her over who ran the company. 'He opened up China,' he says.

'And what a can of worms that's turned out to be,' Stavros says. 'At least all those years they were hating our guts they didn't cost us a nickel. This party of his wasn't cheap either. Everybody was there – Red Skelton, Buzz Aldrin.'

'You know I think it broke Fred's heart,' Ma Springer pronounces. 'Watergate. He followed it right to the end, when he could hardly lift his head from the pillows, and he used to say to me, "Bessie, there's never been a President who hasn't done worse. They just have it in for him because he isn't a glamour boy. If that had been Roosevelt or one of the Kennedys," he'd say, "you would never have heard 'boo' about Watergate." He believed it, too.'

Harry glances at the gold-framed photograph and imagines it nodded. 'I believe it,' he says. 'Old man Springer never steered me wrong.' Bessie glances at him to see if this is sarcasm. He keeps his face motionless as a photograph.

'Speaking of Kennedys,' Charlie puts in, he really is talking too much, on that one Kool-Aid, 'the papers are sure giving Chappaquiddick another go-around. You wonder, how much more they can say about a guy on his way to neck who drives off a bridge instead?'

Bessie may have had a touch of sherry, too, for she is working herself up to tears. 'Fred,' she says, 'would never settle on it's being that simple. "Look at the result," he said to me more than once. "Look at the result, and work backwards from that."' Her berry-dark eyes challenge them to do so, mysteriously. 'What was the result?' This seems to be in her own voice. 'The result was, a poor girl from up in the coal regions was killed.'

'Oh Mother,' Janice says. 'Daddy just had it in for Democrats. I loved him dearly, but he was absolutely hipped on that.'

Charlie says, 'I don't know, Jan. The worst things I ever heard your father say about Roosevelt was that he tricked us into war and died with his mistress, and it turns out both are true.' He looks in the candlelight after saying this like a cardsharp who has snapped down an ace. 'And what they tell us now about how Jack Kennedy carried on in the White House with racketeers' molls and girls right off the street Fred Springer in his wildest dreams would never come up with.' Another ace. He looks, Harry thinks, like old man Springer in a way: that hollow-templed, well-combed look. Even the little dabs of eyebrows sticking out like toy artillery.

Harry says, 'I never understood what was so bad about Chappaquiddick. He *tried* to get her out.' Water, flames, the tongues of God, a man is helpless.

'What was bad about it,' Bessie says, 'was he put her in.'

'What do you think about all this, Melanie?' Harry asks, playing cozy to get Charlie's goat. 'Which party do you back?'

'Oh the parties,' she exclaims in a trance. 'I think they're both evil.' *Ev-il*: a word in the air. 'But on Chappaquiddick a friend of mine spends every summer on the island and she says she wonders why more people don't drive off that bridge, there are no guard rails or anything. This is lovely soup,' she adds to Janice.

'That spinach soup the other day was terrific,' Charlie tells Melanie. 'Maybe a little heavy on the nutmeg.'

Janice has been smoking a cigarette and listening for a car door to slam. 'Harry, could you help me clear? You might want to carve in the kitchen.'

The kitchen is suffused with the strong, repugnant smell of roasting lamb. Harry doesn't like to be reminded that these are living things, with eyes and hearts, that we eat; he likes salted nuts, hamburger, Chinese food, mince pie. 'You know I can't carve lamb,' he says. 'Nobody can. You're just having it because you think it's what Greeks eat, showing off for your old lover boy.'

She hands him the carving set with the bumpy bone handles. 'You've done it a hundred times. Just cut parallel slices perpendicular to the bone.'

'Sounds easy. You do it if it's so fucking easy.' He is thinking, stabbing someone probably harder than the movies make it look, cutting underdone meat there's plenty of resistance, rubbery and tough. He'd rather hit her on the head with a rock, if it came to that, or that green glass egg Ma has as a knickknack in the living room.

'Listen,' Janice hisses. A car door has slammed on the street. Footsteps pound on a porch, their porch, and the reluctant front door pops open with a bang. A chorus of voices around the table greet Nelson. But he keeps coming, searching for his parents, and finds them in the kitchen. 'Nelson,' Janice says. 'We were getting worried.'

The boy is panting, not with exertion but the shallow-lunged pant of fear. He looks small but muscular in his grape-colored tie-dyed T-shirt: a burglar dressed to shinny in a window. But caught, here, in the bright kitchen light. He avoids looking Harry in the eye. 'Dad. There's been a bit of a mishap.'

'The car. I knew it.'

'Yeah. The Toyota got a scrape.'

'My Corona. Whaddeya mean, a scrape?'

'Nobody was hurt, don't get carried away.'

'Any other car involved?'

'No, so don't worry, nobody's going to *sue*.' The assurance is contemptuous.

'Don't get smart with *me*.'

'O.K., O.K., Jesus.'

'You drove it home?'

The boy nods.

Harry hands the knife back to Janice and leaves the kitchen to address the candlelit group left at the table – Ma at the head, Melanie bright-eyed next to her, Charlie on Melanie's other side, his square cufflink reflecting a bit of flame. 'Keep calm, everybody. Just a mishap, Nelson says. Charlie, you want to come carve some lamb for me? I got to look at this.'

He wants to put his hands on the boy, whether to give him a push or comfort his instinct is obscure; the actual touch might prove which, but Nelson stays just ahead of his father's fingertips, dodging into the summer night. The streetlights have come on, and the Corona's tomato color looks evil by the poisonous sodium glow – a hollow shade of black, its metallic lustre leeched away. Nelson in his haste has parked it illegally, the driver's side along the curb. Harry says, 'This side looks fine.'

'It's the *other* side, Dad.' Nelson explains: 'See Billy and I were coming back from Allenville where his girlfriend lives by this windy back road and because I knew I was getting late for supper I may have been going a little fast, I don't know, you can't go too fast on those back roads anyway, they wind too much. And this woodchuck or whatever it was comes out in front of me and in trying to avoid it I get off the road a little and the back end slides into this telephone pole. It happened so fast, I couldn't believe it.'

Rabbit has moved to the other side and by lurid light views the damage. The scrape had begun in the middle of the rear door and deepened over the little gas-cap door; by the time the pole reached the tail signal and the small rectangular sidelight, it had no trouble ripping them right out, the translucent plastic torn and shed like Christmas wrapping, and inches of pretty color-coded wiring exposed. The urethane bumper, so black and mat and trim, that gave Harry a small sensuous sensation whenever he touched the car home against the concrete parking-space divider at the place on the lot stencilled ANGSTROM, was pulled out from the frame. The dent even carried up into the liftback door, which would never seat exactly right again.

Nelson is chattering, 'Billy knows this kid who works in a body shop over near the bridge to West Brewer and he says you should get some real expensive rip-off place to do the estimate and then when you get the check from the insurance company give it to him and he can do it for less. That way there'll be a profit everybody can split.'

'A profit,' Harry repeated numbly.

Nails or rivets in the pole have left parallel longitudinal gashes the length of the impact depression. The chrome-and-rubber stripping has been wrenched loose at an angle, and behind the wheel socket on this side – hooded with a slightly protruding flare like an eyebrow, one of the many snug Japanese details he has cherished – a segment of side strip has vanished entirely, leaving a chorus of tiny holes. Even the many-ribbed hubcap is dented and besmirched. He feels his own side has taken a wound. He feels he is witnessing in evil light a crime in which he has collaborated.

'Oh come *on*, Dad,' Nelson is saying. 'Don't make such a big deal of it. It'll cost the insurance company, not you, to get it fixed, and anyway you can get a new one for almost nothing, don't they give you a terrific discount?'

'Terrific,' Rabbit says. 'You just went out and smashed it up. My Corona.'

'I didn't *mean* to, it was an *ac*cident, shit. What do you want me to do, piss blood? Get down on my knees and cry?'

'Don't bother.'

'Dad, it's just a *thing*; you're looking like you lost your best friend.'

A breeze, too high to touch them, ruffles the treetops and makes the streetlight shudder on the deformed metal. Harry sighs. 'Well. How'd the woodchuck do?'

# II

Once that first weekend of riots and rumors is over, the summer isn't so bad; the gas lines never get so long again. Stavros says the oil companies have the price hike they wanted for now, and the government has told them to cool it or face an excess profits tax. Melanie says the world will turn to the bicycle, as Red China has already done; she has bought herself a twelve-speed Fuji with her waitress's wages, and on fair days pedals around the mountain and down, her chestnut curls flying, through Cityview Park into Brewer. Toward the end of July comes a week of record heat; the papers are full of thermal statistics and fuzzy photographs of the time at the turn of the century when the trolley tracks warped in Weiser Square, it was so hot. Such heat presses out from within, against our clothes; we want to break out, to find another self beside the sea or in the mountains. Not until August will Harry and Janice go to the Poconos, where the Springers have a cottage they rent to other people for July. All over Brewer, air-conditioners drip onto patios and into alleyways.

On an afternoon of such hot weather, with his Corona still having bodywork done, Harry borrows a Caprice trade-in from the lot and drives southwest toward Galilee. On curving roads he passes houses of sandstone, fields of corn, a cement factory, a billboard pointing to a natural cave (didn't natural caves go out of style a while ago?), and another billboard with a great cutout of a bearded Amishman advertising 'Authentic Dutch Smorgasbord.' Galilee is what they call a string town, a hilly row of houses with a feed store at one end and a tractor agency at the other. In the middle stands an old wooden inn with a deep porch all along the second story and a renovated restaurant on the first with a window full of credit card stickers to catch the busloads of tourists that come up from Baltimore, blacks most of them, God knows what they hope to see out here in the sticks. A knot of young locals is hanging around in front of the Rexall's, you never used to see that in farm country, they'd be too busy with the chores. There is an old stone trough, a black-lacquered row of hitching posts, a glossy new bank, a traffic island with a monument Harry cannot make out the meaning of, and a small brick post office with its bright silver letters GALILEE up a side street that in a block dead-ends at the edge of a field. The woman in the post office tells Harry where the Nunemacher farm is, along R. D. 2. By the landmarks she gives him – a vegetable stand, a pond rimmed with willows, a double silo close to the road – he feels his way through the tummocks and swales of red earth crowded with shimmering green growth, merciless vegetation that allows not even the crusty eroded road embankments to rest barren but makes them bear tufts and mats of vetch and honeysuckle vines and fills the stagnant hot air with the haze of exhaled vapor. The Caprice windows are wide open and the Brewer disco station fades and returns in twists of static as the land and electrical wires obtrude. NUNEMACHER is a faded name on a battered tin mailbox. The house and barn are well back from the road, down a long dirt lane, brown stones, buried in pink dust.

Rabbit's heart rises in his chest. He cruises the road, surveying the neighboring mailboxes; but Ruth gave him, when he once met her by accident in downtown Brewer a dozen years ago, no clue to her name, and the girl a month ago refused to write hers in his showroom ledger. All he has to go by, other than Nunemacher's being his daughter's neighbor, if she is his daughter, is Ruth mentioning that her husband besides being a farmer ran a fleet of school buses. He was older than she and should be dead now, Harry figures. The school buses would be gone. The mailboxes alone this length of road say BLANKENBILLER, MUTH, and BYER. It is not easy to match the names with the places, as glimpsed in their hollows, amid their trees, at the end of their lanes of grass and dirt. He feels conspicuous, gliding along in a magenta Caprice, though no soul emerges from the wide landscape to observe him. The thick-walled houses hold their inhabitants in, in this hazy mid-afternoon too hot for work. Harry drives down a lane at random and stops and backs around in the beaten, rutted space between the buildings while some pigs he passed in their pen set up a commotion of snorting and a fat woman in an apron comes out of a door of the house. She is shorter than Ruth and younger than Ruth would be now, with black hair pulled tight beneath a Mennonite cap. He waves and keeps going. This was the Blankenbillers, he sees by the mailbox as he pulls onto the road again.

The other two places are nearer the road and he thinks he might get closer on foot. He parks on a widened stretch of shoulder, packed earth scored by the herringbone of tractor tire treads. When he gets out of the car, the powerful sweetish stench of the Blankenbillers' pigsty greets him from a distance, and what had seemed to be silence settles into his ear as a steady dry hum of insects, an undercoat to the landscape. The flowering weeds of mid-summer, daisies and the Queen Anne's lace and chicory, thrive at the side of the road and tap his pants legs as he hops up onto the bank. In his beige summerweight salesman's suit he prowls behind a hedgerow of sumac and black gum and wild cherry overgrown with poison ivy, shining leaves of it big as valentines and its vines having climbed to the tips of strangled trees. The roughly shaped sandstones of a tumbled old wall lie within this hedgerow, hardly one upon another. At a gap where wheeled vehicles have been driven through he stands surveying the cluster of buildings below him – barn and house, asbestos-sided chicken house and slat-sided corn crib, both disused, and a newish building of cement-block with a roof of corrugated overlapped Fiberglas. Some kind of garage, it looks like. On the house roof has been mounted a copper lightning rod oxidized green and an H-shaped television aerial, very tall to catch the signals out here. Harry means only to survey, to relate this layout to the Nunemacher spread across the next shaggy rise, but a soft clinking arising from somewhere amid the buildings, and the ripples a little runnel makes pouring itself into a small pond perhaps once for ducks, and an innocent clutter of old tractor seats and axles and a rusted iron trough in a neglected patch between the woodpile and the mowed yard lure him downward like a species of music while he churns in his head the story he will tell if approached and challenged. This soft dishevelled farm feels like a woman's farm, in need of help. An unreasonable expectancy brings his heart up to the pitch of the surrounding insect-hum.

Then he sees it, behind the barn, where the woods are encroaching upon what had once been a cleared space, sumac and cedar in the lead: the tilted yellow shell of a school bus. Its wheels and windows are gone and the snub hood of its cab has been torn away to reveal a hollow space where an engine was cannibalized; but like a sunken galleon it testifies to an empire, a fleet of buses whose proprietor has died, his widow left with an illegitimate daughter to raise. The land under Rabbit seems to move, with the addition of yet another citizen to the subterrain of the dead.

Harry stands in what once had been an orchard, where even now lopsided apple and pear trees send up sprays of new shoots from their gutted trunks. Though the sun burns, wetness at the root of the orchard grass has soaked his suede shoes. If he ventures a few steps farther he will be in the open and liable to be spotted from the house windows. There are voices within the house he can hear now, though they have the dim steady rumble that belongs to voices on radio or television. A few steps farther, he could distinguish these voices. A few steps farther still, he will be on the lawn, beside a plaster birdbath balanced off-center on a pillar of blue-tinted fluting, and then he will be committed to stride up bravely, put his foot on the low cement porch, and knock. The front door, set deep in its socket of stone, needs its green paint refreshed. From the tattered composition shingles of its roof to the dreary roller shades that hang in its windows the house exhales the dead breath of poverty.

What would he say to Ruth if she answered his knock?

*Hi. You may not remember me . . .*

*Jesus. I wish I didn't.*

*No, wait. Don't close it. Maybe I can help you.*

*How the hell would you ever help me? Get out. Honest to God, Rabbit, just looking at you makes me sick.*

*I have money now.*

*I don't want it. I don't want anything that stinks of you. When I did need you, you ran.*

*O.K., O.K. But let's look at the present situation. There's this girl of ours –*

*Girl, she's a woman. Isn't she lovely? I'm so proud.*

*Me too. We should have lots. Great genes.*

*Don't be so fucking cute. I've been here for twenty years, where have you been?*

It's true, he could have tried to look her up, he even knew she lived around Galilee. But he hadn't. He hadn't wanted to face her, the complicated and accusing reality of her. He wanted to hold her in his mind as just fucked and satisfied, lifting white and naked above him on an elbow. Before he drifted off to sleep she got him a drink of water. He does not know if he loved her or not, but with her he had known love, had experienced that cloudy inflation of self which makes us infants again and tips each moment with a plain excited purpose, as these wands of grass about his knees are tipped with packets of their own fine seeds.

A door down below slams, not on the sides of the house he can see. A voice sounds the high note we use in speaking to pets. Rabbit retreats behind an apple sapling too small to hide him. In his avidity to see, to draw closer to that mysterious branch of his past that has flourished without him, and where lost energy and lost meaning still flow, he has betrayed his big body, made it a target. He crowds so close to the little tree that his lips touch the bark of its crotch, bark smooth as glass save where darker ridges of roughness at intervals ring its gray. The miracle of it: how things grow, always remembering to be themselves. His lips have flinched back from the unintended kiss. Living microscopic red things – mites, aphids, he can see them – will get inside him and multiply.

'Hey!' a voice calls. A woman's voice, young on the air, frightened and light. Could Ruth's voice be so young after so many years?

Rather than face who it is, he runs. Up through the heavy orchard grass, dodging among the old fruit trees, breaking through as if a sure lay-up waits on the other side of the ragged hedgerow, onto the red tractor path and back to the Caprice, checking to see if he tore his suit as he trots along, feeling his age. He is panting; the back of his hand is scratched, by raspberries or wild rose. His heart is pounding so wildly he cannot fit the ignition key into the lock. When it does click in, the motor grinds for a few revolutions before catching, overheated from waiting in the sun. The female voice calling 'Hey' so lightly hangs in his inner ear as the motor settles to its purr and he listens for pursuing shouts and even the sound of a rifle. These farmers all have guns and think nothing of using them, the years he worked as a type-setter for the *Vat* hardly a week went by without some rural murder all mixed in with sex and booze and incest.

But the haze of the country around Galilee hangs silent above the sound of his engine. He wonders if his figure had been distinct enough to be recognized, by Ruth who hadn't seen him since he'd put on all this weight or by the daughter who has seen him once, a month ago. They report this to the police and use his name it'll get back to Janice and she'll raise hell to hear he's been snooping after this girl. Won't wash so good at Rotary either. Back. He must get back. Afraid of getting lost the other way, he dares back around and head back the way he came, past the mailboxes. He decides the mailbox that goes with the farm he spied on down in its little tousled valley with the duck pond is the blue one saying BYER. Fresh sky blue, painted this summer, with a decal flower, the sort of decoration a young woman might apply.

Byer. Ruth Byer. His daughter's first name Jamie Nunemacher never pronounced, that Rabbit can recall.

He asks Nelson one night, 'Where's Melanie? I thought she was working days this week.'

'She is. She's gone out with somebody.'

'Really? You mean on a date?'

The Phillies have been rained out tonight and while Janice and her mother are upstairs watching a *Waltons* rerun he and the kid find themselves in the living room, Harry leafing through the August *Consumer Reports* that has just come ('*Are hair dyes safe?*' '*Road tests: 6 pickup trucks*' '*An alternative to the $2000 funeral*') while the boy is looking into a copy of a book he has stolen from Fred Springer's old office at the lot, which has become Harry's. He doesn't look up. 'You could call it a date. She just said she was going out.'

'But *with* somebody.'

'Sure.'

'That's O.K. with you? Her going out with somebody?'

'Sure. Dad, I'm trying to read.'

The same rain that has postponed the Phils against the Pirates at Three Rivers Stadium has swept east across the Commonwealth and beats on the windows here at 89 Joseph Street, into the low-spreading branches of the copper beech that is the pride of the grounds, and at times thunderously upon the roof and spouting off the front porch roof. 'Lemme see the book,' Harry begs, and from within the Barcalounger holds out a long arm. Nelson irritably tosses over the volume, a squat green handbook on automobile dealership written by some crony of old man Springer's who had an agency in Paoli. Harry has looked into it once or twice: mostly hot air, hotshot stuff geared to the greater volume you can expect in the Philly area. 'This tells you,' he tells Nelson, 'more than you need to know.'

'I'm trying to understand,' Nelson says, 'about the financing.'

'It's very simple. The bank owns the new cars, the dealer owns the used cars. The bank pays the Mid-Atlantic Toyota when the car leaves Maryland; also there's something called holdback that the manufacturer keeps in case the dealer defaults on parts purchases, but that he rebates annually, and that to be frank about it has the effect of reducing the dealer's apparent profit in case he gets one of these wiseass customers who takes a great interest in the numbers and figures he can jew you down. Toyota insists we sell everything at their list so there's not much room for finagling, and that saves you a lot of headaches in my opinion. If they don't like the price they can come back a month later and find it three hundred bucks higher, the way the yen is going. Another wrinkle about financing, though, is when the customer takes out his loan where we send him – Brewer Trust generally, and though this magazine right here had an article just last month about how you ought to shop around for loans instead of going where the agency recommends it's a hell of a hassle actually to buck the system, just to save maybe a half of a per cent – the bank keeps back a percentage for our account, supposedly to cover the losses of selling repossessed vehicles, but in fact it amounts to a kickback. Follow me? Why do you care?'

'Just interested.'

'You should have been interested when your granddad Springer was around to be talked to. He ate this crap up. By the time he had sold a car to a customer the poor bozo thought he was robbing old Fred blind when the fact is the deal had angles to it like a spider web. When he wanted Toyota to give him the franchise, he claimed sixty thousand feet of extra service space that was just a patch of weeds, and then got a contractor who owed him a favor to throw down a slab and put up an uninsulated shell. That shop is impossible to heat in the winter, you should hear Manny bitch.'

Nelson asks, 'Did they used to ever chop the clock?'

'Where'd you learn that phrase?'

'From the book.'

'Well...' This isn't so bad, Harry thinks, talking to the kid sensibly while the rain drums down. He doesn't know why it makes him nervous to see the kid read. Like he's plotting something. They say you should encourage it, reading, but they never say why. 'You know chopping the clock is a felony. But maybe in the old days sometimes a mechanic, up in the dashboard anyway, kind of had his screwdriver slip on the odometer. People who buy a used car know it's a gamble anyway. A car might go twenty thousand miles without trouble or pop a cylinder tomorrow. Who's to say? I've seen some amazing wear on cars that were running like new. Those VW bugs, you couldn't kill 'em. The body so rotten with rust the driver can see the road under his feet but the engine still ticking away.' He tosses the chunky green book back. Nelson fumbles the catch. Harry asks him, 'How do you feel, about your girlfriend's going out with somebody else?'

'I've told you before, Dad, she's not my girlfriend, she's my friend. Can't you have a friend of the opposite sex?'

'You can try it. How come she settled on moving back here with you then?'

Nelson's patience is being tried but Harry figures he might as well keep pushing, he's not learning anything playing the silent game. Nelson says, 'She needed to blow the scene in Colorado and I was coming east and told her my grandmother's house had a lot of empty rooms. She's not been any trouble, has she?'

'No, she's charmed old Bessie right out of her sneakers. What was the matter with the scene in Colorado that she needed to blow it?'

'Oh, you know. The wrong guy was putting a move on her, and she wanted to get her head together.'

The rain restates its theme, hard, against the thin windows. Rabbit has always loved that feeling, of being inside when it rains. Shingles in the attic, pieces of glass no thicker than cardboard keeping him dry. Things that touch and yet not.

Delicately Harry asks, 'You *know* the guy she's out with?'

'Yes, Dad, and so do you.'

'Billy Fosnacht?'

'Guess again. Think older. Think Greek.'

'Oh my God. You're kidding. That old crock?'

Nelson watches him with an alertness, a stillness of malice. He is not laughing, though the opportunity has been given. He explains, 'He called up the Crêpe House and asked her, and she thought Why not? It gets pretty boring around here, you have to admit. Just for a meal. She didn't promise to go to bed with him. The trouble with your generation, Dad, you can only think along certain lines.'

'Charlie Stavros.' Harry says, trying to get a handle on it. The kid seems in a pretty open mood. Rabbit dares go on, 'You remember he saw your mother for a while.'

'I remember. But everybody else around here seems to have forgotten. You all seem so cozy now.'

'Times change. You don't think we should be? Cozy.'

Nelson sneers, sinking lower into the depths of the old sofa. 'I don't give that much of a damn. It's not my life.'

'It was,' Harry says. 'You were right there. I felt sorry for you, Nelson, but I couldn't think what else to do. That poor girl Jill –'

'Dad –'

'Skeeter's dead, you know. Killed in a Philadelphia shoot-out. Somebody sent me a clipping.'

'Mom wrote me that. I'm not surprised. He was crazy.'

'Yeah, and then not. You know he said, he'd be dead in ten years. He really did have a certain –'

110

'Dad. Let's cool this conversation.'

'O.K. Suits me. Sure.'

Rain. So sweet, so solid. In the garden the smallest scabs of earth, beneath the lettuce and lopsided bean leaves perforated by Japanese beetles, are darkening, soaking, the leaves above them glistening, dripping, in the widespread vegetable sharing of this secret of the rain. Rabbit returns his eyes to his magazine from studying Nelson's stubborn clouded face. The best type of four-slice toaster, he reads, is the one that has separate controls for each pair of toast slots. Stavros and Melanie, can you believe? Charlie had kept saying he had liked her style.

As if in apology for having cut his father off when the rain was making him reminiscent, Nelson breaks the silence. 'What's Charlie's title over there, anyway?'

'Senior Sales Rep. He's in charge of the used cars and I take care of the new. That's more or less. In practice, we overlap. Along with Jake and Rudy, of course.' He wants to keep remind-ing the kid of Jake and Rudy. No rich men's sons, they give a good day's work for their dollar.

'Are you satisfied with the job Charlie does for you?'

'Absolutely. He knows the ropes better than I do. He knows half the county.'

'Yeah, but his health. How much energy you think he has?'

The question has a certain collegiate tilt to it. He hasn't asked Nelson enough about college, maybe that's the way through to him. All these women around, it's too easy for Nelson to hide. 'Energy? He has to watch himself and take it easy, but he gets the job done. People don't like to be hustled these days, there was too much of that, the way the car business used to be. I think a salesman who's a little – what's the word? – laid back, people trust more. I don't mind Charlie's style.' He wonders if Melanie does. Where are they, in some restaurant? He pictures her face, bright-eyed almost like a thyroid bulge and her cheeks that look always rouged, rosy with exertion even before she bought the Fuji, her young face dense and smooth as she smiles and keeps smiling opposite old Charlie's classic con-man's profile, as he puts his move on her. And then later that business down below, his thick cock that blue-brown of Mediterranean types and, he wonders if her hair there is as curly as the hair on her head, in and out, he can't believe it will happen, while the rest of them sit here listening to the rain.

Nelson is saying, 'I was wondering if something couldn't be done with convertibles.' A heavy shamed diffidence thickens his words so they seem to drop one by one from his face, downturned where he sits in the tired gray sofa with his muskrat cut.

'Convertibles? How?'

'You know, Dad, don't make me say it. Buy 'em and sell 'em. Detroit doesn't make 'em anymore, so the old ones are more and more valuable. You could get more than you paid for Mom's Maverick.'

'If you don't wreck it first.'

This reminder has the effect Rabbit wants. 'Shit,' the boy exclaims, defenseless, darting looks at every corner of the ceiling looking for the escape hatch, 'I didn't wreck your damn precious Corona, I just gave it a little dent.'

'It's still in the shop. Some dent.'

'I didn't do it on purpose. Christ, Dad, you act like it was some divine chariot or something. You've gotten so uptight in your old age.'

'Have I?' He asks sincerely, thinking this might be information.

'Yes. All you think about is money and *things*.'

'That's not good, is it?'

'No.'

'You're right. Let's forget about the car. Tell me about college.'

'It's yukky,' is the prompt response. 'It's Dullsville. People think because of that shooting ten years ago it's some great radical place but the fact is most of the kids are Ohio locals whose idea of a terrific time is drinking beer till they throw up and having shaving cream fights in the dorms. Most of 'em are going to go into their father's business anyway, they don't care.'

Harry ignores this, asking, 'You ever have reason to go over to the big Firestone plant? I keep reading in the paper where they kept making those steel-belted radial five hundreds even after they kept blowing up on everybody.'

'Typical,' the boy tells him. 'All the products you buy are like that. All the American products.'

'We used to be the best,' Harry says, staring into the distance as if toward a ground where he and Nelson can agree.

'So I'm told.' The boy looks downward into his book.

'Nelson, about work. I told your mother we'd make a summer job for you over there on wash-up and maintenance. You'd learn a lot, just watching Manny and the boys.'

'Dad, I'm too old for wash-up. And maybe I need more than a summer job.'

'Are you trying to tell me you'd drop out of college with one lousy year to go?'

His voice has grown loud and the boy looks alarmed. He stares at his father open-mouthed, the dark ajar spot making with his two eyesockets three holes, in a hollow face. The rain drums on the porch roof spout. Janice and her mother come down from *The Waltons* weeping. Janice wipes at her eyes with her fingers and laughs. 'It's so stupid, to get carried away. It was in *People* how all the actors couldn't stand each other, that's what broke up the show.'

'Well, they have lots of reruns,' Ma Springer says, dropping onto the gray sofa beside Nelson, as if this little trip downstairs has been all her legs can bear. 'I'd seen that one before, but still they get to you.'

Harry announces, 'The kid here says he may not go back to Kent.'

Janice had been about to walk into the kitchen for a touch of Campari but freezes, standing. She is wearing just her short see-through nightie over underpants in the heat. 'You knew that, Harry,' she says.

Red bikini underpants, he notices, that show through as dusty pink. At the height of the heat wave last week she got her hair cut in Brewer by a man Doris Kaufmann goes to. He exposed the back of her neck and gave her bangs; Harry isn't used to them yet, it's as if a strange woman was slouching around here nearly naked. He almosts shouts, 'The hell I did. After all the money we've put into his education?'

'Well,' Janice says, swinging so her body taps the nightie from within, 'maybe he's got what he can out of it.'

'I don't get all this. There's something fishy going on. The kid comes home with no explanation and his girlfriend goes out with Charlie Stavros while he sits here hinting to me I should can Charlie so I can hire him instead.'

'Well,' Ma Springer pronounces peacefully, 'Nelson's of an age. Fred made space for you, Harry, and I know if he was here he'd make space for Nelson.'

In on the sideboard, dead Fred Springer listens to the rain, misty-eyed.

'Not at the top he wouldn't,' Harry says. 'Not to somebody who quits college a few lousy credits short of graduating.'

'Well Harry,' Ma Springer says, as calm and mellow as if the TV show had been a pipe of pot, 'some would have said you weren't so promising when Fred took you on. More than one person advised him against it.'

Out in the country, under the ground, old Farmer Byer mourns his fleet of school buses, rotting in the rain.

'I was a forty-year-old man who'd lost his job through no fault of his own. I sat and did Linotype as long as there was Linotype.'

'You worked at your father's trade,' Janice tells him, 'and that's what Nelson's asking to do.'

'Sure, *sure*,' Harry shouts, 'when he gets out of college if that's what he wants. Though frankly I'd hoped he'd want more. But what is the *rush*? What'd he come home for anyway? If I'd ever been so lucky at his age to get to a state like Colorado I'd sure as hell have stayed at least the summer.'

Sexier than she can know, Janice drags on a cigarette. 'Why don't you want your own son home?'

'He's too *big* to be home! What's he running from?' From the look on their faces he may have hit on something, he doesn't know what. He's not sure he wants to know what. In the silence that answers him he listens again to the downpour, an incessant presence at the edge of their lamplight domain, gentle, insistent, unstoppable, a million small missiles striking home and running in rivulets from the face of things. Skeeter, Jill, and the Kent State Four are out there somewhere, bone dry.

'Forget it,' Nelson says, standing up. 'I don't want any job with this creep.'

'What's he so hostile for?' Harry beseeches the women. 'All I've said was I don't see why we should fire Charlie so the kid can peddle convertibles. In time, sure. In 1980, even. Take over, young America. Eat me up. But one thing at a time, Jesus. There's tons of time.'

'Is there?' Janice asks strangely. She does know something. All cunts know something.

He turns to her directly. 'You. I'd think *you'd* be loyal to Charlie at least.'

'More than to my own son?'

'I'll tell you this. I'll tell you all this. If Charlie goes, I go.' He struggles to stand, but the Barcalounger has a sticky grip.

'Hip, hip hooray,' Nelson says, yanking his denim jacket from the clothes tree inside the front door and shrugging it on. He looks humpbacked and mean, a rat going out to be drowned.

'Now he's going out to wreck the Maverick.' Harry struggles to his feet and stands, taller than them all.

Ma Springer slaps her knees with open palms. 'Well this discussion has ruined my mood. I'm going to heat up water for a cup of tea, the damp has put the devil in my joints.'

Janice says, 'Harry, say goodnight to Nelson nicely.'

He protests, 'He hasn't said goodnight nicely to me. I was down here trying to talk nicely to him about college and it was like pulling teeth. What's everything such a secret for? I don't even know what he's majoring in now. First it was pre-med but the chemistry was too hard, then it was anthropology but there was too much to memorize, last I heard he'd switched to social science but it was too much bullshit.'

'I'm majoring in geography,' Nelson admits, nervous by the door, tense to scuttle.

'Geography! That's something they teach in the third grade! I never heard of a grownup studying geography.'

'Apparently it's a great specialty out there,' Janice says.

'Whadde they do all day, color maps?'

'Mom, I got to split. Where's your car keys?'

'Look in my raincoat pocket.'

Harry can't stop getting after him. 'Now remember the roads around here are slippery when wet,' he says. 'If you get lost just call up your geography professor.'

'Charlie's taking Melanie out really bugs you doesn't it?' Nelson says to him.

'Not at all. What bugs me is why it doesn't bug you.'

'I'm queer,' Nelson tells him.

'Janice, what have I done to this kid to deserve this?'

She sighs. 'Oh, I expect you know.'

He is sick of these allusions to his tainted past. 'I took care of him, didn't I? While you were off screwing around who was it put his breakfast cereal on the table and got him off to school?'

'My daddy did,' Nelson says in a bitter mincing voice.

Janice intervenes. 'Nellie, why don't you go now if you're going to go? Did you find the keys?'

The child dangles them.

'You're committing automotive suicide,' Harry tells her. 'This kid is a car killer.'

'It was just a fucking *dent*,' Nelson cries to the ceiling, 'and he's going to make me suffer and *suf*fer.' The door slams, having admitted a sharp gust of the aroma of the rain.

'Now who else would like some tea?' Ma Springer calls from the kitchen. They go in to her. Moving from the stuffy over-furnished living room to the kitchen with its clean enamelled surfaces provides a brighter perspective on the world. 'Harry, you shouldn't be so hard on the boy,' his mother-in-law advises. 'He has a lot on his mind.'

'Like what?' he asks sharply.

'Oh,' Ma says, still mellow, setting out plates of comfort, Walton-style, 'the things young people do.'

Janice has on underpants beneath her nightie but no bra and in the bright light her nipples show inside the cloth with their own pink color, darker, more toward wine. She is saying, 'It's a hard age. They seem to have so many choices and yet they don't. They've been taught by television all their lives to want this and that and yet when they get to be twenty they find money isn't so easy to come by after all. They don't have the opportunities even we had.'

This doesn't sound like her. 'Who have *you* been talking to?' Harry asks scornfully.

Janice is harder to put down than formerly; she tidies her bangs with a fiddling raking motion of her fingers and answers, 'Some of the girls at the club, their children have come home too and don't know what to do with themselves. It even has a name now, the back-to-the-nest something.'

'Syndrome,' he says; he is being brought round. He and Pop and Mom sometimes after Mim had been put to bed would settle like this around the kitchen table, with cereal or cocoa if not tea. He feels safe enough to sound plaintive. 'If he'd just *ask* for help,' he says, 'I'd try to give it. But he doesn't ask. He wants to take without asking.'

'And isn't that just human nature,' Ma Springer says, in a spruced-up voice. The tea tastes to her satisfaction and she adds as if to conclude, 'There's a lot of sweetness in Nelson, I think he's just a little overwhelmed for now.'

'Who isn't?' Harry asks.

In bed, perhaps it's the rain that sexes him up, he insists they make love, though at first Janice is reluctant. 'I would have taken a bath,' she says, but she smells great, deep jungle smell, of precious rotting mulch going down and down beneath the ferns. When he won't stop, crazy to lose his face in this essence, the cool stern fury of it takes hold of her and combatively she comes, thrusting her hips up to grind her clitoris against his face and then letting him finish inside her beneath him. Lying spent and adrift he listens again to the rain's sound, which now and then quickens to a metallic rhythm on the window glass, quicker than the throbbing in the iron gutter, where ropes of water twist.

'I like having Nelson in the house,' Harry says to his wife. 'It's great to have an enemy. Sharpens your senses.'

Murmurously beyond their windows, yet so close they might be in the cloud of it, the beech accepts, leaf upon leaf, shelves and stairs of continuous dripping, the rain.

'Nelson's not your enemy. He's your boy and needs you more now than ever though he can't say it.'

Rain, the last proof left to him that God exists. 'I feel,' he says, 'there's something I don't know.'

Janice admits, 'There is.'

'What is it?' Receiving no answer, he asks then, 'How do you know it?'

'Mother and Melanie talk.'

'How bad is it? Drugs?'

'Oh Harry no.' She has to hug him, his ignorance must make him seem so vulnerable. 'Nothing like that. Nelson's like you are, underneath. He likes to keep himself pure.'

'Then what the fuck's up? Why can't I be told?'

She hugs him again, and lightly laughs. 'Because you're not a Springer.'

Long after she has fallen into the steady soft rasping of sleep he lies awake listening to the rain, not willing to let it go, this sound of life. You don't have to be a Springer to have secrets. Blue eyes so pale in the light coming into the back seat of that Corolla. Janice's taste is still on his lips and he thinks maybe it wouldn't be such a good idea for Sealtest. Twice as he lies awake a car stops outside and the front door opens: the first time from the quietness of the motor and the lightness of the steps on the porch boards. Stavros dropping off Melanie; the next time, not many minutes later, the motor brutally raced before cut-off and the footsteps loud and defiant, must be Nelson, having had more beers than was good for him. From the acoustical quality surrounding the sounds of this second car Rabbit gathers that the rain is letting up. He listens for the young footsteps to come upstairs but one set seems to trap the other in the kitchen, Melanie having a snack. The thing about vegetarians, they seem always hungry. You eat and eat and it's never the right food. Who told him that, once? Tothero, he seemed so old there at the end but how much older than Harry is now was he? Nelson and Melanie stay in the kitchen talking until the eavesdropper wearies and surrenders. In his dream, Harry is screaming at the boy over the telephone at the lot, but though his mouth is open so wide he can see all his own teeth spread open like in those dental charts they marked your cavities on that looked like a scream, no sound comes out; his jaws and eyes feel frozen open and when he awakes it seems it has been the morning sun, pouring in violently after the rain, that he has been aping.

The display windows at Springer Motors have been recently washed and Harry stands staring through them with not a fleck of dust to show him he is not standing outdoors, in an air-conditioned outdoors, the world left rinsed and puddled by last night's rain, with yet a touch of weariness in the green of the tree across Route 111 behind the Chuck Wagon, a dead or yellow leaf here and there, at the tips of the crowded branches that are dying. The traffic this weekday flourishes. Carter keeps talking about a windfall tax on the oil companies' enormous profits but that won't happen, Harry feels. Carter is smart as a whip and prays a great deal but his gift seems to be the old Eisenhower one of keeping much from happening, just a little daily seepage.

Charlie is with a young black couple wrapping up a sale of a trade-in, unloading a '73 Buick eight-cylinder two-tone for three K on good folks too far behind in the rat race to know times have changed, we're running out of gas, the smart money is into foreign imports with sewing machine motors. They even got dressed up for the occasion, the wife wears a lavender suit with the skirt old-fashionedly short, her calves hard and high up on her skinny bow legs. They really aren't shaped like we are; Skeeter used to say they were the latest design. Her ass is high and hard along the same lines as her calves as she revolves gleefully around the garish old Buick, in the drench of sunshine, on the asphalt still wet and gleaming. A pretty sight, out of the past. Still it does not dispel the sour unease in Harry's stomach after his short night's sleep. Charlie says something that doubles them both up laughing and then they drive the clunker off. Charlie comes back to his desk in a corner of the cool showroom and Harry approaches him there.

'How'd you dig Melanie last night?' He tries to keep the smirk out of his voice.

'Nice girl.' Charlie keeps his pencil moving. 'Very straight.'

Harry's voice rises indignantly. 'What's straight about her? She's kooky as a bluebird, for all I can see.'

'Not so, champ. Very level head. She's one of those women you worry about, that they see it all so clearly they'll never let themselves go.'

'You're telling me she didn't let herself go with you.'

'I didn't expect her to. At my age – who needs it?'

'You're younger than I am.'

'Not at heart. You're still learning.'

It is as when he was a boy in grade school, and there seemed to be a secret everywhere, flickering up and down the aisles, bouncing around like the playground ball at recess, and he could not get his hands on it, the girls were keeping it from him, they were too quick. 'She mention Nelson?'

'A fair amount.'

'Whatcha think is going on between them?'

'I think they're just buddies.'

'You don't think anymore they got to be fucking?'

Charlie gives up, slapping his desk and pushing back from his paperwork. 'Hell, I don't know how these kids have it organized. In our day if you weren't fucking you'd move on. With them it may be different. They don't want to be killers like we were. If they *are* fucking, from the way she talks about him it has about the charge of cuddling a one-eyed teddy bear before you go to sleep.'

'She sees him that way, huh? Childish.'

'Vulnerable is the way she'd put it.'

Harry offers, 'There's some piece missing here. Janice was dropping hints last night.'

Stavros delicately shrugs. 'Maybe it's back in Colorado. The piece.'

'Did she say anything specific?'

Stavros ponders before answering, pushing up his amber glasses with a forefinger and then resting that finger on the bridge of his nose. 'No.'

Harry tries outright grievance. 'I can't figure out what the kid *wants*.'

'He wants to get started at the real world. I think he wants in around here.'

'I *know* he wants in, and I don't *want* him in. He makes me uncomfortable. With that sorehead look of his he couldn't sell –'

'Coke in the Sahara,' Charlie finishes for him. 'Be that as it may, he's Fred Springer's grandson. He's *engonaki*.'

'Yeah, both Janice and Bessie are pushing, you saw that the other night. They're driving me wild. We have a nice symmetrical arrangement here, and how many cars'd we move in July?'

Stavros checks a sheet of paper under his elbow. 'Twenty-nine, would you believe. Thirteen used, sixteen new. Including three of those Celica GTs for ten grand each. I didn't think it would go, not against all the little sports coming out of Detroit at half the price. Those Nips, they know their market research.'

'So to hell with Nelson. There's only one month left in the summer anyway. Why screw Jake and Rudy out of some commission just to accommodate a kid too spoiled to take a job in the shop? He wouldn't even have had to dirty his hands, we could have put him in Parts.'

Stavros says, 'You could put him on straight salary here on the floor. I'd take him under my wing.'

Charlie doesn't seem to realize he is the one to get pushed out. You try to defend somebody and he undermines you while you're doing it. But Charlie sees the problem after all; he expresses it: 'Look. You're the son-in-law, you can't be touched. But me, the old lady is my connection here, and it's sentimental at that, she likes me because I remind her of Fred, of the old days. Sentiment doesn't beat out blood. I'm in no position to hang tough. If you can't beat 'em, join 'em. Furthermore I think I can talk to the kid, do something for him. Don't worry, he'll never stick in this business, he's too twitchy. He's too much like his old man.'

'I see no resemblance,' Harry says, though pleased.

'You wouldn't. I don't know, it seems to be hard these days, being a father. When I was a kid it seemed simple. Tell the kid what to do and if he doesn't do it sock him. Here's my thought. When you and Jan and the old lady are taking your weeks in the Poconos, has Nelson been planning to come along?'

'They've asked him, but he didn't seem too enthusiastic. As a kid he was always lonely up there. Jesus, it'd be hell, in that little space. Even around the house every time you come into a little room it seems he's sitting there with a beer.'

'Right. Well how about buying him a suit and tie and letting him come in here? Give him the minimum wage, no commission and no draw. He wouldn't be getting on your nerves, or you on his.'

'How could I be getting on his nerves? He walks all over me. He takes the car all the time and tries to make me feel guilty besides.'

Charlie doesn't dignify this with an answer; he knows too much of the story.

Harry admits, 'Well, it's an idea. Then he'd be going back to college?'

Charlie shrugs. 'Let's hope. Maybe you can make that part of the bargain.'

Looking down upon the top of Charlie's fragile, striped skull, Rabbit cannot avoid awareness of his own belly, an extensive suit-straining slope; he has become a person and a half, where the same years have pared Charlie's shape, once stocky, bit by bit. He asks him, 'You really want to do this for Nelson?'

'I like the kid. To me, he's just another basket case. At his age now they're all basket cases.'

A couple has parked out in the glare and is heading for the showroom doors, a well-dressed Penn Park sort of pair that will probably collect the literature and sneak off to buy a Mercedes, as an investment. 'Well, it's your funeral,' Harry tells Charlie. Actually it might be nice all around. Melanie wouldn't be left alone in that big house all by herself. And it occurs to him that this all may be Melanie's idea, and Charlie's way of keeping his move on her alive.

In bed Melanie asks Nelson, 'What are you learning?'

'Oh, stuff.' They have decided upon her bed in the front room for these weeks when the old people are in the Poconos. Melanie in the month and more of her tenancy here has gradually moved the headless dress dummy to a corner and hidden some of the Springers' other ugly possessions – slid some rolled-up hall carpeting beneath the bed, tucked a trunkful of old curtains and a broken foot-pedalled Singer into the back of the closet, already crammed with outgrown and outmoded clothes in polyethylene cleaner bags. She has Scotch-taped a few Peter Max posters to the walls and made the room her own. They have used Nelson's room up to now, but his childhood bed is single and in truth he feels inhibited there. They had not intended to sleep together at all in this house but out of their long and necessary conversations it had been inevitable they sink into it. Melanie's breasts are indeed, as Charlie had noticed at a glance, large; their laden warm sway sometimes sickens Nelson, reminding him of a more shallow-breasted other, abandoned. He elaborates: 'Lots of things. There's all these pressures that don't show, like between the agency and the manufacturer. You got to buy sets of their special tools, for thousands of dollars, and they keep loading their base models with what used to be extras, where the dealer used to make a lot of his profit. Charlie told me a radio used to cost the dealer about thirty-five dollars and he'd add about one-eighty on to the sales price. See then by the manufacturer getting greedy and taking these options away from the dealer the dealers have to think up more gimmicks. Like undercoating. And rustproofing. There's even a treatment they'll give the vinyl upholstery to keep it from wearing supposedly. All that stuff. It's all cutthroat but kind of jolly at the same time, all these little pep talks people keep giving each other. My grandfather used to have a performance board but Dad's let it drop. You can tell Charlie thinks Dad's really lazy and sloppy.'

She pushes herself more upright in the bed, her breasts sluggish and silver in the half-light the maples filter from the sodium lamps on Joseph Street. There is that something heavy and maternal and mystical in her he cannot escape. 'Charlie's asked me out on another date,' she says.

'Go,' Nelson advises, enjoying the altered feeling of the bed, Melanie's lifting her torso above him deepening the rumpled trough in which he lies. When he was a little child and Mom and Dad were living in that apartment high on Wilbur Street and they would come visit here he would be put to bed in this very room, his grandmother's hair all black then but the patterns of light carved on the ceiling by the window mullions just the same as they are now. Mom-mom would sing him songs, he remembers, but he can't remember what they were. In Pennsylvania Dutch, some of them. *Reide, reide, Geile . . .*

Melanie pulls a hairpin from the back of her head and fishes with it in the ashtray for a dead roach that may have a hit or two left in it. She holds it to her red lips and lights it; the paper flares. When she lifted her arm to pull the hairpin, the hair in her armpit, unshaved, has flared in Nelson's field of vision. Despite himself, to no purpose, his prick with little knocks of blood begins to

123

harden down in the trough of childish warmth. 'I don't know,' Melanie says. 'I think with them away, he's psyched to score.'

'How do you feel about that?'

'Not so great.'

'He's a pretty nice guy,' Nelson says, snuggling deeper beside her abstracted body, enjoying the furtive growth of his erection. 'Even if he did screw Mom.'

'Suppose it kills him, how would I feel then? I mean, one of the reasons for my coming with you was to clean my head of all this father-figure shit.'

'You came along because Pru told you to.' Saying the other's name is delicious, a cool stab in the warmth. 'So I wouldn't get away.'

'Well, yeah, but I wouldn't have if I hadn't had reasons of my own. I'm glad I came. I like it here. It's like America used to be. All these brick houses built so solid, one against the other.'

'I hate it. Everything's so humid and stuffy and, so *closed*.'

'You really feel that Nelson?' He likes it when she kind of purrs his name. 'I thought you acted frightened, in Colorado. There was too much space. Or maybe it was the situation.'

Nelson loses Colorado in awareness of his erection, like a piece of round-ended ivory down there, and of the womanly thick cords in her throat swelling as she sucks one last hit from the tiny butt held tight against her painted lips. Melanie always wears make-up, lipstick and touches of red to her cheeks to make her complexion less olive, where Pru never wore any, her lips pale as her brow, and everything about her face precise and dry as a photograph. Pru: the thought of her is a gnawing in his stomach, like somebody rolling a marble around over grits of sand. He says, 'Maybe what I mind about around here is Dad.' At the thought of Dad the abrasion intensifies. 'I can't stand him, the way he sits there in the living room hogging the Barcalounger. He' – he can hardly find words, the discomfort is so great – 'just sits there in the middle of the whole fucking world, taking and taking. He doesn't know anything the way Charlie does. What did he ever do, to build up the lot? My granddad was grubbing his way up while my father wasn't doing anything but being a lousy husband to my mother. That's all he's done to deserve all this money: be

124

too lazy and shiftless to leave my mother like he wanted to. I think he's queer. You should have seen him with this black guy I told you about.'

'You loved your granddad, didn't you Nelson?' When she's high on pot her voice gets husky and kind of trancy, like one of these oracles sitting over her tripod they talked about in anthro at Kent. Kent: more sand rubbing in his stomach.

'He liked *me*,' Nelson insists, writhing a little and noticing with his hand that his erection has slightly wilted, possessing no longer the purity of ivory but the compromised texture of flesh and blood. 'He wasn't always criticizing me because I wasn't some great shakes athlete and ten feet tall.'

'I've never heard your father criticize you,' she says, 'except when you cracked up his car.'

'Goddam it I *did*n't crack it up, I just dented the bastard and he's going through the whole big deal, weeks in the body shop while I'm supposed to feel guilty or inept or something. And there *was* an animal in the road, some little thing I don't know what it was, a woodchuck, I would have seen the stripes if it had been a skunk, I don't know why they don't make these dumb animals with longer legs, it *waddled*. Right into the headlights. I wish I'd killed it. I wish I'd smashed up all Dad's cars, the whole fucking inventory.'

'This is really crazy talk Nelson,' Melanie says from within her amiable trance. 'You need your father. We all need fathers. At least yours is where you can find him. He's not a bad man.'

'He *is* bad, really bad. He doesn't know what's up, and he doesn't *care*, and he thinks he's so great. That's what gets me, his *hap*piness. He is so fucking *hap*py.' Nelson almost sobs. 'You think of all the misery he's caused. My little sister dead because of him and then this Jill he let die.'

Melanie knows these stories. She says in a patient singsong, 'You mustn't forget the circumstances. Your father's not God.' Her hand follows down inside the bedsheet where his has been exploring. She smiles. Her teeth are perfect. She's had orthodonture, and poor Pru never did, her people were too poor, so she hates to smile, though the irregularity isn't really that noticeable, just a dog tooth slightly overlapping on one side. 'You're feeling frustrated right now,' Melanie tells him, 'because of your situation. But your situation is not your father's fault.'

'It *is*,' Nelson insists. 'Everything's his fault, it's his fault I'm so fucked up, and he en*joys* it, the way he looks at me sometimes, you can tell he's really eating it up, that I'm fucked up. And then the way Mom waits on him, like he's actually *done* something for her, instead of the other way around.'

'Come on Nelson, let it go,' Melanie croons. 'Forget everything for now. I'll help you.' She flips down the sheet and turns her back. 'Here's my ass. I love being fucked from behind when I have a buzz on. It's like I'm occupying two planes of being.'

Melanie hardly ever tries to come when they make love, takes it for granted she is serving the baby male and not herself. With Pru, though, the woman was always trying, breathing 'Wait' in his ear and squirming around with her pelvis for the right contact, and even when he couldn't wait and failed, this was somehow more flattering. Remembering Pru this way he feels the nibble of guilt in the depths of his stomach take a sharper bite, like the moment in *Jaws* when the girl gets pulled under.

Water. Rabbit distrusts the element though the little brown hourglass-shaped lake that laps the gritty beach in front of the Springers' old cottage in the Poconos seems friendly and tame, and he swims in it every day, taking a dip before breakfast, before Janice is awake, and while Ma Springer in her quilty bathrobe fusses at the old oil stove to make the morning coffee. On weekdays when there aren't so many people he walks down across the coarse imported sand wrapped in a beach towel and, after a glance right and left at the cottages that flank theirs back in the pines, slips into the lake naked. What luxury! A chill silver embrace down and through his groin. Gnats circling near the surface shatter and reassemble as he splashes through them, cleaving the plane of liquid stillness, sending ripples right and left toward muddy rooty banks city blocks away. A film of mist sits visible on the skin of the lake if the hour is early enough. He was never an early-to-rise freak but sees the point of it now, you get *into* the day at the start, before it gets rolling, and roll with it. The film of mist tastes of evening chill, of unpolluted freshness in a world waking with him. As a kid Rabbit never went to summer camps, maybe Nelson is right they were too poor, it never occurred to them. The hot cracked sidewalks and dusty playground of Mt Judge were summer enough, and the few trips to the Jersey Shore his parents organized stick up in his remembrance as almost torture, the hours on poky roads in the old Model A and then the mud-brown Chevy, his sister and mother adding to the heat the vapors of female exasperation, Pop dogged at the wheel, the back of his neck sweaty and scrawny and freckled while the flat little towns of New Jersey threw back at Harry distorted echoes of his own town, his own life, for which he was homesick after an hour. Town after town numbingly demonstrated to him that his life was a paltry thing, roughly duplicated by the millions in settings where houses and porches and trees mocking those in Mt Judge fed the illusions of other little boys that their souls were central and dramatic and invisibly cherished. He would look at the little girls on the sidewalks they drove alongside wondering which of them he would marry, for his idea of destiny was to move away and marry a girl from another town. The traffic as they neared the Shore became thicker, savage, metropolitan. Cars, he has always found cars, their glitter, their exhalations, cruel. Then at last arriving in a burst of indignities – the parking lot full, the bathhouse attendant rude – they would enter upon a few stilted hours on the alien beach whose dry sand burned the feet and scratched in the crotch and whose wet ribs where the sea had receded had a deadly bottomless smell, a smell of vast death. Every found shell had this frightening faint stink. His parents in bathing suits alarmed him. His mother didn't look obscenely fat like some of the other mothers but bony and long and hard, and as she stood to call him or little Mim back from the suspect crowd of strangers or the dangerous rumour of undertow her arms seemed to be flapping like featherless wings. Not Rabbit then, he would be called as 'Hassy! Hassy!' And his father's skin where the workclothes always covered it seemed so tenderly white. He loved his father for having such whiteness upon him, secretly, a kind of treasure; in the bathhouse he and Pop changed together rapidly, not looking at one another, and at the end of the day changed again. The ride back to Diamond County was always long enough for the sunburn to start hurting. He and Mim would start slapping each other just to hear the other yell and to relieve the boredom of this wasted day that could have been spent among the fertile intrigues and perfected connections of the Mt Judge playground.

In his memory of these outings they always seem to be climbing toward the ocean as toward a huge blue mountain. Sometimes at night before falling to sleep he hears his mother say with a hiss, 'Hassy.' He sees now that he is rich that these were the outings of the poor, ending in sunburn and stomach upset. Pop liked crabcakes and baked oysters but could never eat them without throwing up. When the Model A was tucked into the garage and little Mim tucked into bed Harry could hear his father vomiting in a far corner of the yard. He never complained about vomiting or about work, they were just things you had to do, one more regularly than the other.

So as a stranger to summer places Rabbit had come to this cottage Fred Springer had bought rather late in his life, after the Toyota franchise had made him more than a used-car dealer, after his one child was married and grown. Harry and Janice used to come for just visits of a week. The space was too small, the tensions would begin to rub through, with Nelson bored and bug-eaten after the first day or so. When old man Springer died Harry became the man of the place and at last understood that Nature isn't just something that pushes up through the sidewalk cracks and keeps the farmers trapped in the sticks but is an elixir, a luxury that can be bought and fenced off and kept pure for the more fortunate, in an impure age. Not that this five-room, dark-shingled cottage, which Ma Springer rents for all but these three weeks of August, taking the Labor Day gravy and renting into hunting season if she can, was in any league with the gabled estates and lodges and resort hotels that are all around them tumbling down or being broken up by developers; but it has two acres of woods behind it and a dock and rowboat of its own, and holds out to Harry the possibility that life can be lived selectively, as one chooses from a menu, or picks a polished fruit from a bowl. Here in the Poconos food, exercise, and sleep, no longer squeezed into the margins of the day, swell to sumptuous importance. The smell of fresh coffee drifting to greet him as he walks still wet back from his swim; the kiss of morning fog through a rusted window screen; the sight of Janice with bare brown feet wearing the same tennis shorts and kid's black T-shirt day after day; the blue jay switching stances on the porch rail; the smooth rose-veined rock holding shut the upstairs door that has lost its latch; the very texture of root-riddled mud and reeds where the fresh cedar dock pilings have been driven: he feels love for each phenomenon and not for the first time in his life seeks to bring himself into harmony with the intertwining simplicities that uphold him, that were woven into him at birth. There must be a good way to live.

He eases off on the gin and snacks. He swims and listens to Ma Springer reminisce over the morning coffee and goes down into the village with Janice each day to shop. At night they play three-handed pinochle by the harsh light of bridge lamps, the light feeling harsh because when he had first come to this place they lit kerosene lamps, with fragile interior cones of glowing ash, and went to bed soon after dark, the crickets throbbing. He does not like to fish, nor does he much like playing tennis with Janice against one of the other couples that have access to the lake community's shared court, an old rectangle of clay in the pines, the edges coated with brown needles and the chicken-wire fencing drooping like wet ash. Janice plays every day at the Flying Eagle, and beside her efficient grace he feels cumbersome and out of it. The ball hops at him with a fury his racket cannot match. Her black T-shirt has on it in faded 3-D script the word *Phillies*; it is a shirt he bought Nelson on one of their excursions to Veterans Stadium, and the boy left it behind when he went away to Kent, and Janice in her middle-aged friskiness found it and made it hers. Typical of the way things have gone, that the kid's growing up should seem a threat and a tragedy to him and to her an excuse to steal a T-shirt. Not that it would fit Nelson anymore. It fits her fine; he feels her beside him in the corner of his eye nimbler and freer than he in her swarthy thick-middled old girl's shape with her short hair and bounding bangs. The ball arcs back steadily from her racket while he hits it too hard or else, trying to 'stroke' it like she tells him, pops it weakly into the net. 'Harry, don't try to steer it,' she says. 'Keep your knees bent. Point your hip toward the net.' She has had a lot of lessons. The decade past has taught her more than it has taught him.

What has he done, he wonders as he waits to receive the serve, with this life of his more than half over? He was a good boy to his mother and then a good boy to the crowds at the basketball games, a good boy to Tothero his old coach, who saw in Rabbit something special. And Ruth saw in him something special too, though she saw it winking out. For a while Harry had kicked against death, then he gave in and went to work. Now the dead are so many he feels for the living around him the camaraderie of survivors. He loves the people with him, penned in among the lines of the tennis court. Ed and Loretta: he's an electrical contractor from Easton specializing in computer installations. Harry loves the treetops above their heads, and the August blue above these. What does he know? He never reads a book, just the newspaper to have something to say to people, and then mostly human interest stories, like where the Shah is heading next and how sick he really is, and that Baltimore doctor. He loves Nature, though he can name almost nothing in it. Are these pines, or spruces, or firs? He loves money, though he doesn't understand how it flows to him, or how it leaks away. He loves men, uncomplaining with their pot bellies and cross-hatched red necks, embarrassed for what to talk about when the game is over, whatever the game is. What a threadbare thing we make of life! Yet what a marvellous thing the mind is, they can't make a machine like it, though some of these computers Ed was telling about fill rooms; and the body can do a thousand things there isn't a factory in the world can duplicate the motion. He used to love screwing, though more and more he's willing just to think about it and let the younger people mess with it, meeting in their bars and cars, amazing how many of them there are now, just walking down the street or getting into a movie line he often seems to be the oldest guy in sight. At night when he's with Janice, she needing a touch of cock to lead her into sleep, he tries to picture what will turn him on, and he's running out of pictures; the last that works is of a woman on all fours being fucked by one man while she blows another. And it's not clear in the picture if Harry is doing the fucking or is the man being blown, he is looking at all three from outside, as if up on a screen

130

at one of these movie theatres on upper Weiser with titles like *Harem Girls* and *All the Way*, and the woman's sensations seem nearer to him than the man's, the prick in his mouth like a small wet zucchini, plus the other elsewhere, in and out, in and out, a kind of penance at your root. Sometimes he prays a few words at night but a stony truce seems to prevail between himself and God.

He begins to run. In the woods, along the old logging roads and bridle trails, he ponderously speeds in tennis shoes first, orange with clay dust, and then in gold-and-blue Nikes bought at a sporting goods shop in Stroudsburg especially for this, running shoes with tipped-up soles at toe and heel, soles whose resilient circlets like flattened cleats lift him powerfully as, growing lighter and quicker and quieter, he runs. At first he feels his weight like some murderous burden swaddled about his heart and lungs and his thigh muscles ache in the morning so that he staggers in leaving the bed and laughs aloud in surprise. But as over the days, running after supper in the cool of the early evening while all the light has not ebbed from the woods, he accustoms his body to this new demand, his legs tighten, his weight seems less, his chest holds more air, the twigs fly past his ears as if winged on their own, and he extends the distance he jogs, eventually managing the mile and a half to the waist of the hourglass, where the gates of an old estate bar the way. Carbon Castle the locals call the estate, built by a coal baron from Scranton and now little utilized by his scattered and dwindled descendants, the swimming pool drained, the tennis court overgrown, energy gone. The glass eyes of the stuffed deer heads in the hunting lodge stare through cobwebs; the great main house with its precipitous slate roofs and diamond-paned windows is boarded up, though ten years ago one of the grandsons tried to make of it a commune, the villagers say. The young people vandalized the place, the story runs, and sold off everything they could move, including the two bronze brontosaurs that guarded the main entrance, emblems of the Coal Age. The heavy iron gates to Carbon Castle are double-chained and padlocked; Rabbit touches the forbidding metal, takes a breath for a still second while the world feels still to be rushing on, pouring through the tremble of his legs, then turns and jogs back, casting his mind wide, so as to become unconscious of his heaving body. There is along the way an open space, once a meadow, now spiked with cedars and tassle-headed weeds, where swallows dip and career, snapping up insects revived in the evening damp. Like these swallows Rabbit, the blue and gold of his new shoes flickering, skims, above the earth, above the dead. The dead stare upwards. Mom and Pop are lying together again as for so many years on that sway-backed bed they'd bought second-hand during the Depression and never got around to replacing though it squeaked like a tricycle left out in the rain and was so short Pop's feet stuck out of the covers. Papery-white feet that got mottled and marbled with veins finally: if he'd ever have exercised he might have lived longer. Tothero down there is all eyes, eyes big as saucers staring out of his lopsided head while his swollen tongue hunts for a word. Fred Springer, who put Harry where he is, eggs him on, hunched over and grimacing like a man with a poker hand so good it hurts. Skeeter, that that newspaper clipping claimed had fired upon the Philly cops first even though there were twenty of them in the yard and hallways and only some pregnant mothers and children on the commune premises, Skeeter black as the earth turns his face away. The meadow ends and Harry enters a tunnel, getting dark now, the needles a carpet, he makes no sound, Indians moved without sound through the trees without end where a single twig snapping meant death, his legs in his fatigue cannot be exactly controlled but flail against the cushioned path like arms of a loose machine whose gears and joints have been bevelled by wear. Becky, a mere seed laid to rest, and Jill, a pale seedling held from the sun, hang in the earth, he imagines, like stars, and beyond them there are myriads, whole races like the Cambodians, that have drifted into death. He is treading on them all, they are resilient, they are cheering him on, his lungs are burning, his heart hurts, he is a membrane removed from the hosts below, their filaments caress his ankles, he loves the earth, he will never die.

The last hundred feet, up their path to the tilting front porch, Rabbit sprints. He opens the front screen door and feels the punky floorboards bounce under him. The milk-glass shades of the old kerosene lamps, increasingly valuable as antiques, tremble, like the panes in the breakfront. Janice emerges barefoot from the kitchen and says, 'Harry, you're all red in the face.'

'I'm – all – right.'

'Sit down. For heaven's sakes. What are you training for?'

'The big bout,' he pants. 'It feels great. To press against. Your own limitations.'

'You're pressing too hard if you ask me. Mother and I thought you got lost. We want to play pinochle.'

'I got to take. A shower. The trouble with running is. You get all sweaty.'

'I still don't know what you're trying to prove.' With that Phillies shirt on she looks like Nelson, before he filled out and needed to shave.

'It's now or never,' he tells her, the blood of fantasy rushing through his brain. 'There's people out to get me. I can lie down now. Or fight.'

'*Who's* out to get you?'

'You should know. You hatched him.'

The hot water here runs off a little electric unit and is scalding for a few minutes and then cools with lightning speed. Harry thinks, A good way to kill somebody would be to turn off the cold water while they're in the shower. He dances out before the hot expires totally, admires the wet prints of his big feet on the bare pine floors of this attic-shaped upstairs, and thinks of his daughter, her feet in those cork-soled platforms. With her leggy pallor and calm round face she glows like a ghost but unlike the dead shares the skin of this planet with him, breathes air, immerses herself in water, moves from element to element, and grows. He goes into the bedroom he and Janice have here and dresses himself in Jockey shorts, an alligator shirt, and soft Levi's all washed and tumble-dried at the laundromat behind the little Acme in the village. Each crisp item seems another tile of his well-being he is fitting into place. As he sits on the bed to put on fresh socks a red ray of late sun slices through a gap in the pines and falls knifelike across his toes, the orangish corns and the little hairs between the joints and the nails translucent like the thin sheets in furnace peepholes. There are feet that have done worse than his, on a lot of women's in summer sandals you notice how the little toes have been bent under by years of pointy high-heeled shoes, and the big toes pushed over so the joint sticks out like a broken bone; thank God since he is a man that has never had to happen to him. Nor to Cindy Murkett either, come to think of it: toes side by side like candies in a box. Suck. That lucky stiff Webb. Still. It's good to be alive. Harry goes downstairs and adds the fourth element to his happiness; he lights a fire. Ma Springer, riding shrewdly with the times, has bought a new wood stove. Its bright black flue pipe fits snugly into the smudged old fireplace of ugly fieldstones. Old man Springer had installed baseboard electric heat when the cottage was connected for electricity, but his widow begrudges the expense of turning it on, even though by August the nights bring in a chill from the lake. The stove comes from Taiwan and is clean as a skillet, installed just this summer. Harry lays some rough sticks found around the cottage on top of a crumpled Sports page from the Philadelphia *Bulletin* and watches them catch, watches the words EAGLES READY ignite and blacken, the letters turning white on the crinkling ash; then he adds some crescent-shaped scraps of planed fruitwood a local furniture-maker sells by the bushel outside his factory. This fire greets the dark as Janice and her mother, the dishes done, come in and get out the pinochle deck.

As she deals, Ma Springer says, the words parcelled out in rhythm with the cards, 'Janice and I were saying, really we don't think it's so wise, for you to be running like this, at your age.'

'My age is the age to do it. Now's the time to start taking care of myself, I've had a free ride up to now.'

'Mother says you should have your heart checked first,' Janice says. She has put on a sweater and jeans but her feet are still bare. He glances at them under the card table. Pretty straight, the toes are. Not too much damage, considering. Bony and brown and boyish. He likes it, that up here in the Poconos she looks so often like a boy. His playmate. As when a child he is staying over at a playmate's house.

'Your father, you know,' Ma Springer is telling him, 'was taken off by his heart.'

'He'd been suffering for years,' Harry says, 'with a lot of things. He was seventy. He was ready to go.'

'You may not think so when your time comes.'

'I've been thinking about all the dead people I know lately,' Harry says, looking at his cards. Ace, ten, king, and jack of spades, but no queen. No pinochle either therefore. No runs. No four of anything. A raft of low clubs. 'I pass.'

'Pass,' Janice says.

'I'll take it at twenty-one,' Ma Springer sighs, and lays down a run in diamonds, and the nine, and a queen of spades to go with the jack.

'Wow,' Harry tells her. 'What power.'

'Which dead, Harry?' Janice asks.

She is afraid he means Becky. But he really rarely thinks of their dead infant, and then pleasantly, as of a brief winter day's sun on last night's snowfall, though her name was June. 'Oh, Pop and Mom mostly. Wondering if they're watching. You do so much to get your parents' attention for so much of your life, it seems weird to be going on without them. I mean, who cares?'

'A lot of people care,' Janice says, clumsily earnest.

'You don't know what it feels like,' he tells her. 'You still have your mother.'

'For just a little while yet,' Bessie says, playing an ace of clubs. Gathering in the trick with deft rounding motion of her hand she pronounces, 'Your father now was a good worker, who never gave himself airs, but your mother I must confess I never could abide. A sharp tongue, in a plain body.'

'Mother. Harry loved his mother.'

Bessie snaps down the ace of hearts. 'Well that's right and proper I guess, at least they say it is, for a boy to like his mother. But I used to feel sorry for him when she was alive. She drove him to have an uncommon high opinion of himself and yet could give him nothing to grab ahold of, the way Fred and I could you.'

She talks of Harry as if he too is dead. 'I'm still here, you know,' he says, flipping on the lowest heart he has.

Bessie's mouth pinches in and her face slightly bloats as her black eyes stare down at her cards. 'I know you're still here, I'm not saying anything I won't say to your face. Your mother was an unfortunate woman who caused a lot of devilment. You and Janice when you were starting out would never have had such a time of it if it hadn't been for Mary Angstrom, and that goes for ten years ago too. She thought too much of herself for what she was.' Ma has that fanatic tight look about the cheeks women get when they hate one another. Mom didn't think that much of Bessie Springer either – *little upstart married to that crook, a woman without enough brains to grease a saucepan living in that big house over on Joseph Street looking down her nose. The Koerners were dirt farmers and not even the good dirt, they farmed the hills.*

'Mother, Harry's mother was bedridden all through that time the house had burned down. She was dying.'

'Not so dying she didn't stir up a lot of mischief before she went. If she'd have let you two work out your relations with these others there would never have been a separation and all the grief. She was envious of the Koerners and had been since Day One. I knew her when she was Mary Renninger two classes ahead of me in the old Thad Stevens School before they built the new high school where the Morris farm used to be, and she thought too much of herself then. The Renningers weren't country people, you see, they came right out of Brewer and had that slum mentality, that cockiness. Too tall for her sex and too big for her britches. Your sister, Harry, got all her looks from your father's side. Your father's father they say was one of those very fair Swedes, a plasterer.' With a thump of her thumb she lays down the ace of diamonds.

'You can't lead trump until after the third trick,' Harry reminds her.

'Oh, foolish.' She takes the ace back and stares at her cards through the unbecoming though fashionable eyeglasses she bought recently – heavy blue shell frames hinged low to S-shaped temples and with a kind of continuous false eyebrow of silvery inlay. They aren't even comfortable, she has to keep touching the bridge to push them up on her little round nose.

Her agony is so great pondering the cards, Harry reminds her, 'You only need one point to make your bid. You've already made it.'

'Yes, well . . . make all you can while you can, Fred used to say.' She fans her cards a little wider. 'Ah. I thought I had another one of those.' She lays down a second ace of clubs.

But Janice trumps it. She pulls in the trick and says, 'Sorry, Mother. I only had a singleton of clubs, how could you know?'

'I had a feeling as soon as I put down that ace. I had a premonition.'

Harry laughs; you have to love the old lady. Cabined with these two women, he has grown soft and confiding, as when he was a little boy and asked Mom where ladies went wee-wee. 'I used to sometimes wonder,' he confides to Bessie, 'if Mom had ever, you know, been false to Pop.'

'I wouldn't have put it past her,' she says, grim-lipped as Janice leads out her own aces. Her eyes flash at Harry. 'See, if you'd have let me play that diamond she wouldn't have gotten in.'

'Ma,' he says, 'you can't take every trick, don't be so greedy. I know Mom must have been sexy, because look at Mim.'

'What do you hear from your sister?' Ma asks to be polite, staring down at her cards again. The shadows thrown by her ornate spectacle frames score her cheeks and make her look old, dragged down, where there is no anger to swell the folds of her face.

'Mim's fine. She's running this beauty parlor in Las Vegas. She's getting rich.'

'I never believed half of what people said about her,' Ma utters absently.

'Now Janice has run through her aces and plays a king of spades to the ace she figures Harry must have. Since she joined up with that bridge-and-tennis bunch of witches over at the Flying Eagle, Janice isn't as dumb at cards as she used to be. Harry plays the expected ace and, momentarily in command, asks Ma Springer, 'How much of my mother do you see in Nelson?'

'Not a scrap,' she says with satisfaction, whackingly trumping his ten of spades. 'Not a whit.'

'What can I do for the kid?' he asks aloud. It is as if another has spoken, through him. Fog blowing through a window screen.

'Be patient,' Ma answers, triumphantly beginning to run out the trumps.

'Be loving,' Janice adds.

'Thank God he's going back to college next month.'

Their silence fills the cottage like cool lake air. Crickets.

He accuses, 'You both know stuff I don't.'

They do not deny it.

He gropes. 'What do you both think of Melanie, really? I think she depresses the kid.'

'I dare say the rest are mine,' Ma Springer announces, laying down a raft of little diamonds.

'Harry,' Janice tells him. 'Melanie's not the problem.'

'If you ask me,' Ma Springer says, so firmly they both know she wants the subject changed, 'Melanie is making herself altogether too much at home.'

On television Charlie's angels are chasing the heroin smugglers in a great array of expensive automobiles that slide and screech, that plunge through fruit carts and large panes of glass and finally collide one with another, and then another, tucking into opposing fenders and grilles in a great slow-motion climax of bent metal and arrested motion and final justice. The angel who had replaced Farrah Fawcett-Majors gets out of her crumbled Malibu and tosses her hair: this becomes a freeze-frame. Nelson laughs in empathetic triumph over all those totalled Hollywood cars. Then the more urgent tempo and subtly louder volume of the commercial floods the room; a fresh palette of reflected light paints the faces, chubby and clownish side by side, of Melanie and Nelson as they sit on the old sofa of gray nappy stuff cut into a pattern and gaze at the television set where they have placed it in the re-arranged living room, where the Barcalounger used to be. Beer bottles glint on the floor beneath their propped-up feet; hanging drifts of sweetish smoke flicker in polychrome as if the ghosts of Charlie's angels are rising to the ceiling. 'Great smash-up,' Nelson pronounces, with difficulty rising and fumbling the television off.

'I thought it was stupid,' Melanie says in her voice of muffled singing.

'Oh shit, you think everything is stupid except what's his name, Kerchief.'

'G. I. Gurdjieff.' She has a prim mode of withdrawal, into mental regions where she knows he cannot reach. At Kent it became clear there were realms real for others not real to him –

not just languages he didn't know, or theorems he couldn't grasp, but drifting areas of unprofitable knowledge where nevertheless profits of a sort were being made. Melanie was mystical, she ate no meat and felt no fear, the tangled weedy gods of Asia spelled a harmony to her. She lacked that fury against limits that had been part of Nelson since he had known he would never be taller than five nine though his father was six three, or perhaps before that since he had found himself helpless to keep his father and mother together and to save Jill from the ruin she wanted, or perhaps before that since he had watched grownups in dark suits and dresses assembling around a small white coffin, with silvery handles and something sparkly in the paint, that they told him held what had been his baby sister, born and then allowed to die without anybody asking *him*; nobody ever asked him, the grown-up world was like that, it just ground on, and Melanie was part of that world, smugly smiling out at him from within that bubble where the mystery resided that amounted to power. It would be nice, as long as he was standing, to take up one of the beer bottles and smash it down into the curly hair of Melanie's skull and then to take the broken half still in his hand and rotate it into the smiling plumpnesses of her face, the great brown eyes and cherry lips, the mocking implacable Buddha calm. 'I don't care what the fuck his dumb name is, it's all bullshit,' he tells her instead.

'You should read him,' she says. 'He's wonderful.'

'Yeah, what does he say?'

Melanie thinks, unsmiling. 'It's not easy to sum up. He says there's a Fourth Way. Besides the way of the yogi, the monk, and the fakir.'

'Oh, great.'

'And if you go this way you'll be what he calls awake.'

'Instead of asleep?'

'He was very interested in somehow grasping the world as it is. He believed we all have plural identities.'

'I want to go out,' he tells her.

'Nelson, it's ten o'clock at night.'

'I promised I might meet Billy Fosnacht and some of the guys down at the Laid-Back.' The Laid-Back is a new bar in Brewer at the corner of Weiser and Pine, catering to the young. It used to be called the Phoenix. He accuses her, 'You go out all the time with Stavros leaving me here with nothing to do.'

'You could read Gurdjieff,' she says, and giggles. 'Anyway I haven't gone out with Charlie more than four or five times.'

'Yeah, you work all the other nights.'

'It isn't as if we ever *do* anything, Nelson. The last time we sat and watched television with his mother. You ought to see her. She looks younger than he does. All black hair.' She touches her own dark, vital, springy hair. 'She was wonderful.'

Nelson is putting on his denim jacket, bought at a shop in Boulder specializing in the worn-out clothes of ranch hands and sheep herders. It had cost twice what a new one would have cost. 'I'm working on a deal with Billy. One of the other guys is going to be there. I gotta go.'

'Can I come along?'

'You're working tomorrow, aren't you?'

'You know I don't care about sleep. Sleep is giving in to the body.'

'I won't be late. Read one of your books.' He imitates her giggle.

Melanie asks him, 'When have you last written to Pru? You haven't answered any of her recent letters.'

His rage returns; his tight jacket and the very wallpaper of this room seem to be sqeezing him smaller and smaller. 'How can I, she writes twice every fucking day, it's worse than a newspaper. Christ, she tells me her temperature, what she's eaten, when she's taken a crap practically –'

The letters are typewritten, on stolen Kent stationery, page after page, flawlessly.

'She thinks you're interested,' Melanie says in reproach. 'She's lonely and apprehensive.'

Nelson gets louder. '*She's* apprehensive! What does she have to be apprehensive about? Here I am, good as gold, with you such a goddam watchdog I can't even go into town for a beer.'

'Go.'

He is stabbed by guilt. 'Honest, I did promise Billy; he's going to bring this kid whose sister owns a '76 TR convertible with only fifty-five thousand miles on it.'

'Just go,' Melanie says quietly. 'I'll write to Pru and explain how you're too busy.'

'Too busy, too busy. Who the hell am I doing all this for except for fucking silly-ass Pru?'

'I don't know, Nelson. I honestly don't know what you're doing or who you're doing it for. I do know that I found a job, according to our plan, whereas you did nothing except finally bully your poor father into making up a job for you.'

'My *poor* father! *Poor* father! Listen who do you think put him where he is? Who do you think owns the company, my mother and grandmother own it, my father is just their front man and doing a damn lousy job of it too. Now that Charlie's run out of moxie there's nobody over there with any drive or creativity at all. Rudy and Jake are stooges. My father's running that outfit into the ground; it's sad.'

'You can say all that, Nelson, and that Charlie's run out of moxie which I think I'm in a better position than you to know, but you haven't shown me much capacity for responsibility.'

He hears, though frustrated and guilty to the point of tears, a deliberate escalation in her 'capacity for responsibility' in answer to his mention of 'creativity.' Against the Melanies of the world he will always come in tongue-tied. 'Bullshit' is all he can say.

'You have a lot of *feel*ings, Nelson,' she tells him. 'But feelings aren't actions.' She stares at him as if to hypnotize him, batting her eyes once.

'Oh Christ. I'm doing exactly what you and Pru wanted me to do.'

'You see, that's how your mind works, putting everything off on others. We didn't *want* you to *do* anything specific, we just wanted you to cope like an adult. You couldn't seem to do it out there so you came back here to put yourself in phase with reality. I don't see that you've done it.' When she bats her eyelids like that, her head becomes a doll's, all hollow inside. Fun to smash. 'Charlie says,' Melanie says, 'you're overanxious as a salesman; when the people come in, they're scared away.'

'They're scared away by the lousy tinny Japanese cars that cost a fortune because of the shit-eating yen. I wouldn't buy one, I don't see why anybody else should buy one. It's Detroit. Detroit has let everybody down, millions of people depending for jobs on Detroit's coming up with some decent car design and the assholes won't do it.'

'Don't swear so much, Nelson. It doesn't impress me.' As she gazes steadily up at him her eyeballs show plenty of white; he pictures the also plentiful white orbs of her breasts and he doesn't want this quarrel to progress so far she won't comfort him in bed. She hasn't ever sucked him off but he bets she does it for Charlie, that's the only way these old guys can get it up. Smiling that hollow-headed Buddha smile, Melanie says, 'You go off and play with the other little boys, I'll stay here and write Pru and won't tell her you said her ass is silly. But I'm getting very tired, Nelson, of covering for you.'

'Well who asked you to? You're getting something out of it too.' In Colorado she had been sleeping with a married man who was also the partner of the crumb Nelson was supposed to spend the summer working for, putting up condominiums in ski country. The man's wife was beginning to make loud noises though she had been around herself and the other guy Melanie was seeing had visions of himself as a cocaine supplier to the beautiful people at Aspen and yet lacked the cool and the contacts, and seemed headed for jail or an early grave depending on which foot he tripped over first. Roger the guy's name was and Nelson had liked him, the way he sidled along like a lanky yellow hound who knows he's going to be kicked. It had been Roger who had gotten them into hang gliding, Melanie too prudent but Pru surprisingly willing to try, joking about how this would be one way to solve all their problems. Her face so slender in the great white crash helmet they rented you at the Highlands base, up on the Golden Horn, she would give him in the second before the launch into astonishing, utterly quiet space that same wry sharp estimating look sideways he had seen the first time she had decided to sleep with him, in her little studio apartment in that factorylike highrise over in Stow, her picture window above a parking lot. He had met Melanie first, in a course they both took called the Geography of Religions: Shintō, shamanism, the Jains, all sorts of antique superstitions thriving, according to the maps, in overlapping patches, like splotches of disease, and in some cases even spreading, the world in such a desperate state. Pru was not a student but a typist for the Registrar's office over in Rockwell Hall; Melanie had gotten to know her during a campaign by the Students' League for a Democratic Kent to create discontent among the university employees, especially the secretaries. Most of such friendships withered when the next cause came along but Pru had stuck. She wanted something. Nelson had been drawn to her grudging crooked smile, as if she too had trouble spinning herself out for display, not like these glib kids who had gone from watching TV straight to the classroom with never a piece of the world's real weather to stop their tongues. And also her typist's hard long hands, like the hands of his grandmother Angstrom. She had taken her portable Remington west with her in hopes of finding some free-lance work out of Denver, so she typed her letters telling him when she went to sleep and when she woke up and when she felt like vomiting, whereas he has to respond in his handwriting that he hates, it is such a childish-looking scrawl. The fluent perfection of her torrent of letters overwhelms him, he couldn't have known she would be the source of such a stream. Girls write easier than boys somehow: he remembers the notes in green ink Jill used to leave around the house in Penn Villas. And he remembers, suddenly, more of the words of the song Mom-mom used to sing: *'Reide, reide, Geile | Alle Schtunn en Meili | Geht's iwwer der Schtumbe | Fallt's Bubbli nunner!'* with the last word, where Baby falls down, *nunner*, not sung but spoken, in a voice so solemn he always laughed.

'What am I getting out of it, Nelson?' Melanie asks with that maddening insistent singingness.

'Kicks,' he tells her. 'Safe kicks, too, the kind you like. Controlling me, more or less. Charming the old folks.'

Her voice relaxes and she sounds sad. 'I think that's wearing thin. Maybe I've talked too much to your grandmother.'

'Could be.' As he stands there he feels some advantage return to him. This is his house, his town, his inheritance. Melanie is an outsider here.

'Well, I *liked* her,' she says, strangely using the past tense. 'I'm always drawn to older people.'

'She makes more sense at least than Mom and Dad.'

'What do you want me to tell Pru if I write?'

'I don't *know*.' His shoulders shiver in his jacket as if the taut little coat is an electric contact; he feels his face cloud, even his breath grow hot. Those white envelopes, the white of the crash helmet she put on, the white of her belly. Space would open up immensely under you after you launched but was not menacing somehow, the harness holding you tight and the trees falling away smaller along the grassy ski trails and tilted meadows below and the great nylon wing responsive to every tug on the control bar. 'Tell her to hold on.'

Melanie says, 'She's *been* holding on, Nelson, she can't keep holding on forever. I mean, it *shows*. And I can't stay on here much longer either. I have to visit my mother before I go back to Kent.'

Everything seems to complicate, physically, in front of his mouth, so he is conscious of the effort of breathing. 'And *I* gotta get to the Laid-Back before everybody leaves.'

'Oh, go. Just go. But tomorrow I want you to help me start tidying up. They'll be back Sunday and you haven't once weeded the garden or mowed the lawn.'

Driving Ma Springer's cushy old Newport up Jackson to where Joseph Street intersects, the first thing Harry sees is his tomato-red Corona parked in front, looking spandy-new and just washed besides. They had got it fixed at last. It was cute of the kid to have had it washed. Loving, even. A surge of remorse for all the ill will he has been bearing Nelson gives a quickening countercurrent to the happiness he feels at being back in Mt Judge, on a sparkling Sunday noon late in August with the dry-grass smell of football in the air and the maples thinking of turning gold. The front lawn, even that awkward little section up by the azalea bushes and the strip between the sidewalk and the curb where roots are coming to the surface and hand-clippers have to be used, has been mowed. Harry knows how those hand-clippers begin to chafe in the palm. When the boy comes out on the porch and down to the street to help with the bags, Harry shakes Nelson's hand. He thinks of kissing him but the start of a frown scares him off; his impulse to be extra friendly flounders and drowns amidst the clutter of greetings. Janice embraces Nelson and, more lightly, Melanie. Ma Springer, overheated from the car ride, allows herself to be kissed on the cheek by both young people. Both are dressed up, Melanie in a peach-colored linen suit Harry didn't know she owned and Nelson in a gray sharkskin he knows the boy didn't have before. A new suit to be a salesman in. The effect is touchingly trimmer; in the tilt of the child's combed head his father is startled to see a touch of the dead Fred Springer, con artist.

Melanie looks taller than he remembers: high heels. In her pleased croon of a voice she explains, 'We went to church,' turning toward Ma Springer. 'You had said over the phone you might try to make the service and we thought we'd surprise you in case you did.'

'Melanie, I couldn't get them up in time,' Bessie says. 'They were just a pair of lovebirds up there.'

'The mountain air, nothing personal,' Rabbit says, handing Nelson a duffel bag full of dirty sheets. 'It was supposed to be a vacation and I wasn't going to get up at dawn the last day we were there just so Ma could come make cow eyes at that fag.'

'He didn't seem that faggy, Dad. That's just how ministers talk.'

'To me he seemed pretty radical,' Melanie says. 'He went on about how the rich have to go through a camel's eye.' To Harry she says, 'You look *thin*ner.'

'He's been running, like an idiot,' Janice says.

'Also not having to eat lunch at a restaurant every day,' he says. 'They give you too much. It's a racket.'

'Mother, be careful of the curb,' Janice says sharply. 'Do you want an arm?'

'I've been managing this curb for thirty years, you don't need to tell me it's here.'

'Nelson, help Mother up the steps,' Janice nevertheless says.

'The Corona looks great,' Harry tells the boy. 'Better than new.' He suspects, though, that that annoying bias in the steering will still be there.

'I really got on 'em about it, Dad. Manny kept giving it bottom priority because it was yours and you weren't here. I told him by the time you *were* here I wanted that car *done*, period.'

'Take care of the paying customers first,' Harry says, vaguely obliged to defend his service chief.

'Manny's a jerk,' the boy calls over his shoulder as he steers his grandmother and the duffel bag through the front door, under the stained-glass fanlight that holds among leaded foliate shapes the number 89.

Toting suitcases, Harry follows them in. This house had faded in his mind. 'Oh boy,' he breathes. 'Like an old shoe.'

Ma is dutifully admiring the neatness, the flowers from the border beds arranged in vases on the sideboard and dining-room table, the vacuumed rugs and the laundered antimacassars on the nappy gray sofa and matching easy chair. She touches the tufted chenille. 'These pieces haven't looked so good since Fred fought with the cleaning woman, old Elsie Lord, and we had to let her go.'

Melanie explains, 'If you use a damp brush, with just a dab of rug cleaner –'

'Melanie, you know how to do a job,' Harry says. 'The only trouble with you, you should have been a man.' This comes out rougher than he had intended, but a sudden small vexation had thrown him off balance when he stepped into the house. His house, yet not his. These stairs, those knickknacks. He lives here like a boarder, a rummy old boarder in his undershirt, too fuddled to move. Even Ruth has her space. He wonders how his round-faced girl is doing, out in that overgrown terrain, in her sandstone house with its scabby green door.

Ma Springer is sniffing the air. 'Something smells sweet,' she says. 'It must be the rug cleaner you used.'

Nelson is at Harry's elbow, closer than he usually gets. 'Dad, speaking of jobs, I have something I want to show you.'

'Don't show me anything till I get these bags upstairs. It's amazing how much crap you need just to walk around barefoot in the Poconos.'

Janice bangs the kitchen door, coming in from the outside. 'Harry, you should see the garden, it's all beautifully weeded! The lettuce comes up to my knees, the kohlrabi has gotten *enor*mous!'

Harry says to the young people, 'You should have eaten some, the kohlrabi gets pulpy if you let it grow too big.'

146

'It *never* has any taste, Dad,' Nelson says.

'Yeah. I guess nobody much likes it except me.' He likes to nibble, is one reason he's fat. While growing up he had many sensitive cavities and now that he has his molars crowned eating has become perhaps too much of a pleasure. No more twinges, just everlasting gold.

'Kohlrabi,' Melanie is saying dreamily, 'I wondered what it was, Nelson kept telling me turnips. Kohlrabi is rich in vitamin C.'

'How're the crêpes cooking these days?' Harry asks her, trying to make up for having told the girl she should have been a man. He may have hit on something, though; in her a man's normal bossiness has had to turn too sweet.

'Fine. I've given them my notice and the other waitresses are going to give me a party.'

Nelson says, 'She's turned into a real party girl, Dad. I hardly ever saw her when we were here together. Your pal Charlie Stavros keeps taking her out, he's even coming for her this afternoon.'

You poor little shnook, Rabbit thinks. Why is the kid standing so close? He can hear the boy's worried breath.

'He's taking me to Valley Forge,' Melanie explains, bright-eyed, those bright eyes concealing what mischief, Rabbit may never know now. The girl is pulling out: smart girl. 'I'm about to leave Pennsylvania and I really haven't seen any of the sights, so Charlie's being nice enough to take me to some of the places. Last weekend we went into Amish country and saw all the buggies.'

'Depressing damn things, aren't they?' Harry says, going on, 'Those Amish are mean bastards – mean to their kids, to their animals, to each other.'

'Dad –'

'If you're going as far as Valley Forge you might as well go look at the Liberty Bell, see if it still has a crack in it.'

'We weren't sure it was open Sundays.'

'Philly in August is a sight to see anyhow. One big swamp of miserable humanity. They cut your throat for a laugh down there.'

'Melanie, I'm so sorry to hear you're leaving,' Janice intervenes smoothly. It sometimes startles Harry, how smooth Janice can be in her middle age. Looking back, he and Jan were pretty rough customers – kids with a grudge, and not much style. No style, in fact. A little dough does wonders.

'Yeah,' the guest of their summer says, 'I should visit my family. My mother and sisters, I mean, in Carmel. I don't know if I'll go up to see my father or not, he's gotten so *strange*. And then back to college. It's been wonderful staying here, you were all so kind. I mean, considering that you didn't even *know* me.'

'No problem,' Harry says, wondering about her sisters, if they all have such eyes and ruby lips. 'You did it yourself; you paid your way.' Lame, lame. Never could talk to her.

'I know Mother will really miss your company,' Janice says, and calls over, 'Isn't that right, Mother?'

But Ma Springer is examining the china in her breakfront, to see if anything has been stolen, and doesn't seem to hear.

Harry asks Nelson abruptly, 'So what did you want to show me in such a hurry?'

'It's over at the lot,' the boy says. 'I thought we could drive over when you came back.'

'Can't I even have lunch first? I hardly had any breakfast, with all this talk of making church. Just a couple of Pecan Sandies that the ants hadn't gotten to.' His stomach hurts to think of it.

'I don't think there is that much for lunch,' Janice says.

Melanie offers, 'There's some wheat germ and yogurt in the fridge, and some Chinese vegetables in the freezer.'

'I have no appetite,' Ma Springer announces. 'And I want to try my own bed. Without exaggerating I don't believe I had more than three hours sleep in a row all that time up there. I kept hearing the raccoons.'

'She's just sore about missing church,' Rabbit tells the others. He feels trapped by all this fuss of return. There is a tension here that wasn't here before. You never return to the same place. Think of the dead coming back on Resurrection Day. He goes out through the kitchen into his garden and eats a kohlrabi raw, tearing off the leaves with his hands and stripping the skin from the bland crisp bulb with his front teeth. The butch women up the street are still hammering away – what can they be building? How did that poem used to go? *Build thee more stately something O my soul*. Lotty Bingaman would have known, waving her hand in the air. The air feels nice. A flatter noon than earlier, the summer settling to its dust. The trees have dulled down from the liquid green of June and the undertone of insect hum has deepened to a constant dry rasp, if you listen. The lettuce is tall and seedy, the beans are by, a carrot he pulls up is stubby as a fat man's prick, all its push gone upwards into greens. Back in the kitchen Janice has found some salami not too dried-out to eat and has made sandwiches for him and Nelson. This excursion to the lot seems bound to happen, when Harry had hoped to get over to the club this afternoon and see if the gang has missed him. He can see them gathered by the shuddering bright pool of chlorinated aqua, laughing, Buddy and his dog of the month, the Harrisons, foxy old Webb and his little Cindy. Little Cindy Blackbottom Babytoes. Real people, not these shadows in the corners of Ma's glum house. Charlie honks out front but doesn't come in. Embarrassed, and he should be, the babysnatcher. Harry looks at Janice to see how she takes it when the front door slams. Not a flicker. Women are tough. He asks her, 'So what're *you* going to do this afternoon?'

'I was going to tidy up the house, but Melanie seems to have done it all. Maybe I'll go over to the club and see if I can get into a game. At least I could swim.' She swam at Hourglass Lake, and in truth does look more supple through the middle, longer from hips to breasts. Not a bad little bride, he sometimes thinks, surprised by their connivance in this murky world of old blood and dark strangers.

'How'd you like that, about Charlie and Melanie?' he asks.

She shrugs, imitating Charlie. 'I like it fine, why not? More power to him. You only live once. They say.'

'Whyn't you go over and Nellie and I'll come join you after I look at this thing of his, whatever it is?'

Nelson comes into the kitchen, mouth ajar, eyes suspicious.

Janice says, 'Or I could come with you and Nelson to the lot and then we all three could go to the club together and save gas by using only the one car.'

'Mom, it's *bus*iness,' Nelson protests, and from the way his face clouds both parents see that they had better let him have his way. His gray suit makes him seem extra vulnerable, in the way of children placed in unaccustomed clothes for ceremonies they don't understand.

So Nelson and Harry, behind the wheel of his Corona for the first time in a month, drive through the Sunday traffic the route they both know better than the lines in their palms, down Joseph to Jackson to Central and around the side of the mountain. Harry says, 'Car feels a little different, doesn't it?' This is a bad start; he tries to patch it with, 'Guess a car never feels the same after it's been banged up.'

Nelson bridles. 'It was just a dent, it didn't have anything to do with the front end, that's where you'd feel the difference if there was any.'

Harry holds his breath and then concedes, 'Probably imagining it.'

They pass the view of the viaduct and then the shopping center where the four-theatre complex advertises AGATHA MANHATTAN MEATBALLS AMITYVILLE HORROR. Nelson asks, 'Did you read the book, Dad?'

'What book?'

'*Amityville Horror*. The kids at Kent were all passing it around.'

Kids at Kent. Lucky stiffs. What he could have done with an education. Been a college coach somewhere. 'It's about a haunted house, isn't it?'

'Dad, it's about Satanism. The idea is some previous occupant of the house had conjured up the Devil and then he wouldn't go away. Just an ordinary-looking house on Long Island.'

'You believe this stuff?'

'Well – there's evidence that's pretty hard to get around.'

Rabbit grunts. Spineless generation, no grit, nothing solid to tell a fact from a spook with. Satanism, pot, drugs, vegetarianism. Pathetic. Everything handed to them on a platter, think life's one big TV, full of ghosts.

Nelson reads his thoughts and accuses: 'Well *you* believe all that stuff they say in church and that's really sick. You should have seen it, they were giving out communion today and it was incredible, all these people sort of patting their mouths and looking serious when they come back from the altar rail. It was like something out of anthropology.'

'At least,' Harry says, 'it makes people like your grandmother feel better. Who does this Amityville horror make feel better?'

'It's not sup*posed* to, it's just something that *hap*pened. The people in the house didn't want it to happen either, it just *did*.' From the pitch of his voice the kid is feeling more in a corner than Rabbit had intended. He doesn't want to think about the invisible anyway, every time in his life he's made a move toward it somebody has gotten killed.

In silence father and son wind along Cityview Drive, with its glimpses through trees grown too tall of the flowerpot-colored city that German workers built on a grid laid out by an English surveyor and where now the Polacks and spics and blacks sit crammed in listening to each other's television sets through the walls, and each other's babies cry, and each other's Saturday nights turn ugly. Tricky to drive now, all these bicycles and mopeds and worst of all the roller skaters in jogging shirts with earphones on their heads, looking like boxers, all doped up, roller-skating as though they owned the street. The Corona coasts along Locust, where the doctors and lawyers hole up in their long brick single-family dwellings, set back and shady, with retaining walls and plantings of juniper fighting the slope of the ground, and passes on the right Brewer High, that he thought of as a kid as a castle, the multiple gyms and rows of lockers you wouldn't believe, receding to infinity it seemed, the few times he went there, the times the Mt Judge varsity played the Brewer J V squad, more or less for laughs (theirs). He thinks of telling Nelson about this, but knows the kid hates to have him reminisce about his sporting days. Brewer kids, Rabbit remembers in silence, were mean, with something dirty-looking about their mouths, as if they'd all just sucked raspberry popsicles. The girls fucked and some of the really vicious types smoked things called reefers in those days. Now even Presidents' kids, that Ford son and who knows about Chip, fuck and smoke reefers. Progress. In a way, he sees now, he grew up in a safe pocket of the world, like Melanie said, like one of those places you see in a stream where the twigs float backward and accumulate along the mud.

As they swing down into the steep part of Eisenhower, Nelson breaks the silence and asks, 'Didn't you used to live up on one of these cross streets?'

'Yeah. Summer. For a couple of months, ages ago. Your mother and I were having some problems. What makes you ask?'

'I just remembered. Like when you feel you've been someplace before, only it must have been in a dream. When I'd miss you real bad Mom used to put me in the car and we'd drive over here and look at some house hoping you'd come out. It was in a row that all looked alike to me.'

'And did I? Come out.'

'Not that I can ever remember. But I don't remember much about it, just being there in the car, and Mom having brought some cookies along to keep me entertained, and her starting to cry.'

'Jesus, I'm sorry. I never knew about this before, that she drove you over.'

'Maybe it just happened once. But it feels like more than once. I remember her being so big.'

Eisenhower flattens out and they pass without comment number 1204, where Janice years later had fled to Charlie Stavros, and where Nelson used to come on his bicycle and look up at the window. The kid had been desperate for a mini-bike at the time, and now Harry wishes he had got him one, it would be junk now in any case, and a good feeling might survive. Funny about feelings, they seem to come and go in a flash yet outlast metal.

Down over the abandoned car yards they go, through the factory outlet district, and left on Third, then right on lower Weiser, past white windowless Schoenbaum Funeral Directors, and then over the bridge. The traffic is mostly composed of old ladies poking back from their restaurant lunch they owed themselves after church and of carloads of kids already beered-up heading for the ballgame in the stadium south of Brewer where the Blasts play. Left on Route 111. DISCO. FUEL ECONOMY. They have forgotten to turn on the radio, so distracting has the tension between them been. Harry clears his throat and says, 'So Melanie's getting set to go back to college. You must be too.'

Silence. The subject of college is hot, too hot to touch. He should have been asking the kid what he's been learning at the lot. SPRINGER MOTORS. They pull in. Three weeks since Harry's seen it, and as with the house there's been a pollution. That Caprice he sometimes drove when the Corona was out of action isn't there, must have been sold. Six new Corollas are lined up next to the highway in their sweet and sour colors. Harry can never quite get over how small their wheels look, almost like tricycle wheels compared to the American cars he grew up with. Still, they're the guts of the line: buy cheap, most people are still poor, face it. You don't get something for nothing but hope springs eternal. Like a little sea of melting candy his cars bake in the sun. Since it's Sunday Harry parks right next to the hedge that struggles up front around the entrance and that collects at its roots all the stray wrappers and napkins that blow across 111 from the Chuck Wagon. The display windows need washing again. A paper banner bearing the slogan of the new TV campaign, OH WHAT A FEELING, fills the top half of the lefthand pane. The showroom has two new Celicas, one black with a yellow side stripe and one blue with a white one. Under the OH WHAT A FEELING poster, featuring some laughing cunt in a bathing suit splashing around in some turquoise pool with an Alp or Rocky in the background, lurks something different, a little low roachlike car that is no Toyota. Harry has no key; Nelson lets them in the double glass door with his. The strange car is a TR-6 convertible, polished up for sale but unmistakably worn, the windshield dull with the multiplied scratches of great mileage, the fender showing that slight ripple where metal has been bruised and healed. 'What the hell is this?' Harry asks, lifted to a great height by the comparative lowness of this intruding automobile.

'Dad, that's my idea we talked about, to sell convertibles. Honest, hardly anybody makes 'em anymore, even Jaguar has quit, they're bound to go up and up. We're asking fifty-five hundred and already a couple of guys have almost bought it.'

'Why'd the owner get rid of it if it was worth so much? What'd you give him on the trade?'

'Well, it wasn't a trade-in exactly –'

'What was it, exactly?'

'We bought it –'

'You *bought* it!'

'A friend of Billy Fosnacht's has this sister who's marrying some guy who's moving to Alaska. It's in great shape, Manny went all over it.'

'Manny and Charlie let you go ahead with this?'

'Why shouldn't they? Charlie's been telling me how he and old man Springer used to do all these crazy things, they'd give away stuffed animals and crates of oranges and have these auctions with girls in evening gowns where the highest bid got the car even if it was only five dollars – guys from car rodeos used to come –'

'That was the good old days. These are the bad new days. People come in here looking for Toyotas, they don't want some fucking British sports car –'

'But they will, once we have the name.'

'We *have* a name. Springer Motors, Toyota and used. That's what we're known for and that's what people come in here for.' He hears his voice straining, feels that good excited roll of anger building in him, like in a basketball game when you're down ten points and less then five minutes left on the clock and you've just taken one too many elbows in the ribs, and all the muscles go loose suddenly and something begins lifting you and you know nothing is impossible, with faith. He tries to hold himself back, this is a fragile kid and his son. Still, this has been his lot. 'I don't remember discussing any convertibles with you.'

'One night, Dad, we were sitting in the living room just the two of us, only you got sore about the Corona and changed the subject.'

'And Charlie really gave you the green light?'

'Sure; he kind of shrugged. With you gone he had the new cars to manage, and this whole shipment came in early –'

'Yeah. I saw. That close to the road they'll pick up all the dust.'

'– and anyway Charlie's not my boss. We're equals. I told him Mom-mom had thought it was a good idea.'

'Oh. You talked to Ma Springer about this?'

'Well not exactly at the time, she was off with you and Mom, but I know she wants me to plug into the lot, so it'll be three generations and all that crap.'

Harry nods. Bessie will back the kid, they're both black-eyed Springers. 'O.K., I guess no harm done. How much you pay for this crate?'

'He wanted forty-nine hundred but I jewed him down to forty-two.'

'Jesus. That's way over book. Did you look at the book? Do you know what the book is?'

'Dad of course I know what the fucking book is, the point is convertibles don't go by the book, they're like antiques, there's only so many and there won't be any more. They're what they call collectibles.'

'You paid forty-two for a '76 TR that cost six new. How many miles on it?'

'A girl drove it, they don't drive a car hard.'

'Depends on the girl. Some of the tootsies I see on the road are really pushing. How many miles did you say?'

'Well, it's kind of hard to say; this guy who went to Alaska was trying to fix something under the dashboard and I guess he didn't know which –'

'Oh boy. O.K., let's see if we can unload it for wholesale and chalk it up to experience. I'll call Hornberger in town tomorrow, he still handles TR and MG, maybe he'll take it off our hands as a favor.'

Harry realizes why Nelson's short haircut troubles him: it reminds him of how the boy looked back in grade school, before all that late Sixties business soured everything. He didn't know how short he was going to be then, and wanted to become a baseball pitcher like Jim Bunning, and wore a cap all summer that pressed his hair in even tighter to his skull, that bony freckled unsmiling face. Now his necktie and suit seem like that baseball cap to be the costume of doomed hopes. Nelson's eyes brighten as if at the approach of tears. 'Take it off our hands for cost? Dad, I *know* we can sell it, and clear a thousand. And there're two more.'

'Two more TRs?'

'Two more convertibles, out back.' By now the kid is scared, white in the face so his eyelids and eartips look pink. Rabbit is scared too, he doesn't want any more of this, but things are rolling, the kid has to show him, and he has to react. They walk back along the corridor past the parts department, Nelson leading the way and picking a set of car keys off the pegboard fastened next to the metal doorframe, and then they let themselves into the great hollow space of the garage, so silent on Sunday, a bare-girdered ballroom with its good warm stink of grease and acetylene. Nelson switches off the burglar alarm and pushes against the crash bar of the back door. Air again. Brewer far across the river, the tip of the tall courthouse with its eagle in concrete relief peeking above the forest of weeds, thistle and poke, at the lot's unvisited edge. This back area is bigger then it should be and always reminds Rabbit somehow of Paraguay. Making a little island of their own on the asphalt, two extinct American convertibles sit: a '72 Mercury Cougar, its top a tattered cream and its body that intense pale scum-color they called Nile Green, and a '74 Olds Delta 88 Royale, in color the purply-red women wore as nail polish in the days of spy movies. They were gallant old boats, Harry has to admit to himself, all that stretched tin and aerodynamical razzmatazz, headed down Main Street straight for a harvest moon with the old accelerator floored. He says, 'These are here on spec, or what? I mean, you haven't paid for them yet.' He senses that even this is the wrong thing to say.

'They're bought, Dad. They're ours.'

'They're mine?'

'They're not yours, they're the *com*pany's.'

'How the hell'd you work it?'

'What do you mean, how the hell? I just asked Mildred Kroust to write the checks and Charlie told her it was O.K.'

'Charlie said it was O.K.'

'He thought we'd all *agreed*. Dad, cut it out. It's not such a big deal. That's the idea here, isn't it – buy cars and sell 'em at a profit?'

'Not those crazy cars. How much were they?'

'I bet we make six, seven hundred on the Merc and more on the Olds. Dad, you're too uptight. It's only money. Was I supposed to have any responsibility while you were away, or not?'

'How much?'

'I forget exactly. The Cougar was about two thousand and the

156

Royale, some dealer toward Pottsville that Billy knows had it but I thought we should be able to offer, you know, a selection, it came to I think around two-five.'

'Two thousand five hundred dollars.'

Just repeating the numbers slowly makes him feel good, in a bad kind of way. Any debt he ever owed Nelson is being paid back now. He goes at it again: 'Two thousand five hundred good American –'

The child almost screams. 'We'll get it back, I promise! It's like antiques, it's like gold! You can't lose, Dad.'

Harry can't stop adding. 'Forty-two hundred for the little chop-clock TR, four thousand five hundred –'

'The boy is begging. 'Leave me alone, I'll do it myself. I've already put an ad in the paper, they'll be gone in two weeks. I promise.'

'You promise. You'll be back in college in two weeks.'

'Dad. I won't.'

'You won't?'

'I want to quit Kent and stay here and work.' This little face all frightened and fierce, so pale his freckles seem to be coming forward and floating on the surface, like flecks in a mirror.

'Jesus, that's all I need,' Harry sighs.

Nelson looks at him shocked. He holds up the car keys. His eyes blur, his lower lip is unsteady. 'I was going to let you drive the Royale for fun.'

Harry says, 'Fun. You know how much gas these old hot rods burn? You think people today with gas a dollar a gallon are going to want these eight-cylinder inefficient guzzlers just to feel the wind in their hair? Kid, you're living in a dream world.'

'They don't *care*, Dad. People don't *care* that much about money anymore, it's all shit anyway. Money is shit.'

'Maybe to you but not to me I'll tell you that now. Let's keep calm. Think of the parts. These things sure as hell need some work, the years they've been around. You know what six-, seven-year-old parts cost these days, when you can get 'em at all? This isn't some fancy place dealing in antiques, we sell Toyotas. Toyotas.'

The child shrinks beneath his thunder. 'Dad, I won't buy any more, I promise. These'll sell, I promise.'

'You'll promise me nothing. You'll promise me to keep your nose out of my car business and get your ass back to Ohio. I hate to be the one telling you this, Nelson, but you're a disaster. You've gotta get yourself straightened out and it isn't going to happen here.'

He hates what he's saying to the kid, though it's what he feels. He hates it so much he turns his back and tries to get back into the door they came out of but it has locked behind them, as it's supposed to do. He's locked out of his own garage and Nelson has the keys. Rabbit rattles the knob and thumps the metal door with the heel of his hand and even as in a blind scrimmage knees it; the pain balloons and coats the world in red so that though he hears a car motor start up not far away he doesn't connect it to himself until a squeak of rubber and a roar of speed slam metal into metal. That black gnashing cuts through the red. Rabbit turns around and sees Nelson backing off for a second go. Small parts are still settling, tinkling in the sunshine. He thinks the boy might now aim to crush him against the door where he is paralyzed but that is not the case. The Royale rams again into the side of the Mercury, which lifts up on two wheels. The pale green fender collapses enough to explode the headlight; the lens rim flies free.

Seeing the collision coming, Harry expected it to happen in slow motion, like on television, but instead it happened comically fast, like two dogs tangling and then thinking better of it. The Royale's motor dies. Through the windshield's granular fracture Nelson's face looks distorted, twisted by tears, twisted small. Rabbit feels a wooden sort of choked hilarity rising within him as he contemplates the damage. Pieces of glass finer than pebbles, bright grit, on the asphalt. Shadows on the broad skins of metal where shadows were not designed to be. The boy's short haircut looking like a round brush as he bends his face to the wheel sobbing. The whisper of Sunday traffic continuing from the other side of the building. These strange awkward blobs of joy bobbing in Harry's chest. Oh what a feeling.

Within a week, at the club, it has become a story he tells on himself. 'Five thousand bucks' worth of metal, *crunch*. I had this terrible impulse to laugh, but the kid was in there crying, they were *his* cars after all, the way he saw it. The only thing I could think of to do was go stand by the Olds with my arms out like *this*.' He spreads his arms wide, under the benign curve of the mountain. 'If the kid'd come out swinging my gut would've been wide open. But sure enough he stumbles out all blubbery and I could take him into my arms. I haven't felt so close to Nelson since he was about two. What makes me really feel rotten, he was right. His ad for the convertibles ran that same Sunday and we must have had twenty calls. The TR was gone by Wednesday, for fifty-five Cs. People aren't counting their pennies anymore, they're throwin' 'em out the window.'

'Like the Arabs,' Webb Murkett says.

'Jesus, those Arabs,' Buddy Inglefinger says. 'Wouldn't it be bliss just to nuke 'em all?'

'Did you see what gold did last week?' Webb smiles. 'That's the Arabs dumping their dollars in Europe. They smell a rat.'

Buddy asks, 'D'you see in today's paper where some investigation out of Washington showed that absolutely the government rigged the whole gas shortage last June?'

'We knew it at the time, didn't we?' Webb asks back, the red hairs that arc out of his eyebrows glinting.

Today is the Sunday before Labor Day, the day of the members-only fourball. Their foursome has a late starting time and they are having a drink by the pool waiting, with their wives. With some of their wives: Buddy Inglefinger has no wife, just that same dumb pimply Joanne he's been dragging around all summer, and Janice this morning said she'd go with her mother to church and show up at the club around drink time, for the after-the-fourball banquet. This is strange. Janice loves the Flying Eagle even more than he does. But ever since Melanie left the house this last Wednesday something is cooking. Charlie has taken two weeks off now that Harry is back from the Poconos, and with Nelson being persona non grata around the lot the Chief Sales Representative has his hands full. There is always a little upbeat at the end of summer, what with the fall models being advertised and raised prices already in the wind and the standing inventory beginning to look like a bargain, what with inflation worse and worse. There always comes in September a parched brightness to the air that hits Rabbit two ways, smelling of apples and blackboard dust and marking the return to school and work in earnest, but then again reminding him he's suffered another promotion, taken another step up the stairs that has darkness at the head.

Cindy Murkett hoists herself out of the pool. Dry sun catches in every drop beaded on her brown shoulders, so tan the skin bears a flicker of iridescence. Her boyishly cut hair is plastered in a fringe of accidental feathers halfway down the back of her skull. Standing on the flagstones, she tilts her head to twist water from this hair. Hair high inside her thigh merges with the black triangle of her string bikini. Walking over to their group, Cindy leaves plump wet footprints, heel and sole pad and tiny round toes. Little circular darkdab sucky toes.

'You think gold is still a good thing to buy?' Harry asks Webb, but the man has turned his narrow creased face to gaze up at his young wife. The fat eaves of her body drip onto his lap, the checks of his golf pants, darkening their lime green by drops. From the length of those eyebrow hairs of Webb's that curve out it's a wonder some don't stab him in the eye. He hugs her hips sideways; the Murketts look framed as for an ad against the green sweep of Mt Pemaquid. Behind them a diver knifes supple into the chlorine. Harry's eyes sting.

Thelma Harrison has been listening to his story, its sad undertone. 'Nelson must have been desolated by what he'd done,' she says.

He likes the word 'desolated,' so old-fashioned, coming from this mousy sallow woman who somehow keeps the lid on that jerk Harrison. 'Not so's you'd notice,' he says. 'We had that moment right after it happened, but he's been mean as hell to everybody since, especially since I made the mistake of telling him his ad had produced some results. He wants to keep coming to the lot but I told him to stay the hell away. You know what he did borders on crazy.'

Thelma offers, 'Maybe there's more on his mind than he can tell you.' The sun must be right behind his head from the way she shields her eyes to look up at him, even though she has on her sunglasses, big rounded brown ones that darken at the top like windshields. They hide the top half of her face so her lips seem to move with a strange precise independence; though thin, they have a dozen little curves that might fit sweetly around Harrison's thick prick, if you try to think what her hold on him might be, though this is hard to imagine. She's such a school-teacher with her little pleated skirt and studied way of holding herself and pronouncing words. For all of her lotions her nose is pink and the pinkness spreads into the area below her eyes, that her sunglasses all but hide.

In his floating wifeless state beside the pool, near the bottom of his g-and-t with its wilted sprig of mint, waiting for his fourball to start, he finds Thelma's solemn staring mottled look a bit befuddling. 'Yeah,' he says, eyes on the sprig. 'Janice keeps suggesting that. But she won't tell me what it might be.'

'Maybe she can't,' Thelma says, pressing her legs together tighter and tugging the skirt of her bathing suit down over an inch of thigh. She has these little purple veins women her age get but Harry can't see why she'd be self-conscious with an old pot-bellied pal like him.

He tells her, 'He doesn't seem to want to go back to college so maybe he's flunked out and never told us. But wouldn't we have gotten a letter from the dean or something? These letters from Colorado, boy, we see plenty of them.'

'You know Harry,' Thelma tells him, 'a lot of fathers Ronnie and I know complain how the boys don't *want* to come into the family business. They have these businesses and no one to carry them on. It's a tragedy. You should be glad Nelson does care about cars.'

'All he cares about is smashing 'em up,' Harry says. 'It's his revenge.' He lowers his voice to confide, 'I think one of the troubles between me and the kid is every time I had a little, you know, slip-up, he was there to see it. That's one of the reasons I don't like to have him around. The little twerp knows it, too.'

Ronnie Harrison, trying to put some kind of a move on poor old Joanne, looks up and shouts across, 'What's the old hotshot trying to sell ya, hon? Don't let him do a number on ya.'

Thelma ignores her husband with a dim smile and tells Harry

matter-of-factly, 'I think that's more in you than in Nelson. I'm wondering, could he be having girl trouble? Nelson.'

Harry is wondering if another g-and-t might erase a little headache that's beginning. Drinking in the middle of the day always does that to him. 'Well I can't see how. These kids, they just drift in and out of each other's beds like a bunch of gerbils. This girl he brought with him, Melanie, they didn't seem to have any contact really, in fact were getting pretty short with each other toward the end. She took some kind of a crazy shine to Charlie Stavros, of all people.'

'Why "of all people"?' Her smile is less dim, its thin curves declare that she knows Charlie had been Janice's lover, in the time before this club existed.

'Well he's old enough to be her father for one thing and he has one foot in the grave for another. He had rheumatic fever as a kid and it left him with a bum ticker. You ought to see him toddle around the lot now, it's pathetic.'

'Having an ailment doesn't mean you want to give up living,' she says. 'You know I have what they call lupus; that's why I try to protect myself against the sun and can't get nice and tan like Cindy.'

'Oh. Really?' Why is she telling him this?

Thelma from a wryness in her smile sees that she's presumed. 'Some men with heart murmurs live forever,' she says. 'And now the girl and Charlie are out of the county together.'

This is a new thought also. 'Yeah, but in totally different directions. Charlie goes to Florida and Melanie's visiting her family on the West Coast.' But he remembers Charlie talking up Florida to her at the dinner table and he finds the possibility that they are together depressing. You can't trust anybody not to fuck. He turns his head to let the sun strike the skin of his face; his eyes close, the lids glowing red. He should be practicing chipping for the fourball instead of lying here drowning in these voices. He heard on the radio driving over that a hurricane is approaching Florida.

Ronnie Harrison's voice, close at hand, shouts, 'What's that hon, you say I'm going to live forever? You bet your sweet bippy I am!'

Rabbit opens his eyes and sees that Ronnie has changed the position of his chair to make room for Cindy Murkett, who is at home enough now among them all not to fuss covering her lap with the towel the way she did earlier in the summer; she just sits there on the wire grid of her poolside chair naked but for a few black strings and the little triangles they hold in place, letting her boobs wobble the way they will as she pushes back the wet hair from her ears and temples, not once but several times, self-conscious at that. In her happiness with Webb she is letting her weight slip up, there is almost too much baby fat; when she stands, Harry knows, the pattern of the chair bottom will be printed in the backs of her thighs like a waffle iron releasing two warm slabs of dark dough. Still, that wobble: to lick and suck and let them fall first one and then the other into your eye-sockets. He closes his eyes. Ronnie Harrison is trying to entrance Joanne and Cindy at once with a story that involved a lot of deep-pitched growling as the hero-self talks back to the villain-other. What a conceited shit.

Webb Murkett leans forward to tell Harry, 'In answer to your question, yes, I think gold is an excellent buy. It's up over sixty per cent in less than a year and I see no reason for it not to appreciate at the same rate as long as the world energy situation holds. The dollar is bound to keep leaking, Harry, until they figure out how to get gasoline cheap out of grain alcohol, which'll put us back in the driver's seat. Grain we've got.'

From the other side of the group, Buddy Inglefinger calls over, 'Nuke 'em, I say; let's take their oil from the Arabs the same way we took it from the Eskimos.' Joanne gives this an obligatory giggle, Ronnie's story having been overridden for a minute. Buddy sees Harry as his straight man and calls, 'Hey Harry, did you see in *Time* where people stuck with their big old American cars are giving 'em to charity and taking a deduction or leaving 'em on the street to be stolen so they can collect the insurance? It said some dealer somewhere is giving you a free Chevette if you buy a Cadillac Eldorado.'

'We don't get *Time*,' Harry tells him coolly. Looked at a certain way, the world is full of twerps. Oh to close your eyes and just flicker out with your tongue for Cindy's nipples as she swung them back and forth, back and forth, teasing.

Joanne tries to join in: 'Meanwhile the President is floating down the Mississippi.'

'What else can he do?' Harry asks her, himself feeling floating and lazy and depressed.

'Hey Rabbit,' Harrison calls, 'whaddidya think when he was attacked by that killer rabbit?'

This gets enough of a laugh so they let him alone. Thelma speaks softly at his side. 'Children are hard. Ron and I have been lucky with Alex, once we gave him an old television set he could take apart he's known what he's wanted to do, electronics. But now our other boy Georgie sounds a lot like your Nelson, though he's a few years younger. He thinks what his father does is gruesome, betting against people that they're going to die, and Ron can't make him understand how life insurance is really such a small part of the whole business.'

'They're disillusioned,' Webb Murkett asserts in that wise voice of tumbling gravel. 'They've seen the world go crazy since they were age two, from JFK's assassination right through Vietnam to the oil mess now. And here the other day for no good reason they blow up this old guy Mountbatten.'

'Huh,' Rabbit grunts, doubting. According to Skeeter the world was never a pleasant place.

Thelma intervenes, saying, 'Harry was saying about how Nelson wants to come into the car business with him, and his negative feelings about it.'

'Be the very worst thing you could do for him,' Webb says. 'I've had five kids, not counting the two tykes Cindy has given me, and when any of them mentioned the roofing business to me I'd say, "Go get a job with another roofer, you'll never learn a thing staying with me." I couldn't give 'em an order, and if I did they wouldn't obey it anyway. When those kids turned twenty-one, boy or girl, I told each one of them, "It's been nice knowing you, but you're on your own now." And not one has ever sent me a letter asking for money, or advice, or anything. I get a Christmas card at Christmastime if I'm lucky. One once said to me, Marty the oldest, he said, "Dad, thanks for being such a bastard. It's made me fit for life."'

Harry contemplates his empty glass. 'Webb, whaddeya think?

Should I have another drink or not? It's fourball, you can carry the team.'

'Don't do it, Harry, we need you. You're the long knocker. Stay sober.'

He obeys, but can't shake his depression, thinking of Nelson. Thanks for being such a bastard. He misses Janice. With her around, his paternity is diluted, something the two of them did together, conniving, half by accident, and can laugh together about. When he contemplates it by himself, bringing a person into the world seems as terrible as pushing somebody into a furnace. By the time they finally get out onto the golf course, green seems a shade of black. Every blade of grass at his feet is an individual life that will die, that has flourished to no purpose. The fairway springy beneath his feet blankets the dead, is the roof of a kingdom where his mother stands at a cloudy sink, her hands red and wearing sleeves of soap bubbles when she lifts them out to give him some sort of warning. Between her thumb and knobby forefinger, the hands not yet badly warped by Parkinson's, a bubble pops. Mountbatten. And this same week their old mailman has died, Mr Abendroth, a cheerful overweight man with his white hair cut in a whiffle, dead of a thrombosis at sixty-two. Ma Springer had heard about it from the neighbors, he'd been bringing the neighborhood their bills and magazines ever since Harry and Janice had moved in; it had been Mr Abendroth who had delivered last April that anonymous envelope containing the news that Skeeter was dead. As he held that clipping that day the letters of type like these blades of grass drew Harry's eyes down, down into a blackness between them, as the ribs of a grate reveal the unseen black river rushing in the sewer. The earth is hollow, the dead roam through caverns beneath its thin green skin. A cloud covers the sun, giving the grass a silver sheen. Harry takes out a seven-iron and stands above his ball. Hit *down*. One of the weaknesses of Harry's game is he cannot make himself take a divot, he tries with misapplied tenderness to skim it off the turf, and hits it thin. This time he hits the ball fat, into a sand bunker this side of the tenth green. Must have rocked forward onto his toes, another fault. His practice swing is always smooth and long but when the pressure is on anxiety and hurry enter in. 'You dummy,'

Ronnie Harrison shouts over at him. 'What'd you do that for?'

'To annoy you, you creep,' Rabbit tells him. In a fourball one of the foursome must do well on every hole or the aggregate suffers. Harry here had the longest drive. Now look at him. He wriggles his feet to root himself in the sand, keeping his weight back on his heels, and makes himself swing through with the wedge, pick it up and swing it *through*, blind faith, usually he picks it clean in his timidity and flies it over the green but in this instance with his fury at Ronnie and his glum indifference it all works out: the ball floats up on its cushioning spray of sand, bites, and crawls so close to the pin the three others of his foursome cackle and cheer. He sinks the putt to save his par. Still, the game seems long today, maybe it's the gin at noon or the end-of-summer doldrums, but he can't stop seeing the fairways as chutes to nowhere or feeling he should be somewhere else, that something has happened, *is* happening, that he's late, that an appointment has been made for him that he's forgotten. He wonders if Skeeter had this feeling in the pit of his stomach that moment when he decided to pull his gun out and get blasted, if he had that feeling when he woke on the morning of that day. Tired flowers, goldenrod and wild carrot, hang in the rough. The millions of grass blades shine, ready to die. This is what it all comes to, a piece of paper that itself turns yellow, a news item you cut out and mail to another with no note. File to forget. History carves these caverns with a steady drip-drip. Dead Skeeter roams below, cackling. Time seeps up through the blades of grass like a colorless poison. He is tired, Harry, of summer, of golf, of the sun. When he was younger and just taking up the game twenty years ago and even when he took it up again eight years or so ago there were shots that seemed a miracle, straight as an edge of glass and longer than any power purely his could have produced, and it was for the sake of collaboration with this angle that he kept playing, but as he improved and his handicap dwindled from sky's-the-limit to a sane sixteen, these super shots became rarer, even the best of his drives had a little tail or were struck with a little scuff, and a shade off line one way or another, and the whole thing became more like work, pleasant work but work, a matter of approximations in the realm of the imperfect, with nothing breaking through but normal healthy happiness. In pursuit of such happiness Harry feels guilty, out on the course as the shadows lengthen, in the company of these three men, who away from their women loom as boring as they must appear to God.

Janice is not waiting for him in the lounge or beside the pool when at last around 5:45 they come in from playing the par-5 eighteenth. Instead one of the girls in their green and white uniforms comes over and tells him that his wife wants him to call home. He doesn't recognize this girl, she isn't Sandra, but she knows his name. Everybody knows Harry at the Flying Eagle. He goes into the lounge, his hand lifted in continuous salute to the members there, and puts the same dime he's been using as a ball marker on the greens into the pay phone and dials. Janice answers after a single ring.

'Hey come on over,' he begs. 'We miss you. I played pretty good, the second nine, once I got into the mood. With our handicap strokes Webb figures our best ball to be a sixty-three, which ought to be good for an alligator shirt at least. You should have seen my sand shot on the tenth.'

'I'd like to come over,' Janice says, her voice sounding so careful and far away the idea crosses his mind she's being held for ransom and so must be careful what she says, 'but I can't. There's somebody here.'

'Who?'

'Somebody you haven't met yet.'

'Important?'

She laughs. 'I believe so.'

'Why are you being so fucking mysterious?'

'Harry, just come.'

'But there's going to be the banquet, and the prizes. I can't desert my foursome.'

'If you won any prize Webb can give it to you later. I can't keep talking forever.'

'This better be good,' he warns her, hanging up. What can it be? Another accident for Nelson, the police have come for him. The kid has a criminal slouch. Harry goes back to the pool and tells the others, 'Crazy Janice says I have to come home but she won't say why.'

The women's faces show concern but the men are on their second round of drinks now and feeling no pain. 'Hey Harry,' Buddy Inglefinger shouts. 'Before you go, here's one you might not have heard up in the Poconos. Why did the Russian ballet dancer defect to the U.S.A.?'

'I don't know, why?'

'Because Communism wasn't Goodunov.'

The obliging laughter of the three women, as they all gaze upward in the reddening slant sun toward Harry's face, is like some fruit, three different ripenesses on the same branch, still hanging there when he turns his back. Cindy has put on over her bare shoulders a peach-colored silken shirt and in the V of its throat her little gold cross burns, that he hadn't noticed when she was nearly naked. He changes out of his golf shoes in the locker room and instead of showering just takes the hanger holding the sports coat and slacks he was going to put on for the banquet out to the parking lot on his arm. The Corona still doesn't feel right. He hears on the radio the Phillies have eked out a victory in Atlanta, 2–1. The gang never mentions the Phillies anymore, they're in fifth place, out of it. Get out of it in this society and you're as good as dead, an embarrassment. Not Goodunov. Keep Our City Clean. The radio announcer is not that wiseass woman but a young man with a voice like bubbles of fat in water, every syllable. Hurricane David has already left six hundred dead in the Caribbean region, he says, and, finally, life may exist, some scientists are coming to believe, on Titan, Saturn's largest moon. Harry passes the old box factory and enjoys yet once again the long view of the town of Mt Judge you get coming in the Route 422 way. The row houses ascending the slope of the mountain like stairs, their windows golden with setting sun like holes in a Hallowe'en pumpkin. Suppose he had been born on Titan instead, how different would he feel down deep? He thinks of those cindery lunar surfaces, the chunky men in their white suits hopping, the footprints they left in the dust there forever. He remembers how when they'd come visiting the Springers or after the fire the first years they lived here he and Nelson used to watch *Lost in Space* together on the gray sofa, how they'd squirm and groan when Doctor Smith did some dumb imperilling egotistical thing, and only that manly-voiced robot and the little boy Will with enough sense to pull the thing off, the spaceship fighting free of man-eating plants or whatever the week's villains were. He wonders now if Nelson saw himself as Will, saving the grownups from themselves, and he wonders where the boy actor is now, what he is, Rabbit hopes not a junkie the way so many of these child stars seem to end up. That was good solid space they were lost in, not this soupy psychedelic space they have on TV now, all tricks with music and lights, tricks he associates with the movie *2001*, an unpleasant association since that was the time Janice ran off with Charlie and all hell broke loose on the home front. The problem is, even if there is a Heaven how can there be one we can stand forever? On Earth, when you look up from being bored, things have changed, you're that much closer to the grave, and that's exciting. Imagine climbing up and up into that great tree of night sky. Dizzying. Terrible. Rabbit didn't even like to get too high into these little maples around town, though with the other kids as witnesses he pushed himself up, gripping tighter and tighter as the branches got smaller. From a certain angle the most terrifying thing in the world is your own life, the fact that it's yours and nobody else's. A loop is rising in his chest as in a rope when you keep twisting. Whatever can have happened bad enough to make Janice miss the fourball banquet?'

He accelerates along Jackson as the streetlights come on, earlier each day now. Janice's Maverick is out along the curb with the top down, she must have gone somewhere after church, she wouldn't take Bessie to church with the top down. Inside the front door, a wealth of duffel bags and suitcases has been deposited in the living room as by a small army. In the kitchen there is laughter and light. The party comes to meet him halfway, in the shadowy no-man's land between the staircase and the breakfront. Ma Springer and Janice are overtopped by a new female, taller, with a smoothly parted head of hair from which the kitchen light strikes an arc of carrot color, where Melanie's hair would have caught in its curls a straggly halo. He had grown used to Melanie. It is Nelson who speaks. 'Dad, this here is Pru,' the 'this here' a little scared joke.

'Nelson's fiancée,' Janice amplifies in a voice tense but plump, firmly making the best of it.

'Is that a fact?' Harry hears himself ask. The girl saunters forward, a slender slouching shape, and he takes the bony hand she extends. In the lingering daylight the dining-room windows admit she stands plain, a young redhead past girlhood, with arms too long and hips too wide for the boniness of her face, an awkward beauty, her body helplessly not only hers but somehow theirs, overcommitted, a look about her of wry, slightly twisted resignation, of having been battered by life young as she is, but the battering having not yet reached her eyes, which are clear green, though guarded. As she entrusts her hand to his her smile is a fraction slow, as if inside she must make certain there is something to smile at, but then comes forth eagerly enough, with a crimp in one corner. She wears a baggy brown sweater and the new looser style of jeans, bleach spattered across the thighs. Her hair, swept back behind her ears to form a single fanning sheaf down her back, looks ironed, it is so straight, and dyed, it is so vivid a pallid red.

'I wouldn't say fiancée exactly,' Pru says, directly to Harry. 'There's no ring, look.' She holds up a naked trembling hand.

Harry in his need to get a fix on this new creature glances from Nelson right through Janice, whom he can grill later in bed, to Ma Springer. Her mouth is clamped shut; if you tapped her she'd ring like a gong, rigid in her purple church dress. Nelson's mouth is ajar. He is a sick man fascinated by the ministration of doctors around him, his illness at last confessed and laid open to cure. In Pru's presence he looks years younger than when Melanie was about, a nervous toughness melted all away. It occurs to Harry that this girl is older than the boy, and another, deeper, instinctive revelation pounds in upon him even as he hears himself saying, as humorous paternal host, 'Well in any case it's nice to meet you, Pru. Any friend of Nelson's, we put up with around here.' This maybe falls flat, so he adds, 'I bet you're the girl's been sending all those letters.'

Her eyes glance down, the demure plane of her cheek reddened as if he's slapped her. 'Too many I suppose,' she says.

'No bother to me,' he assures her, 'I'm not the mailman.'

She lifts her eyes, a flourishing green.

Pru is pregnant. One of the few advantages of not having been born yesterday is that a man acquires, like a notion of tomorrow's weather from the taste of the evening air, some sense of the opposite sex's physiology, its climate. She has less waist than a woman so young should, and that uncanny green clarity of her eyes and a soft slowed something in her motions as she turns away from Harry's joke to take a cue from Nelson bespeak a burden beyond disturbing, a swell beneath the waves. In her third or fourth month, Rabbit guesses. And with this guess a backwards roll of light illumines the months past. And the walls of this house, papered with patterns sunk into them like stains, change meaning, containing this seed between them. The fuzzy gray sofa and the chair that matches and the Barcalounger and the TV set (an Admiral) and Ma Springer's pompous lamps of painted porcelain and tarnished brass and the old framed watercolors sunk to the tint of dust from never being looked at, the table runners Ma once crocheted and her collection of brittle bright knickknacks stored on treble corner shelves nicked and sanded to suggest antique wood but stemming from an era of basement carpentry in Fred Springer's long married life: all these souvenirs of the dead bristle with new point, with fresh mission, if as Harry imagines this intruder's secret is a child to come.

He feels swollen. His guess has been like a fist into him. As was not the case with Melanie he feels kinship with this girl, is touched by her, turned on: *he* wants to be giving her his baby.

In bed he asks Janice, 'How long have you known?'

'Oh,' she says, 'about a month. Melanie let some of the cat out of the bag and then I confronted Nelson with it. He was relieved to talk, he cried even. He just didn't want *you* to know.'

'Why not?' He is hurt. He is the boy's father.

Janice hesitates. 'I don't know, I guess he was afraid you'd be mad. Or laugh at him.'

'Why would I laugh at him? The same thing happened to me.'

171

'He doesn't know that, Harry.'

'How could he not? His birthday keeps coming around seven months after our anniversary.'

'Well, yes.' In her impatience she sounds much like her mother, setting the heel of her voice into each word. The bed creaks as she flounces in emphasis. 'Children don't want to know these things, and by the time they're old enough to care it's all so long ago.'

'When did he knock the girl up, does he remember that much?'

'Weren't you funny, guessing so quickly she was in a family way? We weren't going to tell you for a while.'

'Thanks. It was the first thing that hit me. That baggy sweater. That, and that she's taller than Nelson.'

'Harry, she isn't. He's an inch taller, he's told me himself, it's just that his posture is so poor.'

'And how much older is she? You can see she's older.'

'Well, a year or a little more. Don't forget he's old for his class, what with all those terms off. She was a secretary in the Registrar's office –'

'Yeah and why wasn't he fucking another student? What does he have to get mixed up in the secretarial pool for?'

'Harry, you should talk to *them* if you want to know every in and out of it all. You know though how he used to say how phony these college girls were, he never felt comfortable in that atmosphere. He's from business people on my side and working people on yours and there hasn't been much college in his background.'

'Or in his future from the way it looks.'

'It's not such a bad thing the girl can do a job. You heard her say at supper she'd like him to go back to Kent and finish, and she could take in typing in their apartment.'

'Yeah and I heard the little snot say he wanted no part of it.'

'You won't get him to go back by shouting at him.'

'I didn't shout.'

'You got a look on your face.'

'Well, Jesus. Because the kid gets a girl pregnant he thinks he's entitled to run Springer Motors.'

'Harry, he doesn't want to run it, he just wants a place in it.'

'You can't give him a place without taking a place from somebody else.'

'Mother and I think he should have a place,' Janice says, so definitely it seems her mother has spoken, out of the dark air of this bedroom where the old lady's presence was always felt as a rumble of television or a series of snores coming through the wall.

He reverts to his question, 'When did he get her pregnant?'

'Oh, when these things happen, in the spring. She missed her first period in May, but they waited till they got to Colorado to do the urine test. It was positive and Pru told him she wasn't going to get an abortion, she didn't believe in them and too many of her friends had had their insides messed up.'

'In this day and age, she said all that.'

'Also I believe there's Catholicism in her background, on her mother's side.'

'Still, she looks like she has some common sense.'

'Maybe it was common sense talking. If she goes ahead and has the baby then Nelson has to do something.'

'Poor little devil. How come she got pregnant in the first place? Don't they all have the Pill, and loops, and God knows what else now? I was reading in *Consumer Reports* about these temporary polyurethane tube ties.'

'Some of these new things are getting a bad name in the papers. They give you cancer.'

'Not at her age they wouldn't. So then she sat out there in the Rocky Mountains hatching this thing while Melanie kept him on a short leash around here.'

Janice is growing sleepy, whereas Harry fears he will be awake forever, with this big redhead out of the blue across the hall. Ma Springer had made it clear she expected Pru to sleep in Melanie's old room and had stomped upstairs to watch *The Jeffersons*. The old crow had just sat there pretty silent all evening, looking like a boiler with too much pressure inside. She plays her cards tight. Harry nudges Janice's sleepy soft side to get her talking again.

She says, 'Melanie said Nelson became very hard to manage, once the test came back positive – running around with a bad crowd out there, making Pru take up hang gliding. Then when he saw she wouldn't change her mind all he wanted to do was run back here. They couldn't take him out of it, he went and quit this job he had with a man building condominiums. Melanie I guess had some reasons of her own to get away so she invited herself along. Nelson didn't want her to but I guess the alternative was Pru letting her parents and us know what the situation was and instead of that he begged for time, trying to get some kind of nest ready for her here and maybe still hoping it would all go away, I don't know.'

'Poor little Nelson,' Harry says. Sorrow for the child bleeds upward to the ceiling with its blotches of streetlight shuffling through the beech. 'This has been Hell for him.'

'Well Melanie's theory was not Hell enough; she didn't like the way he kept going out with Billy Fosnacht and his crowd instead of facing us with the facts and telling us why he really wanted to go to work at the lot.'

Harry sighs. 'So when's the wedding?'

'As soon as it can be arranged. I mean, it's her fifth month. Even you spotted it.'

*Even you*, he resents this, but doesn't want to tell Janice of the instinctive bond he has with this girl. Pru is like his mother, awkward and bony, with big hands, but less plain.

'One of the reasons I took Mother to church this morning was so we could have a word with Reverend Campbell.'

'That fag? Lordy-O.'

'Harry you know nothing about him. He's been uncommonly sweet to Mother and he's really done a lot for the parish.'

'The little boys' choir especially, I bet.'

'You are so un-open. Mother with all her limitations is more open than you.' She turns her face away and says into her pillow, 'Harry, I'm very tired. All this upsets me too. Was there anything else you wanted to ask?'

He asks, 'Does he love the girl, do you think?'

'You've seen her. She's striking.'

'I can see that, but can Nelson? You know they say history repeats but it never does, exactly. When we got married everybody was doing it but now when these kids hang back and just live together it must be a bigger deal. I mean, it must be more frightening.'

Janice turns her head back again and offers, 'I think it's good, that she's a little older.'

'Why?'

'Well, Nelson needs steadying.'

'A girl who gets herself knocked up and then pulls this right-to-life act isn't my idea of steady. What kind of parents does she come from anyway?'

'They're just average people in Ohio. I think the father works as a steamfitter.'

'A-*ha*,' he says. 'Blue collar. She's not marrying Nelson, she's marrying Springer Motors.'

'Just like you did,' Janice says.

He should resent this but he likes it, her new sense of herself as a prize. He lays his hand in that soft place where her waist dips. 'Listen,' he says, 'when I married you you were selling salted nuts at Kroll's and my parents thought your dad was a shifty character who was going to wind up in jail.'

But he didn't, he wound up in Heaven. Fred Springer made that long climb into the tree of the stars. Lost in space. Now Janice is following, his touch tipping her into sleep just as he feels below his waist a pulsing that might signal a successful erection. Nothing like the thought of fucking money. He doesn't fuck her enough, his poor dumb moneybags. She has fallen asleep naked. When they were newly married and for years thereafter she wore cotton nighties that made her look like that old-fashioned Time to Retire ad, but sometime in the Seventies she began to come to bed in just her skin, her little still-tidy snake-smooth body brown wherever the tennis dress didn't cover, with a fainter brown belly where that Op-pattern two-piece bathing suit exposed her middle. How quickly Cindy's footprints dried on the flagstones behind her today! The strange thing is he can never exactly picture fucking her, it is like looking into the sun. He turns on his back, frustrated yet relieved to be alone in the quiet night where his mind can revolve all that is new. In middle age you are carrying the world in a sense and yet it seems out of control more than ever, the self that you had as a boy all scattered and distributed like those pieces of bread in the miracle. He had been struck in Kruppenbach's Sunday School by the verse that tells of the clean-up, twelve baskets full of the fragments. Keep Your City Clean. He listens for the sound of footsteps slithering out of

Melanie's – no, Pru's – room, she'd come a long way today and had met a lot of new faces, what a hard thing for her this evening must have been. While Ma and Janice had scraped together supper, another miracle of sorts, the girl had sat there in the bamboo basket chair brought in from the porch and they all eased around her like cars easing past an accident on the highway. Harry could hardly take his eyes from this grown woman sitting there so demure and alien and perceptibly misshapen. She breathed that air he'd forgotten, of high-school loveliness, come uninvited to bloom in the shadow of railroad overpasses, alongside telephone poles, within earshot of highways with battered aluminum center strips, out of mothers gone to lard and fathers ground down by gray days of work and more work, in an America littered with bottlecaps and pull-tabs and pieces of broken muffler. Rabbit remembered such beauty, seeing it caught here in Pru, in her long downy arms and skinny bangled wrists and the shining casual fall of her hair, caught as a stick snags the flow of a stream with a dimpled swirl. Janice sighs in her sleep. A car swishes by, the radio trailing disco through the open window. Labor Day Eve, the end of something. He feels the house swell beneath him, invading presences crowding the downstairs, the dead awakened. Skeeter, Pop, Mom, Mr Abendroth. The photograph of Fred Springer fading on the sideboard fills with the flush of hectic color Fred carried on his cheeks and where the bridge of his nose pressed. Harry buries his mind in the girls of Mt Judge High as they were in the Forties, the fuzzy sweaters and dimestore pearls, the white blouses that let the beige shadow of the bra show through, the skirts, always skirts, long as gowns when the New Look was new, swinging in the locker-lined halls, and then out along the pipe rail that guarded the long cement wells that let light into the basement windows of the shop and home ec and music rooms, the long skirts in rows, the saddle shoes and short white socks in rows, the girls exhaling winter breath like cigarette smoke, their pea jackets, nobody wore parkas then, the dark lipstick of those girls, looking all like Rita Hayworth in the old yearbooks. The teasing of their skirts, open above their socks, come find me if you can, the wild fact of pubic hair, the thighs timidly parted in the narrow space of cars, the damp strip of underpants, Mary Ann his first girl, her underpants down around her saddle shoes like an animal trap, the motor running to keep the heater on in Pop's old De Soto, that they let him borrow one night a week in spite of all Mim's complaining and sarcasm. Mim a flat-chested brat until about seventeen when she began to have her own secrets. Between Mary Ann's legs a locker-room aroma turned delicate, entrusted to him. Married another while he was in the Army. Invited another into that secret space of hers, he couldn't believe it. Lost days, buried at the back of his brain, deep inside, gray cells of which millions die every day he has read somewhere, taking his life with them into blackout, his only life, trillions of electric bits they say, makes even the biggest computer look sick: having found and entered again that space he notices his prick has stayed hard and grown harder, the process there all along, little sacs of blood waiting for the right part of the brain to come alive again. Left-handedly, on his back so as not to disturb Janice, he masturbates, remembering Ruth. Her room on Summer. The first night, having run, all that sad craziness with dead Tothero, then the privacy of this room. This island, their four walls, her room. Her fat white body out of her clothes and her poking fun of his Jockey underpants. Her arms seemed thin, thin, pulling him down and rising above him, one long underbelly erect in light.

*Hey.*

*Hey.*

*You're pretty.*

*Come on. Work.*

He shoves up and comes, the ceiling close above him, his body feeling curved as if tied to a globe that is growing, growing as his seed bucks up against the sheet. More intense than pumping down into the darkness. Weird behavior for an old guy. He stealthily slides from the bed and gropes after a handkerchief in a drawer, not wanting the scrape to wake Janice or Ma Springer or this Pru, cunts all around him. Back in bed, having done his best, though it's always queer where the wet is, maybe it doesn't come out when you feel it does, he composes himself for sleep by thinking of his daughter, her pale round face floating in what appeared to be a milky serene disposition. A voice hisses, *Hassy.*

*

The Reverend Archie Campbell comes visiting a few nights later, by appointment. He is short and slight, but his voice compensates by being deep and mellow; he enunciates with such casual smiling sonorousness that his sentences seem to keep travelling around a corner after they are pronounced. His head is too big for his body. His lashes are long and conspicuous and he sometimes shuts his eyes as if to display the tremor in his closed lids. He wears his collar with a flimsy black buttonless shirt and a seersucker coat. When he smiles, thick lips like Carter's reveal even but tiny teeth with fine black lines between them, like seeds lifted from a stain. Harry is fascinated by fags, what makes them tick, why they have done this to themselves.

Ma Springer offers him a cup of coffee but he says, 'Dear me, no thank you, Bessie. This is my third call this evening and any more caffeine intake will positively give me the shakes.' The sentence travels around a corner up Joseph Street.

Harry says to him, 'A real drink then, Reverend. Scotch? A g-and-t? It's still summer officially.'

Campbell glances around for their reaction – Nelson and Pru side by side on the gray sofa, Janice perched on a straight chair brought in from the dining room, Ma Springer uneasy on her legs, her offer of coffee spurned. 'Well as a matter of fact yes,' the minister drawls. 'A touch of the sauce might be sheer bliss. Harry, do you have a vodka, perchance?'

Janice intervenes, 'Way in the back of the corner cupboard, Harry, the bottle with the silver label.'

He nods. 'Anybody else?' He looks at Pru especially, since in these few days of living with them she's shown herself to be no stranger to the sauce. She likes liqueurs; she and Nelson the other day brought back from a shopping expedition along with the beer sixpacks Kahlúa, Cointreau, and Amaretto di Saronno; chunky little bottles, there must have been between twenty and thirty dollars invested in that stuff. Also they have found in the corner cupboard some crème de menthe left over from a dinner party Harry and Janice gave for the Murketts and Harrisons last February and a little bright green gleam of it appears by Pru's elbow at surprising times, even in the morning, as she and Ma watch *Edge of Night*. Nelson says he wouldn't turn down a beer.

178

Ma Springer says she's going to have coffee anyway, she even has decaffeinated if the rector would prefer. But Archie sticks to his guns, with a perky little bow of thanks to her and a wink all around. The guy is something of a card, Rabbit can see that. Probably the best way to play it, at this late date A.D. They had figured him for the gray easy chair that matches the sofa, but he foxes them by pulling out the lopsided old Syrian hassock from behind the combination lamp and table, where Ma keeps some of her knickknacks, and squatting down. Thus situated, the minister grins up at them all and, nimble as a monkey, fishes a pipe from his front coat pocket and stuffs its bowl with a brown forefinger.

Janice gets up and goes with Harry into the kitchen while he makes the drinks. 'That's some little pastor you've got there,' he tells her softly.

'Don't be snide.'

'What's snide about that?'

'Everything.' She pours herself some Campari in an orange juice glass and without comment fills with crème de menthe one of the set of eight little cylindrical liqueur glasses that came as a set with a decanter she had bought at Kroll's years ago, about the same time they joined the Flying Eagle. They hardly ever have used them. When Harry returns to the living room with Campbell's vodka-and-tonic and Nelson's beer and his own g-and-t Janice follows him in and sets this cylinder of gaudy green on the end table next to Pru's elbow. Pru gives no sign of noticing.

Reverend Campbell has persuaded Ma Springer to take the Barcalounger, where Harry had anticipated sitting, and to raise up its padded extension for her legs. 'I must say,' she says, 'that does wonders for the pressure in my ankles.'

Thus laid back the old lady looks vulnerable, and absurdly reduced in importance within the family circle. Janice, seeing her mother stretched out helpless, volunteers, 'Mother, I'll fetch you your coffee.'

'And that plate of chocolate-chip cookies I set out. Though I don't suppose anybody with liquor wants cookies too.'

'I do, Mom-mom,' Nelson says. He wears a different expression since Pru arrived – the surly clotted look has relaxed into an

179

expectant emptiness, a wide-eyed docility that Harry finds just as irritating.

Since the minister declined to take the gray easy chair, Harry must. As he sinks into it his legs stretch out, and Campbell without rising jumps the hassock and himself together a few feet to one side, like a bullfrog hopping, pad and all, to avoid being touched by Harry's big suede shoes. Grinning at his own agility, the little man resonantly announces, 'Well now. I understand somebody here wants to get married.'

'Not me, I'm married already,' Rabbit says quickly, as a joke of his own. He has the funny fear that Campbell, one of whose little hands (they look grubby, like his teeth, a line of shadow encircling each nail) rests on the edge of the hassock inches from the tips of Harry's shoes, will suddenly reach down and undo the laces. He moves his feet over, some more inches away.

Pru had smiled sadly at his joke, gazing down, her green-filled glass as yet untouched. Nelson beside her stares forward, solemnly unaware of the dabs of beer on his upper lip. Baby eating: Rabbit remembers how Nelson used to batter with the spoon, held left-handed in his fist though they tried to get him to take it in his right, on the tray of the high chair in the old apartment on Wilbur Street, high above the town. He was never one of the messier babies, though – always wanting to be good. A solemn look came natural to him. Harry wants to cry, gazing at the innocently ignored mustache of foam on the kid's face. They're selling him down the river. Pru touches her glass furtively, without giving it a glance.

Ma Springer's voice sounds weary, rising from the Barca-lounger. 'Yes they'd like to have it be in the church, but it won't be one of your dressy weddings. Just family. And as soon as convenient, even next week we were thinking.' Her feet in their dirty aqua sneakers, with rounded toes and scuffed rims of white rubber, look childish and small off the floor, up on the padded extension.

Janice's voice sounds hard, cutting in. 'Mother there's no need for such a rush. Pru's parents will need time to make arrangements to come from Ohio.'

Her mother says, with a flip of her tired hand toward Pru, 'She says her folks may not be bothering to come.'

The girl blushes, and tightens her touch on the glass, as if to pick it up when attention has moved past her. 'We're not as close as this family is,' she says. She lifts her eyes, with their translucent green, to the face of the minister, to explain, 'I'm one of seven. Four of my sisters are married already, and two of those marriages are on the rocks. My father's sour about it.'

Ma Springer explains, 'She was raised Catholic.'

The minister smiles broadly. 'Prudence seems such a Protestant name.'

The blush, as if quickened by a fitful wind, deepens again. 'I was baptized Teresa. My friends in high school used to think I was prudish, that's where Pru came from.'

Campbell giggles. '*Real*ly! That's *fas*cinating!' The hair on the top of his head, Rabbit sees, is gettin thin, young as he is. Thank God that's one aspect of aging Harry doesn't have to worry about: good lasting heads of hair on both sides of his family, though Pop's toward the end had gone through gray to yellow, finer than cornsilk, and too dry to comb. They say the mother's genes determine. One of the things he never liked about Janice was her high forehead, like she might start to go bald. Nelson's too young to tell yet. Old man Springer used to slick his hair back so he always looked like a guy in a shirt collar ad, even on Saturday mornings, and in the coffin they got the parting all wrong, the newspaper obituary had reversed the photo in doing the halftone and the mortician had worked from that. With Mim, one of the first signs of her rebellion as he remembers was she bleached stripes into her hair, 'Protestant rat' she used to call the natural color, in tenth grade, and Mom would get after her saying, 'Better that than look like a skunk.' It was true, with those blond pieces Mim did look tough, suddenly – besmirched. That's life, besmirching yourself. The young clergyman's voice is sliding from syllable to syllable smoothly, his surprising high giggle resettled in the back of his throat. 'Bessie, before we firm up particulars like the date and the guest list, I think we should investigate some basics. Nelson and Teresa: do you love one another, and are you both prepared to make the eternal commitment that the church understands to exist at the heart of Christian marriage?'

The question is a stunner. Pru says 'Yes' in a whisper and takes the first sip from her glass of crème de menthe.

Nelson looks so glazed his mother prompts, 'Nelson.'

He wipes his mouth and whines, 'I *said* I'd do it, didn't I? I've been here all summer trying to work things out. I'm not going back to school, I'll never graduate now, because of this. What more do you people want?'

All flinch into silence but Harry, who says, 'I thought you didn't like Kent.'

'I didn't, much. But I'd put in my time and would just as soon have gotten the degree, for what it's worth, which isn't much. All summer, Dad, you kept bugging me about college and I wanted to say, O.K., O.K., you're right, but you didn't know the story, you didn't know about *Pru*.'

'Don't marry me then,' Pru says quickly, quietly.

The boy looks sideways at her on the sofa and sinks lower into the cushions. 'I'd just as soon,' he says. 'It's time I got serious.'

'We can get married and still go back for a year and have you finish.' Pru has transferred her hands to her lap and with them the little glass of green; she gazes down into it and speaks steadily, as if she is drawing out of its tiny well words often rehearsed, her responses to Nelson's complaints.

'Naa,' Nelson says, shamed. 'That seems silly. If I'm gonna be married, let's really do it, with a job and clunky old station wagon and a crummy ranch house and all that drill. There's nothing I can get at Kent'll make me better at pushing Dad's little Japanese kiddy cars off on people. If Mom and Mom-mom can twist his arm so he'll take me in.'

'Jesus, how you distort!' Harry cries. 'We'll all take you in, how can we help but? But you'd be worth a helluva lot more to the company and what's more to your*self* if you'd finish up at college. Because I keep saying this I'm treated around here like a monster.' He turns to Archie Campbell, forgetting how low the man is sitting and saying over his head, 'Sorry about all this chitchat, it's hardly up your alley.'

'No,' the young man mellifluously disagrees, 'it's part of the

182

picture.' Of Pru he asks, 'What would be *your* preference, of where to live for the coming year? The first year of married life, all the little books say, sets the tone for all the rest.'

With one hand Pru brushes back her long hair from her shoulders as if angry. 'I don't have such happy associations with Kent,' she allows. 'I'd be happy to begin in a fresh place.'

Campbell's pipe is filling the room with a sweetish tweedy perfume. Probably less than thirty and there's nothing they can throw at him that he hasn't fielded before. A pro: Rabbit can respect that. But how did he let himself get queer?

Ma Springer says in a spiteful voice, 'You may wonder now why they don't wait that year.'

The small man's big head turns and he beams. 'No, I hadn't wondered at that.'

'She's got herself in a family way,' the old lady declares, needlessly.

'With Nelson's help, of course,' the minister smiles.

Janice tries to intervene: 'Mother, these things happen.'

Ma snaps back, 'Don't tell me. I haven't forgotten it happened to you.'

'*Mother.*'

'This is horrible,' Nelson announces from the sofa. 'What'd we drag this poor guy in here for anyway? Pru and I didn't ask to be married in a church, I don't believe any of that stuff anyway.'

'You don't?' Harry is shocked, hurt.

'No, Dad. When you're dead, you're dead.'

'You are?'

'Come off it, you know you are, everybody knows it down deep.'

'Nobody knows for sure,' Pru points out in a quiet voice.

Nelson asks her furiously, 'How many dead people have you seen?'

Even as a child, Harry remembers, Nelson's face would get white around the gills when he was angry. He would get nervous stomach aches, and clutch at the edge of the bannister on his way upstairs to get his books. They would send him off to school anyway. Harry still had his job at Verity and Janice was working part-time at the lot and they had no babysitter. School was the babysitter.

Reverend Campbell, puffing unruffled on his aromatic pipe, asks Pru another question. 'How do your parents feel about your being married outside of the Roman faith?'

That tender blush returns, deepening the green of her eyes. 'Only my mother was a Catholic actually, and I think by the time I came along she had pretty much given up. I was baptized but never confirmed, though there was this confirmation dress my sisters had worn. Daddy had beaten it out of her I guess you could say. He didn't like having all the children to feed.'

'What was his denomination?'

'He was a nothing.'

Harry remembers out loud, 'Nelson's grandfather came from a Catholic background. His mother was Irish. *My* dad, I'm talking about. Hell, what I think about religion is –'

All eyes are upon him.

'– is without a little of it, you'll sink.'

Saying this, he gazes toward Nelson, mostly because the child's vivid pale-gilled face falls at the center of his field of vision. That muskrat haircut: it suggests to Harry a convict's shaved head that has grown out. The boy sneers. 'Well don't sink, Dad, whatever you do.'

Janice leans forward to speak to Pru in that mannerly mature woman's bosomy voice she can produce now. 'I *wish* you could persuade your parents to come to the wedding.'

Ma Springer says, trying a more placating tone, since she has got the minister here and the conference is not delivering for her, 'Around here the Episcopalians are thought the next thing to the Catholics anyway.'

Pru shakes her head, her red hair flicking, a creature at bay. She says, 'We had a break. They didn't approve of something I did before I met Nelson, and they wouldn't approve of this, the way I am now.'

'What did you do?' Harry asks.

She doesn't seem to have heard, saying as if to herself, 'I've learned to take care of myself without them.'

'I'll say this,' Campbell says pleasantly, his pipe having gone dead and its relighting having occupied his attention for the last minute. 'I'm experiencing some difficulty wrapping my mind around' – the phrase brings out his mischievous grin, stretched like that guy's on *Mad* – 'performing a church ceremony for two persons one of whom belongs to the Church of Rome and the other, he has just told us, is an atheist.' He gives a nod to Nelson. 'Now the bishop gives us more latitude in these matters than we used to have. The other day I married a divorced Japanese man, but with an Episcopal background, to a young woman who originally wanted the words "Universal Mother" substituted for "God" in the service. We talked her out of that. But in this case, good people, I really don't see much indication that Nelson and his *very* charming fiancée are at all prepared for, or desirous of, what you might call our brand of magic.' He releases a great cloud of smoke and closes his lips in that prissy way of pipe-smokers, waiting to be contradicted.

Ma Springer is struggling as if to rise from the Barcalounger. 'Well no grandson of Fred Springer is going to get married in a Roman Catholic church!' Her head falls back on the padded headrest. Her gills look purple.

'Oh,' Archie Campbell says cheerfully. 'I don't think my dear friend Father McGahern could handle them either. The young lady was never even confirmed. You know,' he adds, knitting his hands at one knee and gazing into space, 'a lot of wonderful, dynamic marriages have been made in City Hall. Or a Unitarian-Universalist service. My friend Jim Hancock of the fellowship in Maiden Springs has more than once taken some of our problem betrothals.'

Rabbit jumps up. Something awful is being done here, he doesn't know exactly what, or to whom. 'Anybody besides me for another drink?'

Without looking at Harry, Campbell holds out a glass which has become empty, as has Pru's little glass of crème de menthe. The green of it has all gone into her eyes. The minister is telling her, and Nelson, 'Truly, under some circumstances, even for the most devout it can be the appropriate recourse. At a later date, the wedding can be consecrated in a church; we see a number now of these reaffirmations of wedding vows.'

'Why don't they just keep living in sin right here?' Harry asks. 'We don't mind.'

'We do indeed,' Ma says, sounding smothered.

'Hey Dad,' Nelson calls, 'could you bring me another beer?'

'Get it yourself. My hands are full.' Yet he stops in front of Pru and takes up the little liqueur glass. 'Sure it's good for the baby?'

She looks up with an unexpected coldness. He was feeling so fatherly and fond and the eyes she gives him are frozen grass. 'Oh yes,' she tells him. 'It's the beer and wine that are bad; they bloat you.'

By the time Rabbit returns from the kitchen, Campbell is allowing himself to be brought around. He has what they want: a church wedding, a service acceptable in the eyes of the Grace Stuhls of this world. Knowing this, he is in no hurry. Beneath the girlish lashes his eyes are as dark as Janice's and Ma's, the Koerner eyes. Ma Springer is holding forth, the little rounded toes of her aqua sneakers bouncing. 'You must take what the boy says with a grain of salt. At his age I didn't know what I believed myself, I thought the government was foolish and the gangsters had the right idea. This was back in Prohibition days.'

Nelson looks at her with his own dark eyes, sullen. 'Mom-mom, if it matters so much to you, I don't care that much, one way or another.'

'What does Pru think?' Harry asks, giving her her poison. He wonders if the girl's frozen stiffness of manner, and those little waits while her smile gets unstuck, aren't simply fear: it is she who is growing another life within her body, and nobody else.

'I think,' she responds slowly, so quietly the room goes motionless to hear, 'it would be nicer in a church.'

Nelson says, 'I know I sure don't want to go down to that awful concrete City Hall they've built behind where the Bijou used to be, some guy I know was telling me the contractor raked off a million and there's cracks in the cement already.'

Janice in her relief says, 'Harry, I could use some more Campari.'

Campbell lifts his replenished glass from his low place on the hassock. 'Cheers, good people.' He states his terms: 'The customary procedure consists of at least three sessions of counseling and Christian instruction after the initial interview. This I suppose we can consider the interview.' As he addresses Nelson particularly, Harry hears a seductive note enrich the great mellow voice. 'Nelson, the church does not expect that every couple it marries be a pair of Christian saints. It does ask that the participants have some understanding of what they are undertaking. *I* don't take the vows; you and Teresa do. Marriage is not merely a rite; it is a sacrament, an invitation from God to participate in the divine. And the invitation is not for one moment only. Every day you share is meant to be sacramental. Can you feel a meaning in that? There were wonderful words in the old prayer book; they said that marriage was not "to be entered into unadvisedly or lightly; but reverently, discreetly, advisedly, soberly, and in the fear of God."' He grins, having intoned this, and adds, 'The new prayer book omits the fear of God.'

Nelson whines, 'I *said*, I'd go along.'

Janice asks, a little prim, 'How long would these sessions of instruction take?' It is like she is sitting, in that straight-backed dining-room chair, on an egg that might hatch too soon; Harry tells himself he should try to fuck her tonight, just to keep her loose.

'Oh,' Campbell says, rolling his eyes toward the ceiling, 'I should think considering the various factors, we could get three of them in in two weeks. I just happen, the officious clergyman said, to have my appointment book here.' Before reaching into the breast pocket of the seersucker coat, Campbell taps out the bowl of his pipe with a finicky calm that conveys to Harry the advantages of being queer: the world is just a gag to this guy. He walks on water; the mud of women, of making babies, never dirties his shoes. You got to take off your hat: nothing touches him. That's real religion.

Some rebellious wish to give him a poke, to protest the smooth bargain that has been struck, prompts Harry to say, 'Yeah, we want to get 'em in before the baby comes. He'll be here by Christmas.'

'God willing,' Campbell smiles, adding, 'He or she.'

'January,' Pru says in a whisper, after putting down her glass. Harry can't tell if she is pleased or displeased by the gallant way he keeps mentioning the baby, that everybody else wants to ignore. While the appointments are being set up she and Nelson sit on that sofa like a pair of big limp Muppets, with invisible arms coming up through the cushions into their torsos and heads.

'Fred had his birthday in January,' Ma Springer announces, grunting as she tried to get out of the Barcalounger, to see the minister off.

'Oh Mother,' Janice says. 'One twelfth of the world has January birthdays.'

'*I* was born in January,' Archie Campbell says, rising. He grins to show his seedy teeth. 'In my case, after much prayer. My parents were *an*cient. It's a wonder I'm here at all.'

The next day a warm rain is beginning to batter the yellowing leaves down from the trees in the park along Cityview Drive as Harry and Nelson drive through Brewer to the lot. The kid is still persona non grata but he's asked to check on the two convertibles he crunched, one of which, the Royale, Manny is repairing. The '72 Mercury, hit twice from the side, was more severely damaged, and parts are harder to get. Rabbit's idea had been when the kid went off to school to sell it for junk and write off the loss. But he didn't have the heart not to let the boy look at the wrecks at least. Then Nelson is going to borrow the Corona and visit Billy Fosnacht before he goes back to Boston to become an endodontist. Harry had a root canal job once; it felt like they were tickling the underside of his eyeball. What a hellish way to make a living. Maybe there's no entirely good way. The Toyota's windshield wipers keep up a steady rubbery singsong as the Brewer traffic slows, brake lights burning red all along Locust Boulevard. The Castle has started up again and yellow school buses loom ahead in the jam. Harry switches the wipers from Fast to Intermittent and wishes he still smoked cigarettes. He wants to talk to the kid.

'Nelson.'

'Unhh?'

'How do you feel?'

'O.K. I woke up with a soreness in my throat but I took two of those five-hundred-milligram vitamin Cs Melanie talked Bessie into getting.'

'She was really a health nut, wasn't she? Melanie. We still have all that Granola in the kitchen.'

'Yeah, well. It was part of her act. You know, mystical gypsy. She was always reading this guru, I forget his name. It sounded like a sneeze.'

'You miss her?'

'Melanie? No, why would I?'

'Weren't you kind of close?'

Nelson avoids the implied question. 'She was getting pretty grouchy toward the end.'

'You think she and Charlie went off together?'

'Beats me,' the boy says.

The wipers, now on Intermittent, startle Rabbit each time they switch across, as if someone other than he is making decisions in this car. A ghost. Like in that movie about Encounters of the Third Kind the way the truck with Richard Dreyfuss in it begins to shake all over and the headlights behind rise up in the air instead of pulling off to one side. He readjusts the knob from Intermittent to Slow. 'I didn't mean your physical health exactly. I meant more your state of mind. After last night.'

'You mean about that sappy minister? I don't mind going over to listen to his garbage a couple times if it'll satisfy the Springer honor or whatever.'

'I guess I mean more about marriage in general. Nellie, I don't want to see you railroaded into anything.'

The boy sits up a little in the side of Harry's vision; the yellow buses ahead pull into the Brewer High driveway and the line of cars begins to move again, slowly, beside a line of parked cars whose rooftops are spattered with leaves the rain has brought down. 'Who says I'm being railroaded?'

'Nobody says it. Pru seems a fine girl, if you're ready for marriage.'

'You don't think I'm ready. You don't think I'm ready for anything.'

He lets the hostility pass, trying to talk meditatively, like Webb Murkett. 'You know, Nelson, I'm not sure any man is ever a hundred per cent ready for marriage. I sure as hell know I wasn't, from the way I acted toward your mother.'

'Yeah, well,' the boy says, in a voice a little crumbled, from his father's not taking the bait. 'She got her own back.'

'I never could hold that against her. Or Charlie either. You ought to understand. After we got back together that time we've both been pretty straight. We've even had a fair amount of fun, in our dotage. I'm just sorry we had so much working out to do, with you still on the scene.'

'Yeah, well.' Nelson's voice sounds breathy and tight, and he keeps looking at his knees, even when Harry hangs that tricky left turn onto Eisenhower Avenue. The boy clears his throat and volunteers, 'It's the times, I guess. A lot of the kids I got to know at Kent, they had horror stories worse than any of mine.'

'Except that thing with Jill. They couldn't top that, I bet.' He doesn't quite chuckle. Jill is a sacred name to the boy; he will never talk about it. Harry goes on clumsily, as the car gains momentum down hill and the spic and black kids strolling uphill to school insolently flirt with danger as his fenders brush their bodies, or seem to, 'There's something that doesn't feel right to me in this new development. The girl gets knocked up, O.K., it takes two to tango, you have some responsibility there, nobody can deny it. But then as I understand it she flat out refuses to get the abortion, when one of the good things that's come along in twenty years along with a lot that's not so good is you can go have an abortion now right out in the open, in a hospital, safe and clean as having your appendix out.'

'So?'

'So why didn't she?'

The boy makes a gesture that Rabbit fears might be an attempt to grab the wheel; his grip tightens. But Nelson is merely waving to indicate a breadth of possibilities. 'She had a lot of reasons. I forget what all they were.'

'I'd like to hear them.'

'Well for one thing she said she knew of women who had their insides all screwed up by abortions, so they could *never* have a baby. You say it's easy as an appendix but you've never had it done. She didn't be*lieve* in it.'

'I thought she wasn't that much of a Catholic.'

190

'She wasn't, she isn't, but still. She said it wasn't natural.'

'What's natural? In this day and age getting knocked up like that isn't natural.'

'Well she's *shy*, Dad. They don't call her Pru for nothing. Going to a doctor like that, and having him scrape you out, she just didn't want to do it.'

'You bet she didn't. Shy. She wanted to have a baby, and she wasn't too shy to manage that. How much younger're you than she?'

'A year. A little more. What does it matter? It wasn't just a baby she wanted to have, it was *my* baby. Or so she said.'

'That's sweet. I guess. What did you think about it?'

'I thought it was O.K., probably. It was her body. That's what they all tell you now, it's their body. I didn't see much I could do about it.'

'Then it's sort of her funeral, isn't it?'

'How do you mean?'

'I mean,' Harry says, in his indignation honking at some kids at the intersection of Plum Street who saunter right out toward him, this early in the school year the crossing guards aren't organized yet, 'so she decides to keep pregnant till there's no correcting it while this other girl babysits for you, and your mother and grandmother and now this nance of a minister all decide when and how you're going to marry the poor broad. I mean, where do you come in? Nelson Angstrom. I mean, what do *you* want? Do you know?' In his frustration he hits the rim of the steering wheel with the heel of his hand, as the avenue dips down beneath the blackened nineteenth-century stones of the underpass at Eisenhower and Seventh, that in a bad rainstorm is flooded but not today. The arch of this underpass, built without a keystone, by masons all long dead, is famous, and from his earliest childhood has reminded Rabbit of a crypt, of death. They emerge among the drooping wet pennants of low-cost factory outlets.

'Well, I want –'

Fearing the kid is going to say he wants a job at Springer Motors, Harry interrupts: 'You look scared, is all I see. Scared to say No to any of these women. I've never been that great at saying No either, but just because it runs in the family doesn't mean you have to get stuck. You don't necessarily have to lead my life, I guess is what I want to say.'

'Your life seems pretty comfy to me.' Cocky and cool, Nelson's voice has climbed up onto a ledge from which rescue will be difficult. They turn down Weiser, the forest of the inner-city mall a fogged green smear in the rearview mirror.

'Yeah, well,' Harry says, 'it's taken me a fair amount of time to get there. And by the time you get there you're pooped. The world,' he tells his son, 'is full of people who never knew what hit 'em, their lives are over before they wake up.'

'Dad, you keep talking about yourself but I don't see what it has to do with *me*. What *can* I do with Pru except marry her? She's not so bad, I mean I've known enough girls to know they all have their limits. But she's a person, she's a friend. It's as if you want to deny her to me, as if you're jealous or something. The way you keep mentioning her baby.'

This kid should have been spanked at some point. 'I'm not jealous, Nelson. Just the opposite. I feel sorry for you.'

'Don't feel sorry for me. Don't waste your feelings on me.'

They pass Schoenbaum Funeral Directors. Nobody out front in this rain. Harry swallows and asks, 'Don't you want out, if we could rig it somehow?'

'How could we rig it? She's in her fifth month.'

'She could go ahead have the baby without you marrying her. These adoption agencies are crying for white babies, you'd be doing somebody else a favor.'

'Pru would never consent.'

'Don't be too sure. We could ease the pain. She's one of seven, she knows the value of a dollar.'

'Dad, this is crazy talk. You're forgetting this baby is a person. An Angstrom!'

'Jesus, how could I forget that?'

The light at the foot of Weiser, before the bridge, is red. Harry looks over at his son and gets an impression of something freshly hatched, wet and not quite unfolded. The light turns green. A bronze plaque on a pillar of pebbled concrete names the mayor for whom the bridge was named but it is raining too hard to read it.

He starts up again, 'Or you could just, I don't know, not make any decision, just disappear for a while. I'd give you the money for that.'

'Money, you're always offering me money to stay away.'

'Maybe because when I was your age I wanted to get away and I couldn't. I didn't have the money. I didn't have the sense. We tried to send you away to get some sense and you've thumbed your nose at it.'

'I haven't thumbed my nose, it's just that there's not that much out there. It isn't what you think, Dad. College is a rip-off, the professors are teaching you stuff because they're getting paid to do it, not because it does you any good. They don't give a fuck about geography or whatever any more than you do. It's all phony, they're there because parents don't want their kids around the house past a certain age and sending them to college makes them look good. "My little Johnny's at Haavahd." "My little Nellie's at Kent." '

'Really, that's how you see it? In my day kids *wanted* to get out in the world. We were scared but not so scared we kept running back to Mama. And Grandmama. What're you going to do when you run out of women to tell you what to do?'

'Same thing you'll do. Drop dead.'

DISCO. DATSUN. FUEL ECONOMY. Route 111 has a certain beauty in the rain, the colors and the banners and the bluish asphalt of the parking lots all run together through the swish of traffic, the beat of wipers. Rubbery hands flailing, *Help, help*. Rabbit has always liked rain, it puts a roof on the world. 'I just don't like seeing you caught,' he blurts out to Nelson. 'You're too much me.'

Nelson gets loud. 'I'm not you! I'm not caught!'

'Nellie, you're caught. They've got you and you didn't even squeak. I hate to see it, is all. All I'm trying to say is, as far as I'm concerned you don't have to go through with it. If you want to get out of it, I'll help you.'

'I don't want to be helped that way! I *like* Pru. I like the way she looks. She's great in bed. She needs me, she thinks I'm neat. She doesn't think I'm a baby. You say I'm caught but I don't feel caught, I feel like I'm becoming a man!'

193

*Help, help.*

'Good,' Harry says then. 'Good luck.'

'Where I want your help, Dad, you won't give it.'

'Where's that?'

'Here. Stop making it so hard for me to fit in at the lot.'

They turn into the lot. The tires of the Corona splash in the gutter water rushing toward its grate along the highway curb. Stonily Rabbit says nothing.

# III

A new shop has opened on Weiser Street in one of those
scruffy blocks between the bridge and the mall, opposite the
enduring old variety store that sells out-of-town newspapers,
warm unshelled peanuts, and dirty magazines for queers as well
as straights. From the look of it the new store too might be
peddling smut, for its showcase front window is thoroughly
masked by long thin blond Venetian blinds, and the lettering on
its windows is strikingly discreet. Gold letters rimmed in black
and very small simply say FISCAL ALTERNATIVES and below
that, smaller yet, *Old Coins, Silver, and Gold Bought and Sold*.
Harry passes the place by car every day, and one day, there being
two empty metered spaces he can slide into without holding up
traffic, he parks and goes in. The next day, after some business
at his bank, the Brewer Trust two blocks away, he comes out of
Fiscal Alternatives with thirty Krugerrands purchased for
$377.14 each, including commission and sales tax, coming to
$11,314.20. These figures had been run off inside by a girl with
platinum hair; her long scarlet fingernails didn't seem to hamper
her touch on the hand computer. She was the only person visible,
at her long glass-topped desk, with beige sides and swivel chair
to match. But there were voices and monitoring presences in other
rooms, back rooms into which she vanished and from which she
emerged with his gold. The coins came in cunning plastic cylinders of fifteen each, with round blue-tinted lids that suggested
dollhouse toilet seats; indeed, bits of what seemed toilet paper
were stuffed into the hole of this lid to make the fit tight and to
conceal even a glimmer of the sacred metal. So heavy, the cylinders threaten to tear the pockets off his coat as Harry hops up Ma
Springer's front steps to face his family. Inside the front door, Pru

195

sits knitting on the gray sofa and Ma Springer has taken over the Barcalounger to keep her legs up while some quick-lipped high yellow from Philly is giving her the six o'clock news. Mayor Frank Rizzo has once again denied charges of police brutality, he says, in a rapid dry voice that pulls the rug out from every word. Used to be Philadelphia was a distant place where no one dared visit, but television has pulled it closer, put its muggy murders and politics right next door. 'Where's Janice?' Harry asks.

Ma Springer says, 'Shh.'

Pru says, 'Janice took Nelson over to the club, to fill in with some ladies' doubles, and then I think they were going to go shopping for a suit.'

'I thought he bought a new suit this summer.'

'That was a business suit. They think he needs a three-piece suit for the wedding.'

'Jesus, the wedding. How're you liking your sessions with what's-his-name?'

'I don't mind them. Nelson hates them.'

'He says that just to get his grandmother going,' Ma Springer calls, twisting to push her voice around the headrest. 'I think they're really doing him good.' Neither woman notices the hang of his coat, though it feels like a bull's balls tugging at his pockets. It's Janice he wants. He goes upstairs and snuggles the two dense, immaculate cylinders into the back of his bedside table, in the drawer where he keeps a spare pair of reading glasses and the rubber tip on a plastic handle he is supposed to massage his gums with to keep out of the hands of the periodontist and the pink wax earplugs he stuffs in sometimes when he has the jitters and can't tune out the house noise. In this same drawer he used to keep condoms, in that interval between when Janice decided the Pill was bad for her and when she went and had her tubes burned, but that was a long while ago and he threw them all away, the whole tidy tin box of them, after an indication, the lid not quite closed, perhaps he imagined it, that Nelson or somebody had been into the box and filched a couple. From about that time on he began to feel crowded, living with the kid. As long as Nelson was socked into baseball statistics or that guitar or even the rock records that threaded their sound through all the fibers of the house, his occupation of the room down the hall was no more uncomfortable than the persistence of Rabbit's own childhood in an annex of his brain; but when the stuff with hormones and girls and cars and beers began, Harry wanted out of fatherhood. Two glimpses mark the limits of his comfort in this matter of men descending from men. When he was about twelve or thirteen he walked into his parents' bedroom in the half-house on Jackson Road not expecting his father to be there, and the old man was standing in front of his bureau in just socks and an undershirt, innocently fishing in a drawer for his undershorts, that boxer style that always looks sad and dreary to Harry anyway, and here was his father's bare behind, such white buttocks, limp and hairless, mute and helpless flesh that squeezed out shit once a day and otherwise hung there in the world like linen that hadn't been ironed; and then when Nelson was about the same age, a year older he must have been for they were living in this house already and they moved when the kid was thirteen, Harry had wandered into the bathroom not realizing Nelson would be stepping out of the shower and had seen the child frontally: he had pubic hair and, though his body was still slim and pint-sized, a man-sized prick, heavy and oval, unlike Rabbit's circumcised and perhaps because of this looking brutal, and big. Big. This was years before the condoms were stolen. The drawer rattles, stuck, and Harry tries to ease it in, hearing that Janice and Nelson have come into the house, making the downstairs resound with news of their tennis and of the outer world. Harry wants to save his news for Janice. To knock her out with it. The drawer suddenly eases shut and he smiles, anticipating her astonished reception of his precious, lustrous, lead-heavy secret.

As with many anticipated joys it does not come exactly as envisioned. By the time they climb the stairs together it is later than it should be, and they feel unsettled and high. Dinner had to be early because Nelson and Pru were going over to Soupy, as they both call Campbell, for their third session of counseling. They returned around nine-thirty with Nelson in such a rage they had to break out the dinner wine again while with a beer can in hand he did an imitation of the young minister urging the church's way into the intimate space between these two. 'He keeps

talking about the church being the be-riide of Ke-riist. I kept
wanting to ask him, Whose little bride are you?'

'Nelson,' Janice said, glancing toward the kitchen, where her
mother was making herself Ovaltine.

'I mean, it's ob*scene*,' Nelson insisted. 'What does He do, fuck
the church up the ass?'

Pru laughed, Harry noticed. Did Nelson do that to her? It was
about the last thing left a little out of the ordinary for these kids,
blowing all over the magazines these days, giving head they call
it, there was that movie *Shampoo* where Julie Christie who you
associate with costume dramas all decked out in bonnets announced right on the screen she wanted to blow Warren Beatty,
actually said it, and it wasn't even an X, it was a simple R, with
all these teen-age dating couples sitting there holding hands as
sweetly as if it was a rerun of *Showboat* with Kathryn Grayson and
Howard Keel, the girls laughing along with the boys. Pru's long-
boned mute body does not declare what it does, nor her pale lips,
that in repose have a dry, pursed look, an expression maybe you
learn in secretarial school. *Great in bed*, Nelson had said.

'I'm sorry, Mom, but he really pisses me off. He gets me to say
these things I don't believe and then he grins and acts jolly like
it's all some kind of crappy joke. Mom-mom, how can you and
those other old ladies stand him?'

Bessie had come in from the kitchen, her mug of Ovaltine
steaming as she stared it steady and her hair pinned tight up
against her skull with a net over it all, for bed. 'Oh,' she said, 'he's
higher than some, and lower than others. At least he doesn't choke
us on all the incense like the one that became a Greek Orthodox
priest finally. And he did a good job of getting the diehards to
accept the new form. My tongue still sticks at some of the
responses.'

Pru offered, 'Soupy seemed quite proud that the new service
doesn't have "obey." '

'People never did obey, I guess they might as well leave it out,'
Ma said.

Janice seemed determined to have a go at Nelson herself.
'Really you shouldn't put up such resistance, Nelson. The man
is leaning over backwards to give us a church service, and I think

from the way he acts he sincerely likes you. He really does have a feel for young people.'

'Does he ever,' Nelson said, soft enough for Ma Springer not to hear, then mimicking loudly, 'Dear Mater and Pater were *ain*cient. It's such a *whun*der I got here at all. In case you *whun*der why I have this *toad*stool look.'

'You shouldn't mind people's physical appearance,' Janice said.

'Oh but Mater, one simply *does*.' For some while they went on in this way, it was as good as television, Nelson imitating Soupy's mellow voice, Janice pleading for reason and charity, Ma Springer drifting in some world of her own where the Episcopal Church has presided since Creation; but Harry felt above them all, a golden man waiting to take his wife upstairs and show her their treasure. When the joking died, and a rerun of $M\star A\star S\star H$ came on that Nelson wanted to see, the young couple looked tired and harried suddenly, sitting there on the sofa, being beaten into one. Already each took an accustomed place, Pru over on the end with the little cherry side table for her crème de menthe and her knitting, and Nelson on the middle cushion with his feet in their button-soled Adidas up on the reproduction cobbler's bench. Now that he didn't go to the lot he didn't bother to shave every day, and the whiskers came in as reddish bristle on his chin and upper lip but his cheeks were still downy. To hell with this scruffy kid. Rabbit has decided to live for himself.

When Janice comes back from the bathroom naked and damp inside her terrycloth robe, he has locked their bedroom door and arranged himself in his underpants on the bed. He calls in a husky and insinuating voice, 'Hey. Janice. Look. I bought us something today.'

Her dark eyes are glazed from all that drinking and parenting downstairs; she took the shower to help clear her head. Slowly her eyes focus on his face, which must show an intensity of pleasure that puzzles her.

He tugs open the sticky drawer and is himself startled to see the two tinted cylinders sliding toward him, still upright, still there. He would have thought something so dense with preciousness would broadcast signals bringing burglars like dogs to a bitch in

199

heat. He lifts one roll out and places it in Janice's hand; her arm dips with the unexpected weight, and her robe, untied, falls open. Her thin brown used body is more alluring in this lapsed sheath of rough bright cloth than a girl's; he wants to reach in, to where the shadows keep the damp fresh.

'What is it, Harry?' she asks, her eyes widening.

'Open it,' he tells her, and when she fumbles too long at the transparent tape holding on the toilet-seat-shaped little lid he pries it off for her with his big fingernails. He removes the wad of tissue paper and spills out upon the quilted bedspread the fifteen Krugerrand. Their color is redder than gold in his mind had been. 'Gold,' he whispers, holding up close to her face, paired in his palm, two coins, showing the two sides, the profile of some old Boer on one and a kind of antelope on the other. 'Each of these is worth about three hundred sixty dollars,' he tells her. 'Don't tell your mother or Nelson or anybody.'

She does seem bewitched, taking one into her fingers. Her nails scratch his palm as she lifts the coin off. Her brown eyes pick up flecks of yellow. 'Is it all right?' Janice asks. 'Where on earth did you get them?'

'A new place on Weiser across from the peanut store that sells precious metals, buys and sells. It was simple. All you got to do is produce a certified check within twenty-four hours after they quote you a price. They guarantee to buy them back at the going rate any time, so all you lose is their six per cent commission and the sales tax, which at the rate gold is going up I'll have made back by next week. Here. I bought two stacks. Look.' He takes the other thrillingly hefty cylinder from the drawer and undoes the lid and spills those fifteen antelopes slippingly upon the bed-spread, thus doubling the riches displayed. The spread is a light-weight Pennsylvania Dutch quilt, small rectangular patches sewed together by patient biddies, graded from pale to dark to form a kind of dimensional effect, of four large boxes having a lighter and darker side. He lies down upon its illusion and places a Krugerrand each in the sockets of his eyes. Through the chill red pressure of the gold he hears Janice say, 'My God. I thought only the government could have gold. Don't you need a license or anything?'

'Just the bucks. Just the fucking bucks, Wonder Woman.'
Blind, he feels amid the pure strangeness of the gold his prick
firming up and stretching the fabric of his Jockey shorts.

'Harry. How much did you spend?'

He wills her to lift down the elastic of his underpants and suck,
suck until she gags. When she fails to read his mind and do this,
he removes the coins and gazes up at her, a dead man reborn and
staring. No coffin dark greets his open eyes, just his wife's out-
of-focus face, framed in dark hair damp and stringy from the
shower and fringy across the forehead so that Mamie Eisenhower
comes to mind. 'Eleven thousand five hundred more or less,' he
answers. 'Honey, it was just sitting in the savings account drawing
a lousy six per cent. At only six per cent these days you're losing
money, inflation's running about twelve. The beauty of gold is,
it loves bad news. As the dollar sinks, gold goes up. All the Arabs
are turning their dollars into gold. Webb Murkett told me all
about it, the day you wouldn't come to the club.'

She is still examining the coin, stroking its subtle relief, when
he wants her attention to turn to him. He hasn't had a hard-on
just blossom in his pants since he can't remember when. Lotty
Bingaman days. 'It's pretty,' Janice admits. 'Should you be
supporting the South Africans though?'

'Why not, they're making jobs for the blacks, mining the stuff.
The advantage of the Krugerrand, the girl at this fiscal alternatives place explained, is it weighs one troy ounce exactly and is
easier to deal with. You can buy Mexican pesos if you want, or
that little Canadian maple leaf, though there she said it's so fine
the gold dust comes off on your hands. Also I liked the look of
that deer on the back. Don't you?'

'I do. It's exciting,' Janice confesses, at last looking at him,
where he lies tumescent amid scattered gold. 'Where are you
going to keep them?' she asks. Her tongue sneaks forward in
thought, and rests on her lower lip. He loves her when she tries
to think.

'In your great big cunt,' he says, and pulls her down by the
lapels of her rough robe. Out of deference to those around them
in the house – Ma Springer just a wall's thickness away, her
television a dim rumble, the Korean War turned into a joke –

Janice tries to suppress her cries as he strips the terrycloth from her slippery body and the coins on the bedspread come in contact with her skin. The cords of her throat tighten; her face darkens as she strains in the grip of indignation and glee. His underwear off, the overhead light still on, his prick up like a jutting piece of pink wreckage, he calms her into lying motionless and places a Krugerrand on each nipple, one on her navel, and a number on her pussy, enough to mask the hair with a triangle of unsteady coins overlapping like snake scales. If she laughs and her belly moves the whole construction will collapse. Kneeling at her hips, Harry holds a Krugerrand by the edge as if to insert it in a slot. '*No!*' Janice protests, loud enough to twitch Ma Springer awake through the wall, loud enough to jar loose the coins so some do spill between her legs. He hushes her mouth with his and then moves his mouth south, across the desert, oasis to oasis, until he comes to the ferny jungle, which his wife lays open to him with a humoring toss of her thighs. A kind of interest compounds as, seeing red, spilled gold pressing on his forehead, he hunts with his tongue for her clitoris. He finds what he thinks is the right rhythm but doesn't feel it take; he thinks the bright overhead light might be distracting her and risks losing his hard-on in hopping from the bed to switch it off over by the door. Turning then in the half-dark he sees she has turned also, gotten up onto her knees and elbows, a four-legged moonchild of his, her soft cleft ass held high to him in the gloom as her face peeks around one shoulder. He fucks her in this position gently, groaning in the effort of keeping his jism in, letting his thoughts fly far. The pennant race, the recent hike in the factory base price of Corollas. He fondles her underside's defenseless slack flesh, his own belly massive and bearing down. Her back looks so breakable and brave and narrow – the long dent of its spine, the cross-bar of pallor left by her bathing-suit bra. Behind him his bare feet release a faraway sad odor. Coins jingle, slithering in toward their knees, into the depressions their interlocked weights make in the mattress. He taps her ass and asks, 'Want to turn over?'

'Uh-huh.' As an afterthought: 'Want me to sit on you first?'

'Uh-huh.' As an afterthought: 'Don't make me come.'

Harry's skin is bitten as by ice when he lies on his back. The coins: worse than toast crumbs. So wet he feels almost nothing, Janice straddles him, vast and globular in the patchy light that filters from the streetlight through the big copper beech. She picks up a stray coin and places it glinting in her eye, as a monocle. Lording it over him, holding him captive, she grinds her wet halves around him; self to self, bivalve and tuber, this is what it comes to. 'Don't come,' she says, alarmed enough so that her mock-monocle drops to his tense abdomen with a thud. 'Better get underneath,' he grunts. Her body then seems thin and black, silhouetted by the scattered circles, reflecting according to their tilt. Gods bedded among stars, he gasps in her ear, then she in his.

After this payoff, regaining their breaths, they can count in the semi-dark only twenty-nine Krugerrands on the rumpled bedspread, its landscape of ridged green patches. He turns on the overhead light. It hurts their eyes. By its harshness their naked skins seem also rumpled. Panic encrusts Harry's drained body; he does not rest until, naked on his knees on the rug, a late strand of spunk looping from his reddened glans, he finds, caught in the crack between the mattress and the bed side-rail, the precious thirtieth.

He stands with Charlie gazing out at the bleak September light. The tree over beyond the Chuck Wagon parking lot has gone thin and yellow at its top; above its stripped twigs the sky holds some diagonal cirrus, bands of fat in bacon, promising rain tomorrow. 'Poor old Carter,' Harry says. 'D'ya see where he nearly killed himself running up some mountain in Maryland?'

'He's pushing,' Charlie says. 'Kennedy's on his tail.' Charlie has returned from his two weeks' vacation with a kiss of Florida tan undermined by some essential pallor and maybe by the days intervening. He did not come from Florida directly. Simultaneously with his return Monday a card sent from Ohio arrived at Springer Motors, saying in his sharply slanted book-keeper's hand,

> Hi Gang –
>       Detoured on way
> back from Fla. thru Gt.
> Smokies. Southern belles,

mile after mile. Now near
Akron, exploded radial
capital of the world. Fuel
economy a no-no out here,
big fins & V-8s still reign.
Miss you all lots.     Chas.

The joke especially for Harry was on the other side: a picture of
a big flat-roofed building like a quarter of a pie, identified as
KENT STATE STUDENT COMPLEX, *embracing the largest open-
stack library in northeastern Ohio.*

'Sort of pushing yourself these days, aren't you?' Harry asks
him. 'How was Melanie all the while?'

'Who says I was with Melanie?'

'You did. With that card. Jesus, Charlie, a young kid like that
grinding your balls could kill you.'

'What a way to go, huh champ? You know as well as I do it's
not the chicks that grind your balls, it's these middle-aged broads
time is running out on.'

Rabbit remembers his bout with Janice amid their gold, yet still
remains jealous. 'Whajja do in Florida with her?'

'We moved around Sarasota, Venice, St Pete's. I couldn't talk
her out of the Atlantic side so we drove over from Naples on 75,
old Alligator Alley, and did the shmeer – Coral Gables, Ocean
Boulevard, up to Boca and West Palm. We were going to take in
Cape Canaveral but ran out of time. The bimbo didn't even bring
a bathing suit, the one we bought her was one of these new ones
with the sides open. Great figure. Don't know why you didn't
appreciate her.'

'I *could*n't appreciate her, it was Nelson brought her into the
house. It'd be like screwing your own daughter.'

Charlie has a toothpick left over from lunch downtown, a
persimmon-colored one, and he dents his lower lip with it as he
gazes out the tired window. 'There's worse things!' he offers
bleakly. 'How's Nelson and the bride-to-be?'

'Pru.' Harry sees that Charlie is set to guard the details of his
trip, to make him pull them out one by one. Miles of Southern
belles. Fuck this guy. Rabbit has secrets too. But, thinking this,
he can picture only a farm, its buildings set down low in a hollow.

'Melanie had a lot to say about Pru.'

'Like what?'

'Like she thinks she's weird. Her impression is that shy as she seems she's a tough kid up from a really rocky upbringing and isn't too steady on her feet, emotionally speaking.'

'Yeah well some might say a girl who gets her kicks screwing an old crow like you is pretty weird herself.'

Charlie looks away from the window straight up into his eyes, his own eyes behind their tinted spectacles looking watery. 'You shouldn't say things like that to me, Harry. Both of us getting on, two guys just hanging in there ought to be nice to each other.'

Harry wonders from this if Charlie knows how threatened his position is, Nelson on his tail.

Charlie continues, 'Ask me whatever you want about Melanie. Like I said, she's a good kid. Solid, emotionally. The trouble with you, champ, is you have screwing on the brain. My biggest kick was showing this young woman something of the world she hadn't seen before. She ate it up – the cypresses, that tower with the chimes. She said she'd still take California though. Florida's too flat. She said if this Christmas I could get my ass out to Carmel she'd be happy to show me around. Meet her mother and whoever else is around. Nothing heavy.'

'How much – how much future you think you two have?'

'Harry, I don't have much future with anybody.' His voice is whispery, barely audible. Harry would like to take it and wire-brush it clean.

'You never know,' he reassures the smaller man.

'You *know*,' Stavros insists. 'You know when your time is running out. If life offers you something, take it.'

'O.K., O.K. I will. I do. What'd your poor old mother do, while you were bombing around with Bimbo in the Everglades?'

'Well,' he says, 'funny thing there. A female cousin of mine, five or so years younger, I guess has been running around pretty bad, and her husband kicked her out this summer, and kept the kids. They lived in Norristown. So Gloria's been living in an apartment by herself out on Youngquist a couple blocks away and was happy to babysit for the old lady while I was off and says she'll do it again any time. So I have some freedom now I didn't used to have.'

Everywhere, it seems to Harry, families are breaking up and different pieces coming together like survivors in one great big lifeboat, while he and Janice keep sitting over there in Ma Springer's shadow, behind the times.

'Nothing like freedom,' he tells his friend. 'Don't abuse it now. You asked about Nelson. The wedding's this Saturday. Immediate family only. Sorry.'

'Wow. Poor little Nellie. Signed, sealed, and delivered.'

Harry hurries by this. 'From what Janice and Bessie let drop the mother will probably show up. The father's too sore.'

'You should see Akron,' Charlie tells him. 'I'd be sore too if I had to live there.'

'Isn't there a golf course out there where Nicklaus holds a tournament every year?'

'What I saw wasn't any golf course.'

Charlie has come back from his experiences tenderized, nostalgic it seems for his life even as he lives it. So aged and philosophical he seems, Harry dares ask him, 'What'd Melanie think of me, did she say?'

A very fat couple are prowling the lot, looking at the little cars, testing by their bodies, sitting down on air beside the driver's doors, which models might be big enough for them. Charlie watches this couple move among the glittering roofs and hoods a minute before answering. 'She thought you were neat, except the women pushed you around. She thought about you and her balling but got the impression you and Janice were very solid.'

'You disillusion her?'

'Couldn't. The kid was right.'

'Yeah how about ten years ago?'

'That was just cement.'

Harry loves the way he ticks this off, Janice's seducer; he loves this savvy Greek, dainty of heart beneath his coat of summer checks. The couple have wearied of trying on cars for size and get into their old car, a '77 Pontiac Grand Prix with ivory hardtop, and drive away. Harry asks suddenly, 'How do you feel about it? Think we can live with Nelson over here?'

Charlie shrugs, a minimal brittle motion. 'Can he live with me?

He wants to be a cut above Jake and Rudy, and there aren't that many cuts in an outfit like this.'

'I've told them, Charlie, if you go I go.'

'You can't go, Chief. You're family. Me, I'm old times. I can go.'

'You know this business cold, that's what counts with me.'

'Ah, this isn't selling. It's like supermarkets now: it's shelf-stacking, and ringing it out at the register. When it was all used, we used to try to fit a car to every customer. Now it's take it or leave it. With this seller's market there's no room to improvise. Your boy had the right idea: go with convertibles, antiques, something with a little amusement value. I can't take these Jap bugs seriously. This new thing called the Tercel we're supposed to start pushing next month, have you seen the stats? One point five liter engine, twenty-inch tires. It's like those little cars they used to have on merry-go-rounds for the kids who were too scared to ride the horses.'

'Forty-three m.p.g. on the highway, that's the stat people care about, the way the world's winding.'

Charlie says, 'You don't see too many bugs down in Florida. The old folks are still driving the big old boats, the Continentals, the Toronados, they paint 'em white and float around. Of course the roads, there isn't a hill in the state and never any frost. I've been thinking about the Sun Belt. Go down there and thumb my nose at the heating-oil bills. Then they get you on the air-conditioning. You can't escape.'

Harry say, 'Sodium wafers, that's the answer. Electricity straight from sunlight. It's about five years off, that's what *Consumer Reports* was saying. Then we can tell those Arabs to take their fucking oil and grease their camels with it.'

Charlie says, 'Traffic fatalities are up. You want to know why they're up? Two reasons. One, the kids are pretty much off drugs now and back into alcohol. Two, everybody's gone to compacts and they crumple like paper bags.'

He chuckles and twirls the flavored toothpick against his lower lip as the two men gaze out the window at the river of dirty tin. An old low-slung station wagon pulls into the lot but it has no wooden rack on top; though Harry's heart skips, it is not his daughter. The station wagon noses around and heads out into 111 again, just casing. Burglaries are up. Harry asks Charlie, 'Melanie really thought about' – he balks at 'balling,' it is not his generation's word – 'going to bed with me?'

'That's what the lady said. But you know these kids, they come right out with everything we used to keep to ourselves. Doesn't mean there's more of it. Probably less as a matter of fact. By the time they're twenty-five they're burnt out.'

'I was never attracted to her, to tell you the truth. Now this new girl of Nelson's –'

'I don't want to hear about it,' Charlie says, pivoting to go back to his desk. 'They're about to get married, for Chrissake.'


Running. Harry has continued the running he began up in the Poconos, as a way of getting his body back from those sodden years he never thought about it, just ate and did what he wanted, restaurant lunches downtown in Brewer plus the Rotary every Thursday, it begins to pack on. The town is dark he runs through, full of slanty alleys and sidewalks cracked and tipped from underneath, whole cement slabs lifted up by roots like crypt lids in a horror movie, the dead reach up, they catch at his heels. He keeps moving, pacing himself, overriding the protest of his lungs and making of his stiff muscles and tired blood a kind of machine that goes where the brain directs, uphill past the wide-eaved almost Chinese-looking house where the butch women hammer, their front windows never lit, must watch a lot of television or else snuggle into whatever it is they do early or else saving electricity, women won't get paid the same as men until ERA passes, at least having a nest of them moving into the neighborhood not like blacks or Puerto Ricans, they don't breed.

Norway maples shade these streets. Not much taller than when he was a boy. Grab a low branch and hoist yourself up into a hornets' nest. Split the seeds and stick them to your nose to make yourself a rhinoceros. Panting, he cuts through their shadow. A slim pain cuts through his high left side. Hold on, heart. Old Fred Springer popped off in a blaze of red, anyway Rabbit has always imagined the last thing you'd see in a heart attack would be red, doesn't think that'll be for him somehow, a long slow wrestle with black cancer probably. Amazing, how dark these American houses are, at nine o'clock at night. A kind of ghost town, nobody else on the sidewalk, all the chickens in their coop, only a brownish bit of glow showing through a window crack here and there, night light in a child's room. His mind strides on into a bottomless sorrow, thinking of children. Little Nellie in his room newly moved into Vista Crescent, his teddies stacked in a row beside him, his eyes like theirs unable to close, scared of dying while asleep, thinking of baby Becky who did fall through, who did die. A volume of water still stood in the tub many hours later, dust on the unstirring gray surface, just a little rubber stopper to lift and God in all His strength did nothing. Dry leaves scrape and break underfoot, the sound of fall, excitement in the air. The Pope is coming, and the wedding is Saturday. Janice asks him why is his heart so hard toward Nelson. Because Nelson has swallowed up the boy that was and substituted one more pushy man in the world, hairy wrists, big prick. Not enough room in the world. People came north from the sun belt in Egypt and lived in heated houses and now the heat is being used up, just the oil for the showroom and offices and garage has doubled since '74 when he first saw the Springer Motors books and will double in the next year or two again and when you try to cut it down to where the President says, the men in the garage complain, they have to work with their bare hands, working on a concrete slab they can wear thick socks and heavy soles, he thought at one point he should get them all that kind of golf glove that leaves the fingertips bare but it would have been hard to find ones for the right hand, guys under thirty now just will not work without comfort and all the perks, a whole new ethic, soft, socialism, heat tends to rise in a big space like that and hang up there amid the crossbraces, if they built it now they'd put in twenty inches of insulation, if the Pope is so crazy about babies why doesn't *he* try to keep them warm?

He is running along Potter Avenue now, still uphill, saving the downhill for the homeward leg, along the gutter where the water from the ice plant used to run, an edge of green slime, life tries to get a grip anywhere, on earth that is, not on the moon, that's another thing he doesn't like about the thought of climbing through the stars. Once clowning on the way to school along the gutter that now is dry he slipped on the slime and fell in, got his knickers soaked, those corduroy knickers they used to make you wear, *swish swish*, and the long socks, incredible how far back he goes now, he can remember girls in first grade still wearing high-button shoes: Margaret Schoelkopf, she was so full of life her nose would start to bleed for no reason. When he fell in the gutter of ice-plant water his knickers were so wet he had to run home crying and change, he hated being late for school. Or for anywhere, it was something Mom drummed into him, she didn't so much care where he went but he had to be home on time, and for most of his life this sensation would overtake him, anywhere, in the locker room, on a 16A bus, in the middle of a fuck, that he was late for somewhere and he was in terrible dark trouble, a kind of tunnel would open in his mind with Mom at the end of it with a switch. *Do you want a switching Hassy?* she would ask him as if asking if he wanted dessert, the switches came off the base of the little pear tree in the narrow back yard on Jackson Road; how the yellow-jackets would hover over the fallen rotting fruit. Lately he no longer ever feels he is late for somewhere, a strange sort of peace at his time of life like a thrown ball at the top of its arc is for a second still. His gold is rising in value, ten dollars an ounce or so in the papers every day, ten times thirty is three hundred smackers without his lifting a finger, you think how Pop slaved. Janice putting that monocle on was a surprise, the only trouble with her in bed is she still doesn't like to blow, something mean about her mouth and always was, Melanie had those funny saucy stubborn cherry lips, a wonder Charlie didn't pop his aorta in some motel down there in the sands, how lovely it is when a woman forgets herself and opens her mouth to laugh or exclaim so wide you see the whole round cavern the ribbed pink roof and the tongue like a rug in a hall and the butterfly-shaped blackness in the back that goes down into the throat, Pru did that the other day in the kitchen at something Ma Springer said, her smile usually wider on one side than the other and a bit cautious like she might get burned, but all the girls coming up now blew, it was part of the culture, taken for granted, fuck-and-suck movies they call them, right out in the open, you take your date, ADULT FILMS NEW EACH FRIDAY in the old Baghdad on upper Weiser where in Rabbit's day they used to go see Ronald Reagan being co-pilot against the Japs. Lucky Nelson, in a way. Still he can't envy him. A worn-out world to find his way in. Funny about mouths, they must do so much, and don't tell what went into them, even a minute later. One thing he does hate is seeing bits of food, rice or cereal or whatever, hanging in the little hairs of a face during a meal. Poor Mom in those last years.

His knees are jarring. His big gut jounces. Each night he tries to extend his run among the silent dark houses, through the cones of the streetlights, under the ice-cold lopsided moon, that the other night driving home in the Corona he happened to see through the tinted upper part of the windshield and for a second thought, My God, it *is* green. Tonight he pushes himself as far as Kegerise Street, a kind of alley that turns downhill again, past black-sided small factories bearing mysterious new names like Lynnex and Data Development and an old stone farmhouse that all the years he was growing up had boarded windows and a yard full of tumbledown weeds milkweed and thistle and a fence of broken slats but now was all fixed up with a little neat sign outside saying *Albrecht Stamm Homestead* and inside all sorts of authentic hand-made furniture and quaint kitchen equipment to show what a farmhouse was like around 1825 and in cases in the hall photographs of the early buildings of Mt Judge before the turn of the century but not anything of the fields when the area of the town was in large part Stamm's farm, they didn't have cameras that far back or if they did didn't point them at empty fields. Old man Springer had been on the board of the Mt Judge Historical Society and helped raise the funds for the restoration, after he died Janice and Bessie thought Harry might be elected to take his place on the board but it didn't happen, his checkered past haunting him. Even though a young hippie couple lives upstairs and leads the visitors through, to Harry the old Stamm place is full of ghosts, those old farmers lived weird lives, locking their crazy sisters in the attic and strangling the pregnant hired girl in a fit of demon rum and hiding the body in the potato bin so that fifty years later the skeleton comes to light. Next door the Sunshine Athletic Association used to be, that Harry as a boy had thought was full of athletes, so he hoped he could some day belong, but when twenty years ago he did get inside it smelled of cigar butts and beer gone flat in the bottom of the glass. Then through the Sixties it fell into dilapidation and disrepute, the guys who drank and played cards in there getting older and fewer and more morose. So when the building came up for sale the Historical Society bought it and tore it down and made where it was into a parking lot for the visitors who came by to the Stamm Homestead on their way to Lancaster to look at the Amish or on their way to Philadelphia to look at the Liberty Bell. You wouldn't think people could find it tucked away on what used to be Kegerise Alley but an amazing number do, white-haired most of them. History. The more of it you have the more you have to live it. After a little while there gets to be too much of it to memorize and maybe that's when empires start to decline.

Now he is really rolling, the alley slants down past the body shop and a chicken house turned into a little leather-working plant, these ex-hippies are everywhere, trying to hang on, they missed the boat but had their fun, he has pushed through the first wave of fatigue, when you think you can't drag your body another stride, your thighs pure pain. Then second wind comes and you break free into a state where your body does it by itself, a machine being ridden, your brain like the astronaut in the tip of the rocket, your thoughts just flying. If only Nelson would get married and go away and come back rich twenty years from now. Why can't these kids get out on their own instead of crawling back? Too crowded out there. The Pope, Jesus, you have to hope he isn't shot, just like America to have some nut take a shot to get his name in the papers, that Squeaky Fromme who used to lay the old cowboys for the Manson ranch, all the ass that Manson had you'd think it would have made him nicer since it's being sexually frustrated that causes war, he read somewhere. He knows how the Pope feels about contraception though, he could never stand rubbers, even when they gave them to you free in the Army, this Month's *Consumer Reports* has an article on them page after page, all this testing, some people apparently prefer bright-colored ones with ribs and little nubbins to give the women an added tickle inside, did the staffers on the magazine all ask the secretaries to screw or what, some people even liked ones made out of sheep intestine, the very thought of it makes him crawl down there, with names like Horizon Nuda and Klingtite Naturalamb, Harry couldn't read to the end of the article, he was so turned off. He wonders about his daughter, what she uses, country methods they used to kid about in school, squat on a cornstalk, she looked pretty virginal in that one glimpse of her and who wouldn't be, surrounded by rubes? Ruth would set her straight, what pigs men are. And that barking dog would be a discouragement too.

There is a longer way home, down Jackson to Joseph and over, but tonight he takes the shortcut, diagonally across the lawn of the big stone Baptist church, he likes the turf under his feet for a minute, the church façade so dark, to the concrete steps that take you down onto Myrtle, and on past the red, white, and blue post office trucks parked in a row at the back platform, the American flag hanging limp and bright over the fake gable out front, used to be you shouldn't fly the flag at night but now all the towns do it with a spotlight, waste of electricity, soaking up the last dribble of energy flying the flag. Myrtle leads into Joseph from the other end. They will be sitting around waiting for him, watching the boob tube or going on about the wedding, getting silly about it now that it's so close and Soupy has declared all systems go, they've invited Charlie Stavros after all and Grace Stuhl and a batch of other biddies and a few friends from the Flying Eagle and it turns out Pru or Teresa as they call her in the announcement they want to send out has an aunt and uncle in Binghamton, New York, who will come down even if the father is some sorehead who wants to strangle his daughter and put her in the potato bin. In he will come and Janice will make her usual crack about him killing himself with a heart attack, it's true he does get very red in his white face, he can see in the mirror in the foyer, with his blue eyes, Santa Claus without the whiskers, and has to bend over the back of a chair gasping for a while to get his breath, but that's part of the fun, giving her a scare, poor mutt what would she do without him, have to give up the Flying Eagle and everything, go back to selling nuts in Kroll's. In he will come and there Pru will be sitting on the sofa right next to Nelson like the police officer who takes the criminal from one jail to another on the train without letting the handcuffs show, the one thing Harry is fearful of now that Pru is in the family is stinking up the room with his sweat. Tothero had it that time in the Sunshine, an old man's sour sad body smell, and getting out of bed in the morning sometimes Harry surprises it on himself, this faraway odor like a corpse just beginning to sweeten. Middle age is a wonderful country, all the things you thought would never happen are happening. When he was fifteen, forty-six would have seemed the end of the rainbow, he'd never get there, if a meaning of life was to show up you'd think it would have by now.

Yet at moments it seems it has, there are just no words for it, it is not something you dig for but sits on the top of the table like an unopened dewy beer can. Not only is the Pope coming but the Dalai Lama they bounced out of Tibet twenty years ago is going around the U.S.A. talking to divinity schools and appearing on TV talk shows, Harry has always been curious about what it would feel like to *be* the Dalai Lama. A ball at the top of its arc, a leaf on the skin of a pond. A water strider in a way is what the mind is like, those dimples at the end of their legs where they don't break the skin of the water quite. When Harry was little God used to spread in the dark above his bed like that and then when the bed became strange and the girl in the next aisle grew armpit hair He entered into the blood and muscle and nerve as an odd command and now He had withdrawn, giving Harry the respect due from one well-off gentleman to another, but for a calling card left in the pit of the stomach, a bit of lead true as a plumb bob pulling Harry down toward all those leaden dead in the hollow earth below.

The front lights of Ma Springer's big shadowy stucco house blaze, they are all excited by the wedding, Pru now has a constant blush and Janice hasn't played tennis for days and Bessie evidently gets up in the middle of the night and goes downstairs to watch on the bigger TV the old Hollywood comedies, men in big-brimmed hats and little mustaches, women with shoulders broader than their hips swapping wisecracks in newspaper offices and deluxe hotel suites, Ma must have seen these movies first when she had all black hair and the Brewer downtown was a great white way. Harry jogs in place to let a car pass, one of those crazy Mazdas with the Wankel engine like a squirrel wheel, Manny says they'll never get the seal tight enough, crosses from curb to curb under the streetlight, notices Janice's Maverick isn't parked out front, sprints down the brick walk and up the porch steps, and at last on the porch, under the number 89, stops running. His momentum is such that the world for a second or two streams on, seeming to fling all its trees and housetops outward against star-spangled space.

In bed Janice says, 'Harry.'

'What?' After you run your muscles have a whole new pulled, sheathed feel and sleep comes easy.

'I have a little confession to make.'

'You're screwing Stavros again.'

'Don't be so rude. No, did you notice the Maverick wasn't left out front as usual?'

'I did. I thought, "How nice." '

'It was Nelson who put it out back, in the alley. We really ought to clean out that space in the garage some day, all these old bicycles nobody uses. Melanie's Fuji is still in there.'

'O.K., good. Good for Nelson. Hey, are you going to talk all night, or what? I'm beat.'

'He put it there because he didn't want you to see the front fender.'

'Oh no. That son of a bitch. That little son of a bitch.'

'It wasn't his fault exactly, this other man just kept coming, though I guess the Stop sign was on Nelson's street.'

'Oh Christ.'

'Luckily both hit their brakes, so it really was just the smallest possible bump.'

'The other guy hurt?'

'Well, he said something about whiplash, but then that's what people are trained to say now, until they can talk to their lawyer.'

'And the fender is mashed?'

'Well, it's tipped in. The headlight doesn't focus the same place the other does. But it's fine in the daytime. It's really hardly more than a scratch.'

'Five hundred bucks worth. At least. The masked fender-bender strikes again.'

'He really was terrified to tell you. He made me promise I wouldn't, so you can't say anything to him.'

'I can't? Then why are you telling me? How can I go to sleep now? My head's pounding. It's like he has it in a vise.'

'Because I didn't want you noticing by yourself and making a scene. Please, Harry. Just until after the wedding. He's really very embarrassed about it.'

'The fuck he is, he loves it. He has my head in a vise and he just keeps turning the screw. That he'd do it to *your* car, after you've been knocking yourself out for him, that's really gratitude.'

'Harry, he's about to get married, he's in a state.'

'Well, shit, now I'm in a state. Where're some clothes? I got to go outside and see the damage. That flashlight in the kitchen, did it ever get new batteries?'

'I'm sorry I told you. Nelson was right. He said you wouldn't be able to handle it.'

'Oh did he say that? Our own Mr Cool.'

'So just settle down. I'll take care of the insurance forms and everything.'

'And who do you think pays for the increase in our insurance rates?'

'We do,' she says. 'The two of us.'


St John's Episcopal Church in Mt Judge is a small church that never had to enlarge, built in 1912 in the traditional low-sided steep-roofed style, of a dark gray stone hauled from the north of the county, whereas the Lutheran church was built of local red sandstone, and the Reformed, next to the fire station, of brick. Ivy has been encouraged around St John's pointed windows. Inside, it is dark, with knobby walnut pews and dados and, on the walls between stained-glass windows of Jesus in violet robes making various gestures, marble plaques in memory of the dead gentry who contributed heavily here, in the days when it looked like Mt Judge might become a fashionable suburb. WHITELAW. STOVER. LEGGETT. English names in a German county, gone to give tone to the realms of the departed after thirty years as wardens and vestrymen. Old man Springer had done his bit but the spaces between the windows were used up by then.

Though the wedding is small and the bride an Ohio working-man's daughter, yet in the eyes of passersby the gathering would make a bright brave flurry before the church's rust-red doors, on the verge of four o'clock this September the twenty-second. A person or persons driving past this Saturday afternoon on the way to the MinitMart or the hardware store would have a pang of wanting to be among the guests. The organist with his red robe over his arm is ducking into the side door. He has a goatee. A little grubby guy in green coveralls like a troll is waiting for Harry to show up so he can get paid for the flowers, Ma said it was only decent to decorate the altar at least, Fred would have died to see Nellie married in St John's with a bare altar. Two bouquets of white mums and baby's breath come to $38.50, Rabbit pays him with two twenties, it was a bad sign when the banks started paying out in twenties instead of tens, and yet the two-dollar bill still isn't catching on. People are superstitious. This wasn't supposed to be a wedding at all but in fact it's costing plenty. They've had to take three rooms over at the Four Seasons Motel on Route 422: one for the mother of the bride, Mrs Lubell, a small scared soul who looks like she thinks they'll all stick forks into her if she drops her little smile for a second; and another for Melanie, who came across the Commonwealth with Mrs Lubell from Akron in a bus, and for Pru, who has been displaced from her room – Melanie's old room and before that the sewing dummy's – by the arrival from Nevada of Mim, whom Bessie and Janice didn't want in the house at all but Harry insisted, she's his only sister and the only aunt Nelson has got; and the third room for this couple from Bing-hamton, Pru's aunt and uncle, who were driving down today but hadn't checked in by three-thirty, when the shuttle service Harry has been running in the Corona picked up the two girls and the mother to bring them to the church. His head is pounding. This mother bothers him, her smile has been on her face so long it's as dry as a pressed flower, she doesn't seem to belong to his generation at all, she's like an old newspaper somebody has used as a drawer liner and then in cleaning house you lift out and try to read; Pru's looks must have all come from the father's side. At the motel the woman kept worrying that the messages they were leaving at the front desk for her tardy brother and sister-in-law weren't clear enough, and began to cry, so her smile got damp and ruined. A case of Mumm's second-best champagne waits back in the Joseph Street kitchen for the little get-together afterwards that nobody would call a reception; Janice and her mother decided they should have the sandwiches catered by a grandson of Grace Stuhl's who would bring along this girlfriend in a serving uniform. And then they ordered a cake from some wop over on Eleventh Street who was charging one hundred and eighty-five American dollars for a cake, a *cake* – Harry couldn't believe it. Every time Nelson turns around, it costs his father a bundle.

Harry stands for a minute in the tall ribbed space of the empty church, reading the plaques, hearing Soupy's giggle greet the three dolled-up women off in a side room, one of those out-of-sight chambers churches have where the choir puts itself into robes and the deacons count the collection plates and the communion wine is stored where the acolytes won't drink it and the whole strange show is made ready. Billy Fosnacht was supposed to be best man but he's up at Tufts so a friend of theirs from the Laid-Back called Slim is standing around with a carnation in his lapel waiting to usher. Uncomfortable from the way this young man's slanted eyes brush across him, Rabbit goes outside to stand by the church doors, whose rust-red paint in the September sun gives back heat so as to remind him of standing in his fresh tan uniform on a winter day in Texas at the side of the barracks away from the wind, that incessant wind that used to pour from that great thin sky across the treeless land like the whine of homesickness through this soldier who had never before been away from Pennsylvania.

Standing there thus for a breath of air, in this pocket of peace, he is trapped in the position of a greeter, as the guests suddenly begin to arrive. Ma Springer's stately dark-blue Chrysler pulls up, grinding its tires on the curb, and the three old ladies within claw at the door handles for release. Grace Stuhl has a translucent wart off-center on her chin but she hasn't forgotten how to dimple. 'I bet but for Bessie I'm the only one here went to your wedding too,' she tells Harry on the church porch.

'Not sure I was there myself,' he says. 'How did I act?'

'Very dignified. Such a tall husband for Janice, we all said.'

'And he's kept his looks,' adds Amy Gehringer, the squattest of these three biddies. Her face is enlivened with rouge and a flaking substance the color of Russian salad dressing. She pokes him in the stomach, hard. 'Even added to them some,' the old lady wisecracks.

'I'm trying to take it off,' he says, as if he owes her something. 'I go jogging most every night. Don't I, Bessie?'

'Oh it frightens me,' Bessie says. 'After what happened to Fred And you know there wasn't an ounce extra on him.'

'Take it easy, Harry,' Webb Murkett says, coming up behind with Cindy. 'They say you can injure the walls of your intestines, jogging. The blood all rushes to the lungs.'

'Hey Webb,' Harry says, flustered. 'You know my mother-in-law.'

'My pleasure,' he says introducing himself and Cindy all around. She is wearing a black silk dress that makes her look like a young widow. Would that she were, Jesus. Her hair has been fluffed up by a blow-dryer so it doesn't have that little-headed wet-otter look that he loves. The top of her dress is held together with a pin shaped like a bumblebee at the lowest point of a plunging V-shaped scoop.

And Bessie's friends are staring at gallant Webb with such enchantment Harry reminds them, 'Go right in, there's a guy there leading people to their seats.'

'I want to go right up front,' Amy Gehringer says, 'so I can get a good look at this young minister Bessie raves so about.'

''Fraid this screwed up golf for today,' Harry apologizes to Webb.

'Oh,' Cindy says, 'Webb got his eighteen in already, he was over there by eight-thirty.'

'Who'd you get to take my place?' Harry asks, jealous, and unable to trust his eyes to rest on Cindy's tan décolletage. The tops of tits are almost the best part, nipples can be frightening. Just above the bumblebee a white spot even her bikini bra hides from the sun shows. The little cross is up higher, just under the sexy hollow between her collarbones. What a package.

'The young assistant pro went around with us,' Webb confides. 'A seventy-three, Harry. A seventy-*three*, with a ball into the pond on the fifteenth, he hits it so far.'

Harry is hurt but he has to greet the Fosnachts, who are pushing behind. Janice didn't want to invite them, especially after they decided not to invite the Harrisons, to keep it all small. But since Nelson wanted Billy as best man Harry thought they had no choice, and also even though Peggy has let herself slide there is that aura about a woman who's once upon a time taken off all her clothes for you however poorly it's turned out. What the hell, it's a wedding, so he bends down and kisses Peggy to one side of the big wet hungry mouth he remembers. She is startled, her face broader than he remembers. Her eyes swim up at him in the wake of the kiss, but since one of them is a walleye he never knows which to search for expression.

Ollie's handshake is limp, sinewy, and mean: a mean-spirited little loser, with ears that stick out and hair like dirty straw. Harry crunches his knuckles together a little, squeezing. 'How's the music racket, Ollie? Still tootling?' Ollie is one of these reedy types, common around Brewer, who can pick out a tune on anything but never manage to make it anywhere big. He works in a music store, Chords 'n' Records, renamed Fidelity Audio, on Weiser Street near the old Baghdad, where the adult movies show now.

Peggy, her voice defensive from the kiss, says, 'He sits in on synthesizer sometimes with a group of Billy's friends.'

'Keep at it, Ollie, you'll be the Elton John of the Eighties. Seriously, how've you both been? Jan and I keep saying, we got to have you two over.' Over Janice's dead body. Funny, just that once innocent forlorn screw, and Janice holds a grudge, where he's forgiving as hell of Charlie, just about the only friend he has left in fact.'

And here is Charlie. 'Welcome to the merger,' Harry kids.

Charlie chuckles, his shrug small and brief. He knows the tide is running against him, with this marriage. Still, he has some reserve within him, some squared-off piece of philosophy that keeps him from panicking.

'You seen the bridesmaid?' Harry asks him. Melanie.

'Not yet.'

'The three of 'em went over into Brewer last night and got drunk as skunks, to judge from Nelson. How's that for a way to act on the night before your wedding?'

Charlie's head ticks slowly sideways in obliging disbelief. This elderly gesture is jarred, however, when Mim, dressed in some crinkly pants outfit in chartreuse, with ruffles, grabs him from behind around the chest and won't let go. Charlie's face tenses in fright, and to keep him from guessing who it is Mim presses her face against his back so that Harry fears all her make-up will rub off on Charlie's checks. Mim comes on now any hour of the day or night made up like a showgirl, every tint and curl exactly the way she wants it; but really all the creams and paints in a world of jars won't counterfeit a flexible skin, and rimming your eyes in charcoal may be O.K. for these apple-green babies that go to the disco but over forty it makes a woman look merely haunted, staring, the eyes lassoed. Her teeth are bared as she hangs on, wrestling Charlie from behind like an eleven-year-old with Band-Aids on her knees. 'Jesus,' Charlie grunts, seeing the hands at his chest with their purple nails long as grasshoppers, but slow to think back through all the women he has known who this might be.

Embarrassed for her, worried for him, Harry begs, 'C'mon, Mim.'

She won't let go, her long-nosed tarted-up face mussed and distorted as she maintains the pressure of her grip. 'Gotcha,' she says. 'The Greek heartbreaker. Wanted for transporting a minor across state lines and for misrepresenting used cars. Put the handcuffs on him, Harry.'

Instead Harry puts his hands on her wrists, encountering bracelets he doesn't want to bend, thousands of dollars' worth of gold on her bones, and pulls them apart, having set his own body into the jostle for leverage, while Charlie, looking grimmer every second, holds himself upright, cupping his fragile heart within. Mim is wiry, always was. Pried loose at last, she touches herself rapidly here and there, putting each hair and ruffle back into place.

'Thought the boogyboo had gotten you, didn't you Charlie?' she jeers.

'Pre-owned,' Charlie tells her, pulling his coat sleeves taut to restore his dignity. 'Nobody calls them used cars anymore.'

'Out west we call them shitboxes.'

'Shh,' Harry urges. 'They can hear you inside. They're about to get started.' Still exhilarated by her tussle with Charlie, and amused by the disapproving conscientious man her brother has become, Mim wraps her arms around Harry's neck and hugs him hard. The frills and pleats of her fancy outfit crackle, crushing against his chest. 'Once a bratty sister,' she says breathily in his ear, 'always a bratty sister.'

Charlie has slipped into the church, Mim's eyelids, shut, shine in the sunlight like smears left by some collision of greased vehicles – often on the highways Harry notices the dark swerves of rubber, the gouges of crippled metal left to mark where something unthinkable had suddenly happened to someone. Though it happened the day's traffic continues. *Hold me, Harry*, she used to cry out, little Mim in her hood between his knees as their sled hit the cinders spread at the bottom of Jackson Road, and orange sparks flew. Years before, a child had died under a milk truck sledding here and all the children were aware of this: that child's blank face leaned toward them out of each snowstorm. Now Harry sees a glisten in Mim's eyelids as in the backs of the Japanese beetles that used to cluster on the large dull leaves of the Bolger's grape arbor out back. Also he sees how her earlobes have been elongated under the pull of jewelry and how her ruffles shudder as she pants, out of breath after her foolery. She is sinking through all her sins and late nights toward being a pathetic hag, he sees, one of those women you didn't believe could ever have been loved, with only Mom's strong bones in her face to save her. He hesitates, before going in. The town falls away from this church like a wide flight of stairs shuffled together of roofs and walls, a kind of wreck wherein many Americans have died.

He hears the side door where the organist hurried in open, and peeks around the corner, thinking it might be Janice needing him. But it is Nelson who steps out, Nelson in his cream-colored three-piece marrying suit with pinched waist and wide lapels, that look too big for him, perhaps because the flared pants almost cover the heels of his shoes.

As always when he sees his son unexpectedly Harry feels shame. His upper lip lifts to call out in recognition, but the boy doesn't look his way, just appears to sniff the air, looking around at the grass and down toward the houses of Mt Judge and then up the other way at the sky at the edge of the mountain. *Run*, Harry wants to call out, but nothing comes, just a stronger scent of Mim's perfume at the intake of breath. Softly the child closes the door again behind him, ignorant that he has been seen.

Behind the ajar rust-red portal the church is gathering in silence toward its eternal deed. The world then will be cloven between those few gathered in a Sunday atmosphere and all the sprawling fortunate Saturday remainder, the weekday world going on about its work. From childhood on Rabbit has resented ceremonies. He touches Mim on the arm to take her in, and over the spun glass of her hairdo sees a low-slung dirty old Ford station wagon with the chrome roof rack heightened by rough green boards crawl by on the street. He isn't quick enough to see the passengers, only gets a glimpse of a fat angry face staring from a back window. A fat mannish face yet a woman's.

'What's the matter?' Mim asks.

'I don't know. Nothing.'

'You look like you've seen a ghost.'

'I'm worrying about the kid. How do *you* feel about all this?'

'Me. Aunt Mim? It seems all right. The chick will take charge.'

'That's good?'

'For a while. You must let go, Harry. The boy's life is his, you live your own.'

'That's what I've been telling myself. But it feels like a copout.'

They go in. A pathetic little collection of heads juts up far down front. This mysterious slant-eyed Slim, smoothly as if they were paying him, escorts Mim down the aisle to the second pew and indicates with a graceful sly gesture where Harry should settle in the first, next to Janice. The space has been waiting. On Janice's other side sits the other mother. Mrs Lubell's profile is pale; like her daughter she is a redhead but her hair has been rinsed to colorless little curls, and she never could have had Pru's height and nice rangy bearing. She looks, Harry can't help thinking it, like a cleaning lady. She gives over to him her desiccated but oddly perfect smile, a smile such as flickered from the old black-

223

and-white movie screens, coy and certain, a smile like a thread of pure melody, that when she was young must have seemed likely to lift her life far above where it settled. Janice has pulled back her head to whisper with her mother in the booth behind. Mim has wound up in the same pew as Ma Springer and her biddies. Stavros sits with the Murketts in the third pew, he has Cindy's neckline to look down when he gets bored, let him see what country-club tits look like after all those stuffed grape leaves. In willful awkwardness the Fosnachts were seated or seated themselves across the aisle, on what would have been the bride's side if there had been enough to make a side, and are quarrelling in whispers between themselves: much hissed emphasis from Peggy and stoic forward-gazing mutter from Ollie. The organist is doodling through the ups and downs of some fugue to give everybody a chance to cough and recross their legs. The tip of his little ruddy goatee dips about an inch above the keyboard during the quiet parts. The way he slaps and tugs at the stops reminds Harry of the old Linotype he used to operate, the space adjuster and the way the lead jumped out hot, all done with computer tapes now. To the left of the altar one of the big wall panels with rounded tops opens, it is a secret door like in a horror movie, and out of it steps Archie Campbell in a black cassock and white surplice and stole. He flashes his *What? Me worry?* grin, those sudden seedy teeth.

Nelson follows him out, head down, looking at nobody.

Slim slides up the aisle, light as a cat, to stand beside him. He must be a burglar in his spare time. He stands a good six inches taller than Nelson. Both have these short punk haircuts. Nelson's hair makes a whorl in back that Harry knows so well his throat goes dry, something caught in it.

Peggy Fosnacht's last angry whisper dies. The organ has been silent this while. With both plump hands lifted, Soupy bids them all stand. To the music of their rustle Melanie leads in Pru, from another side room, along the altar rail. The secret knowledge shared by all that she is pregnant enriches her beauty. She wears an ankle-length crêpey dress that Ma Springer calls oatmeal in color and Janice and Melanie call champagne, with a brown sash they decided to leave off her waist lest they have to tie it too high.

It must have been Melanie who wove the little wreath of field flowers, already touched by wilt, that the bride wears as a crown. There is no train or veil save an invisible organic pride. Pru's face, downcast and purse-lipped, is flushed, her carroty hair brushed slick down her back and tucked behind her ears to reveal their crimped soft shell shapes hung with tiny hoops of gold, her eyes imparting green as she glances toward Nelson and then the minister. Harry could halt her with his arm as she paces by but she does not look at him. Melanie gives all the old folks a merry eye; Pru's long red-knuckled fingers communicate a tremble to her little bouquet of baby's breath. Now her bearing as she faces the minister is grave with that gorgeous slowed composure of women carrying more than themselves.

Soupy calls them Dearly Beloved. The voice welling up out of this little man is terrific, Harry had noticed it at the house, but here, in the nearly empty church, echoing off the walnut knobs and memorial plaques and high arched rafters, beneath the tall central window of Jesus taking off into the sky with a pack of pastel apostles for a launching pad, the timbre is doubled, richer, with a rounded sorrowful something Rabbit hadn't noticed hitherto, gathering and pressing the straggle of guests into a congregation, subduing any fear that this ceremony might be a farce. Laugh at ministers all you want, they have the words we need to hear, the ones the dead have spoken. *The union of husband and wife*, he announces in his great considerate organ tones, *is intended by God for their mutual joy*, and like layers of a wide concealing dust the syllables descend, *prosperity*, *adversity*, *procreation*, *nurture*. Soupy bats his eyelids between phrases, is his only flaw. Harry hears a faint groan behind him: Ma Springer standing on her legs too long. Mrs Lubell over past Janice has removed a grubby-looking handkerchief from her purse and dabs at her face with it. Janice is smiling. There is a dark dent at the corner of her lips. With a little white hat on her head like a flower she looks Polynesian.

Ringingly Soupy addresses the rafters: 'If any of you can show just cause why they may not lawfully be married, speak now; or else for ever hold your peace.'

Peace. A pew creaks. The couple from Binghamton. Dead Fred

225

Springer. Ruth. Rabbit fights down a crazy impulse to shout out. His throat feels raw.

The minister now speaks to the couple direct. Nelson, from hanging lamely over on the side, his eyes murky in their sockets and the carnation crooked in his lapel, moves closer to the center, toward Pru. He is her height. The back of his neck looks so thin and bare above his collar. That whorl.

Pru has been asked a question. In an exceedingly small voice she says she will.

Now Nelson is being questioned and his father's itch to shout out, to play the disruptive clown, has become something else, a prickling at the bridge of his nose, a pressure in the two small ducts there.

*Woman, wife, covenant, love her, comfort her, honor and keep her, sickness, health, forsaking all others as long as you both shall live?*

Nelson in a voice midway in size between Soupy's and Pru's says he will.

And the burning in his tear ducts and the rawness scraping at the back of his throat have become irresistible, all the forsaken poor ailing paltry witnesses to this marriage at Harry's back roll forward in hoops of terrible knowing, an impalpable suddenly sensed mass of human sadness concentrated burningly upon the nape of Nelson's neck as he and the girl stand there mute while the rest of them grope and fumble in their thick red new prayer books after the name and number of a psalm announced; Soupy booms angelically above their scattered responses, *wife, a fruitful vine,* to which Rabbit cannot contribute, *the man who fears the Lord,* because he is weeping, weeping, washing out the words, the page, which has become as white and blank as the nape of Nelson's poor mute frail neck. Janice looks up at him in jaunty surprise under her white hat and Mrs Lubell with that wistful cleaning-lady smile passes over her grubby handkerchief. He shakes his head No, he is too big, he will overwhelm the cloth with his effluvia; then takes it anyway, and tries to blot this disruptive tide. There is this place the tears have unlocked that is endlessly rich, a spring.

'May you live to see your children's children,' Soupy intones

226

in his huge mellow encompassing fairy's voice. 'May peace be upon Israel,' he adds.

And outside, when it is done, the ring given, the vows taken in the shaky young voices under the towering Easter-colored window of Christ's space shot and the Lord's Prayer mumbled through and the pale couple turned from the requisite kiss (poor Nellie, couldn't he be just another inch taller?) to face as now legally and mystically one the little throng of their blood, their tribe, outside in the sickly afternoon, clouds having come with the breeze that flows toward evening, the ridiculous tears dried in long stains on Harry's face, then Mim comes into his arms again, a sisterly embrace, all sorts of family grief since the days he held her little hand implied, the future has come upon them darkly, his sole seed married, marriage that daily doom which she may never know; lean and crinkly in his arms she is getting to be a spinster, even a hooker can be a spinster, think of all she's had to swallow all these years, his baby sister, crying in imitation of his own tears, out here where the air quickly dries them, and the after-church smiles of the others flicker about them like butterflies born to live a day.

Oh this day, this holiday they have made just for themselves from a mundane Saturday, this last day of summer. What a great waste of gas it seems as they drive in procession to Ma Springer's house through the slanted streets of the town. Harry and Janice in the Corona follow Bessie's blue Chrysler in case the old dame plows into something, with Mim bringing Mrs Lubell in Janice's Maverick, its headlight still twisted, behind. 'What made you cry so much?' Janice asks him. She has taken off her hat and fiddled her bangs even in the rearview mirror.

'I don't know. Everything. The way Nellie looked from the back. The way the backs of kids' heads *trust* you. I mean they really *liked* that, this little dumb crowd of us gathered to watch.'

He looks sideways at her silence. The tip of her little tongue rests on her lower lip, not wanting to say the wrong thing. She says, 'If you're so full of tears you might try being less mean about him and the lot.'

'I'm not mean about him and the lot. He doesn't give a fuck about the lot, he just wants to hang around having you and your mother support him and the easiest way to put a face on that is to go through some sort of motions over at the lot. You know how much that caper of his with the convertibles cost the firm? Guess.'

'He says you got him so frustrated he went crazy. He says you knew you were doing it, too.'

'Forty-five hundred bucks, that was what those shitboxes cost. Plus now all the parts Manny's had to order and the garage time to fix 'em, you can add another grand.'

'Nelson said the TR sold right off.'

'That was a fluke. They don't make TRs anymore.'

'He says Toyotas have had their run at the market, Datsun and Honda are outselling them all over the East.'

'See, that's why Charlie and me don't want the kid over at the lot. He's full of negative thinking.'

'Has Charlie said he doesn't want Nelson over at the lot?'

'Not in so many words. He's too much of a nice guy.'

'I never noticed he was such a nice guy. Nice in that way. I'll ask him over at the house.'

'Now don't go lighting into poor Charlie, just because he's moved on to Melanie. I don't know what he's ever said about Nelson.'

'Moved *on*! Harry, it's been ten years. You *must* stop living in the past. If Charlie wants to make a fool of himself chasing after some twenty-year-old it couldn't matter to me less. Once you've achieved closure with somebody, all you have is good feelings for them.'

'What's this achieving closure? You've been looking at too many talk shows.'

'It's a phrase people use.'

'Those hussies you hang out with over at the club. Doris Kaufmann. Fuck her.' It stung him, that she thinks he lives in the past. Why should he be the one to cry at the wedding? Mr Nice Guy. Mr Tame Guy. To Hell with them. 'Well at least Charlie's avoiding marriage so that makes him less of a fool than Nelson,' he says, and switches on the radio to shut off their conversation. The four-thirty news: earthquake in Hawaii, kidnapping of two American businessmen in El Salvador, Soviet tanks patrolling the streets of Kabul in the wake of last Sunday's mysterious change of leadership in Afghanistan. In Mexico, a natural-gas pact with the United States signals possible long-term relief for the energy crisis. In California, ten days of brush fire have destroyed more acres than any such fire since 1970. In Philadelphia, publishing magnate Walter Annenberg has donated fifty thousand dollars to the Catholic Archdiocese to help defray costs of the controversial platform from which Pope John Paul the Second is scheduled to celebrate Mass on October the third. Annenberg, the announcer gravely concludes, is a Jew.

'Why did they tell us that?' Janice asks.

God, she is dumb still. The realization comforts him. He tells her, 'To make us alleged Christians feel lousy we've all been such cheapskates about the Pope's platform.'

'I must say,' Janice says, 'it does seem extravagant, to build such a thing you're only going to use once.'

'That's life,' Harry says, pulling up to the curb along Joseph Street. There are so many cars in front of number 89 he has to park halfway up the block, in front of the house where the butch ladies live. One of them, a hefty youngish woman wearing an Army surplus fatigue jacket, is lugging a big pink roll of foil-backed insulation up onto the front porch.

'My son got married today,' Harry calls out to her, on impulse.

His butch neighbor blinks and then calls back, 'Good luck to her.'

'Him.'

'I mean the bride.'

'O.K., I'll tell her.'

The expression on the woman's face, slit-eyed like a cigar-store Indian, softens a little; she sees Janice getting out of the car on the other side, and calls to her, in a shouting mood now, 'Jan, how do *you* feel about it?'

Janice is so slow to answer Harry answers for her, 'She feels great. Why wouldn't she?' What he can't figure out about these butch ladies is not why they don't like him but why he wants them to, why just the distant sound of their hammering has the power to hurt him, to make him feel excluded.

Somehow, this Slim person, driving a canary-yellow Le Car with its name printed a foot high on the side, has made it from the church with bride, groom, and Melanie ahead of Harry and Janice; and Ollie and Peggy too, in their cinnamon-brown '73 Dodge Dart with a Fiberglas-patched fender; and even Soupy has beat their time, because his snappy little black Opel Manta with vanity plate STJOHN is also parked by the curb this side of the maple that Ma Springer has been seeing from her front bedroom for over thirty years. These guests already crowd the living room, while this flustered little fat girl in a stab at a waitress uniform tries to carry around those hors d'oeuvres that are costing a fortune, muddled things that look like cheese melted on Taco Chips with a sprig of parsley added; Harry dodges through, elbows lifted out of old basketball habit in case somebody tries to put a move on him, to get the champagne in the kitchen. Bottles of Mumm's at twelve dollars apiece even at case price fill the whole second shelf of the fridge, stacked 69-style, foil heads by heavy hollow butts, beautiful. CHAMPAGNE PROVIDED AT SHOTGUN WEDDING, he thinks. *Angstrom Foots Bill.* Grace Stuhl's grandson turns out to be a big beefy kid, can't weigh less than two hundred fifty, with a bushy pirate's beard, and he has teeny weenies frying in a pan on the stove and something wrapped in bacon in the oven. Also a beer he took from the fridge open on the counter. The noise in the living room keeps growing, and the front door keeps opening. Stavros and the Murketts following Mim and Ma's brood in, and all the fools come gabbling when the first cork pops. Boy, it's like coming, it can't stop, the plastic hollow-stemmed champagne glasses Janice found at the Acme are on the round Chinese tray on the counter behind Grace Stuhl's grandson's beer, too far away for Harry to reach without some of the tawny foam spilling onto the linoleum. The glasses as he fills them remind him of the gold coins, precious down through the ages, and a latch inside him lifts to let his sorrow out. What the hell, we're all going down the chute together. Back in the living room, in front of the breakfront, Ma Springer proposes a nervous little toast she's worked up, ending with the Pennsylvania Dutch, '*Dir seid nur eins: halt es selle weg.*'

'What does that mean, Mom-mom?' Nelson asks, afraid something's being put over on him, such a child beside the blushing full-grown woman he's crazily gone and married.

230

'I was going to say,' Bessie says irritably. 'You are now one: keep it that way.'

Everybody cheers, and drinks, if they haven't already.

Grace Stuhl glides a step forward, into the circle of space cleared by the breakfront, maybe she was a great dancer fifty years ago, a certain type of old lady keeps her ankles and her feet small, and she is one. 'Or as they always used to say,' she proposes, *Bussie waiirt ows, kocha dut net*. Kissing wears out, cooking don't.'

The cheers are louder. Harry pops another bottle and settles on getting drunk. Those melted Taco Chips aren't so bad, if you can get them to your mouth before they break in your fingers, and the little fat girlfriend has an amazing bosom. All this ass, at least there's no shortage of that, it just keeps arriving. It seems an age since he lay awake disturbed by the entrance into this house of Pru Lubell, now Teresa Angstrom. Harry finds himself standing next to her mother. He asks her, 'Have you ever been to this part of the world before?'

'Just passing through from time to time,' she says, in a wisp of a voice he has to bend over to hear, as at a deathbed. How softly Pru had spoken her vows at the ceremony! 'My people are from Chicago, originally.'

'Well, your daughter does you proud,' he tells her. 'We love her already.' He sounds to himself, saying this, like an impersonator; life, just as we first thought, is playing grownup.

'Teresa tries to do the right thing,' her mother says. 'But it's never been easy for her.'

'It hasn't?'

'She takes after her father's people. You know, always going to extremes.'

'Really?'

'Oh yes. Stubborn. You daren't go against them.'

Her eyes widen. He feels with this woman as if he and she have been set to make a paper chain together, with inadequate glue, and the links keep coming unstuck. It is not easy to hear in this room. Soupy and that Slim are giggling now together.

'I'm sorry your husband can't be here,' Harry says.

'You wouldn't be if you knew him,' Mrs Lubell replies

231

serenely, and waggles her plastic glass as if to indicate how empty it is.

'Lemme get you some more.' Rabbit realizes with a shock that she is his proper date: old as she seems this woman is about his age and instead of naked in dreamland with stacked chicks like Cindy Murkett and Grace Stuhl's grandson's girlfriend he should be in mental bed with the likes of Mrs Lubell. He retreats into the kitchen to look after the champagne supply and finds Nelson and Melanie busy at the bottles. The countertop is strewn with those little wire cages each cork comes trapped in.

'Dad, there may not be *enough*,' Nelson whines.

These two. 'Why don't you kids switch to milk?' he suggests, taking a bottle from the boy. Heavy and green and cold, like money. The label engraved. His own poor dead dad never drank such bubbly in his life. Seventy years of beer and rusty water. To Melanie he says, 'That expensive bike of yours is still in the garage.'

'Oh I know,' she says, innocently staring. 'If I took it back to Kent someone would steal it.' Her bulging brown eyes show no awareness that he has been curt, feeling betrayed by her.

He tells her, 'You ought to go out and say hello to Charlie.'

'Oh, we've *said* hello.' Did she leave the motel room he was paying for to go shack up with Charlie? Harry can't follow it all. As if to make things right Melanie says, 'I'll tell Pru she can use the bike if she wants. It's wonderful exercise for those muscles.'

What muscles? Back in the living room, nobody has been kind enough to take his place beside the mother of the bride. As he refills her readily proffered glass he says to her, 'Thanks for the handkerchief. Back in the church.'

'It must be hard,' she says, looking up at him more cozily now, 'when there's only one.'

There's not only one, he wants to tell her, drunker than he thought. There's a dead little sister lying buried in the hill above us, and a long-legged girl roaming the farmland south of Galilee. Who does she remind him of, Mrs Lubell, when she flirts her head like that, looking up? Thelma Harrison, beside the pool. The Harrisons maybe should have been invited, but then you get into things like Buddy Inglefinger's feelings being hurt. And Ronnie would have been gross. The organist with the goatee (who invited *him*?) has joined Soupy and Slim now and something in the gaiety there leads the minister to remember his duty to others. He comes and joins Harry and the mother, a Christian act.

'Well,' Harry blurts to him. 'What's done is done, huh?'

Becky a skeleton by now, strange to think. The nightie they buried her in turned to cobwebs. Her little toenails and fingernails bits of confetti scattered on the satin.

Reverend Campbell's many small tobacco-darkened teeth display themselves in a complacent smile. 'The bride looked lovely,' he tells Mrs Lubell.

'She gets her height from her father's people,' she says. 'And her straight hair. Mine just curls naturally, where Frank's sticks up all over his head, he can never get it to lay down. Teresa's isn't quite that stubborn, since she's a girl.'

'Just lovely,' Soupy says, his smile getting a glaze.

Harry asks the man, 'How does that Opel of yours do for mileage?'

He takes out his pipe to address the question. 'Up and down on these hills isn't exactly optimum, is it? I'd say twenty-five, twenty-six at best. I do a lot of stopping and starting and with nothing but short trips the carbon builds up.'

Harry tells him, 'You know the Japanese make these cars even though Buick sells 'em. I heard they may not be importing any after the 1980 model. That's going to put a squeeze on parts.'

Soupy is amused, his twinkling eyes tell Mrs Lubell. Toward Harry he slides these eyes with mock severity and asks, 'Are you trying to sell me a Toyota?'

Mom getting to be a skeleton too, come to think of it. Those big bones in the earth like dinosaur bones.

'Well,' Harry says, 'we have a new little front-wheel drive called the Tercel, don't know where they get these names from but never mind, it gets over forty m.p.g. on the highway and is plenty of car for a single man.'

Waiting for the Resurrection. Suppose it never comes?

'But suppose I get *married*,' the small man protests, 'and have an e*nor*mous brood.'

'And indeed you should,' Mrs Lubell unexpectedly pipes up.

'The priests are leaving the church in droves because they've got the itch. All this sex, in the movies, books, everywhere, even on the television if you stay up late enough, no wonder they can't resist. Be grateful you don't have that conflict.'

'I have often thought,' Soupy tells her in a muted return of his great marrying voice, 'I might have made an excellent priest. I adore structure.'

Rabbit says, 'Just now in the car we heard that Annenberg down in Philadelphia gave the Catholics fifty thousand so they could put up this platform for the Pope without all this squawking from the civil liberties people.'

Soupy sniffs. 'Do you know how much publicity that fifty thousand is going to get him? It's a bargain.'

Slim and the organist seem to be discussing clothes, fingering each other's shirts. If he has to talk to the organist Harry can ask why he didn't play 'Here Comes the Bride.'

Mrs Lubell says, 'They wanted the Pope to come to Cleveland but I guess he had to draw the line somewhere.'

'I hear he's going to some farm way out in nowhere,' Harry says.

Soupy touches the mother of the bride on the wrist and tips his head so as to show to Harry the beginnings of his bald spot. 'Mr Annenberg is our former ambassador to the Court of St James in England. The story goes that when presenting his credentials to the Queen she held out her hand to be kissed and he shook it instead and said, "How're ya doin', Queen?"'

His growl is good. Mrs Lubell laughs outright, a titter jumps from her to her shame, for she quickly covers her mouth with her knuckles. Soupy loves it, giving her back a deep laugh as from a barrel-chested old fart. If that's the way they're going to carry on Rabbit figures he can leave them to it, and using Soupy as a pick makes his move away. He scouts over the gathered heads looking for an opening. It's always slightly dark in the living room, no matter how many lights are on or what the time of day, the trees and the porch cut down the sun. He'd like a house some day with lots of light, splashing in across smart square surfaces. Why bury yourself alive?

Ma Springer has Charlie locked in a one-on-one over by the

breakfront, her face puffy and purplish like a grape with the force of the unheard words she is urging into his ear; he politely bows his tidy head, once broad like a ram's but now whittled to an old goat's, nodding almost greedily, like a chicken pecking up grains of corn. Up front, silhouetted against the picture window, the Murketts are holding forth with the Fosnachts, old Ollie no doubt letting these new folks know what a clever musical fellow he is and Peggy gushing, backing him up, holding within herself the knowledge of what a shiftless rat he amounts to domestically. The Murketts belong to the new circle in Harry's life and the Fosnachts to the old and he hates to see them overlap; even if Peggy was a pretty good lay that time he doesn't want those dismal old high-school tagalongs creeping into his country-club set, yet he can see flattery is doing it, flattery and champagne, Ollie ogling Cindy (don't you wish) and Peggy making cow-eyed moos all over Murkett, she'll flop for anybody, Ollie must be very unsatisfying, one of those very thin reedy pricks probably. Harry wonders if he'd better not go over there and break it up, but foresees a wall of razzing he feels too delicate to push through, after all those tears in church, and remembering Becky and Pop and Mom and even old Fred who aren't here. Mim is on the sofa with Grace Stuhl and that other old biddy Amy, and Christ if they aren't having a quiet little ball, the two of them recalling Mim as a child to herself, the Diamond County accent and manner of expressing things making her laugh every minute, and she reminding them, all painted and done up in flowerpot foil, of the floozies they sit and watch all day and night on television, the old souls don't even know they are floozies, these celebrity women playing *Beat the Clock* or *Hollywood Squares* or giving Merv or Mike or Phil the wink sitting in those talk show soft chairs with their knees sticking up naked, they all got there on their backs, nobody cares anymore, the times have caught up with Mim and put her on the gray sofa with the church folk. Nelson and Melanie and Grace Stuhl's lout of a grandson are still in the kitchen and the girlfriend, after going around with the teeny weenies under her tits in a tricky little warmer with a ketchup dip, seems to have given up and joined them; they have in there the little portable Sony Janice sometimes watches the Carol Burnett reruns on as she makes supper, and from the sound of it – cheers, band music – these useless drunken kids have turned on the Penn State-Nebraska game. Meanwhile there's Pru in her champagne-colored wedding dress, the little wreath off her head now, standing alone over by the three-way lamp examining that heavy green glass bauble of Ma Springer's, with the teardrop of air sealed inside, turning it over and over under the wan light with her long pink hands, where a wedding ring now gleams. Laughter explodes from the Fosnacht-Murkett group, which Janice has joined. Webb pushes past Harry towards the kitchen, his fingers full of plastic glasses. 'How about that crazy Rose?' he says, going by, to say something.

Pete Rose has been hitting over .600 lately and only needs four more hits to be the first player ever to get two hundred hits in ten major league seasons. But it doesn't mean that much, the Phillies are twelve and a half games out. 'What a showboat,' Rabbit says, what they used to say about him, nearly thirty years ago.

Perhaps in her conspicuous pregnancy Pru is shy of pushing through the crowd to join the others of her generation in the kitchen. Harry goes to her side and stoops down to kiss her demure warm cheek before she is aware; champagne makes it easy. 'Aren't you supposed to kiss the bride?' he asks her.

She turns her head and gives him that smile that hesitates and then suddenly spreads, one corner tucked awry. Her eyes have taken green from contemplating the glass, that strange glossy egg Harry has more than once thought would be good to pound into Janice's skull. 'Of course,' she says. Held against her belly the bauble throws from its central teardrop a pale knife of light. He senses that she had been aware of his approaching in the side of her vision but had held still like a deer in danger. Among these strange people, her fate sealed by a ceremony, of course she is afraid. Rabbit tries to comfort his daughter-in-law: 'I bet you're beat. Don't you get sleepy as hell? As I remember it Janice did.'

'You feel clumsy,' Pru allows, and with both hands replaces the green glass orb on the round table that is like a wooden leaf all around the stem of the standing lamp. Abruptly she asks, 'Do you think I'll make Nelson happy?'

'Oh sure. The kid and I had a good long talk about it once. He thinks the world of you.'

'He doesn't feel trapped?'

'Well, frankly, that's what I was curious about, 'cause in his position I might. But honest to God, Teresa, it doesn't seem to bother him. From little on up he's always had this sense of fairness and in this case he seems to feel fair is fair. Listen. Don't you worry yourself. The only thing bothering Nelson these days is his old man.'

'He thinks the world of you,' she says, her voice very small, in case this echo is too impudent.

Harry snorts; he loves it when women sass him, and any sign of life from this one is gratefully received. 'It'll all work out,' he promises, though Teresa's aura of fright remains intense and threatens to spread to him. When the girl dares a full smile you see her teeth needed braces and didn't get them. The taste of champagne keeps reminding him of poor Pop. Beer and rusty water and canned mushroom soup.

'Try to have some fun,' he tells Pru, and cuts across the jammed room, around the boisterous Murkett-Fosnacht-Janice crowd, to the sofa where Mim sits between the two old ladies. 'Are you being a bad influence on my little sister?' he asks Amy Gehringer.

While Grace Stuhl laughs at this Amy struggles to get to her feet. 'Don't get up on my account,' Rabbit tells her. 'I just came over to see if I could get any of you anything.'

'What I need,' Amy grunts, still floundering, so he pulls her up, 'I must get for myself.'

'What's that?' he asks.

She looks at him a little glassily, like Melanie when he told her to drink milk. 'A call of nature,' Amy answers, 'you could say.'

Grace Stuhl holds up a hand that when he takes it, to pull her up, feels like a set of worn stones in a sack of the finest driest paper, strangely warm. 'I better say goodbye to Becky,' she says.

'She's over there talking the ear off Charlie Stavros,' Harry tells her.

'Yes, and probably saying too much by now.' She seems to know the subject; or does he imagine that? He drops down onto the sofa beside Mim wearily.

'So,' she says.

'Next I gotta marry you off,' he says.

'I've been asked, actually, now and then.'

'And whajja say?'

'At my age it seemed like too much trouble.'

'Your health good?'

'I make it good. No more smoking, notice?'

'How about those crazy hours you keep, staying up to watch Ol' Blue Eyes? I knew he was called Ol' Blue Eyes, by the way. I just didn't know *which* Ol' Blue Eyes, I thought a new one might have come along.' When he had called her long-distance to invite her to the wedding she said she had a date with a very dear friend to see Ol' Blue Eyes and he had asked, *Who's Ol' Blue Eyes?* She said *Sinatra, ya dummy, where've you been all your life?* and he answered, *You know where I've been, right here* and she said, *Yeah, it shows.* God, he loves Mim; in the end there's nothing to understand you like your own blood.

Mim says, 'You sleep it off during the day. Anyway I'm out of the fast lane now, I'm a businesswoman.' She gestures toward the other side of the room. 'What's Bessie trying to do, keep me from talking to Charlie? She's been at him an hour.'

'I don't know what's going on.'

'You never did. We all love you for it.'

'Drop dead. Hey how do you like the new Janice?'

'What's new about her?'

'Don't you see it? More confident. More of a woman, somehow.'

'Hard as a nut, Harry, and always will be. You were always feeling sorry for her. It was a wasted effort.'

'I miss Pop,' he suddenly says.

'You're getting more and more like him. Especially from the side.'

'He never got a gut like mine.'

'He didn't have the teeth for all those munchies you like.'

'You notice how this Pru looks like him a little? And Mom's big red hands. I mean, she seems more of an Angstrom than Nelson.'

'You guys like tough ladies. She's pulled off a trick I didn't think could be pulled off anymore.'

He nods, imagining through her eyes his father's toothless profile closing in upon his own. 'She's running scared.'

'And how about you?' Mim asks. 'What're *you* doing these days, to feed the inner man?'

'I play golf.'

'And still fuck Janice?'

'Sometimes.'

'You two. Mother and I didn't give it six months, the way she trapped you.'

'Maybe I trapped myself. And what's up with you? How does money work, out in Vegas? You really own a beauty parlor, or you just a front for the big guys?'

'I own thirty-five per cent. That's what I got for being a front for the big guys.'

He nods again. 'Sounds familiar.'

'You fucking anybody else? You can tell me, I'll be on that plane tomorrow. How about the broad bottom over there with the Chinesey eyes?'

He shakes his head. 'Nope. Not since Jill. That shook me up.'

'O.K., but ten years, that's not normal, Harry. You're letting them turn you into a patsy.'

'Remember,' he asks, 'how we used to go sledding on Jackson Road? I often think about it.'

'That happened maybe once or twice, it never *snows* around here, for Cry-eye. Come out to Lake Tahoe; now there's *snow*. We'll go over to Alta or Taos; you should see me ski. Come on out by yourself, we'll fix you up with somebody really nice. Blonde, brunette, redhead, you name it. Good clean small-town girl too; nothing crude.'

'Mim,' he says, blushing, 'you're the limit,' and thinks of telling her how much he loves her, but there is a commotion at the front door.

Slim and the organist are leaving together and they encounter there a dowdy couple who have been ringing the disconnected doorbell for some time. From the look of them they are selling encyclopaedias, except that people don't do that in pairs, or going door-to-door for the Jehovah's Witnesses, except that instead of *The Watchtower* they are holding on to a big silver-wrapped wedding present. This is the couple from Binghamton. They took the wrong turn off the Northeast Extension and found themselves lost in West Philadelphia. The woman sheds tears of relief and exhaustion once inside the foyer. 'Blocks and blocks of blacks,' the man says, telling their story, still staggered by the wonder of it.

'*Oh*,' Pru cries from across the room, 'Uncle Rob!' and throws herself into his arms, home at last.

Ma Springer has made the Poconos place available to the young couple for a honeymoon in these golden last weeks of warm weather – the birches beginning to turn, the floats and canoes pulled in from the lake. All of it wasted on the kid, they'll be lucky if he doesn't burn the cottage down frying his brain and his genes with pot. But it's not Harry's funeral. Now that Nelson is married it's like a door has been shut in his mind, a debt has been finally paid, and his thoughts are turning again to that farm south of here where another child of his may be walking, walking and waiting for her life to begin.

One evening when nothing she likes is on television Ma calls a little conference in the living room, easing her legs wrapped around with flesh-colored bandages (a new thing her doctor has prescribed; when Harry tries to visualize an entire creature made out of the flesh the bandage manufacturers are matching, it would make the Hulk look healthy) up on the hassock and letting the man of the house have the Barcalounger. Janice sits on the sofa with a post-dinner nip of some white creamy poison fermented from coconut milk the kids have brought into the house, looking girlish beside her mother, with her legs tucked up under her. Nice taut legs. She's kept those and he has to take his hat off to her, tiddly half the time or not. What more can you ask of a wife in a way than that she stick around and see with you what happens next?

Ma Springer announces, 'We must settle now what to do with Nelson.'

'Send him back to college,' Harry says. 'She had an apartment out there, they can both move into one.'

'He doesn't want to go,' Janice tells them, not for the first time.

'And why the hell not?' Harry asks, the question still exciting to him, though he knows he's beaten.

'Oh Harry,' Janice says wearily, 'nobody knows. You didn't go to college, why should he?'

'That's the reason. Look at me. I don't want him to live my life. I'm living it and that's enough.'

'Darling, I said that from his point of view, not to argue with you. Of course Mother and I would have preferred he had graduated from Kent and not got so involved with this secretary. But that's not the way it is.'

'He can't go back to college with a wife as if nothing happened,' Bessie states. 'They knew her out there as one of the employees and I think he'd be embarrassed. He needs a job.'

'Great,' Harry says, enjoying being perverse, letting the women do the constructive thinking. 'Maybe his father-in-law can get him a job out in Akron.'

'You saw the mother,' Ma Springer says. 'There's no help there.'

'Uncle Rob was a real swinger, though. What does he do up in the shoe factory? Punch the holes for the laces?'

Janice imitates her mother's flat, decided rhythm. 'Harry. Nelson must come to work at the lot.'

'Oh Christ. Why? *Why?* This is a huge country. It has old factories, new factories, farms, stores, why can't the lazy brat get a job at one of *them?* All those summers he was back from Kent he never got a job. He hasn't had a job since that paper route when he was fourteen and needed to buy records.'

Janice says, 'Going up to the Poconos a month every summer meant he couldn't get anything too serious, he used to complain about it. Besides, he did do some things. He babysat for a time there, and he helped that high-school teacher who was building his own home, with the solar panels and the cellar full of rocks that stored heat.'

'Why doesn't he go into something like that? That's where the future is, not selling cars. Cars have had it. The party's over. It's going to be all public transportation twenty years from now. Ten years from now, even. Why doesn't he take a night course and learn how to program a computer? If you look at the want ads, that's all there is, computer programmers and electronic engineers. Remember when Nelson rigged up all those hi-fi components and even had speakers hooked up on the sunporch? He could do all that, what happened?'

'What happened is, he grew up,' Janice says, finishing off the coconut liqueur, tilting her head back so far her throat shows the pale rings that when her head is held normally are wrinkles. Her tongue probes the bottom of the glass. With Nelson and Pru part of the household, Janice drinks more freely; they sit around getting silly and waiting up for Johnny Carson or *Saturday Night Live*, her smoking has gotten back up to over a pack a day in spite of Harry's nagging to get her to quit. Now in this discussion she's acting as if he is some natural disturbance they must let boringly run its course.

He is getting madder. 'I *off*ered to take him on in Service, there's the department they can always use an extra man, Manny'd have him trained as a full-fledged mechanic in no time. You know what mechanics pull down an hour now? Seven bucks, and it costs me over eight to pay 'em that what with all this fringe stuff. And once they can work faster than the flat rate they get bonuses. Our top men take home over fifteen thousand a year and a couple of them aren't much older than Nelson.'

'Nelson doesn't want,' Janice says, 'to be a grease monkey any more than you do.'

'Happiest days of my life,' he lies, 'were spent working with my hands.'

'It isn't easy,' Ma Springer decides to tell them, 'being old, and a widow. In everything I do, after I pray about it, I try to ask myself, "Now what would Fred want?" And I know with absolute certainty in this instance he would want little Nellie to come work on the lot if that's what the boy desired. A lot of these young men now wouldn't want such a job, they don't have the thick skins a salesman has to have, and it's not so glamorous, unless you began by following the hind end of a horse around all day the way the people of my generation did.'

Rabbit bristles, impatient. 'Bessie, every generation has its problems, we all start behind the eight ball. Face the facts. How much you gonna pay Nelson? How much salary, how much commission? You know what a dealer's profit margin is. Three per cent, three lousy little per cent, and that's being cut down to nothing by a lot of new overhead you can't pass on the customer with these fixed prices Toyota has. Oil going up takes everything up with it; in the five years I've been in charge heating costs have doubled, electricity is way up, delivery costs are up, plus all these social security hikes and unemployment to pay so the bums in this country won't have to give up their yacht, half the young people in the country go to work just enough to collect unemployment, and now the interest on the inventory is going out of sight. It's just like the Weimar thing, people's savings are being washed right down the tube, everybody agrees there's a recession coming to curl your hair. The economy is *shot*, Ma, we can't hack it, we don't have the discipline the Japs and Germans do, and on top of this you want me to hire a piece of dead weight who happens to be my son.'

'In answer to your question,' Ma says, grunting a little as she shifts the sorer leg on the hassock, 'the minimum wage is going to be three-ten an hour so if he works forty hours a week you'll have to give him a hundred twenty-five a week, and then the bonuses you'd have to figure on the usual formula, isn't it now something like twenty per cent of the gross profit on the sale, and then going to twenty-five over a certain minimum? I know it used to be a flat five per cent of the net amount of the sale, but Fred said you couldn't do that with foreign cars for some reason.'

'Bessie, with all respect, and I love you, but you are crazy. You pay Nelson five hundred a month to start with and set commission on top of that he's going to be taking home a thousand a month for bringing in the company only twenty-five hundred. To pay Nelson that amount it should mean he sells, depending on the proportion of new to used, between seven to ten cars a month for an agency that doesn't move twenty-five a month overall!'

'Well, maybe with Nelson there you'll move more,' Ma says.

'*Dreamer*,' Harry says to her. 'Detroit's getting tooled up finally to turn out subcompacts a dime a dozen, and there's going to be stiffer import taxes any day now. Twenty-five a month is optimum, honest to God.'

'The people that remember Fred will like to see Nelson there,' she insists.

Janice says, 'Nelson says the mark-up on the new Toyotas is at least a thousand dollars.'

'That's a loaded model, with all the extras. The people who buy

Toyotas aren't into extras. Basic Corollas are what we sell mostly, four to one. And even on the bigger models the carrying costs amount to a couple hundred per unit with money going to Hell the way it is.'

She is obstinate and dumb. 'A thousand a car,' she says, 'means he has to sell only five a month, the way you figure it.'

'What about Jake and Rudy!' he cries. 'How could the kid sell even five without cutting into Jake and Rudy? Listen, if you two want to know who your loyal employees are, it's Jake and Rudy. They work all the shit hours you ask 'em to, on the floor nights and weekends, they moonlight to make up for all the low hours you tell 'em to stay away, Rudy runs a little bike repair shop out of his garage, in this day and age, everybody else begging for handouts, they're still taking a seventy-five base and a one-fifty draw. You can't turn guys like that out in the cold.'

'I wasn't thinking so much of Jake and Rudy,' Ma Springer says, with a frown resting one ankle on top of the other. 'How much now does Charlie make?'

'Oh no you don't. We've been through this. Charlie goes, I go.'

'Just for my information.'

'Well, Charlie pulls down around three-fifty a week – rounds out to over twenty thousand a year with the bonuses.'

'Well, then,' Ma Springer pronounces, easing the ankle back to where it was, 'you'd actually save money, taking Nelson on instead. He has this interest in the used cars, and that's Charlie's department, hasn't it been?'

'Bessie, I can't believe this. Janice, talk to her about Charlie.'

'We've talked, Harry. You're making too much of it. Mother has talked to me and I thought it might do Charlie good to make a change. She also talked to Charlie and he agreed.'

Harry is disbelieving. '*When* did you talk to Charlie?'

'At the reception,' Ma Springer admits. 'I saw you looking over at us.'

'Well my God, whajja say?'

This is some old lady, Rabbit thinks, sneakers, Ace bandages, cotton dress up over her knees, puffy throat, funny silver-browed eyeglasses, and all. Once in a while, in the winters since old Fred cashed in, she has visited the lot wearing the mink coat he gave her for their twenty-fifth wedding anniversary, and there was a glitter on that fur like needles of steel, like a signal crackling out of mission control. She says, 'I asked him how his health was.'

'The way we worry about Charlie's health you'd think he was in a wheelchair.'

'Janice has told me, even ten years ago he was taking nitro-glycerine. For a man only in his thirties then, that's not good.'

'Well what did *he* say, how his health was?'

'Fair,' Ma Springer answers, giving it the local two syllables, *Fai-ir*. 'Janice herself claims you complain he doesn't do his share anymore, just sits huddled at the desk playing with paperwork he should leave for Mildred to do.'

'Did I say all that?' He looks at Janice, his betrayer. He has always thought of her darkness as a Springer trait but of course old man Springer was fair, thin-skinned pink; it is her mother's blood, the Koerners', that has determined her coloring.

She flicks her cigarette at the ashtray impatiently. 'More than once,' she says.

'Well I didn't mean your mother should go fire the guy.'

'Fire was never used as a word,' Ma Springer says. 'Fred would never have fired Charlie, unless his personal life got all out of hand.'

'You got to go pretty far to get out of hand these days,' Harry says, resenting that this is the case.

Ma Springer rolls her weight uncomfortably on the sofa. 'Well I must say, this chasing that girl out to Ohio –'

'He took her to Florida, too,' Harry says, so quickly both women stare at him with their button-black eyes. It's true, it galls him more than it should, since he could never warm to Melanie himself and had nowhere to take her anyhow.

'We talked about Florida,' Ma Springer says. 'I asked him if now that winter's coming he mightn't be better off down there. Amy Gehringer's son-in-law, that used to work in an asbestos plant in New Jersey until they got that big scare, has retired down there on the compensation, and he's under fifty. She says he tells her there are a lot of young people coming down there now, to get away from the oil crisis, it's not just the old people like in all the jokes, and of course there are jobs to be had there too. Charlie's clever. Fred recognized that from the start.'

'He has this mother, Ma. An old Greek lady who can't speak English and who's never been out of Brewer hardly.'

'Well maybe it's time she was. You know people think we old people are such sticks in the mud but Grace Stuhl's sister, older than she is, mind you, and buried two husbands right in the country, went out to visit her son in Phoenix and loved it so she's bought her own little condominium and even, Grace was telling me, her burial plot, that's how much she pulled up her roots.'

'Charlie's not like you, Harry,' Janice explains. 'He's not scared of change.'

He could take that green glass egg and in one stride be at the sofa and pound it down into her dense skull. Instead he ignores her, saying to Ma, 'I still haven't heard exactly what you said to Charlie, and he said to you.'

'Oh, we reminisced. We talked about the old days with Fred and we agreed that Fred would want Nellie to have a place at the lot. He was always one for family, Fred, even when family let him down.'

That must mean him, Rabbit thinks. Letting that shifty little wheeler-dealer down is about the last thing on his conscience.

'Charlie understands family,' Janice interposes, in that smooth matronly voice she can do now but that sounds phony at this moment. 'All the time I was, you know, seeing him, he was absolutely ready to stand aside and have me go back.'

Bragging about her affair to her own mother. The world is running down fast.

'And so,' Ma Springer sighs – she is wearying of this, her legs hurt and aren't improving, old people need their privacy – 'we tried to come to an understanding of what Fred would want and came up with this idea of a leave for Charlie, for six months with half pay, and then at the end we'd see how Nellie was working out. In the meantime if the offer of another job comes Charlie's way he's to be free to take it, and then we'll settle at that point with two months' pay as a bonus, plus whatever his Christmas bonus would be for all of 1979. This wasn't just worked out at the party, I was over there today while you were playing golf.'

He had been carrying an 83 into the last hole and then hooked into the creek and took an 8. It seems he'll never break 90 there, unless he does it in his sleep. Webb Murkett's relaxed swing is getting on his nerves. 'Sneaky,' he says. 'I thought you didn't trust yourself to drive the Chrysler in Brewer traffic anymore.'

'Janice drove me over.'

'Aha.' He asks his wife, 'How did Charlie like seeing you there on this mission of mercy?'

'He was sweet. This has all been between him and Mother. But he knows Nelson is our son. Which is more than you seem to.'

'No, no, I know he is, that's the trouble,' Harry tells her. To old lady Springer he says, 'So you're paying Charlie thousands to hand Nelson a job he probably can't do. Where's the savings for the firm in that? And you're going to lose sales without Charlie, I don't have half the contacts around town he does. Not just Greeks, either. Being single he's been in a lot of bars, that's where you win people's trust around here.'

'Well, it may be.' Ma Springer gets herself to her feet and stamps each one softly on the carpet, testing if either is asleep. 'It may all be a mistake, but in this life you can't always be afraid of mistakes. I never liked that about Charlie, that he was unwilling to get married. It bothered Fred too, I know. Now I must get myself upstairs and see my Angels. Though it's not been the same since Farrah left.'

'Don't I get a vote?' Harry asks, almost yelling, strapped as he feels into the Barcalounger. 'I vote against it. I don't *want* to be bothered with Nelson over there.'

'Well,' Ma says, and in her long pause he has time to appreciate how big she is, how broad from certain angles, like a tree trunk seen suddenly in terms of all the toothpicks it would make, all those meals and days gone into this bulk, the stiff heavy seesaw of her hips, the speckled suet of her arms, 'as I understand Fred's will, he left the lot to me and Janice, and I think we're of a mind.'

'Two against three, Harry, in any case,' Janice says, with a winning smile.

'Oh screw you,' he says. 'Screw Springer Motors. I suppose if I don't play dead doggie you two'll vote to can me too.'

They don't deny it. While Ma's steps labor up the staircase, Janice, beginning to wear that smudged look she gets when the day's intake catches up with her, gets to her feet and tells him confidentially, 'Mother thought you'd take it worse than you did. Want anything from the kitchen? This CocoRibe is really addictive.'

October first falls on a Monday. Autumn is starting to show its underside: out of low clouds like a row of torn mattresses a gray rain is knocking the leaves one by one off the trees. That lonely old maple behind the Chuck Wagon across Route 111 is bare now down to its lower branches, which hang on like a monk's fringe. Not a day for customers: Harry and Charlie gaze together through the plate glass windows where the posters now say COMING, ALL NEW COROLLAS · *New 1.8-liter engine · New aerodynamic styling · Aluminum wheels on SR5 models · Removable sunroof/moonroof · Best selling car in the world!* Another paper banner proclaims THE COROLLA TERCEL · *First Front-Wheel Drive Toyota · Toyota's Lowest Price & Highest Mileage · 33 Est. MPG · 43 EPA Estimated Highway MPG.* 'Well,' Harry says, after clearing his throat, 'the Phillies went out with a bang.' By shutting out the Montreal Expos on the last day of the season, 2–0, they enabled Pittsburgh to win the championship of the National League East.

'I was rooting for the Expos,' Charlie says.

'Yeah, you hate to see Pittsburgh win again. They're so fucking jivey. All that Family crap.'

Stavros shrugs. 'Well, a team of blacks like that, you need a slogan. They all grew up on television commercials, the box was the only mother they had. That's the tragedy of blacks these days.'

It relieves Harry, to hear Charlie talk. He came in half expecting to find him crushed. 'At least the Eagles screwed the Steelers,' he says. 'That felt good.'

'They were lucky. That fumble going into the end zone. Bradshaw you can expect to throw some interceptions, but you don't expect Franco Harris to fumble going into the end zone.'

Harry laughs aloud, in remembered delight. 'How about that barefoot rookie kicker the Eagles got? Wasn't that beautiful?'

Charlie says, 'Kicking isn't football.'

'A forty-eight-yard field goal barefoot! That guy must have a big toe like a rock.'

'For my money they can ship all these old soccer players back

248

to Argentina. The contact in the line, that's football. The Pit. That's where the Steelers will get you in the end. I'm not worried about the Steelers.'

Harry sniffs anger here and changes the subject, looking out at the weather. Drops on the glass enlarge and then abruptly dart down, dodgingly, leaving trails. The way he wept. Ever since earliest childhood, his consciousness dawning by the radiators in the old half-house on Jackson Road, it has been exciting for Harry to stand near a window during a rain, his face inches from the glass and dry, where a few inches away it would be wet. 'Wonder if it's going to rain on the Pope.' The Pope is flying into Boston that afternoon.

'Never. He'll just wave his arms and the sky'll be full of blue-birds. Bluebirds and horseshit.'

Though no Catholic, Harry feels this is a bit rude; no doubt about it, Charlie is prickly this morning. 'Ja see those crowds on television? The Irish went wild. One crowd was over a million, they said.'

'Micks are dumb,' Charlie says, and starts to turn away. 'I gotta get hot on some NV-1s.'

Harry can't let him go. He says, 'And they gave the old Canal back last night.'

'Yeah. I get sick of the news. This country is sad, everybody can push us around.'

'You were the guy wanted to get out of Vietnam.'

'That was sad too.'

'Hey.'

'Yeah?'

'I hear you had a talk with Ma Springer.'

'The last of a long series. She's not so sad. She's tough.'

'Any thoughts about where you're going to be going?' Nelson and Pru are due back from the Poconos Friday.

'Nowhere, for a while. See a few movies. Hit a few bars.'

'How about Florida, you're always talking about Florida.'

'Come on. I can't ask the old lady to move down there. What would she do, play shuffleboard?'

'I thought you said you had a cousin taking care of her now.'

'Gloria. I don't know, something's cooking there. She and her husband may be getting back together. He doesn't like scrambling his own eggs in the morning.'

'Oh. Sorry.' Harry pauses. 'Sorry about everything.'

Charlie shrugs. 'What can *you* do?'

This is what he wants to hear; relief bathes him like a kind of light. When you feel better, you see better; he sees all the papers, wrappers and take-out cup lids that have blown across the highway from the Chuck Wagon, lying in the bushes just outside the window, getting soaked. He says, 'I could quit myself.'

'That's crazy, champ. What would you do? Me, I can sell anywhere, that's no worry. Already I've had some feelers. News travels fast in this business. It's a scared business.'

'I told her, "Ma, Charlie's the heart of Springer Motors. Half the clients come in because of him. More than half." '

'I appreciate your putting in a word. But you know, there comes a time.'

'I guess.' But not for Harry Angstrom. Never, never.

'How about Jan? What'd *she* have to say about giving me the gate?'

A tough question. 'Not much, that I heard. You know she can't stand up to the old lady; never could.'

'If you want to know what I think cooked my goose, it was that trip with Melanie. That cooled it with both the Springer girls.'

'You think Janice still cares that much?'

'You don't stop caring, champ. You still care about that little girl whose underpants you saw in kindergarten. Once you care, you always care. That's how stupid we are.'

A rock in space, is the image these words bring to Rabbit's mind. He is interested in space, and scans the paper every day for more word on these titanic quasars on the edge of everything, and in the Sunday section studies the new up-close photos of Jupiter, expecting to spot a clue that all those scientists have missed; God might have a few words to say yet. In the vacuum of the heart love falls forever. Janice jealous of Charlie, we get these ideas and can't let go, it's been twenty years since he slept with Ruth but whenever in some store downtown or along Weiser he sees from behind a woman with gingery hair bundled up carelessly behind, a few loops flying loose, his heart bumps up. And Nelson, he was young at the time but you're never too young to fall, he loved Jill and come to think of it Pru has some of the hippie style, long hair flat down the back and that numb look daring you to hurt her, though Jill of course was of a better class, she was no Akron steamfitter's daughter. Harry says to Charlie, 'Well at least now you can run out to Ohio from time to time.'

Charlie says, 'There's nothing out there for me. Melanie's more like a daughter. She's smart, you know. You ought to hear her go on about transcendental meditation and this crazy Russian philosopher. She wants to go on and get a Ph.D. if she can worm the money out of her father. He's out there on the West Coast fucking Indian maidens.'

Coast to coast, Rabbit thinks, we're one big funhouse. It's done with mirrors. 'Still,' he tells Charlie, 'I wish I had some of your freedom.'

'You got freedom you don't even use. How come you and Jan keep living in that shabby old barn with her mother? It's not doing Jan any good, it's keeping her childish.'

Shabby? Harry had never thought of the Springer place as shabby: old-fashioned maybe but with big rooms full of the latest and best goods, just the way he saw it the first time, when he began to take Janice out, the summer they were both working at Kroll's. Everything looked new and smelled so clean, and in the side room off the living room a long wrought-iron table held a host of tropical plants, a jungle of their own that seemed the height of luxury. Now the table stands there hollow and you can see where it's stained the hardwood floor with rusty drippings. And he thinks of the gray sofa and the wallpaper and watercolors that haven't changed since the days he used to pick Jan up for a night of heavy petting in the back of Pop's old De Soto and maybe it is shabby. Ma doesn't have the energy she did and what she does with all her money nobody knows. Not buy new furniture. And now that it's fall the copper beech outside their bedroom window is dropping its nuts, the little triangular seedpods explode and with all the rustling and crackling it's not so easy to sleep. That room has never been ideal. 'Childish, huh?'

'Speaking of which,' Charlie says, 'remember those two kids who came in at the beginning of the summer, the girl that turned you on? The boy came back Saturday, while you were out on the golf course, I can't think of his name.'

'Nunemacher.'

'Right. He bought that orange Corolla liftback with standard transmission out on the lot. No trade-in, and these new models coming in, I quoted him two hundred off the list. I thought you'd want me to be nice to him.'

'Right. Was the girl with him?'

'Not that I could see.'

'And he didn't trade in that County Squire?'

'You know these farmers, they like to keep junk in their yards. Probably hitch it up to a band saw.'

'My God,' Harry says. 'Jamie bought the orange Corolla.'

'Well come on, it's not that much of a miracle. I asked him why he waited so long and he said he thought if he waited to fall the '79s would be down in price a little. And the dollar would be worth less. The yen too as it turns out.'

'When's he taking delivery?'

'He said around noon tomorrow. That's one of the NV-1s I gotta do.'

'Shit. That's when I have Rotary.'

'The girl wasn't with him, what do you care? You talk about me; she was younger than Melanie. That girl might have been as young as sixteen, seventeen.'

'Nineteen is what she'd be,' Rabbit says. 'But you're right. I don't care.' Rain all around them leads his heart upward by threads; he as well as Charlie has his options.

Tuesday after Rotary with the drinks still working in him Harry goes back to the lot and sees the orange Corolla gone and can hardly focus with happiness, God has kissed him out of space. Around four-thirty, with Rudy on the floor and Charlie over in Allenville trying to wrap up a used-car package with a dealer there to clear the books a little before Nelson takes over, he eases out of his office and down the corridor and through the shop where Manny's men are still whacking metal but their voices getting louder as the bliss of quitting time approaches and out the back door, taking care not to dirty his shirt cuffs on the crash bar, and out into air. Paraguay. On this nether portion of the asphalt the Mercury with its mashed-in left side and fender and grille still waits upon a decision. It turns out Charlie was able to unload the repaired Royale for thirty-six hundred to a young doctor from Royersford, he wasn't even a regular doctor but one of these homeopathic or holistic doctors as they call it now who looks at your measles and tells you to eat carrots or just hum at a certain pitch for three hours a day, he must be doing all right because he snapped up that old Olds, said a guy he admired at college had driven one like it and he'd always wanted one just that color, evidently – that purply-red nail-polish color. Harry squeezes himself into his Corona the color of tired tomato soup and slides out of the lot softly and heads down 111 the way away from Brewer, toward Galilee. Springer Motors well behind him, he turns on the radio and that heavy electrified disco beat threatens to pop the stereo speakers. Tinny sounds, wiffling sounds, sounds like a kazoo being played over the telephone come at him from the four corners of the vinyl-upholstered interior, setting that hopeful center inside his ribs to jingling. He thinks back to the Rotary luncheon and Eddie Pastorelli of Pastorelli Realty with his barrel chest and stiff little bow legs now, that used to do the 440 in less than fifty seconds, giving them a slide show on the proposed planned development of the upper blocks of Weiser, which were mostly parking lots and bars these days, and little businesses like vacuum-cleaner repair and pet supplies that hadn't had the capital to move out to the malls, Eddie trying to tell them that some big glass boxes and a corkscrew-ramped concrete parking garage are going to bring the shoppers back in spite of all the spic kids roaming around with transistors glued to their ears and knives up their wrists. Harry has to laugh, he remembers Eddie when he was a second-string guard for Hemmigtown High, a meaner grease-ball never stayed out of reform school. Donna Summer comes on singing, *Dim all the lights sweet darling* ... When you see pictures of her she's much less black than you imagine, a thin-cheeked yellow staring out at you like what are you going to do about it. The thing about those Rotarians, if you knew them as kids you can't stop seeing the kid in them, dressed up in fat and baldness and money like a cardboard tuxedo in a play for high-school assembly. How can you respect the world when you see it's being run by a bunch of kids turned old? That's the joke Rabbit always enjoys at Rotary. With a few martinis inside him Eddie can be funny as hell, when he told that joke about the five men in the airplane the tip of his nose bent down like it was on a little string and his laugh came out as an old woman's wheeze. *Knapsack! hee hee hee*. Rabbit must try to remember and try it out on the gang at the Flying Eagle. Five men: a hippie, a priest, a policeman, and Henry Kissinger, the smartest man in the world. But who was the fifth? Donna Summer says to turn her brown body white, at least that's what he thinks she's said, you can't be sure with all this disco *wowowow*, some doped-up sound engineer wiggling the knobs to give that sound, the words don't matter, it's that beat pushed between your ribs like a knife, making the soul jingle.

Houses of sandstone. A billboard pointing to a natural cave. He wonders who goes there anymore, natural caves a thing of the past, like waterfalls. Men in straw hats. Women with not even their ankles showing. Natural wonders. That smartass young female announcer – he hasn't heard her for a while, he thought maybe the station had fired her, too sassy or got pregnant – comes on and says that the Pope has addressed the UN and is stopping in Harlem on his way to Yankee Stadium. Harry saw the cocky little guy on television last night, getting soaked in Boston in his white robes, you had to admire his English, about his seventh language, and who was the deadpan guy standing there holding the umbrella over him? Some Vatican bigwig, but Pru didn't seem to know any more than he did, what's the good of being raised a Catholic? In Europe, gold rose today to a new high of four hundred forty-four dollars an ounce while the dollar slipped to new lows. The station fades and returns as the road twists among the hilly fields. Harry calculates, up eighty dollars in less than three weeks, thirty times eighty is two thousand four hundred, when you're rich you get richer, just like Pop used to say. In some of the fields the corn stands tall, others are stubble. He glides through the ugly string town of Galilee, on the lookout for the orange Corolla. No need to ask at the post office this time. The vegetable stand is closed for the season. The pond has some geese on it, he doesn't remember those, migrating already, the green little turds they leave all over the fairways, maybe that was the reason that doctor ... He turns off the radio. BLANKENBILLER. MUTH. BYER. He parks on the same widened spot of red dirt road shoulder. His heart is pounding, his hands feel swollen and numb, resting on the steering wheel. He turns off the ignition, digging himself in deeper. It's not as if he's doing anything illegal. When he gets out of the car, the pigsty whiff isn't in the air, the wind is from the other direction, and there is no insect hum. They have died, millions. Across the silence cuts the far-off whine and snarl of a chain saw. The new national anthem. *Oho say can you saw* ... The woods are a half-mile off and can't be part of the Byer farm. He begins to trespass. The hedgerow that has swallowed the stone wall is less leafy, he is less hidden. A cool small wind slips through the tangled black gum and wild cherry and licks his hands. Poison ivy leaves have turned, a Mercurochrome red, some of them half-dyed as if dipped. As he ventures down through the old orchard, a step at a time, he treads on fallen apples lying thick in the grass grown to hay. Mustn't turn an ankle, lie up here and rot as well. Poor trees, putting out all this wormy fruit for nothing. Perhaps not nothing from their point of view, when men didn't exist they were doing the same. Strange thought. Harry looks down upon the farmhouse now, the green door, the birdbath on its pale blue pillar. Smoke is rising from the chimney; the nostalgic smell of burning wood comes to him. So close, he gets behind a dying apple tree with a convenient fork at the height of his head. Ants are active in the velvety light brown rot inside the trunk, touching noses, telling the news, hurrying on. The tree trunk is split open like an unbuttoned overcoat but still carries life up through its rough skin to the small round leaves that tremble where the twigs are young and smooth. Space feels to drop away not only in front of him but on all sides, even through the solid earth, and he wonders what he is doing here in his good beige suit, his backside exposed to any farmer with a shotgun who might be walking along in the field behind him and his face posed in this fork like a tin can up for target practice were anybody to look up from the buildings below, he who has an office with his name on the door and CHIEF SALES REPRESENTATIVE on his business cards and who a few hours back was entertaining other men in suits with the expense and complications of his son's wedding, the organist going off with this Slim and the couple turning up so late he thought they were Jehovah's Witnesses; and for some seconds of panic cannot answer himself why, except that out here, in the air, nameless, he feels purely alive. Then he remembers: he hopes to glimpse his daughter. And what if he were to gather all his nerve and go down and knock at the green door in its deep socket of wall and she were to answer? She would be in jeans this time of year, and a sweat-shirt or sweater. Her hair would be less loose and damp than in its summer do, maybe pulled back and held by a rubber band. Her eyes, widely spaced, would be pale blue little mirrors.

*Hi. You don't remember me –*

*Sure I do. You're the car dealer.*

*I'm more than that, I think.*

*Like what?*

*Is your mother's name by any chance Ruth Byer?*

*Well . . . yes.*

*And has she ever talked to you about your father?*

*My father's dead. He used to run the school buses for the township.*

*That wasn't your father. I'm your father.*

And that broad pale face in which he saw his own would stare at him furious, disbelieving, fearful. And if he did at last make her believe, she would be angry at him for taking from her the life she had lived and substituting for it one she could never live now. He sees that these fields where his seed may have taken hold hold nothing of harvest for him but, if he seize it, the space at his back to escape in. Yet he stands, in his tired summer suit – time to have it cleaned and stored in the big plastic clothes bag until next April – transfixed by the motionlessness of the scene below, but for the rising smoke. His heart races in steady alarm at his having strayed so far off track. You have a life and there are these volumes on either side that go unvisited; some day soon as the world winds he will lie beneath what he now stands on, dead as those insects whose sound he no longer hears, and the grass will go on growing, wild and blind.

His idling heart jumps at a rustle close behind him in the orchard. He has lifted his arms and framed the first words of his self-explanation before he sees that the other presence is not a person but a dog, an old-looking collie with one red eye and its coat loaded with burrs. Rabbit is uncomfortable with dogs anyway and knows collies to be especially nervous and prone to attack, Lassie to the contrary. This dog is blacker than Lassie. It stands the length of a long putt away, head cocked, the hair behind its ears electric, set to bark.

'Hi,' Harry says, his voice a hoarse shade above a whisper, lest it carry down to the house.

The collie cocks it narrow head at a sharper tilt, as if to favor the sore eye, and the long white hair around its throat like a bib riffles where the breeze flattens it.

'You a good doggie?' Harry asks. He envisions the distance to the car, sees himself running, the dog at his legs in two seconds, the tearing of cloth, the pointed yellowish canines, the way dogs lift that black split upper lip to bare the little front teeth in fury; he feels his ankle pinned as if between two grinding cogwheels, his fall, his arm up in a futile attempt to save his face.

But the dog makes a decision in its narrow skull. Its dropped tail cautiously wags, and it lopes forward with that horrible silent lightness of four-footed animals through the orchard grass. It sniffs at Harry's knees and then leans against his legs, allowing its neck to be scratched as Harry keeps up a whispered patter. 'Nice boy, good girl, where'd you get all these burrs, *baaad* burrs.' Don't let them smell your terror. You sure know you're out in the country when you meet dogs running around without collars just like bears.

Distantly, a car door slams. The sound echoes off the barn wall so that at first he looks in the wrong spot. Then he sees through the fork of the apple tree, about a six-iron away allowing for the slope, the orange Corolla in the big bare spot between the house and the garage, which has the yellow shell of the school bus behind it.

So a wild hope is confirmed, but most of his mind stays with the opaque bundle of muscle and teeth at his knees, how to keep it from barking, how to keep it from biting. Tiny brains, change in a second, a collie belonging to old Mrs Haas down Jackson Road lived in a barrel, snapped one time when nobody expected it, he still has the faint white scar on two middle fingers, pulling them loose felt like skinning a carrot, he can still feel it.

The dog too hears the car door slam and, flattening its ears, rockets down through the orchard. Around the Corolla it sets up a barking that is frantic but remote, delayed by echo and space. Harry seizes the moment to scurry back to a tree farther away. From there he sees the car's driver step out, lanky Jamie, no longer wearing dirty dungarees but pinkish bell-bottoms and a red turtleneck shirt. The collie jumps up and down, greeting, apologizing for barking at the unfamiliar car. The boy's drawl drifts up through the orchard, doing singsong dog talk, the words indistinct. Rabbit drops his eyes a moment to the earth, where two yellowjackets are burrowing into a rotten apple. When he looks again, a girl, the girl, her round white face unmistakable, her hair shorter than in June, steps out of the Corolla's passenger side and hunkers down to the dog, mingling herself with its flurry. She turns her face away from a thrust of the dog's muzzle and stares upwards at the exact spot from which Harry, frozen, watches. He sees when she stands that she is dressed trimly, in dark brown skirt and russet sweater, a little plaid jacket squaring up her shoulders so she looks sharp, collegiate, a city girl. Still there is that certain languor of her legs as she takes a stride or two toward the house. Her voice lifts in calling. Both their young faces have turned to the house, so Rabbit takes the opportunity to retreat to yet a farther tree, slimmer than the one previous. But he is close to the tangled hedgerow now and perhaps against this invisible in his light suit, camouflaged among pieces of sky.

Down below, echoing off the stucco and cinder-block walls, the cries of greeting and pleasure have a melancholy, drifting sound. From out of the house, following a thin slam of its door, a fat elderly woman has emerged, moving under the burden of her own weight so cautiously that the collie, herding, nudges her forward, encircling her legs. This might be the woman he glimpsed in the old station wagon when it went by the church on the day of the wedding, but it cannot be Ruth, for her hair, that had been a kind of soft and various wiry fire, is an iron cap of gray fitted to her head, and her body is enormous, so big her clothes from this distance seem wide as a sail. In pants and shirt this person advances plodding to admire the new car. There is no exchange of kisses, but from the way they all rotate and slide one past another these three are well acquainted. Their voices drift to Harry unintelligibly.

The boy demonstrates the liftback. The girl taps the old woman, as if to say, *Go on*; she is being teased. Then they fish from the car's interior two tall brown paper bags, groceries, and the collie dog, bored with these proceedings, lifts its head and points its nose in the direction where Harry, his heart thunderous, is holding as still as the man concealed in the tangled lines of those puzzle drawings that used to be in Sunday papers.

The dog begins to bark and races up into the orchard toward him; Harry has no choice but to turn and run. Perhaps he makes it through the hedgerow before the people look up and see him. They call out for the dog – 'Fritzie! Fritzie!' – in two female voices. Twigs scratch his hands; the loose stones of the old wall nearly trip him, and scuff one shoe. Now he flies. The red earth marred by tractor treads skims underfoot. Yet the dog, he sees glancing behind, will overtake him before he can reach the car; already the creature, its hair and ears swept flat by its speed, has broken through the hedgerow and is streaming along beside the corn stubble. Oh Christ. Rabbit stops, wraps his arms around his face, and waits. The house is out of sight below the rise of land; he is all alone with this. He hears the dog's claws rattle past him in momentum and a bark dies to a growl in its throat. He feels his legs being nosed through his trousers, then leaned on. The dog doesn't want to bring him down but to gather him in, to herd him also.

'Nice Fritzie,' Harry says. 'Good Fritzie. Let's go to my car. Let's trot along.' Foot by careful foot he consumes the little distance to the shoulder of the road, the dog bumping and sniffing him all the way. The cries from the house, invisible, persist raggedly; the collie's tail, uncertainly wagging, pats Harry's calves while the long skull inquires upward with its sick red eye. Harry pulls his hand up to the level of his lapels. Dirty yellow drooly teeth would skin his fingers like a carrot grater. He tells Fritzie, 'You're a beautiful girl, a wonderful girl,' and eases around the back of the Corona. The chain saw is still zipping along. He opens the driver's door and slides in. Slams it. The collie stands on the overgrown banking of red earth looking puzzled, her shepherding come to an end. Harry finds the car key in his pocket, the engine starts. His heart is still pounding. He leans over toward the passenger's window and scrabbles his fingers on the glass. 'Hey Fritzie!' he shouts and keeps up the scrabbling until the dog starts to bark again. *Bark*. *Bark bark bark*. Laughing, Rabbit pops the clutch and digs out, the thing inside his chest feeling fragile and iridescent like a big soap bubble. Let it pop. He hasn't felt so close to breaking out of his rut since Nelson smashed those convertibles.

Webb Murkett is handy about the house; he has a cellar full of expensive power tools and subscribes to magazines with titles like *Fine Woodworking* and *Homecraft*. In every corner of the garrison colonial he and Cindy have shared for the seven years of their marriage there are hand-made refinements of rounded, stained, and varnished wood – shelves, cabinets, built-in lazy susans with as many compartments as a seashell – expressing the patience and homelovingness of the house's master. There is a way of working with rotten wood, and making it as solid as marble, and like marble swirled and many-shaded; this art is on display in the base of several lamps and in a small bowl holding an untouched spiral of cigarettes on the butler's-tray table, which Webb has also fashioned, down to its gleaming copper hinges shaped like butterflies. Some of these objects must have come from the homes of Webb's previous marriages, and Harry wonders what these phantom women have kept, that so much remains. Webb's previous marriages are represented in his great long sunken living room only by color photographs, in ensemble frames of unusual proportion that Webb himself has cut and grooved and cemented together of Lucite, of children too old to be his and Cindy's, caught in a moment of sunshine on the flagstone stoop of another suburban house, or in a sailboat against the blue of a lake that the Kodak chemicals are permitting to fade to yellow, or at a moment of marriage or graduation – for some of these children were now adult, older than Nelson, and infants of a third generation stare out unsmiling, propped on a pillow or held in firm young arms, from among the many smiles of these family groups. Harry has several times in Webb's house slyly searched these photos for the sight of a former wife; but though there are women beheaded or sliced to a splinter by the edge of a frame or another picture, and here and there an unidentifiable mature hand and forearm intrudes behind a set of children's heads, no face seems preserved of the vanished mistresses of all this fleeting family happiness.

When Webb and Cindy entertain, built-in speakers bathe the downstairs rooms in a continuous sweetness of string music and spineless arrangements, of old show tunes or mollified rock classics, voiceless and seamless and with nagging dental associations for Harry. Behind a mahogany bar that Webb salvaged from the tavern of a farmer's hotel being demolished in Brewer and then transported with its brass rail to a corner of his living room, he has constructed a kind of altar to booze, two high doors with rounded tops that meet in a point and shelves that come forward on a lazy-tongs principle with not only the basics of whiskey, gin, and vodka but exotic drinks like rum and tequila and saki and all the extras you could want from bitters to powdered Old-Fashioned mix in little envelopes. And the bar has its own small refrigerator, built in. Much as he admires Webb, Harry thinks when he gets his own dream house he will do without the piped music and such elaborate housing for the liquor.

The bathroom, though, enchants him, with its little enamelled dishes of rosebud-shaped soap and furry blue toilet seat cover and its dazzling mirror rimmed with naked light bulbs like actors have in their dressing rooms. Everything in here that doesn't shine is tinted and scented. The toilet paper, very dulcet, is printed with old comic strips, each piece a panel. Poor Popeye, eating shit instead of spinach. And the towels have W and M and L for Lucinda intertwined in such a crusty big monogram he hates to think what it would do to Cindy's sweet underparts if she forgot and rubbed herself hard. But Harry wonders if this downstairs bathroom is ever used by the Murketts and their rather pasty-looking little kids or is set up primarily for guests. Certain mysterious artifacts in it – a big sort of sugar bowl, white, with a knobbed lid painted with two women dressed in filmy gowns sitting on clouds or a sofa that fades into nothing, and their feet in pink ballerina shoes and their ankles crossed and the toes of one woman touching the other's and one bare arm of each intertwined above the knob, yet when the lid is lifted utterly empty, so empty you feel nothing has ever been put inside; and a pink plastic hand on a stick, meant maybe for a comic backscratcher; and an egg-shaped jar a third full of lavender crystalline salts; and a kind of tiny milkman's carrier of what he takes to be bath oils; and a flexible plastic cylinder holding a pastel rainbow of powder puffs like a stack of pancakes – all seem put there, on the set of open shelves hung on two black dowels between the bathtub and the toilet, for exhibit more than use. To think of little Cindy though, pouring that oil into her bath and then just soaking there, playing with herself with the backscratcher, her nipples poking through the blanket of soapsuds. Harry feels sexy. In the mirror that makes things too vivid his eyes stare with a pallor almost white like the little frost-flowers that appear on the skin of a car in the morning and his lips look bluish; he is drunk. He has had two tequila fizzes before dinner, as much Gallo Chablis as he could grab during the meal, and a brandy and a half afterwards. In the middle of the second brandy the need to urinate came upon him like yet another pressure of happiness, added to his health and prosperity and the privilege of being there sitting across a coffee table from Cindy watching her body rotate within the strange coarse cloth of the exotic Arab-looking thing she is wearing, her wrists and her feet, bare but for sandals, as exciting in this outfit as the insides of her thighs in a bikini. Besides himself and Janice the Murketts have invited the Harrisons and for a new thrill the moronic Fosnachts, whom they just met at Nelson's wedding two weeks ago. Harry doesn't suppose the Murketts know he and Peggy had a fling years back when Ollie had done one of his copouts, but maybe they do, people know more than you ever think they do, and it turns out it doesn't much matter. Look at what you read every week in *People* magazine, and you still keep watching television, the actors all dope addicts and adulterers. He has an urge to look into the medicine cabinet framed by the rim of showbiz bulbs and waits until a gale of laughter from the drunken bunch in the living room arises to drown out any possible click of him opening the mirror-door. Click. The cabinet has more in it than he would have supposed: thick milk-glass jars of skin cream and flesh-tint squeeze bottles of lotion and brown tubes of suntan lotion, Parepectolin for diarrhea, Debrox for ear wax control, menthol Chloraseptic, that mouthwash called Cēpacol, several kinds of aspirin, both Bayer and Anacin, and Tylenol that doesn't make your stomach burn, and a large chalky bottle of liquid Maalox. He wonders which of the Murketts needs Maalox, they both always look so relaxed and at peace. The pink poison ivy goo would be downstairs handy for the kids, and the Band-Aids, but how about the little flat yellow box of Preparation H for hemorrhoids? Carter of course has hemorrhoids, that grim over-motivated type who wants to do everything on schedule ready or not, pushing, pushing, but old Webb Murkett with that gravelly voice and easy swing, like the swing you see crooners use at celebrity tournaments, unwrapping one of those little wax bullets and poking it up his own asshole? You have to go into a squat and the place is not easy to find, Rabbit remembers from his own experience, years ago, when he was sitting all day at the Linotype on that hard steel bench, under tension, the matrices rattling down in response to the touch of his fingertips, every slip a ruined slug, everybody around him unhappy, the kid still small, his own life closed in to a size his soul had not yet shrunk to fit. And what of these amber pill bottles with *Lucinda R. Murkett* typed in pale blue script face on the prescription labels? White pills, lethally small. He should have brought his reading glasses. Harry is tempted to lift one of these containers off its shelf in hopes of deciphering what illness might have ever found its way into that plump and supple delectable body, but a superstitious fear of fingerprints restrains him. Medicine cabinets are tragic, he sees by this hard light, and closes the door so gently no one will hear the click. He returns to the living room.

They are discussing the Pope's visit, loudly. 'Did you *see*,' Peggy Fosnacht is shouting, 'what he said in Chicago yesterday about *sex*!' The years since Harry knew her have freed her to stop wearing dark glasses to hide her walleye and to be sloppy in her person and opinions both; she's become the kind of woman who looks permanently out of press, as a protest of sorts. 'He said everything outside marriage was *wrong*. Not just if you're married, but *before* you're married too. What does that man *know*? He doesn't know anything about *life*, life as she is lived.'

Webb Murkett offers in a soft voice, trying to calm his guest down, 'I liked what Earl Butz said some years ago. "He no play-a the game, he no make-a the rules."' Webb is wearing a maroon turtleneck under a coarse yarny gray sweater that has something to do, Rabbit thinks, with Scandinavian fishermen. The way the neck is cut. Harry and Ronnie came in suits; Ollie was with-it enough to know you don't wear suits out even on a Saturday night anymore. He came in tight faded jeans and an embroidered shirt that made him look like a cowboy too runty to be out on the range.

'No play-a the game!' Peggy Fosnacht yells. 'See if you're a pregnant slum mother and can't get an abortion legally if you think it's such a game.'

Rabbit says to her, 'Webb's agreeing with you,' but she doesn't hear him, babbling on headlong, face flushed by wine and the exciting class of company, her hairdo coming uncurled like taffy softening in the sun.

'Did any of you watch except me – I can't stop watching, I get so furious – the performance he put on in Philly where he said absolutely No to women priests? And he kept smiling, what really got my goat, he kept smiling while spouting all this sexist crap about only men in the priesthood and how it was the conviction of the church and God's decision and all that, so solly. He's so *smooth* about it, I think is what gets to me, at least somebody like Nixon or Hitler had the decency to be frantic.'

'He is one smooth old Polack,' Ollie says, uneasy at this outburst by his wife. He is into cool, you can see. Music, dope. Just on the fringes, but enough to give you the pitch.

'He sure can kiss those nigger babies,' Ronnie Harrison comes in with, maybe trying to help. It's fascinating to Rabbit how long those strands of hair are Ronnie is combing over his bald spot these days, if you pulled one the other way it would go below his ear. In this day and age why fight it? There's a bald look, go for it. Blank and pink and curved, like an ass. Everybody loves an ass. Those wax bullets in the yellow box – could they have been for Cindy? Sore there from, but would Webb? Harry has read somewhere that male homosexuals have a lot of trouble with hemorrhoids. Amazing the things they try to put up – fists, light bulbs. He squirms on his cushion.

'I think he's very sexy,' Thelma Harrison states firmly. Everything she says sounds like a schoolteacher, enunciated. He looks at her through the enhancing lens of liquor: thin lips and that unhealthy yellow color. Harry can hardly ever look at her without seeing Ronnie's prick, flat like a board on the upper side it's so thick. 'He is a beautiful man,' Thelma insists. Her eyes are half-shut. She's had a glass or two too many herself. Her throat rises absolutely straight, like a person trying not to hiccup. He has to look down the front of her dress, velvet that mousy blue of old movie seats, the way she's holding herself. Nothing much there. That little stocky guy in white with all those gold buttons and different funny hats, to see him as sexy you'd have to be a nun. Ronnie is stocky like that, actually. She likes thick men. He looks down the front of her dress again. Maybe more there than you'd think.

Janice is saying, she has known Peggy for ages and is trying to save her from herself, 'What I liked today, I don't know if you were watching, Peggy, was when he came out on the balcony of that cathedral in Washington, before he went to the White House, to this crowd that was shouting, "We want the Pope, we want the Pope," and he came out on the balcony waving and shouted, "John Paul Two, he wants you!" Actually.'

'Actually' because the men had laughed, it was news to them. Three of them had been out on the Flying Eagle course today, summer had made one last loop back to Diamond County, bringing out fat buds on the magnolias by the sixth tee. Their fourth had been the young assistant pro, the same kid who had shot a 73 the day Nelson got married. He hits a long ball, Webb was right, but Harry doesn't like his swing: too wristy. Give him a few years around his waist he'll be hooking everything. Buddy Inglefinger had been dropped, lately; his golf was a drag and the wives didn't like his tarty girlfriends. But Ollie Fosnacht is no substitute. The only thing he plays is the synthesizer, and his sloppy wife won't stop blabbering.

'I'd *like* to find it amusing,' Peggy says, hoisting her voice above the laughter, 'but to me the issues he's trampling on are too damn serious.'

Cindy Murkett unexpectedly speaks. 'He's been a priest in a Communist country; he's used to taking a stand. The American liberals in the church talk about this *sensus fidelium* but I never heard of it; its been *magisterium* for two thousand years. What is it that offends you, Peggy, if you're not a Catholic and don't have to listen?'

A hush has surrounded her words because they all except the Fosnachts know that she was Catholic until she married Webb. Peggy senses this now but like a white sad heifer having charged in one direction cannot turn herself around. 'You're Catholic?' she bluntly asks.

Cindy tips her chin up, not used to this kind of spotlight, the baby of their group. 'I was raised as one,' she says.

'So was my daughter-in-law, it turns out,' Harry volunteers. He is amused by the idea of having a daughter-in-law at all, a new branch of his wealth. And he hopes to be distracting. He hates to see women fight, he'd be happy to get these two off the spot. Cindy comes up from that swimming pool like a wet dream, and Peggy was kind enough to lay him when he was down.

But no one is distracted. 'When I married a divorced man,' Cindy explains levelly to the other woman, 'I couldn't take communion anymore. But I still go to Mass sometimes. I still believe.' Her voice softens saying this, for she is the hostess, younger though she is.

'And do you use birth control?' Peggy asks.

Back to nowhere, Fosnachts. Harry is just as pleased; he liked his little crowd the way it was.

Cindy hesitates. She can go all girlish and slide and giggle away from the question, or she can sit still and get dignified. With just the smallest of dignified smiles she says, 'I'm not sure that's any of your business.'

'Nor the Pope's either, that's my point!' Peggy sounds triumphant, but even she must be feeling the battle slipping away. She will not be invited here again.

Webb, always the gentleman, perches on the arm of the easy chair in which cumbersome Peggy has set herself up as anti-Pope and leans down a deft inch to say to his guest alone, 'I think Cindy's point, as I understand it, is that John Paul is addressing the doctrinal issues for his fellow Catholics while bringing good will to every American.'

'He can keep his good will along with the doctrine as far as I'm concerned,' Peggy says, trying to shut up but unable. Rabbit remembers how her nipples had felt like gumdrops and how sad her having gotten good at screwing since Ollie left her had seemed to him at the time, ten years ago.

Cindy attacks a little now, 'But he sees the trouble the church has got into since Vatican Two. The priests –'

'The church is in trouble because it's a monument to a lie, run by a bunch of antiquated chauvinists who don't know *any*thing. I'm sorry,' Peggy says, 'I'm talking too much.'

'Well, this is America,' Harry says, coming to her rescue, somewhat, 'Let's all sock it to each other. Today I said goodbye to the only friend I've ever had, Charlie Stavros.'

Janice says, 'Oh, Harry,' but nobody else takes him up on it. The men were supposed to say *they* were his friends.

Webb Murkett tilts his head, his eyebrows working toward Ronnie and Ollie. 'Did either of you see in the paper today where Nixon finally bought a house in Manhattan? Right next to David Rockefeller. I'm no great admirer of tricky Dick's, but I must say the way he's been excluded from apartment houses in a great city is a disgrace to the Constitution.'

'If he'd been a jigaboo,' Ronnie begins.

'Well how would *you* like,' Peggy Fosnacht has to say, 'a lot of secret service men checking your handbag every time you came back from the store?'

The chair Peggy sits in is squared-off ponderous modern with a pale fabric thick as plywood; it matches another chair and a long sofa set around that kind of table with no overhang to the top they call a Parsons table, which is put together in alternating blocks of light and dark wood with a curly knotty grain such as they make golf club heads of. The entire deep space of the room, which Webb added on when he and Cindy acquired this house in the pace-setting development of Brewer Heights, gently brims with appointments chosen all to harmonize. Its tawny wallpaper has vertical threads of texture in it like the vertical folds of the slightly darker pull drapes, and reproductions of Wyeth watercolors lit by spots on track lighting overhead echo with scratchy strokes the same tints, and the same lighting reveals little sparkles, like mica on a beach, in the overlapping arcs of the rough-plastered ceiling. When Harry moves his head these sparkles in the ceiling change location, wave upon wave of hidden silver. He announces, 'I heard a kind of funny story at Rotary the other day involving Kissinger. Webb, I don't think you were there. There were these five guys in an airplane that was about to crash – a priest, a hippie, a policeman, somebody else, and Henry Kissinger. And only four parachutes.'

Ronnie says, 'And at the end the hippie turns to the priest and says, "Don't worry, Father. The Smartest Man in the World just jumped out with my knapsack." We've all heard it. Speaking of which, Thel and I were wondering if you'd seen this.' He hands him a newspaper clipping, from an Ann Landers column printed in the Brewer *Standard*, the respectable paper, not the *Vat*. The second paragraph is marked in tidy ballpoint. 'Read it aloud,' Ronnie demands.

He doesn't like being given orders by sweaty skinheads like Harrison when he's come out for a pleasant low-key time with the Murketts, but all eyes are on him and at least it gets them off the Pope. He explains, more to the Fosnachts than the others, since the Murketts seem to be in on the joke already, 'It's a letter to Ann Landers from somebody. The first paragraph tells about a news story about some guy whose pet python bit him in the stomach and wouldn't let go, and when the paramedics came he yelled at them to get out of his apartment if they're going to hurt his snake.' There is a little laughter at that and the Fosnachts, puzzled, try to join in. The next paragraph goes:

> The other news story was about a Washington, D.C., physician who beat a Canadian goose to death with his putter on the 16th green of a country club. (The goose honked just as he was about to sink one.) The reason for printing those letters was to demonstrate that truth is stranger than fiction.

Having read this aloud, he explains to the Fosnachts, 'The

reason they're razzing me with this is last summer I heard about the same incident on the radio and when I tried to tell them about it at the club they wouldn't listen, nobody believed me. Now here's proof it happened.'

'You chump, *that's* not the point,' Ronnie Harrison says.

'The point is, Harry,' Thelma says, 'it's so *different*. You said he was from Baltimore and this says he was from Washington. You said the ball hit the goose accidentally and the doctor put him out of his misery.'

Webb says, 'Remember – "A mercy killing, or murder most foul?" That really broke me up.'

'You didn't show it at the time,' Harry says, pleased however.

'According to Ann Landers, then, it *was* murder most foul,' Thelma says.

'Who cares?' Ronnie says, getting ugly. This clipping was clearly her idea. Her touch on the ballpoint too.

Janice has been listening with that glazed dark look she gets when deep enough into the booze. She and Webb have been trying some new imported Irish liqueur called Greensleeves. 'Well not if the goose honked,' she says.

Ollie Fosnacht says, 'I can't believe a goose honking would make that much difference on a putt.'

All the golfers there assure him it would.

'Shit,' he says, 'in music, you do your best work at two in the morning, stoned half out of your mind and a lot of drunks acting up besides.'

His mention of music reminds them all that in the background Webb's hidden speakers are incessantly performing; a Hawaiian melody at the moment, with Vibra-Harp.

'Maybe it wasn't a goose at all,' Harry says. 'Maybe it was a very little caddy with feathers.'

'That's music,' Ronnie sneers, of Ollie's observation. 'Hey Webb, how come there isn't any beer in this place?'

'There's beer, there's beer. Miller Lite and Heineken's. What can I get everybody?'

Webb acts a little jumpy, and Rabbit worries that the party is in danger of flattening out. He misses, whom he never thought he would, Buddy Inglefinger, and tries to say the kind of thing

Buddy would if he were here. 'Speaking of dead geese,' he says, 'I noticed in the paper the other day where some anthropologist or something says about a fourth of the animal species on earth right now will be extinct by the year 2000.'

'Oh *don't*,' Peggy Fosnacht protests loudly, shaking herself ostentatiously, so the fat on her upper arms jiggles. She is wearing a short-sleeved dress, out of season. 'Don't mention the year 2000, just the thought of it gives me the *creeps*.'

Nobody asks her why.

Rabbit at last says, 'Why? You'll still be alive.'

'No I won't,' she says flatly, wanting to make an argument even of that.

The heated flush the papal argument roused in Cindy still warms her throat and upper chest, that with its tiny gold cross sits half-exposed by the unbuttoned two top buttons or string-latches of the Arab-style robe, her tapering forearms looking childishly fragile within its wide sleeves, her feet bare but for the thinnest golden sandals below the embroidered hem. In the commotion as Webb takes drink orders and Janice wobbles up to go to the john, Harry goes over and sits on a straight chair beside their young hostess. 'Hey,' he says, 'I think the Pope's pretty great. He really knows how to use T V.'

Cindy says, with a sharp quick shake of her face as if stung, 'I don't like a lot of what he says either, but he's got to draw the line somewhere. That's his job.'

'He's running scared,' Rabbit offers. 'Like everybody else.'

She looks at him, her eyes a bit Chinesey like Mim said, the fatty pouches of her lower lids giving her a kind of squint, as if she's been beaten or is suffering from ragweed, so she twinkles even as she's being serious, her pupils large in this shadowy center of the room away from the track lighting. 'Oh, I can't think of him that way, though you're probably right. I've still too much parochial school in me.' The ring of brown around her pupils is smooth chocolate, without flecks or fire. 'Webb's so gentle, he never pushes me. After Betsey was born, and we agreed he's been father enough, Webb, I couldn't make myself use a diaphragm, it seemed so evil, and he didn't want me on the Pill, what he'd read about it, so he offered to get himself fixed, you know, like the men are paid to do in India, what do they call it, a vasectomy. Rather than have him do that and do God knows what to his psyche, I went impulsively one day and got myself fitted for the diaphragm, I still don't know if I'm putting it in right when I do it, but poor Webb. You know he had five other children by his other wives, and they're both after his money *con*stantly. Neither has married though they're living with men, that's what I would call immoral, to keep bleeding him that way.'

This is more than Harry had bargained for. He tries to confess back at her. 'Janice had her tubes cauterized the other year, and I must say, it's great not to have to worry about it, whenever you want it, night or day, no creams or crap or anything. Still, sometimes she starts crying, for no reason. At being sterile.'

'Well of course, Harry. I would too.' Cindy's lips are long and in their lipstick lie together with a wised-up closeness of fit, a downward tug at the end of sentences, he has never noticed before tonight.

'But you're a baby,' he tells her.

Cindy gives him a wise slanting look and almost toughly says, 'I'm getting there, Harry. I'll be thirty this April.'

Twenty-nine, she must have been twenty-two when Webb started fucking her, what a sly goat, he pictures her body all brown with its little silken slopes and rolls of slight excess inside the rough loose garment, shadowy spaces you could put your hand in, for the body to breathe in that desert heat, it goes with the gold threads on her feet and the bangles around her wrists, still small and round as a child's, veinless. The vehemence of his lust dries his mouth. He stands to go after his brandy but loses his balance so his knee knocks against Peggy Fosnacht's ponderous square chair. She is not in it, she is standing at the top of the two steps that lead upward out of the living room, with the out-of-date dull green loden coat she came in draped around her shoulders. She looks down at them like one placed above and beyond, driven away.

Ollie, though, is seated around the Parsons table waiting for Webb to bring the beer and oblivious of his wife's withdrawal. Ronnie Harrison, so drunk his lips are wet and the long hair he brushes across his bald spot stands up in a loop, asks Ollie, 'How goes the music racket these days? I hear the guitar craze is over now there's no more revolution.'

'They're into flutes now, it's weird. Not just the girls, but guys too, who want to play jazz. A lot of spades. A spade came in the other day wanted to buy a platinum flute for his daughter's eighteenth birthday, he said he read about some Frenchman who had one. I said, "Man, you're crazy. I can't begin to guess what a flute like that would cost." He said, "I don't give a flying fuck, man," and showed me this roll of bills, there must have been an inch of hundred-dollar bills in it. At least those on top were hundreds.'

Any more feeling-out with Cindy would be too much for now; Harry sits down heavily on the sofa and joins the male conversation. 'Like those gold-headed putters a few years ago. Boy I bet *they've* gone up in value.'

Like Peggy, he is ignored. Harrison is boring in. These insurance salesmen: they have that way of putting down their heads and just boring in until it's either scream or say, sure, you'll take out another fifty thousand of renewable life.

Ronnie says to Ollie, 'How about electric stuff? You see this guy on television even has an electric violin. That stuff must cost.'

'An arm and a leg,' Ollie says, looking up gratefully as Webb sets a Heineken's on a light square of the table in front of him. 'Just the amplifiers take you into the thousands,' he says, pleased to be talking, pleased to sound rich. Poor sap, when most of his business is selling thirteen-year-old dumplings records to make them wet their pants. What did Nelson used to call it? Lollipop music. Nelson used to be be serious about the guitar, that one he saved from the fire and then the one they got him with a big pearl plate on the face, but the chords stopped coming from his room after school when he got his driver's license.

Ronnie has tilted his head to bore in at a different angle. 'You know I'm in client service at Schuylkill Mutual and my boss told me the other day, "Ron, you cost this company eight thousand seven hundred last year." That's not salary, that's benefits. Retirement, health insurance, participation options. How do you handle that in your operation? If you don't have employer-financed insurance and retirement in this day and age, you're in the soup. People expect it and without it they won't perform.'

Ollie says, 'Well, I'm my own employer in a way. Me and my partners –'

'How about Keogh? You gotta have Keogh.'

'We try to keep it simple. When we started out –'

'You gotta be kidding, Ollie. You're just robbing yourself. Schuylkill Mutual offers a terrific deal on Keogh, and we could plug you, in fact we advise plugging you in, on the corporate end so not a nickel comes out of your personal pocket, it comes out of the corporate pocket and there's that much less for Uncle to tax. These poor saps carrying their own premiums with no company input are living in the dark ages. There's nothing shady about rigging it this way, we're just using the laws the government has put there. They *want* people to take advantage, it all works to up the gross national product. You know what I mean by Keogh, don't you? You're looking kind of blank.'

'It's something like social security.'

'A thousand times better. Social security's just a rip-off to benefit the freeloaders now; you'll never see a penny of what you put in. In the Keogh plan, up to seventy-five hundred goes untaxed, every year; you just set it aside, with our help. Our usual suggestion is, depending on circumstances – how many dependents you got? –'

'Two, if you count the wife. My son Billy's out of college and up in Massachusetts studying specialized dentistry.'

Ronnie whistles. 'Boy, you were smart. Limiting yourself to one offspring. I saddled myself with three and only these last few years am I feeling out of the woods. The older boy, Alex, has taken to electronics but the middle boy, Georgie, needed special schools from the start. Dyslexia. I'd never heard of it, but I'll tell you I've heard of it now. Couldn't make any goddam sense at all out of anything written, and you'd never know it from his conversation. He could outtalk me at this job, that's for certain, but he can't see it. He wants to be an artist, Jesus. There's no money there, Ollie, you know that better than I do. But even with just the one kid, you don't want him to starve if you were suddenly out of the picture, or the good woman either. Any man in this day and age carrying less than a hundred, a hundred fifty thousand dollars straight life just isn't being realistic. A decent funeral alone costs four, five grand.'

'Yeah, well —'

'Lemme get back to the Keogh a minute. We generally recommend a forty-sixty split, take the forty per cent of seventy-five hundred in straight life premiums, which generally comes to close to the hundred thou, assuming you pass the exam that is. You smoke?'

'Off and on.'

'Uh-oh. Well, lemme give you the name of a doctor who gives an exam everybody can live with.'

Ollie says, 'I think my wife wants to go.'

'You're kidding, Foster.'

'Fosnacht.'

'You're kidding. This is Saturday night, man. You got a gig or something?'

'No, my wife — she needs to go to some anti-nuclear meeting tomorrow morning at some Universalist church.'

'No wonder she's down on the Pope then. I hear the Vatican and Three-Mile Island are hand-in-glove, just ask friend Harry here. Ollie, here's my card. Could I have one of yours please?'

'Uh —'

'That's O.K. I know where you are. Up there next to the fuck movies. I'll come by. No bullshit, you really owe it to yourself to listen to some of these opportunities. People keep saying the economy is shot but it isn't shot at all from where I sit, it's booming. People are begging for shelters.'

Harry says, 'Come on, Ron. Ollie wants to go.'

'Well, I don't exactly but Peggy —'

'Go. Go in peace man.' Ronnie stands and makes a ham-handed blessing gesture. 'Got pless Ameri-ca,' he pronounces in a thick slow foreign accent, loud, so that Peggy, who has been conferring with the Murketts, patching things up, turns her back. She too went to high school with Ronnie and knows him for the obnoxious jerk he is.

'Jesus, Ronnie,' Rabbit says to him when the Fosnachts have gone. 'What a snow job.'

'Ahh,' Ronnie says. 'I wanted to see how much garbage he could eat.'

'I've never been that crazy about him either,' Harry confesses. 'He treats old Peggy like dirt.'

Janice, who has been consulting with Thelma Harrison about something, God knows what, their lousy children, overhears this and turns and tells Ronnie, 'Harry screwed her years ago, that's why he minds Ollie.' Nothing like a little booze to freshen up old sore points.

Ronnie laughs to attract attention and slaps Harry's knee. 'You screwed that big pig, funny eyes and all?'

Rabbit pictures that heavy glass egg with the interior teardrop of air back in Ma Springer's living room, its smooth heft in his hand, and imagines himself making the pivot from pounding it into Janice's stubborn dumb face to finishing up with a one-handed stuff straight down into Harrison's pink brainpan. 'It seemed a good idea at the time,' he has to admit, uncrossing his legs and stretching them in preparation for an extended night. The Fosnachts' leaving is felt as a relief throughout the room. Cindy is tittering to Webb, clings briefly to his coarse gray sweater in her rough loose Arab thing, like a loving pair advertising vacations abroad. 'Janice had run off at the time with this disgusting greasy Greek Charlie Stavros,' Harry explains to anybody who will listen.

'O.K. O.K.,' Ronnie says, 'you don't need to tell us. We've all heard the story, it's ancient history.'

'What isn't so ancient, you twerpy skinhead, is I had to kiss Charlie goodbye today because Janice and her mother got him canned from Springer Motors.'

'Harry likes to say that,' Janice said, 'but it was as much Charlie's idea as anybody's.'

Ronnie is not so potted he misses the point. He tips his head and looks at Janice with a gaze that from Harry's angle is mostly furry white eyelashes. 'You got your old boyfriend fired?' he asks her.

Harry amplifies, 'All so my shiftless son who won't even finish college with only one year to go can take over this job he's no more qualified for than, than –'

275

'Than Harry was,' Janice finishes for him – in the old days she would never have been quick with sass like that – and giggles. Harry has to laugh too, even before Ronnie does. His cock isn't the only thick thing about Harrison.

'This is what I like,' Webb Murkett says in his gravelly voice above them. 'Old friends.' He and Cindy side by side stand presiding above their circle as the hour settles toward midnight. 'What can I get anybody? More beer? How about a light highball? Scotch? Irish? A CC and seven?' Cindy's tits jut out in that caftan or burnoose or whatever like the angle of a tent. Desert silence. Crescent moon. Put the camel to bed. 'We-ell,' Webb exhales with such pleasure he must be feeling that Greensleeves, 'and what did we think of the Fosnachts?'

'They won't do,' Thelma says. Harry is startled to hear her speak, she has been so silent. If you close your eyes and pretend you're blind, Thelma has the nicest voice. He feels melancholy and mellow, now that the invasion from the pathetic world beyond the Flying Eagle has been repelled.

'Ollie's been a sap from Day One,' he says, 'but she didn't used to be such a blabbermouth. Did she, Janice?'

Janice is cautious, defending her old friend. 'She always had a tendency,' she says. 'Peggy never thought of herself as attractive, and that was a problem.'

'You did, huh?' Harry accuses.

She stares at him, having not followed, her face moistened as by a fine spray.

'Of *course* she did,' Webb gallantly intervenes, 'Janice *is* attractive,' and goes around behind her chair and puts his hands on her shoulders, close to her neck so her shoulders hunch.

Cindy says, 'She was a lot pleasanter just chatting with me and Webb at the door. She said she sometimes just gets carried away.'

Ronnie says, 'Harry and Janice I guess see a lot of 'em. I'll have a brew as long as you're up, Webb.'

'We don't at all. Nelson's best friend is their obnoxious son Billy, is how they got to the wedding. Webb, could you make that two?'

Thelma asks Harry, her voice softly pitched for him alone, 'How *is* Nelson? Have you heard from him in his married state?'

276

'A postcard. Janice has talked to them on the phone a couple times. She thinks they're bored.'

Janice interrupts, 'I don't think, Harry. He *told* me they're bored.'

Ronnie offers, 'If you've done all your fucking before marriage, I guess a honeymoon can be a drag. Thanks, Webb.'

Janice says, 'He said it's been chilly in the cabin.'

'Too lazy no doubt to carry the wood in from the stack outside,' Harry says. 'Yeah, thanks.' The *pffft* of opening a can isn't near as satisfying since they put that safety tab on to keep idiots from choking themselves.

'Harry, he told us they've been having a fire in the wood stove all day long.'

'Burning it all up so somebody else can chop. He's his mamma's boy.'

Thelma, tired perhaps of the tone the Angstroms keep setting, lifts her voice and bends her face far back, exposing a startling length of sallow throat. 'Speaking of the cold, Webb. Are you and Cindy going away at all this winter?' They usually go to an island in the Caribbean. The Harrisons once went with them, years ago. Harry and Janice have never been.

Webb has been circling behind Thelma getting a highball for someone. 'We've talked about it,' he tells Thelma. Through the haze of beer laid over brandy there seems an enchanting conspiracy between her bent-back throat and Webb's arched and lowered voice. Old friends, Harry thinks. Fit like pieces of a puzzle. Webb bends down and reaches over her shoulder to put a tall weak Scotch-and-soda on a dark square in front of her. 'I'd like to go,' he is going on, 'where they have a golf course. You can get a pretty fair deal, if you shop around for a package.'

'Let's all go,' Harry announces. 'The kid's taking over the lot Monday, let's get the hell out of here.'

'Harry,' Janice says, 'he's not taking over the lot, you're being irrational about this. Webb and Ronnie are shocked, to hear you talk about your son this way.'

'They're not shocked. *Their* kids are eating 'em alive too. I want to go to the Caribbean and play golf this winter. Let's bust out. Let's ask Buddy Inglefinger to be the fourth. I hate the winter around here – there's no snow, you can't ice-skate, it's just boring and raw, month after month. When I was a kid, there was snow all the time, what ever happened to it?'

'We had a ton of snow in '78,' Webb observes.

'Harry, maybe it's time to go home,' Janice tells him. Her mouth has thinned to a slot, her forehead under her bangs is shiny.

'I don't want to go home. I want to go to the Caribbean. But first I want to go to the bathroom. Bathroom, home, Caribbean, in that order.' He wonders if a wife like that ever dies of natural causes. Never, those dark wiry types, look at her mother, still running the show. Buried poor old Fred and never looked back.

Cindy says, 'Harry, the downstairs john is plugged, Webb just noticed. Somebody must have used too much toilet paper.'

'Peggy Gring, that's who,' Harry says, standing and wondering why the wall-to-wall carpeting has a curve to it, like the deck of a ship falling away on all sides. 'First she attacks the Pope, then she abuses the plumbing.'

'Use the one in our bedroom,' Webb says to him. 'At the head of the stairs, turn left, past the two closet doors with the slats.'

'. . . wiping away her tears . . . ,' Rabbit hears Thelma Harrison saying dryly as he leaves. Up the two carpeted steps, his head floating far above his feet. Then down a hall and up stairs in different-coloured carpeting, a dirty lime, more wear, older part of the house. Someone else's upstairs always has that hush. Tired nights, a couple talking softly to themselves. The voices below him fade. Turn left, Webb had said. Slatted doors. He stops and peeks in. Female clothes, strips of many colors, fragrant of her. Get Cindy down there in that sand, who can say, talking to him about her diaphragm already. He finds the bathroom. Every light in it is lit. What a waste of energy. Going down with all her lights blazing the great ship America. This bathroom is smaller than the one downstairs, and of a deeper tint, wall tiles and wallpaper and shag carpeting and towels and tinted porcelain all brown, with touches of tangerine. He undoes his fly and in a stream of bliss fills one of this room's bright bowls with gold. His bubbles multiply like coins. He and Janice took their Krugerrands from the bedside table drawer and together went downtown and into the Brewer Trust with them and nestled them in their little cylinders like blue-tinted dollhouse toilets into their stout long safe-deposit box and in celebration had drinks with their lunch at the Crêpe House before he went back to the lot. Because he was never circumcised he tends to retain a drop or two, and pats his tip with a piece of lemon-yellow toilet paper, plain, the comic strips were to amuse guests. Who was Thelma saying would wipe away her tears? The shocking flash of long white throat, muscular, the swallowing muscles developed, she must have something, to hold Harrison. Maybe she meant Peggy using toilet paper to wipe away her tears had clogged the toilet. Cindy's eyes had had a glisten, too shy to like arguing like that with poor Peggy, telling him instead about her diaphragm, Jesus, inviting him to think about it, her sweet red dark deep, could she mean it? *Getting there, Harry:* her voice more wised-up and throaty than he ever noticed before, her eyes pouchy, sexy when women's lower lids are like that, up a little like eggcups, his daughter's lids he noticed that day did that. All around in here are surfaces that have seen Cindy stark naked. Harry looks at his face in this less dazzling mirror, fluorescent tubes on either side, and his lips look less blue, he is sobering up for the drive home. Oh but blue still the spaces in his eyes, encircling the little black dot through which the world flows, a blue with white and gray mixed in from the frost of his ancestors, those beefy blonds in horned helmets pounding to a pulp with clubs the hairy mammoth and the slant-eyed Finns amid snows so pure and widespread their whiteness would have made eyes less pale hurt. Eyes and hair and skin, the dead live in us though their brains are black and their eyesockets of bone empty. His pupils enlarge as he leans closer to the mirror, making a shadow, seeking to see if there truly is a soul. That's what he used to think ophthalmologists were looking at when they pressed that little hot periscope of a flashlight tight against your eye. What they saw, they never told him. He sees nothing but black, out of focus, because his eyes are aging.

He washes his hands. The faucet is one of those single-handed Lavomaster mixers with a knob on the end of the handle like a clown's nose or big pimple, he can never remember which way is hot and which cold, what was wrong with the old two faucets that said H and C? The basin, though, is good, with a wide lip of several ledges to hold soap without its riding off, these little ridges most basins have now don't hold anything, dinky cheap pseudo-marble, he supposes if you're in the roofing industry you know plumbing suppliers who can still provide the good stuff, even though there's not much market for it. The curved lavender bar he has right in his hands must have lost its lettering making lather for Cindy's suntanned skin, suds in her crotch, her hair must be jet black there, her eyebrows are: you should look at a woman's eyebrows not the hair on her head for the color of her pussy. This bathroom has not been so cleaned up for guests as the downstairs one, *Popular Mechanics* on the straw hamper next to the toilet, the towels slung crooked on the plastic towel holders and a touch of damp to them, the Murketts showering just a few hours ago for this party. Harry considers opening this bathroom cabinet as he did the other one but thinking of fingerprints notices the chrome rim and refrains. Nor does he dry his hands, for fear of touching the towel Webb used. He has seen that long yellow body in the Flying Eagle locker room. The man has moles all across his back and shoulders that probably aren't contagious but still.

He can't return downstairs with wet hands. That shit Harrison would make some crack. *Ya still got scum on your hands, ya jerkoff.* Rabbit stands a moment in the hall, listening to the noise of the party rise, a wordless clatter of voices happy without him, the women's the most distinct, a kind of throbbing in it like the melody you sometimes hear in a ragged engine idling, a song so distinct you expect to hear words. The hall is carpeted here not in lime but in a hushed plum, and he moves to follow its color to the threshold of the Murketts' bedroom. Here it happens. It hollows out Harry's stomach, makes him faintly sick, to think what a lucky stiff Webb is. The bed is low in modern style, a kind of tray with sides of reddish wood, and the covers had been pulled up hastily rather than made. Had it just happened? Just before the showers before the party that left the towels in the bathroom damp? In mid-air above the low bed he imagines in afterimage her damp and perfect toes, those sucky little dabtoes whose print he has often spied on the Flying Eagle flagstones, here lifted high to lay her cunt open, their baby dots mingling with the moles on Webb's back. It hurts, it isn't *fair* for Webb to be so lucky, not only to have a young wife but no old lady Springer on the other side of the walls. Where do the Murketts put their kids? Harry twists his head to see a closed white door at the far other end of the plum carpet. There. Asleep. He is safe. The carpet absorbs his footsteps as, silent as a ghost, he follow its color into the bedroom. A cavernous space, forbidden. Another shadowy presence jars his heart: a man in blue suit trousers and rumpled white shirt with cuffs folded back and a loosened necktie, looking overweight and dangerous, is watching him. Jesus. It is himself, his own full-length reflection in a large mirror placed between two matching bureaus of wood bleached so that the grain shows through as through powder. The mirror faces the foot of the bed. Hey. These two. It hasn't been just his imagination. They fuck in front of a mirror. Harry rarely sees himself head to toe except when he's buying a suit at Kroll's or that little tailor on Pine Street. Even there you stand close in to the three-way mirrors and there's not this weird surround of space, so he's meeting himself halfway across the room. He looks mussed and criminal, a burglar too overweight for this line of work.

Doubled in the mirror, the calm room holds few traces of the Murketts' living warmth. No little lacy bits of underwear lying around smelling of Cindy cunt. The curtains are a thick red striped material like a giant clown's pants ballooning, and they have window shades of that room-darkening kind that he keeps asking Janice to get; now that the leaves are letting go the light barrels through the copper beech right into his face at seven in the morning, he's making nearly fifty thousand a year and this is how he has to live, he and Janice will never get themselves organized. The far window here with its shade drawn for a nap must overlook the pool and the stand of woods everybody has up here in this development between the houses, but Harry doesn't want to get himself that deep into the room, already he's betraying hospitality. His hands have dried, he should go down. He is standing near a corner of the bed, its mute plane lower than his knees, the satiny peach bedspread tugged smooth in haste, and he impulsively, remembering the condoms he used to keep in a parallel place, steps to the curly maple bedside table and ever so stealthily pulls out the small drawer. It was open an inch anyway. No diaphragm, that would be in the bathroom. A ballpoint pen, an unlabelled box of pills, some match folders, a few receipts tossed in, a little yellow memo pad with the roofing company logo on it and a diagonally scrawled phone number, a nail clippers, some paper clips and golf tees, and – his thumping heart drowns out the mumble of the party beneath his feet. At the back of the drawer are tucked some black-backed Polaroid instant photos. That SX-70 Webb was bragging about. Harry lifts the little stack out delicately, turns it over, and studies the photos one by one. Shit. He should have brought his reading glasses, they're downstairs in his coat pocket, he must get over pretending he doesn't need them.

The top photo, flashlit in this same room, on this same satiny bedspread, shows Cindy naked, lying legs spread. Her pubic hair is even darker than he imagined, the shape of it from this angle a kind of T, the upright of the T infolded upon a redness as if sore, the underside of her untanned ass making a pale blob on either side. At arm's length he holds the glazed picture closer to the bedside light; his eyes water with the effort to see everything, every crease, every hair. Cindy's face, out of focus beyond her breasts, which droop more to either side than Harry would have hoped, smiles with nervous indulgence at the camera. Her chin is doubled, looking so sharply down. Her feet look enormous. In the next shot, she has turned over, showing a relaxed pair of buttocks, fish-white with an eyelike widening staring from the crack. For the next couple of photos the camera has switched hands, and old Webb, stringy and sheepish, stands as Harry has often seen him after a shower, except without the hard-on, which he is helping with his hand. Not a great hard-on, pointing to ten o'clock, not even ten but more like a little after nine, but then you can't expect a guy over fifty to go for high noon, leave that to the pimply teen-agers: when Rabbit was fourteen in soc sci class, a spot of sun, the shadow of Lotty Bingaman's armpit as she raised her hand with a pencil in it, that sweet strain of cloth and zipper against thick blood. Webb has length but not much bulk at the base; still, there he is, game and even with the pot belly and gnarled skinny legs and shit-eating expression somehow debonair, not a hair on his wavy head out of place. The next shots were in

282

the nature of experiments, by natural light, the shades must have all been up, bold to the day: slabby shapes and shelves of flesh interlocked and tipped toward violet by the spectrum of under-exposure. Harry deciphers one bulge as Cindy's cheek, and then the puzzle fits, she is blowing him, that purply stalk is his prick rooted in her stretched lips and the fuzzy foreground is Webb's chest hair as he takes the picture. In the next one he has improved the angle and light and the focus is perfect on the row of one eye's black lashes. Beyond the shiny tan tip of her nose, her fingers, boneless and blue-knuckled, with grubby nails, hold the veined thing in its place, her little finger lifted as on a flute. What was Ollie saying about flutes? For the next shot Webb had the idea of using the mirror; he is standing sideways with the camera squarely where his face ought to be and Cindy's own dear face impaled, as she kneels naked, on this ten-o'clock hook of his. Her profile is snub-nosed and her nipples jut out stiff. The old bastard's tricks have turned the little bitch on. But her head seems so small and round and brave, stuck on his prick like a candy apple. Harry wants in the next picture to see come like toothpaste all over her face like in the fuck movies, but Webb has turned her around and is fucking her from behind, his prick vanished in the fish-white curve of her ass and his free hand steadying her with his thumb sunk where her asshole would be; her tits hang down pear-shaped in their weight and her legs next to Webb's appear stocky. She's getting there. She will get fatter. She will turn ugly. She is looking into the mirror and laughing. Perhaps in the difficulty of keeping her balance while Webb's one hand operates the camera, Cindy laughed at that moment a big red laugh like a girl on a poster, with this yellow prick in her from behind. The light in the room must have been dying that day for the flesh of both the Murketts appears golden and the furniture reflected in the mirror is dim in blue shadow as if underwater. This is the last picture; there were eight and a camera like this takes ten. *Consumer Reports* had a lot to say a while ago about the SX-70 Land Camera but never did explain what the SX stood for. Now Harry knows. His eyes burn.

The party noise below is lessening, perhaps they are listening for a sound from upstairs, wondering what has happened to him.

He slips the Polaroids back into the drawer, face down, black backs up, and tries to slide shut the drawer to the exact inch it was open by. The room otherwise is untouched; the mirror will erase his image instantly. The only clue remaining, he has given himself an aching great erection. He can't go downstairs like this: he tries to tear his mind loose from that image of her open mouth laughing at the sight of herself being fucked, who would have thought sweet Cindy could be so dirty? It takes some doing to realize that other boys are like you are, that dirty, and then to realize that girls can go right along with it takes more than one lifetime to assimilate. Rabbit tries to fling away that laugh, out of his mind, but it has no more carry to it than a handkerchief. He tries to displace what he has just seen with his other secrets. His daughter. His gold. His son coming down from the Poconos tomorrow to claim his place at the last. That does it, the thing is wilting. Holding gloomy Nelson firmly in his mind, Harry goes into the bathroom and turns on the faucet as if washing his hands in case somebody down below is listening while he undoes his belt and tucks himself properly into his underpants. What is killing, he has seen her laugh that same laugh at poolside, at something he or Buddy Inglefinger or even some joker from outside their group altogether has just said. She'd go down on anybody.

As he descends the stairs his head still feels to be floating on a six-foot string attached to his big shoes. The gang in the long living room has realigned itself in a tighter circle about the Parsons table. There seems to be no place for him. Ronnie Harrison looks up. 'My God, whatcha been doin', jacking off?'

'I'm not feeling so great,' Rabbit says, with dignity.

'Your eyes look red,' Janice says. 'Have you been crying again?'

They are too excited by the topic among themselves to tease him long. Cindy doesn't even turn around. The nape of her neck is thick and brown, soft and impervious. Treading to them on spongy steps across the endless pale carpeting, he pauses by the fireplace mantel to notice what he had failed to notice before, two Polaroid snaps propped up, one each of the Murketts' little children, the five-year-old boy with an outsize fielder's mitt standing sadly on the bricks of their patio, and the three-year-old girl on this same hazily bright summer afternoon, before the

284

parents took a nap, squinting with an obedient and foolish half-smile up toward some light-source that dazzles her. Betsey is wearing both pieces of a play-muddied little bikini and Webb's shadow, arms lifted to his head as if to scare her with horns, fills one corner of the exposed square of film. These are the missing two shots from that pack of ten.

'Hey, Harry, how about the second week of January?' Ronnie hoots at him.

They have all been discussing a shared trip to the Caribbean, and the women are as excited about it as the men.

It is after one when he and Janice drive home. Brewer Heights is a development of two-acre lots off the highway to Maiden Springs, a good twenty minutes from Mt Judge. The road sweeps down in stylish curves; the developer left trees, and six hours ago when they drove up this road each house was lit in its bower of unbulldozed woods like displays in the façade of a long gray department store. Now the houses, all but the Murketts', are dark. Dead leaves swirl in the headlights, pour from the trees in the fall wind as if from bushel baskets. The seasons catch up to you. The sky gets streaky, the trees begin to heave. Harry can think of little to say, intent upon steering on these winding streets called drives and boulevards. The stars flickering through the naked swaying treetops of Brewer Heights yield to the lamp-lit straightaway of the Maiden Springs Pike. Janice drags on a cigarette; the glow expands in the side of his vision, and falls away. She clears her throat and says, 'I suppose I should have stuck up more for Peggy, she being an old friend and all. But she did talk out of turn, I thought.'

'Too much women's lib.'

'Too much Ollie maybe. I know she keeps thinking of leaving him.'

'Aren't you glad we have all that behind us?'

He says it mischievously, to hear her grapple with whether they did or didn't, but she answers simply, 'Yes.'

He says nothing. His tongue feels trapped. Even now, Webb is undressing Cindy. Or she him. And kneeling. Harry's tongue seems stuck to the floor of his mouth like those poor kids every winter who insist on touching their tongues to iron railings.

Janice tells him, 'Your idea of taking this trip in a bunch sure took hold.'

'It'll be fun.'

'For you men playing golf. What'll *we* do all day?'

'Lie in the sun. There'll be things. They'll have tennis courts.' This trip is precious to him, he speaks of it gingerly.

Janice drags again. 'They keep saying now how sunbathing leads to cancer.'

'No faster than smoking.'

'Thelma has this condition where she shouldn't be in the sun at all, it could kill her she's told me. I'm surprised she's so keen on going.'

'Maybe she won't be in the morning on second thought. I don't see how Harrison can afford it, with that kid of theirs in defective school.'

'Can we I wonder? Afford it. On top of the gold.'

'Honey, of course. The gold's already gone up more than the trip will cost. We're so pokey, we should have taken up travelling years ago.'

'You never wanted to go anywhere, with just me.'

'Of course I did. We were running scared. We had the Poconos to go to.'

'I was wondering, it might mean leaving Nelson and Pru just at the time.'

'Forget it. The way she hung on to Nelson, she'll hang on to this baby till the end of January. Till Valentine's Day.'

'It seems mean,' she says. 'And then leaving Nelson at the lot alone with too much responsibility.'

'It's what he wanted, now he's got it. What can happen? Jake and Rudy'll be around. Manny'll run his end.'

Her cigarette glows once more, and then with that clumsy scrabbling motion that always annoys him she stubs it out. He hates having the Corona ashtray dirty, it smells for days even after you've emptied it. She sighs. 'I wish in a way it was just us going, if we must go.'

'We don't know the ropes. Webb does. He's been there before,

I think he's been going since long before Cindy, with his other wives.'

'You can't mind Webb,' she admits. 'He's nice. But to tell the truth I could do without the Harrisons.'

'I thought you had a soft spot for Ronnie.'

'That's you.'

'I hate him,' Rabbit says.

'You like him, all that vulgarity. He reminds you of basketball days. Anyway it's not just him. Thelma worries me.'

'How can she? She's a mouse.'

'I think she's very fond of you.'

'I never noticed. How can she be?' Stay off Cindy, he'll let it all out. He tries to see those photographs again, hair by hair in his mind's eye, and already they are fading. The way their bodies looked golden at the end, like gods.

Janice says with a sudden surprising stiffness, 'Well, I don't know what you think's going to happen down there but we're not going to have any funny stuff. We're too *old*, Harry.'

A pick-up truck with its high beams glaring tailgates him blindingly and then roars around him, kids' voices jeering.

'The drunks are out,' he says, to change the subject.

'What were you *doing* up there in the bathroom so long anyway?' she asks.

He answers primly, 'Waiting for something to happen that didn't.'

'Oh. Were you sick?'

'Heading toward it, I thought. That brandy. That's why I switched to beer.'

Cindy is so much on his mind he cannot understand why Janice fails to mention her, it must be deliberate. All that blowing, Lord. There's birth control. White gobs of it pumping in, being swallowed; those little round teeth and the healthy low baby gums that show when she laughs. Webb on front and him from behind, or the other way around, Harry doesn't care. Ronnie operating the camera. His prick has reawaked, high noon once more in his life, and the steering wheel as they turn into Central Street caresses its swollen tip through the cloth. Janice should appreciate this: if he can get it up to their room intact.

But her mind has wandered far from sex, for as they head down through the cones of limb-raddled light along Wilbur she says aloud, 'Poor Nelson. He seemed so young, didn't he, going off with his bride?'

This town they know so well, every curb, every hydrant, where every mailbox is. It gives way before them like a veil, its houses dark, their headlights low. 'Yeah,' he agrees. 'You sometimes wonder,' he hears himself go on, 'how badly you yourself fucked up a kid like that.'

'We did what we could,' Janice says, firm again, sounding like her mother. 'We're not God.'

'Nobody is,' Rabbit says, scaring himself.

# IV

The hostages have been taken. Nelson has been working at Springer Motors for five weeks. Teresa is seven months pregnant and big as a house, a house within a house as she mopes around Mom-mom's in those maternity slacks with Spandex in front and some old shirts of Dad's he let her have. When she walks down the upstairs hall from the bathroom she blocks out all the light, and when she tries to help in the kitchen she drops a dish. Because there are five of them now they have had to dip into the good china Mom-mom keeps in the breakfront and the dish Pru dropped was a good one. Though Mom-mom doesn't say much you can see by the way her throat gets mottled it's a deal for her, the kind of thing that is a big deal for old ladies, going on about those dishes that she and Fred bought fifty years ago together at Kroll's when the trolley cars ran all up and down Weiser every seven minutes and Brewer was a hot shit kind of place.

What Nelson can't stand about Pru, she farts. And lying on her back in bed because she can't sleep on her stomach, she snores. A light but raspy little rhythmic noise he can't ignore, lying there in the front room with the streetlights eating away at the window-shades and the cars going by on the street below, free. He misses his quiet old room at the back of the house. He wonders if Pru has what they call a deviated septum. Until he married her, he didn't notice that her nostrils aren't exactly the same size: one is more tear-drop-shaped than the other, as if her thin pointy nose with its freckles had been given a sideways tweak when it was still soft back there in Akron. And then she keeps wanting to go to bed early at just the hour after dinner when the traffic outside picks up and he is dying to go out, over to the Laid-Back for a brew or two or even just down to the Superette on Route 422 to check out some new faces after the claustrophobia of hanging around the lot all day trying to deal around Dad and then coming home and having to deal around him some more, his big head grazing the ceiling and his silly lazy voice laying down the law on everything, if you listen, putting Nelson down, looking at him so nervously, with that sad-eyed little laugh, *Did I say that?*, when he thinks he's said something funny. The trouble with Dad is he's lived in a harem too long, Mom and Mom-mom doing everything for him. Any other man around except Charlie who was dying in front of your eyes and those goons he plays golf with, he gets nasty. Nobody except Nelson in the world seems to realize how nasty Harry C. Angstrom is and the pressure of it sometimes makes Nelson want to scream, his father comes into the room all big and fuzzy and sly when he's a killer, a body-count of two to his credit and his own son next if he can figure out how to do it without looking bad. Dad doesn't like to look bad anymore, that was one thing about him in the old days you could admire, that he didn't care that much how he looked from the outside, what the neighbours thought when he took Skeeter in for instance, he had this crazy dim faith in himself left over from basketball or growing up as everybody's pet or whatever so he could say Fuck You to people now and then. That spark is gone, leaving a big dead man on Nelson's chest. He tries to explain it to Pru and she listens but she doesn't understand.

At Kent she was slender and erect and quick in her way of walking, her terrific long carrotty hair up in a sleek twist when it wasn't let flat down her back looking ironed. Going to meet her up at the new part of Rockwell around five, a student out of water, he would feel enlarged to be taking this working woman a year older than he away from the typewriters and files and cool bright light; the administration offices seemed a piece of the sky of the world's real business that hung above the tunnels of the classes he wormed through every day. Pru had none of that false savvy, she knew none of the names to drop, the fancy dead, and could talk only about what was alive now, movies and records and what was on TV and the scandals day to day at work, who burst into tears and who had been propositioned by one of the deans. One of the other secretaries at work was fucking the man she worked for without much liking him but out of a kind of flip indifference to her own life and body and it thrilled Nelson to think how that could be Pru just as well, there was a tightness to lives in Pennsylvania that loosened out here and let people drift where they would. It thrilled him how casually tough she was, with that who-cares? way of walking beside him, smelling of perfume, and a softer scent attached to her clothes, beneath all those trees they kept bragging about at Kent, that and all those gyms in the Student Center Complex and having the biggest campus bus system in the world, all that bullshit heaped on to try to make people forget the only claim to fame Kent State would ever have, which was May 4, 1970, when the Guardsmen fired from Blanket Hill. As far as Nelson was concerned they could have shot all those jerks. When in '77 there was that fuss about Tent City Nelson stayed in his dorm. He didn't know Pru then. At one of the bars along Water Street she would get into the third White Russian and tell him horror stories of her own growing up, beatings and rages and unexplained long absences on her father's part and then the tangled doings of her sisters as they matured sexually and began to kick the house down. His tales seemed pale in comparison. Pru made him feel better about being himself. With so many of the students he knew, including Melanie, he felt mocked, outsmarted by them at some game he didn't want to play, but with Pru Lubell, this secretary, he did not feel mocked. They agreed about things, basic things. They knew that at bottom the world was brutal, no father protected you, you were left alone in a way not appreciated by these kids horsing around on jock teams or playing at being radicals or doing the rah-rah thing or their own thing or whatever. That Nelson saw it was all bullshit gave him for Pru a certain seriousness. Across the plywood booth tables of the workingman's-type bar in north Akron they used to go to in her car – she had a car of her own, a salt-rotted old Plymouth Valiant, its front fender flapping like a flag, and this was another thing he liked about her, her being willing to drive such an ugly old clunker, and having worked for the money to pay for it – Nelson could tell he looked pretty good. In terms of the society she knew he was a step up. And so was she, in terms of this environment, the local geography. Not only a car but an apartment, small but all her own, with a stove she cooked her own dinners on, and liquor she would pour for him after putting on a record. From their very first date, not counting the times they were messing around with Melanie and her freaky SLDK friends, Pru had taken him back to her apartment house in this town called Stow, assuming without making any big deal of it that fucking was what they were both after. She came with firm quick thrusts that clipped him tight and secure into his own coming. He had fucked other girls before but hadn't been sure if they had come. With Pru he was sure. She would cry out and even flip a little, like a fish that flashes to the surface of a gloomy lake. And afterwards cooking him up something to eat she would walk around naked, her hair hanging down her back to about the sixth bump on her spine, even though there were a lot of windows across the apartment courtyard she could be seen from. Who cares? She liked being looked at, actually, in the dancing spots they went to some nights, and in private let him look at her from every angle, her big smooth body like that of a doll whose arms and legs and head stayed where you set them. His intense gratitude for all this, where another might have casually accepted, added to his value in her eyes until he was locked in, too precious to let go of, ever.

Now she sits all day watching the afternoon soaps with Mom-mom and sometimes Mom, *Search for Tomorrow* on Channel 10 and then *Days of Our Lives* on 3 and back to 10 for *As the World Turns* and over to 6 for *One Life to Live* and then 10 again for *The Guiding Light*, Nelson knows the routine from all those days before they let him work at the lot. Now Pru farts because of some way the baby is displacing her insides and drops things and says she thinks his father is perfectly nice.

He has told her about Becky. He told her about Jill. Pru's response is. 'But that was long ago.'

'Not to me. It is to him. He's forgotten, the silly shit, just to look at him you can see he's forgotten. He's forgotten everything he ever did to us. The stuff he did to Mom, incredible, and I don't know the half of it probably. He's so smug and *sat*isfied, is what gets me. If I could *just once* make him see himself for the shit he is, I maybe could let it go.'

'What good would it do, Nelson? I mean, your father's not perfect, but who is? At least he stays home nights, which is more than mine ever did.'

'He's gutless, that's why he stays home. Don't you think he wouldn't like to be out chasing pussy every night? Just the way he used to look at Melanie. It isn't any great love of Mom that holds him back, I tell you that. It's the lot. Mom has the whip hand now, no thanks to herself.'

'Why, honey. I think from what I've seen your parents are quite fond of each other. Couples that have stayed together that long, they must have something.'

To dip his mind into this possibility disgusts Nelson. The wallpaper, its tangled pattern of things moving in and out of things, looks evil. As a child he was afraid of this front room where now they sleep, across the hall from the mumble of Mom-mom's television. Cars passing on Joseph Street, underneath the bare maple limbs, wheel sharp-edged panels around the walls, bright shapes rapidly altering like in those computer games that are everywhere now. When a car brakes at the corner, a patch of red shudders across the wallpaper and a pale framed print of a goateed farmer with a wooden bucket at some stone well: this fading print has always hung here. The farmer too had seemed evil to the child's eyes, a leering devil. Now Nelson can see the figure as merely foolish, sentimental. Still, the taint of malevolence remains, caught somewhere in the transparency of the glass. The red shudders, and winks away; a motor guns, and tires dig out. Go: the fury of this unseen car, escaping, becoming a mere buzz in the distance, gratifies Nelson vicariously.

He and Pru are lying in the old swaybacked bed he used to share with Melanie. He thinks of Melanie, unpregnant, free, having a ball at Kent, riding the campus buses, taking courses in Oriental religion. Pru is dead sleepy, lying there in an old shirt of Dad's buttoned at the breasts and unbuttoned over her belly. He had offered her some shirts of his, now that he has this job he has had to buy shirts, and she said they were too small and pinched. The room is hot. The furnace is directly under it and heat rises, there's nothing they can do about it, here it is the middle of November and they still sleep under a sheet. He is wide awake and will be for hours, agitated by his day. Those friends of Billy's are after him to buy some more convertibles and though the Olds Delta 88 Royale did sell for $3600 to that doctor Dad says and says Manny backs him up on this that by the time you figure in the deductible on the insurance and the carrying costs there really wasn't any profit.

And now the Mercury is in the shop though the insurance man wanted to declare it totalled, he said that would be simplest with a virtual antique like this, parts at a premium and the front end screwed up like somebody had done it deliberately, Manny estimates that the repair costs are going to come in four to five hundred above the settlement check, they can't give you more than car book value, and when he asked Manny if some of the mechanics couldn't do it in their spare time he said, looking so solemn, his brow all furrowed and the black pores in his nose jumping out at you, *Kid, there is no spare time, these men come in here for their bread and butter,* implying he didn't, a rich man's son. Not that Dad backs him up in any of this, he takes the attitude the kid's being taught a lesson, and enjoys it. The only lesson Nelson's being taught is that everybody is out for their own little pile of dollars and nobody can look up to have any vision. He'll show them when he sells that Mercury for forty-five hundred or so, he knows a lot of guys at the Laid-Back money like that is nothing to. This Iranian thing is going to scare gas prices even higher but it'll blow over, they won't dare keep them long, the hostages. Dad keeps telling him how it costs three to five dollars a day every day to carry a car in inventory but he can't see why, if it's just sitting there on a lot you already own, the company even pays rent to itself, he's discovered, to gyp the government.

Pru beside him starts to snore, her head propped up on two pillows, her belly shiny like one of those puffballs you find in the woods attached to a rotten stump. Downstairs Mom and Dad are laughing about something, they've been high as kites lately, worse than kids, going out a lot more with that crummy crowd of theirs, at least kids have the excuse there isn't much else to do. He thinks of those hostages in Tehran and it's like a pill caught in his throat, one of those big dry vitamins Melanie was always pushing on him, when it won't go down or come up. Take a single big black helicopter in there on a moonless night, commandos with black-ened faces, a little piano wire around the throats of those freaky radical Arabs, *uuglh, arg*, you'd have to whisper, women and children first, and lift them all away. Drop a little tactical A-bomb on a minaret as a calling card. Or else a tunnel or some sort of boring machine like James Bond would have. That fantastic scene in *Moonraker* when he's dumped from the plane without a para-chute and free-falls into one of the bad guys and steals his, can't be much worse than hang gliding. By the moonlight Pru's belly-button is casting a tiny shadow, it's been popped like inside out, he never knew a pregnant woman naked before, he had no idea it was that bad. Like a cannonball, that hit from behind and stuck.

Once in a while they get out. They have friends. Billy Fosnacht has gone back to Tufts but the crowd at the Laid-Back still gathers, guys and these scumbags from around Brewer still hang-ing around, with jobs in the new electronics plants or some government boondoggle or what's left of the downtown stores; you go into Kroll's these days, where Mom met Dad in pre-historic days, you go in through that forest where Weiser Square used to be and it's like the deserted deck of a battleship just after the Japs bombed Pearl Harbor, a few scared salesladies standing around cut off at the waist by the On Sale tables. Mom used to work at the salted nut and candy section but they don't have one anymore, probably figured out after thirty years and six people died of worms it wasn't sanitary. But if there hadn't been a nut counter Nelson wouldn't exist, or would exist as somebody else, which doesn't make sense. He and Pru don't know all their friends' first names, they have first names like Cayce and Pam and Jason and Scott and Dody and Lyle and Derek and Slim, and if you show up at the Laid-Back enough you get asked along to some of their parties. They live in places like those new condos with stained rough-planking walls and steep-pitched roofs like a row of silk lodges thrown up on the side of Mt Pemaquid out near the Flying Eagle, or like those city mansions of brick and slate with lots of ironwork and chimneys that the old mill money built along the north end of Youngquist or out beyond the car yards and now are broken up into apartments, where they haven't been made into

295

nursing homes or office buildings for cutesy outfits like hand-crafted-leather shops and do-it-yourself framers and young architects specializing in solar panels and energy saving and young lawyers with fluffy hair and bandit mustaches along with their business suits, that charge their young clients a flat fee of three hundred dollars whether it's for a divorce or beating a possession rap. In these neighborhoods health-food stores have sprung up, and little long restaurants in half-basements serving vegetarian or macrobiotic or Israeli cuisine, and bookstores with names like Karma Paperbacks, and little shops heavy on macramé and batik and Mexican wedding shirts and Indian silk and those drifter hats that make everybody look like the part of his head with the brain in it has been cut off. Old machine shops with cinder-block sides now sell pieces of unpainted furniture you put together yourselves, for these apartments where everybody shares.

The apartment Slim shares with Jason and Pam is on the third floor of a tall old house on the high side of Locust, blocks beyond the high school, in the direction of Maiden Springs. A big bay of three four-paned windows overlooks the deadened heart of the city: where once the neon outlines of a boot, a peanut, a top hat, and a great sunflower formed a garland of advertisement above Weiser Square now only the Brewer Trust's beacons trained on its own granite façade mark the center of the downtown, four great pillars like four white fingers stuck in a rich black pie, the dark patch made by the planted trees of the so-called shopping mall. From this downtown the standard sodium-yellow lamps of the city streets spread outward, a rectilinear web receding down toward the curving river and on into suburbs whose glow flattens to a horizon swallowed by hills that merge with the clouds of night. Slim's front bay windows have in their upper panes the stained-glass transom lights, those simplified flowers of pieces of purple and amber and milky green, that are along with pretzels Brewer's pride. But the old floors of parqueted oak have been covered wall-to-wall with cheap shag carpeting speckled like pimento, and hasty plasterboard partitions have divided up the generous original room. The high ceilings have been lowered, to save heat, and reconstituted in soft white panels of something like pegboard. Nelson sits on the floor, his head tipped back, a can of beer cold between his ankles; he has shared two joints with Pru and the little holes in the ceiling are trying to tell him something, an area of them seems sharp and vivid and aggressive, like the blackheads on Manny's nose the other day, and then this look fades and another area takes it up, as if a jellyfish of intensity is moving transparently across the ceiling. Behind him on the wall is a large grimacing poster of Ilie Nastase. Slim belongs to a tennis club out next to the Hemmigtown Mall and loves Ilie Nastase. Nastase is beaded with sweat, his legs thick as posts. Hairy, knotty posts. The stereo is playing Donna Summer, something about a telephone, very loud. Out in the center of the room between Nelson and some potted ferns and broad-leaved plants like Mom-mom used to have in that side room off the living room (he remembers sitting with his father looking at them some day when an awful thing had happened, a thing enormous and hollow under them while the leaves of the plants drank the sunlight as these bigger plants too must do when the sun comes slanting in the tall bay windows) there is a space and in this space Slim is dancing like a snake on a string with another skinny boy with a short haircut called Lyle. Lyle has a narrow skull with hollows at the back and wears tight jeans and some long-sleeved shirt like a soccer shirt with a broad green stripe down the middle. Slim is queer and though Nelson isn't supposed to mind that he does. He also minds that there are a couple of slick blacks making it at the party and that one little white girl with that grayish kind of sharp-chinned Polack face from the south side of Brewer took off her shirt while dancing even though she has no tits to speak of and now sits in the kitchen with still bare tits getting herself sick on Southern Comfort and Pepsi. At these parties someone is always in the bathroom being sick or giving themselves a hit or a snort and Nelson minds this too. He doesn't mind any of it very much, he's just tired of being young. There's so much wasted energy to it. He sees on the ceiling that the jellyfish intensity flitting across the holes is energy such as flows through the binary bits of computers but he can't take it any further than that. At Kent he was curious about computer science but in just the introductory course Math 10061 in Merrill Hall the math got to be too much for him, all those Jewish kids and Koreans with faces flat as platters just breezing along like it was plain as day, what a function was, it didn't seem to be anything you could actually point to, just the general idea somehow of the equation, another jellyfish, but how to extract it out? It beat him. So he figured he might as well come home and share the wealth. His father was holding him on his lap that day, the sensation of a big warm sad-smelling body all around and under his has stayed with him along with a memory of a beam of sunlight eating into the crescent edge of a furry leaf in that iron table of green plants, it must have been around when Becky died. Mom-mom can't last forever and when she kicks the bucket that leaves him and Mom in charge of the lot, with Dad up front like one of those life-size cardboard cutouts you used to see in car showrooms before cardboard became too expensive. Those blacks mooching around so superior, that decided cool way they have of saying hello, daring you to outstare them, not taking responsibility for anything though, makes him itch with fury, though the joints should be working him around toward mellow by now. Maybe another beer. Then he remembers the beer between his knees, it's cold and heavy because it's full and fresh from Slim's fridge, and takes a sip. Nelson studies his hand carefully because it feels holding the can as though he has a mitten on.

Why doesn't Dad just die? People that age get diseases. Then he and Mom. He knows he can manage Mom.

He's not that young, he's turned twenty-three, and what makes him feel foolish among these people, he's married. Nobody else here looks married. There is sure nobody else pregnant, that it shows. It makes him feel put on display, as a guy who didn't know better. To be fair to her Pru didn't want to come out, she was willing to sit over there like one of these green plants basking in the light of the television set, watching *The Love Boat* and then *Fantasy Island* with poor old Mom-mom, she's been fading lately, Dad and Mom used to sit home with her but now like tonight they're out somewhere with that Flying Eagle crowd, incredible how irresponsible grownups so-called get when they think they're ahead of the game, Mom has told him all about their crazy gold, maybe he should have offered to stay home, him and Pru with Mom-mom, she's the one with all the cards after all, but by that time Pru had gotten herself dolled up thinking she owed Nelson a little social life because he was working so hard and always housebound with her – families, doing everything for each other out of imagined obligation and always getting in each other's way, what a tangle. Then once Pru got here and got a buzz on, the madwoman of Akron took over, she decided to play to the hilt the token pregnant woman, throwing her weight around, dancing in shoes she really shouldn't even be walking in, thick-soled wedgy platforms held on by thin green plastic strapping like that gimp the playground supervisors at the Mt Judge Rec Field used to have you braid lanyards for a whistle out of, there was even he remembers a way of weaving called butterflies, you could make a keyholder this way as if kids ever had keys to hold. Maybe she's doing it out of spite. But he has undergone an abandonment of his own and enjoys watching her from a distance of his own, through the smoke. She has flash, Pru, flash and glitter in this electric-green beltless dress she bought herself at a new shop over on Locust where the old retired people are being forced out by gentrification, the middle class returning to the cities. Sleeves wide as wings lift when she whirls and that cannonball of a stomach sticks out tugging up her dress in front to show more of the orange elastic stockings the doctor told her to wear to save her young veins. Her shiny platforms can barely shuffle on the shag carpeting but she leaves them on, showing she can do it, more spite at him; her body as if skewered through a spot between her shoulder blades writhes to the music while her arms lift green and her fantastic long hair snaps in a circle, again and again.

Nelson cannot dance, which is to say he will not, for all dancing is now is standing in place and letting the devil of the music enter you, which takes more faith than he's got. He doesn't want to appear a fool. Now Dad, Dad would do it if he were here, just like when Jill was there he gave himself to Skeeter and never looked back even when all the worst had happened, such a fool he really believes there is a God he is the apple of the eye of. The dots on the ceiling don't let Nelson take this glimpse higher than this and he returns his eyes to Pru, painfully bright in the dazzle dress, its flow like a jewel turned liquid, her face asleep in the music above her belly, which is solid and not hers alone but also his, so he is dancing too. He hates for a second that in himself which cannot do it, just as he could not join in the flickering mind play of computer science and college generally and could not be the floating easy athlete his father had been. The dark second passes, dissolved by the certainty that some day he will have his revenge on them all.

Pru's partner for some of the dancing has been one of the sassy Brewer blacks, the bigger one, in bib overalls and cowboy boots, and then Slim comes out of a twirl over by the potted plants with Lyle and swings into orbit with Pru, who keeps at it whether or not anybody is there, up and down, little flips of her hands, and a head toss. Her face does look asleep. That hooked nose of hers sharp in profile. People keep touching her belly, as if for luck: in spinning and snapping their fingers their loose fingers trail across the sacred bulge where something that belongs to him too is lodged. But how to fend off their touches, how to protect her and keep her clean? She is too big, he would look like a fool, she likes the dirt, she came out of it. Once she drove him past her old home in Akron, she never took him in, what a sad row, houses with wooden porches with old refrigerators on them. Melanie would have been better, her brother played polo. At least Pru should take off her shoes. He sees himself rising up to tell her but in truth feels too stoned to move, obliged to sit here and mellow between the fluffy worms of the carpet and the worm holes of the ceiling. The music has gas bubbles in it, popping in the speakers, and Donna Summer's zombie voice slides in and out of itself, doubling, taking all parts. *Stuck on you, stuck like glue.* The fairy that Slim stopped dancing with offers Pru a toke and she sucks the wet tip of the joint and holds it deep without losing a beat of the music, belly and feet keeping that twitch. Nelson sees that to an Akron slum kid like this Brewer is a city of hicks and she's showing them all something.

A girl he noticed before, she came here with some big red-faced clod who actually wore a coat and tie to this brawl, comes and sits in the floor beside Nelson under Ilie Nastase and takes the beer from between his ankles to sip from it. Her smiling pale round face looks a little lost here but willing to please. 'Where do *you* live?'

she asks, as if picking up with him a conversation begun with someone else.

'In Mt Judge?' He thinks that's the answer.

'In an apartment?'

'With my parents and my grandmother.'

'Why is that?' Her face shines amiably with sweat. She has been drinking too. But there is a calm about her he is grateful for. Her legs stretch out beside his in white pants that look radiant where that jellyfish of strangeness moves across them.

'It's cheaper.' He softens this. 'We thought no point in looking for a place until the baby comes.'

'You have a wife?'

'There she is.' He gestures toward Pru.

The girl drinks her in. 'She's terrific.'

'You could say that.'

'What does *that* tone of voice mean?'

'It means she's bugging the shit out of me.'

'Should she be bouncing like that? I mean, the baby.'

'Well, they say exercise. Where do *you* live?'

'Not far. On Youngquist. Our apartment isn't near as grand as this, we're on the first floor back, overlooking a little yard where all the cats come. The say our building might be going condo.'

'That good or bad?'

'Good if you have the money, bad if you don't I guess. We just started working in town and my – my man wants to go to college when we get our stake.'

'Tell him, Forget it. I've been to college and it's absolute horse poop.' She has a pleasant puffy look to her upper lip and he's sorry to see, from the way she holds her mouth, that he's left her nothing to say. 'What do you work at?' he asks her.

'I'm a nurses' aide in an old people's home. I doubt if you know it, Sunnyside out toward the old fairgrounds.'

'Isn't it depressing?'

'People say that but I don't mind it. They talk to me, that's mostly what people want, company.'

'You and this man aren't married?'

'Not yet. He wants to get further along in life. I think it's good. We might want to change our minds.'

'Smart. That chick in green out there got herself knocked up and I had no choice.' Not much answer to this either. Yet the girl doesn't show boredom, like so many people do with him. At the lot he watches Jake and Rudy prattle away and he envies how they do it without feeling idiotic. This strange face hangs opposite his calmly, mildly attentive, the eyes a blue paler than you almost ever see and her skin milky and nose slightly tipped up and her gingery hair loosely bundled to the back. Her ears are exposed and pierced but unadorned. In his stoned condition the squarish white folds of these ears seem very vivid. 'You say you just moved to town,' Nelson says. 'Where'd you move from?'

'Near Galilee. Know where that is?'

'More or less. When I was a kid we went down there to the drag race strip a couple times.'

'You can hear the engines from our place, on a quiet night. My room is on the side and I used to always hear them.'

'Where we live there's always traffic going by. My room used to be out in back but now it's up front.' Dear little ears, small like his, though nothing else about her is small, especially. Her thighs really fill those bright white pants. 'What does your father do, he a farmer?'

'My father's dead.'

'Oh. Sorry.'

'No, it was hard, but he was getting along. He was a farmer, you're right, and he had the school bus contract for the township.'

'Still, that's too bad.'

'I have a wonderful mother though.'

'What's wonderful about her?'

In his stupidity he keeps sounding combative. But she doesn't seem to mind. 'Oh. She's just very understanding. And can be very funny. I have these two brothers –'

'You do?'

'Yes, and she's never tried to make me feel I should back down or anything because I'm a girl.'

'Well why would she?' He feels jealous.

'Some mothers would. They think girls should be quiet and

smart. Mine says women get more out of life. With men, it's if you don't win every time, you're nothing.'

'Some momma. She has it all figured.'

'And she's fatter than I am and I love her for that.'

*You're not fat, you're just nice,* he wants to tell her. Instead he says, 'Finish up the beer. I'll get us another.'

'No thanks – what's your name?'

'Nelson.' He should ask her hers but the words stick.

'Nelson. No thanks, I just wanted a sip. I should go see what Jamie's doing. He's in the kitchen with some girl –'

'Who's showing her tits.'

'That's right.'

'My theory on that is, those that got real tits to show don't.' He glances down. The vertical ribs of her russet knit sweater are pushed slightly apart as they pass over the soft ample shelf there. Below that the white cloth of her slacks, taut in wrinkles where belly meets thighs in a triangle, has a radiance that manifests the diagonal run of the threads, the way the cloth was woven and cut. Below that her feet are bare, with a pinkness along the outer edge of each big toe fresh from the pressure of her discarded shoes.

The girl has been made to blush by this survey of her body. 'What do you do since college, Nelson?'

'I just veg out. No, actually, I sell cars. Not your ordinary tacky cars but special old convertibles, that nobody makes anymore. Their value is going to go up and up, it *has* to.'

'Sounds exciting.'

'It is. Jesus, the other day in the middle of town I saw this white Thunderbird parked, with red leather seats, the guy still had the top down though it's getting pretty cold, and I nearly flipped. It looked like a yacht. When they turned out those things there wasn't all this penny-pinching.'

'Jamie and I just bought a Corolla. It's in his name but I'm the one that uses it, there isn't any bus that goes out to the fairgrounds anymore and Jamie has a job he can walk to, in this place that makes bug-killers, you know, those electric grids with a purple light that people put outdoors by their pools or barbecues.'

'Sounds groovy. Must be a slack season for him though.'

'You'd think so but it's not, they're busy making them for next year, and they ship all over the South.'

'Huh.' Maybe they've had enough of this conversation. He doesn't want to hear any more about Jamie's bug-killers.

But the girl keeps going, she's relaxed with him now, and so young everything is new to her. Nelson guesses she's three or four years younger than he is. Pru is over a year older, and that irritates him right now, along with her defiant dancing and her pregnancy and all these blacks and queers she's not afraid of. 'So I really should put in my half,' she is explaining, 'even though he makes twice what I do. His parents and my mother loaned us the down payment equally though I know she couldn't afford it. Next year if I can get a part-time job somewhere I want to begin nurse's training. Those RNs make a fortune doing just what I'm doing now, except they're allowed to give injections.'

'Jesus, you want to spend your whole life around sick people?'

'I like taking care of things. On the farm until my father died there were always animals. I used to shear my own sheep even.'

'Huh.' Nelson has always been allergic to animals.

'Do you dance, Nelson?' she asks him.

'No. I sit and drink beer and feel sorry for myself.' Pru is bouncing around now with a Puerto Rican or something. Manny has a couple of them working for him in the shop now. He doesn't know what disease they get as kids, but their cheeks have worse than pocks – like little hollow cuts all over.

'Jamie won't dance either.'

'Ask one of the fairies. Or just go do it by yourself, somebody'll pick you up.'

'I love to dance. Why do you feel sorry for yourself?'

'Oh . . . my father's a prick.' He doesn't know why this popped out of his mouth. Something about the goody-goody way in which the girl speaks of her own parents. But in thinking of his father, what strikes Nelson about the large bland face that appears to his inner eye is a mournful helplessness. His father's face bloats like an out-of-focus close-up in some war movie in the scramble of battle before floating away. Big and white and vague as on that day when he held him on his lap, when the world was too much for the two of them.

'You shouldn't say that,' the girl says, and stands. Luminous long legs. Her thighs make a kind of lap even when she stands. Her pink-rimmed bare feet sunk in the shag rug so close nearly kill him, they are so sexy. What did she say that for? Making him feel guilty and scolded. Her own father is dead. She makes him feel he's killed his. She can go fuck. She goes and dances, standing shy along the wall for a minute and then moving in, loosening. He doesn't want to watch and get envious; he heaves himself up, to get another beer and steal another look at the girl in the kitchen. Sad, tits by themselves, on a woman sitting up. Little half-filled purses. Jamie's face and hands are broad and scraped-looking and he has loosened his tie to let his bull neck breathe. Another girl is reading his palm; they are all sitting around a little porcelain kitchen table, with spots worn black where place settings were, that Nelson feels he knows from long ago. A poster in here is of Marlon Brando in the black-leather get-up of *The Wild One*. Another shows Alice Cooper with his green eyelids and long fingernails. The refrigerator with its cool shelves of yogurt in paper cups and beer in sharply lettered sixpacks seems an island of decent order amid all this. Nelson is reminded of the lot, its rows of new Toyotas, and his stomach sinks. Sometimes at the lot, standing in the showroom with no customers in sight, he feels return to him from childhood that old fear of being in the wrong place, of life being run by rules nobody would share with him. He returns to the big front room with its fake ceiling and thinks that Pru looks ridiculously older than the other dancers: a little frizzy-haired girl called Dody Weinstein interning in teen fashions at Kroll's and Slim and this Lyle in the soccer shirt back together again and Pam their hostess in a big floppy muu-muu her body is having fits within, while the wan lights of Brewer fall away beyond the bay window, and the girl without a name waits in her white pants to be picked up while she stands to one side shivering from side to side in time to the music. *One night in a lifetime, one life in a night.* She looks a little self-conscious but happy to be here, out of the sticks. The black bubbles in the speakers pop faster and faster, and his wife with her cannonball gut is about to fall flat on her face. He goes to Pru and pulls her by her wrist away. Her spic thug of a partner dead-pan writhes to the girl in white

305

pants and picks her up. *Babe it's gotta be tonight, babe it's gotta be tonight.* Nelson is squeezing Pru's wrist to hurt. She is unsteady, pulled out of the music, and this further angers him, his wife getting tipsy. Defective equipment breaking down on purpose just to show him up. Her brittle imbalance makes him want to smash her completely.

'You're *hurt*ing me,' she says. Her voice arrives, tiny and dry, from a little box suspended in air behind his ear. As she tries to pull her wrist away her bangles pinch his fingers, and this is infuriating.

He wants to get her somewhere out of this. He pulls her across a hallway looking for a wall to prop her up against. He finds one, in a small side room; the light-switch plate beside her shoulder has been painted like an open-mouthed face with an off-on tongue. He puts his own face up against Pru's and hisses, 'Listen. You shape up for Chrissake. You're going to hurt yourself if you don't shape up. And the baby. What're you tryin' to do, shake him loose? Now you calm down.'

'I am calm. You're the one that's not calm, Nelson.' Their eyes are so close her eyes threaten to swallow his with their blurred green. 'And who says it's going to be a him?' Pru gives him her lopsided smirk. Her lips are painted vampire red in the new style and it's not becoming, it emphasizes her hatchet face, her dead calm bloodless look. That blank defiance of the poor: you can't scare them enough.

He pleads, 'You shouldn't be drinking and smoking pot at all, you'll cause genetic damage. You know that.'

She forms her words in response slowly. 'Nelson. You don't give a shit about genetic damage.'

'You silly bitch. I do. Of course I do. It's my kid. Or is it? You Akron kids'll fuck anybody.'

They are in a strange room. Flamingos surround them. Whoever lives in this side room with its view of the brick wall across two narrow sideyards, initially intended for a servant probably, has collected flamingos as a kind of joke. A glossy pink stuffed satin one drapes its ridiculous long black legs over the back of the sofabed, and hollow plastic ones with stick legs are propped along the walls on shelves. There are flamingos worked into ashtrays and coffee mugs and there are little 3-D tableaux of the painted pink birds with lakes and palms and sunsets, souvenirs of Florida. For one souvenir a trio of them were gathered in knickers and Scots caps on a felt putting green. Some of the bigger ones wear on their hollow drooping beaks those limp candylike sunglasses you can get in five and dimes. There are hundreds, others gays must give them to him, it has to be Slim who lives in here, that sofabed wouldn't be enough for Jason and Pam.

'It is,' Pru promises. 'You know it is.'

'I don't know. You're acting awfully whorey tonight.'

'I didn't want to come, remember? You're the one always wants to go out.'

He begins to cry: something about Pru's face, that toughness out of Akron closed against him, her belly bumping his, that big doll-like body he used to love so much, that she might just as easily have entrusted to another, its clefts, its tufts, and might just as easily take from him now, he is nothing to her. All their tender times, picking her up on the hill and walking under the trees, and bars along Water Street, and his going ahead and letting her out there in Colorado make such a sucker of him while he stewed in Diamond County, nothing. He is nothing to her like he was nothing to Jill, a brat, a bug to be humored, and look what happened. Love feels riddled through all his body like rot, down clear to his knees spongy as punk. 'You'll do damage to yourself,' he sobs; tears add their glitter to the green of her dress at the shoulder, yet his own crumpled face hangs as clear in the back of his brain as a face on a TV screen.

'You're strange,' Pru tells him, her voice breathier now, a whispery rag stuffed in his ear.

'Let's get out of this creepy place.'

'That girl you were talking to, what did she say?'

'Nothing. Her boyfriend makes bug-killers.'

'You talked together a long time.'

'She wanted to dance.'

'I could see you pointing and looking at me. You're ashamed of my being pregnant.'

'I'm not. I'm proud.'

'The fuck you are, Nelson. You're embarrassed.'

'Don't be so hard. Come on, let's split.'

'See, you are embarrassed. That's all this baby is to you, an embarrassment.'

'Please come. What're you trying to do, make me get down on my knees?'

'Listen, Nelson. I was having a perfectly good time dancing and you come out and pull this big macho act. My wrist still hurts. Maybe you broke it.'

He tries to lift her wrist to kiss it but she stiffly resists: at times she seems to him, body and soul, a board, flat, with that same abrasive grain. And then the fear comes upon him that this flatness is her, that she is not withholding depths within but there are no depths, this is what there is. She gets on a track sometimes and it seems she can't stop. His pulling at her wrist again, only to kiss it but she doesn't want to see that, has made her altogether mad, her face all pink and pointy and rigid. 'You know what you are?' She tells him, 'You're a little Napoleon. You're a *twerp*, Nelson.'

'Hey don't.'

The space around her vampire lips is tight and her voice is a dead level engine that won't stop. 'I didn't really know you. I've been watching how you act with your family and you're very spoiled. You're spoiled and you're a bully, Nelson.'

'Shut up.' He mustn't cry again. 'I was never spoiled, just the opposite. You don't know what my family did to me.'

'I've heard about it a thousand times and to me it never sounded like any big deal. You expect your mother and poor old grandmother to take care of you no matter what you do. You're horrid about your father when all he wants is to love you, to have a halfway normal son.'

'He didn't want me to work at the lot.'

'He didn't think you were ready and you weren't. You aren't. You aren't ready to be a father either but that's my mistake.'

'Oh, even you make mistakes.' The green she is wearing is a hateful color, shimmery electric arsenic like a big fat black hooker would wear to get attention on the street. He turns his eyes away and sees over on a bureau top some bendable toy flamingos have been arranged in a copulating position, one on top of the other's back, and another pair in what he supposes is a blow job, but the droopy beaks spoil the effect.

'I make plenty,' Pru is going on, 'why wouldn't I, nobody has ever taught me anything. But I'll tell you one thing Nelson Angstrom I'm going to have this baby no matter what you do. You can go to Hell.'

'I can, huh?'

'Yes.' She has to weaken it. Her very belly seems to soften against his, nestling. 'I don't want you to but you can. I can't stop you and you can't stop me, we're two people even if we did get married. You never wanted to marry me and I shouldn't have let you, it turns out.'

'I did though, I did,' he says, fearful that confessing this will make his face crumple again.

'Then stop being a bully. You bullied me to come here and now you're bullying me to go. I like these people. They have better senses of humor than the people in Ohio.'

'Let's stay then.' There are things other than flamingos in the room – hideous things, he sees. A plaster cast of Elvis Presley with votive candles in red cups at its base. An aquarium without fish in it but full of Barbie dolls and polyplike plastic things he thinks are called French ticklers. Tacked-up postcards of women in tinsel triangles somersaulting, mooning, holding giant breasts in their silver-gloved hands, postcards from Germany printed on those tiny ridges that hold two views, one coy and one obscene, depending on how you move your head. The room all over has the distinctness and variousness of vomit that still holds whole green peas and orange carrot dice from the dinner of an hour ago. He can't stop looking.

As he moves from one horror to the next Pru slips away, giving his hand a squeeze that may be apologetic for all they've said. What have they said? In the kitchen the girl with bare tits has put on a T-shirt saying ERA, Jamie has taken off his coat and his necktie. Nelson feels very tall, so tall he can't hear what he himself is saying, but it doesn't matter, and they all laugh. In a dark bedroom off the kitchen someone is watching the eleven-thirty special report from Iran, time slips by in that rapid spasmodic skid of party time. When Pru returns to him asking to go she is dead pale, a ghost with the lipstick on her face like movie blood and worn in the center where her lips meet. Things are being dyed blue by something in his head and her teeth look crooked as she tells him almost inaudibly that she has taken off her shoes like he wanted her to and now she can't find them. She plops down on a kitchen chair and stretches her orange legs out so her belly thrusts up like a prick and laughs with all those around her. What pigs. Nelson in searching for her shoes finds instead in the side room of horrible tinsel and flamingos the girl in white pants asleep on the sofabed. With her face slack she looks even younger than before. Her hand curls beside her snub nose pale palm up. The calm and mildly freckled bulge of her forehead sleeps without a crease. Only her hair holds that deep force of a woman, unbundled from its pins and many-colored in the caves and ridges of its tangle. He wants to cover her up but sees no blanket, just the French ticklers and Barbie dolls brilliant in their aquarium. A sliver of milky bare skin peeps where her russet knit sweater has ridden up from the waist of her slacks. Nelson looks down and wonders, Why can't a woman just be your friend, even with the sex? Why do you have to keep dealing with all this ego, giving back hurt just to defend yoursedf? Gazing down at that milky bit of skin, he forgets what he came in here to find. He needs to urinate, he realizes.

And in the bathroom after his bladder has emptied in those unsteady dribbles that mean it's been allowed to get too full he becomes fascinated by a big slick book sitting on the hamper, belonging to Slim most likely, an album printed of photographs and posters from the Nazi days in Germany, beautiful blond boys in rows singing and a handsome fat man in a white uniform loaded with medals and Hitler looking young and lean and gallant, gazing toward some Alps. Having this here is some kind of swish thing like those tinselled cards showing women as so ugly and there seems no protection against all the ugliness that is in the world, no protection for that girl asleep or for him. Pru has found her horrible green platform shoes and in the kitchen is sitting in a straight chair while that Puerto Rican she picked up with like little knife cuts all over his face kneels at her feet doing up the little buckles on the straps like gimp. When she stands she acts rocky,

310

what have they been giving her? She lets herself be slipped into that velvet jacket she used to wear in fall and spring at Kent, red so with the bright green dress she looks like Christmas six weeks early, all wrapped up. Jason is dancing in that front room where now Jamie and the girl with ERA across her pathetic tits are trying it out too, so they say their goodbyes to Pam and Slim, Pam giving Pru a kiss on the cheek woman to woman as if whispering the code word in her ear and Slim putting his hands together in front of his chest and bowing Buddha-style. That slanty look to his eyes, Nelson wonders if it's natural or comes with doing perverted things. The jellyfish of intensity crawls across Slim's lips. Last little waves and smiles and the door closes on the party noise.

The door to the apartment is an old-fashioned heavy one of yellow oak. He and Pru on this third-floor landing are sealed into something like silence. Rain is tapping on the black skylight of chicken-wire glass above their heads.

'Still think I'm a twerp?' he asks.

'Nelson, why don't you grow up?'

The solid wooden bannister on the right does a dizzying double loop down the two flights to the first floor. Looking down, Nelson can see the tops of two plastic garbage cans set in the basement far below. Impatiently Pru passes him on the left, fed up with him and anxious to be out in the air, and afterwards he remembers her broad hip bumping into his and his anger at what seemed her willful clumsiness, but not if he gives her a bit of hip back, a little vengeful shove. On the left of the stairwell there is no bannister, and the plaster wall here is marred by ragged nail holes where the renovators stripped away what must have been panelling. So when Pru in those wedgy platforms turns her ankle, there is nothing for her to hold on to; she gives a little grunt but her pale face is impassive as in the old days of hang gliding, at the moment of launch. Nelson grabs for her velvet jacket but she is flying beyond his reach, her legs no longer under her; he sees her face skid past these nail holes as she twists toward the wall, clawing for support there, where there is none. She topples then twisting sideways, headfirst, the metal-edged treads ripping at her belly. It is all so fast yet his brain has time to process a number of sensations – the touch of her velvet humming in her fingertips, the scolding bump her hip gave him, his indignation at her clunky shoes and the people who stripped the staircase of its bannister, all precisely layered in his mind. Distinctly he sees the patch of darker orange reinforcing at the crotch of her tights like the center of a flagrant green flower as her dress is flung wide with her legs by first impact. Her arms keep trying to brace her slithering body and one arm ends at an angle when she stops, about halfway down the steep flight, a shoe torn loose on a string of gimp, her head hidden beneath the splayed mass of her beautiful hair and all her long form still.

*Fallt's Bubbli nunner!*

In soft sweeps the rain patters on the skylight. Music leaks through the walls from the party. The noise of her fall must have been huge, for the yellow oak door pops open at once and people thunder all around, but the only sound Nelson heard was a squeak Pru gave when she first hit like one of those plastic floating bath toys suddenly accidentally stepped on.

Soupy is in fine form at the hospital, kidding the nurses and staff and moving through this white world in his black clothes like a happy germ, an exception to all the rules. He comes forward as if to embrace Ma Springer but at the last second holds back and gives her instead a somewhat jaunty swat on the shoulder. To Janice and Harry he gives his mischievous small-toothed grin; to Nelson he turns a graver, but still bright-eyed, face. 'She looks just dandy, except for the cast on her arm. Even there she was fortunate. It's the left arm.'

'She's left-handed,' Nelson tells him. The boy is grouchy and stoops with lack of sleep. He was with her at the hospital from one to three and now at nine-thirty is back again. He called the house around one-fifteen and nobody answered and that has been added to his twenty years of grievances. Mom-mom had been in the house but had been too old and dopey to hear the phone through her dreams and his parents had been out with the Murketts and Harrisons at the new strip joint along Route 422 beyond the Four Seasons toward Pottstown and then had gone back to the Murketts' for a nightcap. So the family didn't hear the news until

Nelson, who had crawled into his empty bed at three-thirty, awoke at nine. On the ride over to the hospital in his mother's Maverick he claimed he hadn't fallen asleep until the birds began to chirp.

'What birds?' Harry said. 'They've all gone south.'

'Dad, don't bug me, there are these black sort of birds right outside the window.'

'Starlings,' Janice offered, peacemaking.

'They don't chirp, they scrawk,' Harry insisted. '*Scrawk, scrawk.*'

'Doesn't it stay dark late now?' Ma Springer interposed. It's aging her, this constant tension between her son-in-law and her grandson.

Nelson sitting there all red-eyed and snuffly and stinking of last night's vapors did annoy Harry, short of sleep and hungover himself. He fought down the impulse to say *Scrawk* again. At the hospital, he asks Soupy, 'How'd you get here so soon?' genuinely admiring. Snicker all you want, the guy *is* magical somehow.

'The lady herself,' the clergyman gaily announces, doing a little side-step that knocks a magazine to the floor from a low table where too many are stacked. *Woman's Day. Field and Stream.* A hospital of course wouldn't get *Consumer Reports.* A killing article in there a while ago about medical costs and the fantastic mark-up on things like aspirin and cold pills. Soupy stoops to retrieve the magazine and comes up slightly breathless. He tells them, 'Evidently, after they calmed the dear girl down and set her arm and reassured her that the fetus appeared unaffected she still felt such concern that she woke up at seven a.m. and knew Nelson would be asleep and didn't know who to call. So she thought of *me.*' Soupy beams. 'I of course was still deep in the arms of Morpheus but got my act together and told her I'd rush over between Holy Communion and the ten o'clock service and, behold, here I am. *Ecce homo.* She wanted to pray with me to keep the baby, she'd been praying *con*stantly, and at least to this point in time as they used to say it seems to have *worked!*' His black eyes click from one to another face, up and down and across. 'The doctor who received her went off duty at eight but the nurse in attendance *sol*emnly swore to me that for all of the mother's bruises that little heartbeat in there is just as strong as ever, and *no* signs of vaginal bleeding or anything nasty like that. That Mother Nature, she is one tough old turkey.' He has chosen Ma Springer to tell this to. 'Now I *must* run, or the hungry sheep will look up and be not fed. Visiting hours here don't really begin until one p.m., but I'm *sure* the authorities wouldn't object if you took a quick peek. Tell them I gave you my blessing.' And his hand reflexively lifts, as if to give them a blessing. But instead he lays the hand on the sleeve of Ma Springer's shimmery fur coat. 'If you can't make the service,' he entreats, 'do come for the meeting afterwards. It's the meeting to advise the vestry on the new tracker organ, and a lot of pennypinchers are coming out of the woods. They put a dollar a week into the plate all year, and their vote is as good as mine or thine.' He flies away, scattering the V-for-peace sign down the hall.

Boy, these boys do love misery, Harry thinks. Well, it's a turf nobody else wants. St Joseph's Hospital is in the tatty north-central part of Brewer where the old Y.M.C.A. was before they tore it down for yet another drive-in bank and where the old wooden railroad bridge has been rebuilt in concrete that started to crack immediately. They used to talk about burying the tracks along through here in a tunnel but then the trains pretty much stopped running and that solved that. Janice had had Rebecca June here when the nurses were all nuns, they may still be nuns but now there's no way of telling. The receptionist for this floor wears a salmon-colored pants suit. Her swollen bottom and slumping shoulders lead the way. Half-open doors reveal people lying emaciated under white sheets staring at the white ceiling, ghosts already. Pru is in a four-bed room and two women in gauzy hospital johnnies scatter back into their beds, ambushed by early visitors. In the fourth bed an ancient black woman sleeps. Pru herself is all but asleep. She still wears flecks of last night's mascara but the rest of her looks virginal, especially the fresh white cast from elbow to wrist. Nelson kisses her lightly on the lips and then, sitting in the one bedside chair while his elders stand, sockets his face in the space on the bed edge next to the curve of Pru's hip. What a baby, Harry thinks.

'Nelson was wonderful,' Pru is telling them. 'So caring.' Her voice is more musical and throaty than Harry has ever heard it. He wonders if just lying down does that to a woman: changes the angle of her voice box.

'Yeah, he felt sick about it,' Harry says. 'We didn't hear the story till this morning.'

Nelson lifts his head. 'They were at a *strip* joint, can you imagine?'

'Jesus,' Harry says to Janice. 'Who's in charge here? What does he want us to do, sit around the house all the time aging gracefully?'

Ma Springer says, 'Now we can only stay a minute, I want to get to church. It wouldn't look right I think just to go to the meeting like Reverend Campbell said.'

'Go to that meeting, Ma,' Harry points out, 'they'll hit you up for a fortune. Tracker organs don't grow on trees.'

Janice says to Pru, 'You poor sweetie. How bad is the arm?'

'Oh, I wasn't paying that much attention to what the doctor said.' Her voice floats, she must be full of tranquilizers. 'There's a bone on the outside, with a funny name –'

'Femur,' Harry suggests. Something about all this has jazzed him up, made him feel nerved-up and defiant. Those strippers last night, some of them young enough to be his daughter. The Gold Cherry, the place was called.

Nelson lifts his head again from burrowing in Pru's side. 'That's in the *thigh*, Dad. She means the humerus.'

'Ha ha,' Harry says.

Pru seems to moan. 'Ulna,' she supplies. 'He said it was just a simple fracture.'

'How long's it gonna be on?' Harry asks.

'He said six weeks if I do what he says.'

'Off by Christmas,' Harry says. Christmas is a big thing in his mind this year, for beyond it, and the mop-up of New Year's, they're going to take their trip, they have the hotel, the plane reservations, they were discussing it all last night again, after the excitement of the strippers.

'You poor sweetie,' Janice repeats.

Pru begins to sing, without music. But the words come out as if sung. 'Oh my God, I don't mind, I'm glad for it, I deserve to

315

be punished somehow. I honestly believe' – she keeps looking straight at Janice, with an authority they haven't seen from her before – 'it's God telling me this is the price He asks for my not losing the baby. I'm glad to pay it, I'd be glad if every bone in my body was broken, I really wouldn't care. Oh my God, when I felt my feet weren't under me and I knew there wasn't anything for me to do but fall down those horrible stairs, the thoughts that ran through my head! You must know.'

Meaning Janice must know what it's like to lose a baby. Janice kind of yelps and falls on the bedridden girl so hard Harry winces, and plucks at her back to pull her off. Feeling the rock of plaster against her breasts, Janice arches her spine under his hands; through the cloth her skin feels taut as a drum, and hot. But Pru shows no pain, smiling her crooked careful smile and keeping her eyelids with their traces of last night's blue closed serenely, accepting the older woman's weight upon her. The hand not captured in a cast Pru sneaks around to pat Janice's back; her fingers come close to Harry's own. Pat, they go, pat pat. He thinks of Cindy Murkett's round fingers and marvels how much more childish and grublike they look than these, bony though young and reddened at the knuckles: his mother's hands had that tough scrubbed look. Janice can't stop sobbing, Pru can't stop patting, the two other women patients awake in the room can't stop glancing over. Moments this complicated rub Harry the wrong way. He feels rebuked, since the official family version is that the baby's dying at Janice's hands was all his fault. Yet now the truth seems declared that he was just a bystander. Nelson, pushed to one side by his mother's assault of grief, sits up and stares, poor frazzled kid. These damn women so intent on communing should leave us out of it entirely. At last Janice rights herself, having snuffled so hard her upper lip is wet with snot.

Harry hands her his handkerchief.

'I'm so happy,' she says with a big runny sniff, 'for Pru.'

'Come on, shape up,' he mutters, taking back the handkerchief.

Ma Springer soothes the waters with, 'It does seem a miracle, all the way down those stairs and nothing worse. Up that high in old Brewer houses the stairs were just for the servants.'

'I didn't go all the way down,' Pru says. 'That's how I broke my arm, stopping myself. I don't remember any pain.'

'Yeah,' Harry offers. 'Nelson said you were feeling no pain.'

'Oh no, no.' Her hair spread out across the pillow by Janice's embrace makes her look like she is falling through white space, singing. 'I'd hardly had anything, the doctors all say you shouldn't, it was those terrible tall platforms they're making us all wear. Isn't that the dumbest style? I'm going to burn them up, absolutely, as soon as I get back.'

'When will that be now?' Ma asks, shifting her black purse to the other hand. She has been dressed for church since before Nelson woke up and the fuss began. She's a slave to that church, God knows what she gets out of it.

'Up to a week, he said,' Pru says. 'To keep me quiet and, you know, to make sure. The baby. I woke up this morning with what I thought were contractions and they scared me so I called Soupy. He was wonderful.'

'Yes, well,' Ma says.

Harry hates the way they all keep calling it the baby. More like a piglet or a wobbly big frog at this stage, as he pictures it. What if she had lost it, wouldn't it have lived? They keep five-month preemies alive now and pretty soon you'll have life in a test tube start to finish. 'We gotta get Ma to church,' he announces. 'Nelson, you want to wake up and come or stay here and sleep?' The boy's head had gone back down onto the hospital mattress again.

'Harry,' Janice says. 'Don't be so rough on everybody.'

'He thinks we're all silly about the baby,' Pru says dreamily, dimly teasing.

'No, hey: I think it's great about the baby.' He bends over to kiss her goodbye for now and wants to whisper in her ear about all the babies he has had, dead and alive, visible and invisible. Instead he tells her, straightening, 'Keep cool. We'll be back after this when we can stay longer.'

'Don't not play golf,' she says.

'Golf's shot. They don't like you to walk on the greens after a certain point.'

Nelson is asking her, 'What do you want me to do, go or stay?'

'Go, Nelson, for heaven's sake. Let me get some sleep.'

'You know, I'm sorry last night if I said anything. I was skunked. When they told me last night they didn't think you'd lost the baby I was so relieved I cried. Honest.' He would cry again but his face clouds with embarrassed awareness that the others have listened. That's why we love disaster, Harry sees, it puts us back in touch with guilt and sends us crawling back to God. Without a sense of being in the wrong we're no better than animals. Suppose the baby had aborted at the very moment he was watching that olive chick with the rolling tongue tug down her tinsel underpants to her knees and peek at the audience from behind her shoulder while tickling her asshole with that ostrich feather: he'd feel terrible.

Pru waves her husband's quavery words and all their worried faces away. 'I'm *fine*. I love all of you so much.' Her hair streams outward as she waits to sink into sleep, into more wild prayer, into the dreaming fluids of her own bruised belly. Her stumpy wing of snow-white plaster lifts a few inches from her chest in farewell. They leave her to the company of antiseptic angels and shuffle back through the hospital corridors, their footsteps clamorous amid their silent determination to save their quarrels for the car.

'A week!' Harry says, as soon as they're rolling in the Maverick. 'Does anybody have any idea how much a week in a hospital costs these days?'

'Dad, how can you keep thinking about money all the time?'

'Somebody has to. A week is a thousand dollars minimum. *Mini*mum.'

'You *have* Blue Cross.'

'Not for daughter-in-laws I don't. Not for you either, once you're over nineteen.'

'Well I don't know,' Nelson says, 'but I don't like her being in a ward with all those other women barfing and moaning all night. One of 'em was even black, did you notice?'

'How did you get so prejudiced? Not from me. Anyway that's not a ward, that's what you call a semi-private,' Harry says.

'I want my wife to have a private room,' Nelson says.

'Is that a fact? You want, you want. And who's going to foot the bill, big shot? Not you.'

Ma Springer says, 'I know when I had my diverticulitis, Fred wouldn't hear of anything but a private room for me. And it was a corner room at that. A wonderful view of the arboretum, the magnolias just in bloom.'

Janice asks, 'How about at the lot, isn't he under the group insurance there?'

Harry tells her, 'Maternity benefits don't start till you've worked for Springer Motors nine months.'

'A broken arm isn't what I'd call maternity,' Nelson says.

'Yeah but if it weren't for her maternity she'd be out walking around with it.'

'Maybe Mildred could look into it,' Janice suggests.

'O.K.,' he concedes, with ill grace. 'I don't know what our exact policy is.'

Nelson should let it go at that. Instead he says, leaning forward from the back seat so his voice presses on Harry's ear, 'Without Mildred and Charlie there isn't much you do know exactly. I mean –'

'I know what you mean and I know a lot more about the car business than you ever will at the rate you're going, if you don't stop futzing around with these old Detroit hotrods that lose us a bundle and start focusing on the line we carry.'

'I wouldn't mind if they were Datsuns or Hondas, but frankly Dad, Toyotas –'

'The Toyota franchise is what old Fred Springer landed and Toyotas are what we sell. Bessie, why doncha slap the kid around a little? I can't reach him.'

His mother-in-law's voice comes from the back seat after a pause. 'I was wondering if I should go to church after all. I know his heart's set on a big drive for the organ and there aren't too many that enthusiastic. If I show up I might get made a committee head and I'm too old for that.'

'Didn't Teresa seem sweet?' Janice asks aloud. 'It seemed like she'd grown up overnight.'

'Yeah,' Harry says, 'and if she'd fallen down all two flights she'd be older than we are.'

'Jesus, Dad,' Nelson says. 'Who *do* you like?'

'I like everybody,' Harry says. 'I just don't like getting boxed in.'

The way from St Joseph's to Mt Judge is to keep going straight over the railroad tracks and then continue right on Locust past Brewer High and on through Cityview Park and then left past the shopping mall as usual. On a Sunday morning the people out in cars are mostly the older American type, the women with hair tinted blue or pink like the feathers of those Easter chicks before they outlawed it and the men gripping the steering wheel with two hands like the thing might start to buck and bray: with no-lead up to a dollar thirteen at some city stations thanks to the old Ayatollah they have to try to squeeze value out of every drop. Actually, people's philosophy seems to be they'll burn it while it's here and when it's fourth down and twenty-seven Carter can punt. The four features at the mall cinema are BREAKING AWAY STARTING OVER RUNNING and '10.' He'd like to see '10,' he knows from the ads this Swedish-looking girl has her hair in corn rows like a black chick out of Zaire. One world: everybody fucks everybody. When he thinks of all the fucking there's been in the world and all the fucking there's going to be, and none of it for him, here he sits in this stuffy car dying, his heart just sinks. He'll never fuck anybody again in his lifetime except poor Janice Springer, he sees this possibility ahead of him straight and grim as the known road. His stomach, sour from last night's fun, binds as it used to when he was running to school late. He says suddenly to Nelson, 'How the hell could you let her fall, why didn't you keep ahold of her? What were you *doing* out so late anyway? When your mother was pregnant with you we never went *any*where.'

'Together at least,' the boy says. 'You went a lot of places by yourself the way I heard it.'

'Not when she was pregnant with *you*, we sat there night after night with the boob tube, *I Love Lucy* and all that crap, didn't we Bessie? And we weren't snorting any dope, either.'

'You don't snort dope, you smoke it. Coke is what you snort.'

Ma Springer responds slowly to his question. 'Oh I don't know how you and Janice managed exactly,' she says wearily, in a voice

320

that is looking out the window. 'The young people are different now.'

'I'll say they are. You fire somebody to give 'em a job and they knock the product.'

'It's an O.K. product if all you want is to get from here to there,' Nelson begins.

Harry interrupts furiously, thinking of poor Pru lying there with a snivelling baby burying his head in her side instead of a husband, of Melanie slaving away at the Crêpe House for all those creeps from the banks that lunch downtown, of his own sweet hopeful daughter stuck with that big red-faced Jamie, of poor little Cindy having to put on a grin at being fucked from behind so old Webb can have his kicks with his SX-70, of Mim going down on all those wop thugs out there all those years, of Mom plunging her old arms in gray suds and crying the kitchen blues until Parkinson's at last took mercy and got her upstairs for a rest, of all the women put upon and wasted in the world as far as he can see so little punks like this can come along. 'Let me tell you something about Toyotas,' he calls back at Nelson. 'They're put together by little yellow guys in white smocks that work in one plant cradle to grave and go crazy if there's a fleck of dust in the fuel injector system and those jalopies Detroit puts out are slapped together by jigaboos wearing headphones pumping music into their ears and so zonked on drugs they don't know a slothead screw from a lug nut and furthermore hate the company. Half the cars come through the Ford assembly line are deliberately sabotaged, I forget where I read all this, it wasn't *Consumer Reports*.'

'Dad, you're so prejudiced. What would Skeeter say?'

Skeeter. In quite another voice Harry says, 'Skeeter was killed in Philly last April, did I tell ya?'

'You *keep* telling me.'

'I'm not blaming the blacks on the assembly line, I'm just saying it sure makes for lousy cars.'

Nelson is on the attack, frazzled and feeling rotten, poor kid. 'And who are you to criticize me and Pru for going out to see some friends when you were off with yours seeing those ridiculous exotic dancers? How could you stand it, Mom?'

Janice says, 'It wasn't as bad as I'd thought. They keep it within bounds. It really wasn't any worse than it used to be at the old fairgrounds.'

'Don't answer him,' Harry tells her. 'Who's he to criticize?'

'The funny thing,' Janice goes on, 'is how Cindy and Thelma and I could agree which girl was the best and the men had picked some girl entirely different. We all liked this tall Oriental who was very graceful and artistic and *they* liked, Mother, the men liked some little chinless blonde who couldn't even dance.'

'She had that look about her,' Harry explains. 'I mean, she meant it.'

'And then that tubby dark one that turned you on. With the feather.'

'Olive-complected. She was nice too. The feather I could have done without.'

'Mom-mom doesn't want to hear all this disgusting stuff,' Nelson says from the back seat.

'Mom-mom doesn't mind,' Harry tells him. 'Nothing fazes Bessie Springer. Mom-mom loves life.'

'Oh I don't know,' the old lady says with a sigh. 'We didn't have such things, when we might have been up to it. Fred I remember used to bring home the *Playboy* sometimes, but to me it seemed more pathetic than not, these eighteen-year-old girls that are really just children except for their bodies.'

'Well who isn't?' Harry asks.

'Speak for yourself, Dad,' Nelson says.

'No now, I meant,' Ma insists, 'you wonder what their parents raised them for, seeing them all naked just the way they were born. And what the parents must think.' She sighs. 'It's a different world.'

Janice says, 'I guess at this same place Monday nights they have ladies' night with male strippers. And they say really the young men become frightened, Doris Kaufmann was telling me, the women grab for them and try to get up on the stage after them. The women over forty they say are the worst.'

'That's so sick,' Nelson says.

'Watch your mouth,' Harry tells him. 'Your mother's over forty.'

'*Dad.*'

'Well I wouldn't behave like that,' she says, 'but I can see how some might. I suppose a lot of it depends on how satisfying the husband you have is.'

'*Mom*,' the boy protests.

They have swung around the mountain and turned up Central and by the electric clock in the dry cleaner's window it is three of ten. Harry calls back, 'Looks like we'll make it, Bessie!'

The town hall has its flag at half-mast because of the hostages. At the church the people in holiday clothes are still filing in, beneath the canopy of bells calling with their iron tongues, beneath the wind-torn gray clouds of this November sky with its scattered silver. Letting Ma out of the Maverick, Harry says, 'Now don't pledge the lot away, just for Soupy's organ.'

Nelson asks, 'How will you get home, Mom-mom?'

'Oh, I guess I can get a ride with Grace Stuhl's grandson, he generally comes for her. Otherwise it won't kill me to walk.'

'Oh Mother,' Janice says. 'You could never walk it. Call us at the house when the meeting's over if you haven't a ride. We'll be home.' The club is down to minimal staff now; they serve only packaged sandwiches and half the tennis court nets are down and already they have relocated the pins to temporary greens. A sadness in all this plucks at Rabbit. Driving home with just Janice and Nelson he remembers the way they used to be, just the three of them, living together, younger. The kid and Janice still have it between them. He's lost it. He says aloud, 'So you don't like Toyotas.'

'It's not a question of like, Dad, there isn't that much about 'em to like or dislike. I was talking to some girl at the party last night who'd just bought a Corolla, and all we could talk about was the old American cars, how great they were. It's like Volvos, they don't have it anymore either, it's not something anybody can con*trol*. It's like, you know, time of life.'

The boy is trying to be conversational and patch things up; Harry keeps quiet, thinking, Time of life, the crazy way you're going, zigzagging around and all those drugs, you'll be lucky to get to my time of life.

'Mazdas,' Nelson says. 'That's what I'd want to have an agency in. That rotary engine is *so* much more efficient than the four-cycle piston, you could run this country on half the gas, once they get the seal perfected.'

'Go over and ask Abe Chafetz for a job then. I heard he was going broke, the Mazdas have so many bugs. Manny says they'll never get the seal right.'

Janice says, placating, 'I think the Toyota ads on television are very clever and glamorous.'

'Oh the *ads* have charisma,' Nelson says. 'The ads are terrific. It's the cars I'm talking about.'

'Don't you love,' Harry asks, 'that new one with Scrooge, the way he cackles and goes off into the distance?' He cackles, and Janice and Nelson laugh, and for the last block home, down Joseph Street beneath the bare maples, their three heads entertain common happy memories, of Toyota commercials, of men and women leaping, average men and women, their clothes lifted in cascading slow-motion folds like angels' robes, like some intimate violence of chemical mating or hummingbird wing magnified and laid bare in its process, leaping and falling, grinning and then in freeze-frame hanging there, defying gravity.

'We got to get out of here,' Harry says hoarsely to Janice in their bedroom some days later, on the eve of Pru's return from her week of grace in the hospital. It is night; the copper beech, stripped of its leaves and clamorous pods, admits more streetlight into their room than in summer. One or two of the panes in the window on the side nearer the street, the side where Rabbit sleeps, hold imperfections, patches of waviness or elongated bubbles, scarcely visible to the eye of day but which at night hurl onto the far wall, with its mothlike shadows of medallion pattern, dramatic amplifications, the tint of each pane also heightened in the enlargement, so that an effect of stained glass haunts the area above Janice's jumbled mahogany dresser descended from the Koerners, beside the four-panelled door that locks out the world. Ten years of habitancy, in the minutes or hours between when the bedside lamps are extinguished and sleep is achieved, have borne these luminous rectangles into Harry's brain as precious entities, diffuse jewels pressed from the air, presences whose company he will miss if he leaves this room. He must leave it. Intermixed with the abstract patterns the imperfect panes project are the unquiet shadows of the beech branches as they shudder and sway in the cold outside.

'Where would we go?' Janice asks.

'We'd buy a house like everybody else,' he says, speaking in a low hoarse voice as if Ma Springer might overhear this breath of treachery through the wall and the mumble and soft roar of her television set as a crisis in her program is reached, then a commercial bursts forth, and another crisis begins to build. 'On the other side of Brewer, close to the lot. That drive through the middle of town every day is driving me crazy. Wastes gas, too.'

'Not Penn Villas,' she says. 'You'll never get me back into Penn Villas.'

'Me neither. What about Penn Park though? With all those nice divorce lawyers and dermatologists? I've always kind of dreamed, ever since we used to play them in basketball, of living over there somewhere. Some house with at least stone facing on the front, and maybe a sunken living room, so we can entertain the Murketts in decent style. It's awkward having anybody back here, Ma goes upstairs after dinner but the place is so damn gloomy, and now we're going to be stuck with Nelson and his crew.'

'He was saying, they plan to get an apartment when things work out.'

'Things aren't going to work out, with his attitude. You know that. The ride is free here and with him around we wouldn't feel so rotten leaving your mother. This is our chance.' His hand has crept well up into her nightie; in his wish to have his vision shared he grips her breasts, familiar handfuls, a bit limp like balloons deflating with her age; but still thanks to all that tennis and swimming and old Fred Springer's stingy lean genes her body is holding up better than most. Her nipples stiffen, and his prick with no great attention paid to it is hardening on the sly. 'Or maybe,' he pursues, his voice still hoarse, 'one of those mock-Tudor jobbies that look like piecrust and have those steep pitched roofs like witches' houses. Jesus, wouldn't Pop be proud, seeing me in one of those?'

'Could we afford it,' Janice asks, 'with the mortgage rates up around thirteen per cent now?'

He shifts his hand down the silvery slick undulations of her belly to the patch of her hair, that seems to bristle at his touch. He ought to eat her sometime. Bed her down on her back with her legs hanging over the side and just kneel and chew her cunt until she came. He used to when they were courting in that apartment of the other girl's with its view of the old gray gas tanks by the river, kneel and just graze in her ferny meadow for hours, nose, eyelids rubbing up against the wonder of it. Any woman, they deserve to be eaten once in a while, they don't come so your mouth is full like with an oyster, how do whores stand it, cock after cock, cuts down on VD, but having to swallow, must amount to pints in the course of a week. Ruth never liked it, but some cunts now if you read the sex tapes in *Oui* lap it up, one said it tasted to her like champagne. Maybe it wouldn't be the living room that would be sunken, it could be the den, just somewhere where there's a carpeted step down or two, so you know you're in a modern home. 'That's the beauty of inflation,' he says seductively to Janice. 'The more you owe, the better you do. Ask Webb. You pay off in shrunken dollars, and the interest Uncle Sam picks up as an income tax deduction. Even after buying the Krugerrand and paying the September taxes we have too much money in the bank, money in the bank is for dummies now. Sock it into the down payment for a house, we'd be letting the bank worry about the dollar going down and have the house appreciating ten, twenty percent a year at the same time.' Her cunt is moistening, its lips growing loose.

'It seems hard on Mother,' Janice says in that weak voice she gets, lovemaking. 'She'll be leaving us this place some day and I know she expects we'd stay in it with her till then.'

'She'll live for another twenty years,' Harry says, sinking his middle finger in. 'In twenty years you'll be sixty-four.'

'And wouldn't it seem strange to Nelson?'

'Why? It's what he wants, me out of the way. I depress the kid.'

'Harry, I'm not so sure it's you that's doing it. I think he's just scared.'

'What's he got to be scared of?'

'The same thing you were scared of at his age. Life.'

Life. Too much of it, and not enough. The fear that it will end some day, and the fear that tomorrow will be the same as yesterday. 'Well he shouldn't have come home if that's the way he was going to feel,' Harry says. He's losing his erection.

'He didn't know,' Janice says. He can feel, his finger still in her, that her mind too is drifting away from their flesh, into sad realms of family. 'He didn't know you'd be so hard on him. Why are you?'

Fucking kid not thirteen years old and tried to take Jill from him, back in Penn Villas after Janice had gone. 'He's hard on me,' Harry says. He has ceased to whisper. Ma Springer's television set, when he listens, is still on – a rumbling, woofing, surging noise less like human voices than a noise Nature would make in the trees or along the ocean shore. She has become a fan of the ABC eleven-thirty special report on the hostages and every morning tells them the latest version of nothing happening. Khomeini and Carter both trapped by a pack of kids who need a shave and don't know shit, they talk about old men sending young men off to war, if you could get the idiotic kids out of the world it might settle down to being a sensible place. 'He gets a disgruntled look on his face every time I open my mouth to talk. Everything I try to tell him at the lot he goes and does the opposite. Some guy comes in to buy this Mercury that was the other one of the convertibles the kid wrecked that time and offers a snowmobile on the trade-in. I thought it was a joke until the other day I go in and the Mercury's gone and this little yellow Kawasaki snowmobile is sitting up in the front row with the new Tercels. I hit the roof and Nelson tells me to stop being so uptight, he allowed the guy four hundred on it and it'll give us more publicity than twice that in ads, the crazy lot that took a snowmobile on trade-in.'

Janice makes a soft noise that were she less tired would be laughter. 'That's the kind of thing Daddy used to do.'

'And then behind my back he's taken on about ten grand's worth of old convertibles that get about ten miles to the gallon nobody'll want and this caper with Pru is running up a fucking fortune. There's no *bene*fits covering her.'

'Shh. Mother can hear.'

'I *want* her to hear, she's the one giving the kid all his high and mighty ideas. Last night, you hear them cooking up how he's going to have his own car for him and Pru, when that old Newport of hers just sits in the garage six days out of seven?' A muffled sound of chanting comes through the papered wall, Iranians outside the Embassy demonstrating for the benefit of the TV cameras. Rabbit's throat constricts with frustration. 'I got to get out, honey.'

'Tell me about the house,' Janice says, returning his hand to her pussy. 'How many rooms would it have?'

He begins to massage, dragging his fingers along the crease on one side, then the other, of the triangle, and then bisecting with a thoughtful stroke, looking for the fulcrum, the nub, of it. Cindy's hair had looked darker than Janice's, less curly, alive maybe with needles of light like the fur of Ma Springer's old coat. 'We wouldn't need a lot of bedrooms,' he tells Janice, 'just a big one for us, with a big mirror you can see from the bed –'

'A mirror! Where'd you get the idea of a mirror?'

'Everybody has mirrors now. You watch yourself fucking in them.'

'Oh, Harry. I couldn't.'

'I think you could. And then at least another bedroom, in case your mother has to come live with us, or we have guests, but not next to ours, with at least a bathroom between so we don't hear her television, and downstairs a kitchen with all new equipment including a Cuisinart –'

'I'm scared of them. Doris Kaufmann says for the first three weeks she had hers everything came out mush. One night it was pink mush and next night green mush was the only difference.'

'You'll learn,' he croons, drawing circles on her front, circles that widen to graze her tits and beaver and then diminish to feather into her navel like the asshole of that olive bitch along 422, 'there are instruction books, and a refrigerator with an automatic ice-maker, and one of those wall ovens that's at the height of your face so you don't have to bend over, and I don't know about all this microwave, I was reading somewhere how they fry your brains even if you're in the next room . . .' Moist, she is so moist her cunt startles him, touching it, like a slug underneath a leaf in the garden. His prick undergoes such a bulbous throb it hurts.

'... and this big sunken living room with lights along the side where we can give parties.'

'Who would we give these parties for?' Her voice is sinking into the pillow like the dust of a mummy's face, so weak.

'Oh ...' His hand continues to glide, around and around, carrying the touch of wetness up to her nipples and adorning first one then the other with it like tinsel on the tips of a Christmas tree. '... everybody. Doris Kaufmann and all those other tennis Lesbians at the Flying Eagle, Cindy Murkett and her trusty sidekick Buddy Inglefinger, all the nice girls who work their pretty asses off for a better America down at the Gold Cherry, all the great macho guys in the service and parts department of Springer Motors –'

Janice giggles, and simultaneously the front door downstairs slams. After visiting Pru, Nelson has been going to that bar that used to be the Phoenix and bumming around with that creepy crowd that kills time there. It oppresses Harry, this freedom: if the kid has been excused from evening floor duty to visit Pru for the week then he has no business going out getting stewed on the time. If the kid was so shook up when she took her tumble he ought to be doing something better than this out of gratitude or penance or whatever. His footsteps below sound drunken, one plunked down on top of the other, bump, bump, across the living room between the sofa and the Barcalounger and past the foot of the stairs, making the china in the sideboard tingle, on into kitchen for one more beer. Harry's breath comes quick and short, thinking of that surly puzzled face sucking the foam out of one more can: drinking and eating up the world, and out of sheer spite at that. He feels the boy's mother at his side listening to the footsteps and puts her hand on his prick; in expert reflex her fingers pump the loose skin of the sides. Simultaneous with Nelson's footsteps below as he treads back into the living room toward the Barcalounger, Harry thrusts as hard as if into that olive chick's ass into the socket Janice's wifely hand makes and speeds up his hypnotic tracing of rapid smooth circles upon the concave expectancy of her belly, assuring her hoarsely, of the house he wants, 'You'll love it. You'll love it.'

*

Nelson says to Pru, as they drive together into Brewer in Ma Springer's stately old navy-blue Chrysler, 'Now guess what. He's talked Mom into them getting a house. They've looked at about six so far, she told me. They all seem too big to her but Dad says she should learn to think big. I think he's flipping out.' Pru says, quietly, 'I wonder how much it has to do with us moving in.' She had wanted them to find an apartment of their own, in the same general neighborhood as Slim and Jason and Pam, and couldn't understand Nelson's need to live with his grandmother.

A defensive fury begins to warm him. 'I don't see why, any decent father would be glad to have us around. There's plenty of room, Mom-mom shouldn't live by herself.'

'I think maybe it's natural,' his wife offers, 'in a couple that age, to want your own space.'

'What's natural, to leave old ladies to die all alone?'

'Well, we're in the house now.'

'Just temporarily.'

'That's what I thought at first, Nelson, but now I don't believe you want us to have a place of our own. I'd be too much for you, just the two of us, you and me.'

'I hate ticky-tacky apartments and condos.'

'It's all right, I'm not complaining. I'm at home there now. I like your grandmother.'

'I hate crummy old inner-city blocks getting all revitalized with swish little stores catering to queers and stoned interracial couples. It all reminds me of Kent. I came back here to get away from all that phony stuff. Somebody like Slim acts so counter-culture sniffing coke and taking mesc and all that, you know what he does for a living? He's a biller for Diamond County Light and Power, he stuffs envelopes and is going to be Head Stuffer if he keeps at if for ten more years, how's that for Establishment?'

'He doesn't pretend to be a revolutionary, he just likes nice clothes and other boys.'

'People ought to be con*s*istent,' Nelson says, 'it isn't *fair* to milk the society and then sneer at it at the same time. One of the reasons I liked you better than Melanie was she was so sold on all this radical stuff and I didn't think you were.'

'I didn't know,' Pru says, even more quietly, 'that Melanie and

I were competing for you. How much sexual *was* there between you two this summer?'

Nelson stares ahead, sorry his confiding has led to this. The Christmas lights are up in Brewer already, red and green and shivering tinsel looking dry and wilted above the snowless streets, the display a shadow of the seasonal glory he remembers as a boy, when there was abundant energy and little vandalism. Then each lamppost wore a giant wreath of authentic evergreen cut in the local hills and a lifelike laughing Santa in a white-and-silver sleigh and a line of eight glassy-eyed reindeer coated in what seemed real fur were suspended along cables stretched from the second story of Kroll's to the roof of the cigar-store building that used to be opposite. The downtown windows from below Fourth up to Seventh were immense with painted wooden soldiers and camels and Magi and golden organ pipes intertwined with clouds of spun glass and at night the sidewalks were drenched with shoppers and carols overflowing from the heated stores into air that prickled like a Christmas tree and it was impossible not to believe that somewhere, in the dark beyond the city, baby Jesus was being born. Now, it was pathetic. City budget has been cut way back and half the downtown stores were shells.

Pru insists. 'Tell me. I know there was some.'

'How do you know?'

'I know.'

He decides to attack: let these young wives get the upper hand now they'll absolutely take over. 'You don't know anything,' he tells her, the only thing you know is how to hang on to that damn thing inside you, *that* you're really good at. Boy.'

Now she stares ahead, the sling on her arm a white blur in the corner of his vision. His eyes are stung by perforations of festive light in the December darkness. Let her play the martyr all she wants. You try to speak the truth and all you get is grief.

Mom-mom's old car feels silky but sluggish under him: all that metal they used to put in, even the glove compartment is lined with metal. When Pru goes silent like this, a kind of taste builds up in his throat, the taste of injustice. He didn't ask her to conceive this baby, nobody did, and now that he's married her she has the nerve to complain he isn't getting her an apartment of her own, give them one thing they instantly want the next. Women. They are holes, you put one thing in after another and it's never enough, you stuff your entire life in there and they smile that crooked little sad smile and are sorry you couldn't have done better, when all is said and done. He's gotten in plenty deep already and she's not getting him in any deeper. Sometimes when he looks at her from behind he can't believe how big she has grown, hips wide as a barn getting set to hatch not some little pink being but a horny-hided white rhinoceros no more in scale with Nelson than the mottled man in the moon, that's what cunts do to you when Nature takes over: go out of control.

The build-up of the taste in his throat is too great; he has to speak. 'Speaking of fucking,' he says, 'what about *us*?'

'I don't think we're supposed to this late. Anyway I feel so ugly.'

'Ugly or not, you're mine. You're my old lady.'

'I get so sleepy, you can't imagine. But you're right. Let's do something tonight. Let's go home early. If somebody asks us back from the Laid-Back to their place let's not go.'

'See if we had an apartment like you're so crazy for *we'd* have to ask people back. At least at Mom-mom's you're safe from that.'

'I do feel safe there,' she says, sighing. Meaning what? He shouldn't be bringing her out at night: he's married now, he works, he's not supposed to have any fun. He dreads work, he wakes every workday morning with a gnawing in his stomach like he's the one with something inside him, that white rhinoceros. Those convertibles staring at him unbought every day and the way Jake and Rudy can't get over his taking that little Kawasaki, as if it's some great joke he's deliberately played on Dad, when he hadn't meant it that way at all, the guy had been so pleading and Nelson was anxious to get the Mercury off the lot, it reminded him every time he saw it of that time Dad had been so scoffing, wouldn't even listen, it wasn't *fair*, he had had to ram the two cars together to wipe that you've-got-to-be-kidding smirk off his face.

On that showroom floor it's like a stage where he hasn't quite learned the lines yet. Maybe it's the stuff he's been taking, too much coke burns the septum out and now they say pot really does rot your brain cells, the THC gets tucked in the fatty tissue and makes you stupid for months, all these teen-age boys coming through with breasts now because something was suppressed when they were turning on at age thirteen, Nelson has these visions lately though he's standing upright with his eyes open, people with holes where their noses should be because of too much coke, or Pru lying there in the hospital with this pink-eyed baby rhinoceros, maybe it has to do with that cast on her arm, dirty and crumbling at the edges now, the gauze underneath the plaster fraying through. And Dad. He's getting bigger and bigger, never jogs anymore, his skin glows like his pores are absorbing some food out of the air.

One of the books Nelson had as a child, with those stiff shiny cartoon covers and a black spine like electrical tape, had a picture in it of a giant, his face all bumpy and green with hairs coming out of it here and there, and smiling – that made it worse, that the giant was grinning, looking in, with those blubbery lips and separated teeth giants have, looking into some cave where two children, a boy and a girl, brother and sister probably, who were the heroes of the story are crouching, silhouettes in shadow, you see only the backs of their heads, they are *you*, looking out, hunted, too scared to move a muscle or breathe a breath as the great bumpy gleeful face fills the sunny mouth of the cave. That's how he sees Dad these days: he Nelson is in a tunnel and his father's face fills the far end where he might get out into the sun. The old man doesn't even know he's doing it, it comes on with that little nibbly sorry smile, a flick of dismissal as he pivots away, disappointed, that's it, he's disappointed his father, he should be something other than he is, and now at the lot all the men, not just Jake and Rudy but Manny and his mechanics all grimy with grease, only the skin around their eyes white, staring, see that too: he is not his father, lacks that height, that tossing off that Harry Angstrom can do. And no witness but Nelson stands in the universe to proclaim that his father is guilty, a cheat and coward and murderer, and when he tries to proclaim it nothing comes out, the world laughs as he stands there with open mouth silent. The giant looks in and smiles and Nelson sinks back deeper into the tunnel. He likes that about the Laid-Back, the tunnel snugness of it, and the smoke and the booze and the joints passed from hand to hand under the tables, and the acceptance, the being all in the smoky tunnel together, rats, losers, who cares, you didn't have to listen to what anybody said because nobody was going to buy a Toyota or insurance policy or anything anyway. Why don't they make a society where people are given what they need and do what they want to do? Dad would say that's fantastic but it's how animals live all the time.

'I still think you fucked Melanie,' Pru says, in her dried-up slum cat's flat voice. One track and that's it.

Without braking Nelson swings the big Chrysler around the corner where that shaggy park blocks the way down Weiser Street. Pine Street has been made one way and you have to approach it from around the block so Pru doesn't have too far to walk. 'Oh, what if I did?' he says. 'You and I weren't married, what does it matter now?'

'It doesn't matter because of *you*, we all know you'll grab anything you can get you're so greedy, it matters because she was my *friend*. I trusted her. I trusted you both.'

'For Chrissake, don't snivel.'

'I'm not snivelling.' But he foresees how she will sit there beside him in the booth sulking and not saying anything, not listening to anything but that kicking in her belly, her broken arm making her look even more ridiculous, belly and sling and all, and picturing it that way makes him feel a little sorry for her, until he tells himself it's his way of taking care of her, bringing her along when a lot of guys wouldn't.

'Hey,' he says gruffly. 'Love you.'

'Love you, Nelson,' she responds, lifting the hand not in a sling from her lap as he lifts one of his from the wheel to give hers a squeeze. Funny, the fatter the middle of her is getting the thinner and drier her hands and face seem.

'We'll leave after two beers,' he promises. Maybe the girl in white pants will be there. She sometimes comes in with that big dumb Jamie and Nelson can tell it is she who gets them here; she digs the scene and he doesn't.

The Laid-Back under this new name is such a success that parking along Pine is hard to find; he wants to spare Pru at least a long walk in the cold, though the doctor says exercise is good.

He hates the cold. When he was little he had loved December because it had Christmas in it toward the end and he was so excited by all the things there were to get in the world that he never noticed how the dark and cold closed in, tighter and tighter. And now Dad is taking Mom off for this fancy holiday on some island with these putrid other couples, to lie there and bask while Nelson freezes and holds the fort at the lot; it's not fair. The girl doesn't always wear white slacks, the last time he saw her she had on one of that new style of skirt with the big slit down the side. There is a space in front of the long low brick building that used to be the Verity Press, between an old two-tone Fairlane and a bronze Honda station wagon, that looks big enough, just. The trick of tight parking is to swing your back bumper square into the other guy's headlights and don't leave yourself too far out from the curb or you'll be forever jockeying in. And don't be afraid to cut it tight on the left, you always have more room than you think. He pulls so close to the Fairlane Pru speaks up sharply, 'Nelson.'

He says, 'I see him, I *see* him, shut up and let me concentrate.' He intends, with that heavy Chrysler's veloured steering wheel, a ratio on the power steering you could turn a cruise ship with, to snap the car into its slot slick as a skater stopping on ice. God, figure skaters' costumes are sexy, the way their little skirts flip up when they skate ass-backwards, and he remembers, straining to see the Honda's rather low little headlights, how that girl's slit skirt fell away to show a whole long load of shining thigh before she arranged herself on the barstool, having given Nelson a brief shy smile of recognition. Mom-mom's ponderous Chrysler slips into reverse and his anticipation of ideal liquid motion is so strong he does not hear the subtle grinding of metal on metal until it has proceeded half the car's length and Pru is yelping, Jesus, like she's having the baby now.

Webb Murkett says gold has gone about as far as it can go for now: the little man in America has caught the fever and when the little man climbs on the bandwagon the smart money gets off. Silver, now that's another story: the Hunt brothers down in Texas are buying up silver futures at the rate of millions a day, and big

335

boys like that must know something. Harry decides to change his gold into silver.

Janice wants to come downtown anyway to do some Christmas shopping, so he meets her at the Crêpe House (that she still calls Johnny Frye's) for lunch, and then they can go to the Brewer Trust with the safe-deposit key and take out the thirty Kruger-rand Harry bought for $11,314.20 three months before. In the cubicle the bank lets you commune with your safe-deposit box in, he fishes out from behind the insurance policies and U.S. Savings Bonds the two blue-tinted cylinders like doll-house toilets, and passes them into Janice's hands, one into each, and smiles when her face as if at the first entry of a good fuck acknowledges with renewed surprise the heft, the weight of the gold. Solid citizens by this extra degree, then, the two of them walk out between the great granite pillars of the Brewer Trust into the frail December sunlight and cross through the forest, where the fountains are dry and the concrete park benches are spray-painted full of young people's names, and on down the east side of Weiser past two blocks of stores doing a thin Christmas business. Underfed little Puerto Rican women are the only ones scuttling in and out of the cut-rate entranceways, and kids who ought to be in school, and bleary retirees in dirty padded parkas and hunter's hats, with whiskery loose jaws; the mills have used these old guys up and spit them out.

The tinsel of the wreaths hung on the aluminum lampposts tingles, audibly shivering, as Harry passes each post. Gold, gold, his heart sings, feeling the weight balanced in the two deep pockets of his overcoat and swinging in time with his strides. Janice hurries beside him with shorter steps, a tidy dense woman warm in a sheepskin coat that comes down to her boots, clutching several packages whose paper rattles in this same wind that stirs the tinsel. He sees them together in the flecked scarred mirror next to a shoestore entrance: him tall and unbowed and white of face, her short and dark and trotting beside him in boots of oxblood leather zippered tight to her ankles, with high heels, so they thrust from her swinging coat with a smartness of silhouette advertising as clear as his nappy black overcoat and Irish bog hat that he is all set, that they are all set, that their smiles as they walk

336

along can afford to discard the bitter blank glances that flicker toward them on the street, then fall away.

Fiscal Alternatives with its long thin Venetian blinds is in the next block, a block that once had the name of disreputable but with the general sinking of the downtown is now no worse than the next. Inside, the girl with platinum hair and long fingernails smiles in recognition of him, and pulls a beige chair over from the waiting area for Janice. After a telephone call to some far-off trading floor, she runs some figures through her little computer and tells them, as they sit bulky in their coats at the corner of her desk, that the price of gold per ounce had nearly touched five hundred this morning but now she can offer them no more than $488.75 per coin, which will come to – her fingers dance unhampered by her nails, the gray display slot of the computer staggers forth with its bland magnetic answer – $14,662.50. Harry calculates inwardly that he has made a thousand a month on his gold and asks her how much silver he can buy for that now. The young woman slides out from under her eyelashes a glance as if she is a manicurist deciding whether or not to admit that she does, in the back room, also give massages. At his side Janice has lit a cigarette, and her smoke pours across the desk and pollutes the relationship this platinum-haired girl and Harry have established.

The girl explains, 'We don't deal in silver bullion. We only handle silver in the form of pre-'65 silver dollars, which we sell under melt value.'

'Melt value?' Harry asks. He had pictured a tidy ingot that would slip into the safe-deposit box snug as a gun into a holster.

The salesgirl is patient, with something sultry about her dispassion. Some of the silky weightiness of precious metals has rubbed off onto her. 'You know, the old-fashioned cartwheel' – she makes an illustrative circle with daggerlike forefinger and thumb – 'the U.S. Mint put out until fifteen years ago. Each one contains point seventy-five troy ounces of silver. Silver this noon was going for' – she consults a slip on her desk, next to the vanilla push dial telephone – '$23.55 a troy ounce, which would make each coin, irrespective of collector value, worth' – the calculator again – '$17.66. But there's some wear on some of the coins, so were you and your wife to decide to buy now I could give you a quote under that.'

'These are old coins?' Janice asks, that Ma Springer edge in her voice.

'Some are, some aren't,' the girl answers coolly. 'We buy them by weight from collectors who have sifted through them for collector value.'

This isn't what Harry had pictured, but Webb had sworn that silver was where the smart money was. He asks, 'How many could we buy with the gold money?'

A flurry of computation follows; $14,662.50 would convert to the magical number of 888. Eight hundred eighty-eight silver dollars priced at $16.50 each, including commission and Pennsylvania sales tax. To Rabbit eight hundred eighty-eight seems like a lot of anything, even matchsticks. He looks at Janice. 'Sweetie. Whaddeya think?'

'Harry, I don't know what to think. It's your investment.'

'But it's our money.'

'You don't want to just keep the gold.'

'Webb says silver could double, if they don't return the hostages.'

Janice turns to the girl. 'I was just wondering, if we found a house we wanted to put a down payment on, how liquid is this silver?'

The blonde speaks to Janice with new respect, at a softer pitch, woman to woman. 'It's very liquid. Much more so than collectibles or land. Fiscal Alternatives guarantees to buy back whatever it sells. These coins today, if you brought them in, we'd pay' – she consults the papers on her desk again – 'thirteen fifty each.'

'So we'd be out three dollars times eight hundred eighty-eight,' Harry says. His palms have started to sweat, maybe it's the overcoat. Make a little profit in this world and right away the world starts scheming to take it from you. He wishes he had the gold back. It was so pretty, that little delicate deer on the reverse side.

'Oh, but the way silver's been going,' the girl says, pausing to scratch at some fleck of imperfection adjacent to the corner of her lips, 'you could make that up in a week. I think you're doing the smart thing.'

'Yeah, but as you say, suppose the Iran thing gets settled,' Harry worries. 'Won't the whole bubble burst?'

'Precious metals aren't a bubble. Precious metals are the ultimate security. I myself think what's brought the Arab money into gold was not so much Iran as the occupation of the Great Mosque. When the Saudis are in trouble, then it's *really* a new ballgame.'

A new ballgame, hey. 'O.K.,' he says. 'Let's do it. We'll buy the silver.'

Platinum-hair seems a bit surprised, for all of her smooth sales talk, and there is a long hassle over the phone locating so many coins. At last some boy she calls Lyle brings in a gray cloth sack like you would carry some leftover mail in; he is swaying with the effort and grunts right out, lifting the sack up onto her desk, but then he has a slender build, with something faggy about him, maybe his short haircut. Funny how that's swung completely around: the squares let their hair grow now and the fags and punks are the ones with butches. Harry wonders what they're doing in the Marines, probably down to their shoulders. This Lyle goes off, after giving Harry a suspicious squint like he's bought not only the massage but the black-leather-and-whip trick too.

At first Harry and Janice think that only the girl with the platinum hair and all but perfect skin may touch the coins. She pushes her papers to one side of her desk and struggles to lift a corner of the bag. Dollars spill out. 'Damn.' She sucks at a fingernail. 'You can help count if you would.' They take off their coats and dig in, counting into stacks of ten. Silver is all over the desk, hundreds of Miss Libertys, some thinned by wear, some as chunky as if virgin from the mint. Handling such a palpable luxury of profiles and slogans and eagles makes Janice titter, and Harry knows what she means: playing in the mud. The muchness. The stacks proliferate and are arranged in ranks of ten times ten. The bag at last yields its final coin, with a smidgeon of lint the girl flicks away. Unsmiling, she waves her red-tipped hand across her stacks. 'I have three hundred and ninety.'

Harry taps his stacks and reports, 'Two forty.'

Janice says of hers, 'Two hundred fifty-eight.' She beat him. He is proud of her. She can become a teller if he suddenly dies.

The calculator is consulted: 888. 'Exactly right,' the girl says, as surprised as they. She performs the paperwork, and gives Harry back two quarters and a ten-dollar bill in change. He wonders if he should hand it back to her, as a tip. The coins fit into three cardboard boxes the size of fat bricks. Harry puts them one on top of another, and when he tries to lift all three Janice and the girl both laugh aloud at the expression on his face.

'My God,' he says. 'What do they weigh?'

The platinum-headed girl fiddles at her computer. 'If you take each one to be a troy ounce at least, it comes to seventy-four pounds. There are only twelve ounces troy measure in a pound.'

He turns to Janice. 'You carry one.'

She lifts one and it's his turn to laugh, at the look on her face, her eyelids stretched wide. 'I can't,' she says.

'You must,' he says. 'It's only up to the bank. Come on, I gotta get back to the lot. Whajja play all that tennis for if you don't have any muscles?'

He is proud of that tennis; he is performing for the blond girl now, acting the role of eccentric Penn Park nob. She suggests, 'Maybe Lyle could walk up with you.'

Rabbit doesn't want to be seen on the street with that fag. 'We can manage.' To Janice he says, 'Just imagine you're pregnant. Come on. Let's go.' To the girl he says, 'She'll be back for her packages.' He picks up two of the boxes and pushes the door open with his shoulder, forcing Janice to follow. Out in the cold sunlight and shimmering wind of Weiser Street he tries not to grimace, or to return the stares of those who glance wonderingly at the two small boxes clutched so fiercely in his two hands at the level of his fly.

A black man in a blue watch cap, with bloodshot eyes like marbles dropped in orange juice, halts on the pavement and stumbles a step toward Harry. 'Hey buddy you wanna hep out a fren' –' Something about these blacks they really zero in on Rabbit. He pivots to shield the silver with his body, and its swung weight tips him so he has to take a step. In moving off, he doesn't dare look behind him to see if Janice is following. But standing on the curb next to a scarred parking meter he hears her breathing and feels her struggle to his side.

'This coat is so heavy too,' she pants.

'Let's cross,' he says.

'In the middle of the block?'

'Don't argue,' he mutters, feeling the puzzled black man at his back. He pushes off the curb, causing a bus halfway down the block to hiss with its brakes. In the middle of the street, where the double white line once wobbled in summer's soft tar, he waits for Janice to catch up. The girl has given her the mail sack to carry the third box of silver in, but rather than sling it over her shoulder Janice carries it cradled in her left arm like a baby. 'How're you doing?' he asks her.

'I'll manage. Keep moving, Harry.'

They reach the far curb. The peanut store now not only has porno magazines inside but has put an array of them on a rack outside. Young muscular oiled boys pose singly or in pairs under titles such as DRUMMER and SKIN. A Japanese in a three-piece pinstripe suit and gray bowler hat steps smartly out of the door, folding a *New York Times* and a *Wall Street Journal* together under his arm. How did the Japanese ever get to Brewer? As the door eases shut, the old circus smell of warm roasted peanuts drifts out to the cold sidewalk. Harry says to Janice, 'We could put all three boxes in the bag and I could lug it over my shoulder. You know, like Santa Claus. Ho ho.'

A small crowd of pocked dark street kids mixed with shaggy rummies in their winter layered look threatens to collect around them as they confer. Harry tightens his grip on his two boxes. Janice hugs her third and says. 'Let's push on this way. The bank's only a block more.' Her face is flushed and bitten by the cold, her eyes squinting and watering and her mouth a determined slot.

'A good block and a half,' he corrects.

Past then the Brewer Wallpaper Company with its display rolls stiffening in the dusty windows like shrouds, past Blimline's Sandwiches and Manderbach Wholesale Office Supplies and a narrow place jammed with flat boxes called Hobby Heaven, past the cigar store with its giant rusting Y-B sign and the ornately iron-barred windows of the old Conrad Weiser Oyster House that now promises *Live Entertainment* in desperate red letters on its

341

dark doors, across Fourth Street when the light at last turns green, past the long glass-block-inlaid façade of the Acme they say is going out of business at the end of the year, past Hollywood Beauty Supplies and Imperial Floor Coverings and Zenith Auto Parts and Accessories with its sweetish baked smell of fresh tires and window of chrome tailpipes they go, man and wife, as the wind intensifies and the sparkling sidewalk squares grow in size.

The squared-off weight in Harry's hands has become a furious thing, burning his palms, knocking against his crotch. Now when he would almost welcome being robbed he feels that the others on this west side of the street are shying from them, as somehow menacing, distorted into struggling shapes by the force-fields of their paper boxes. He keeps having to wait for Janice to catch up, while his own burden, double hers, pulls at his arms. The tinsel wound around the aluminum lampposts vibrates furiously. He is sweating across his back beneath his expensive overcoat and his shirt collar keeps drying to a clammy cold edge. During these waits he stares up Weiser toward the mauve and brown bulk of Mt Judge; in his eyes as a child God had reposed on the slopes of that mountain, and now he can imagine how through God's eyes from that vantage he and Janice might look below: two ants trying to make it up the sides of a bathroom basin.

They pass a camera store advertising Afga Film, the Hexerei Boutique with its mannequins flaunting their nippleless boobs through transparent blouses and vests of gold mail, a Rexall's with pastel vibrators among the suggested Christmas gifts in the windows festooned with cotton and angel hair, the Crêpe House with its lunching couples, the locally famous cigar store saved as an act of historical preservation, and a new store called Pedalease specializing in male and female footwear for jogging and tennis and even racquetball and squash, that young couples or pairs of young singles do together these days, to judge from the big cardboard blow-ups in the window. The Dacron-clad girl's honey-colored hair lifts like air made liquid as she laughingly strokes a ball on easy feet. Next, at last, the first of the four great granite columns of the Brewer Trust looms. Harry leans his aching back against its Roman breadth while waiting for Janice to catch up. If she's robbed in this gap between them it will cost them a third of $14,652 or nearly $5000 but at this point the risk doesn't seem so real. Some distance away he sees spray-painted on the back of one of the concrete benches in the mall of trees a slogan SKEETER LIVES. If he could go closer he could be sure that's what it says. But he cannot move. Janice arrives beside his shoulder. Red-faced, she looks like her mother. 'Let's not stand here,' she pants. Even the circumference of the pillar seems a lengthy distance as she leads him around it and pushes ahead of him through the revolving doors.

Christmas carols are pealing within the great vaulted interior. The high groined ceiling is painted blue here in every season, with evenly spaced stars of gold. When Harry sets his two boxes down on one of the shelves where you write checks, his relieved body seems to rise toward this false sky. The teller, a lady in an orchid pants suit, smiles to be readmitting them to their safe-deposit box so soon. Their box is a four by four – narrower, they discover, than the boxes of silver dollars three rows abreast. Hearts still laboring, their hands still hurting, Harry and Janice are slow to grasp the disparity, once the frosted glass door has sealed them into the cubicle. Harry several times measures the width of one paper lid against the breadth of tin before concluding, 'We need a bigger box.' Janice is delegated to go back out into the bank and request one. Her father had been a good friend of the manager. When she returns, it is with the news that there has been a run lately on safe-deposit boxes, that the best the bank could do was put the Angstroms on a list. The manager that Daddy knew has retired. The present one seemed to Janice very young, though he wasn't exactly rude.

Harry laughs. 'Well we can't sell 'em back to Blondie down there, it'd cost us a fortune. Could we dump everything back in the bag and stuff it in?'

Crowded together in the cubicle, he and Janice keep bumping into each other, and he scents rising from her for the first time a doubt that he has led them well in this new inflated world; or perhaps the doubt he scents arises from him. But there can be no turning back. They transfer silver dollars from the boxes to the bag. When the silver clinks loudly, Janice winces and says, '*Shh.*'

'Why? Who'll hear?'

'The people out there. The tellers.'

'What do they care?'

'I care,' Janice says. 'It's stifling in here.' She takes off her sheepskin coat and in the absence of a hook to hang it on drops it folded to the floor. He takes off his black overcoat and drops it on top. Sweat of exertion has made her hair springier; her bangs have curled back to reveal that high glossy forehead that is so much her, now and twenty years ago, that he kisses it, tasting salt. He wonders if people have ever screwed in these cubicles and imagines that a vault would be a nice place, one of those primped-up young tellers and a lecherous old mortgage officer, put the time-lock on to dawn and ball away. Janice feeds stacks of coins into the coarse gray pouch furtively, suppressing the clink. 'This is so embarrassing,' she says, 'suppose one of those ladies comes in,' as if the silver is naked flesh; and not for the first time in twenty years plus he feels a furtive rush of loving her, caught with him as she is in the narrow places life affords. He takes one of the silver dollars and slips it down the neck of her linen blouse into her bra. As he foresaw, she squeals at the chill and tries to suppress the squeal. He loves her more, seeing her unbutton her blouse a button and frowningly dig into her bra for the coin; old as he is it still excites him to watch women fiddle with their underwear. Make our own coat hook in here.

After a while she announces, 'It simply will *not* go in.' Stuff and adjust as they will, hardly half of the bagged coins can be made to fit. Their insurance policies and Savings Bonds, Nelson's birth certificate and the never-discarded mortgage papers for the house in Penn Villas the burned down – all the scraps of paper preserved as evidence of their passage through an economy and a certain legal time – are lifted out and reshuffled to no avail. The thick cloth of the bag, the tendency of loose coins to bunch in a sphere, the long slender shape of the gray tin box frustrate them as side by side they tug and push, surgeons at a hopeless case. The eight hundred eighty-eight coins keep escaping the mouth of the sack and falling onto the floor and rolling into corners. When they have pressed the absolute maximum into the box, so its tin sides bulge, they are still left with three hundred silver dollars, which Harry distributes among the pockets of his overcoat.

When they emerge from the cubicle, the friendly teller in her orchid outfit offers to take the loaded box off his hands. 'Pretty heavy,' he warns her. 'Better let me do it.' Her eyebrows arch; she backs off and leads him into the vault. They go through a great door, its terraced edges gleaming, into a space walled with small burnished rectangles and floored in waxy white. Not a good place to fuck, he was wrong about that. She lets him slide his long box into the empty rectangle. R.I.P. Harry is in a sweat, bent over with effort. He straightens up and apologizes, 'Sorry we loaded it up with so much crap.'

'Oh no,' the orchid lady says. 'A lot of people nowadays ... all this burglary.'

'What happens if the burglars get in here?' he jokes.

This in not funny. 'Oh ... they *can't*.'

Outside the bank, the afternoon has progressed, and shadows from the buildings darken the glitter of tinsel. Janice taps one of his pockets playfully, to hear him jingle. 'What are you going to do with all these?'

'Give 'em away to the poor. That bitch down the street, that's the last time I buy anything from her.' Cold cakes his face as his sweat dries. Several guys he knows from Rotary come out of the Crêpe House looking punchy on lunch and he gives them the high sign, while striding on. God knows what's happening over on the lot without him, the kid may be accepting roller skates for trade-in.

'You could use the safe at the lot,' Janice suggests. 'They could go into one of these.' She hands him one of the empty cardboard boxes.

'Nelson will steal 'em,' he says. 'He knows the combination now too.'

'Harry. What a thing to say.'

'You know how much that scrape he gave your mother's Chrysler is going to cost? Eight hundred fucking bucks minimum. He must have been out of his head. You could see poor Pru was humiliated, I wonder how long she'll let things cook before she gets smart and asks for a divorce. That'll cost us, too.' His overcoat, so weighted, drags his shoulders down. He feels, as if the sidewalk now is a downslanted plane, the whole year dropping

345

away under him, loss after loss. His silver is scattered, tinsel. His box will break, the janitor will sweep up the coins. It's all dirt anyway. The great sad lie told to children that is Christmas stains Weiser end to end, and through the murk he glimpses the truth that to be rich is to be robbed, to be rich is to be poor.

Janice recalls him to reality, saying, 'Harry, please. Stop looking so tragic. Pru loves Nelson, and he loves her. They won't get a divorce.'

'I wasn't thinking about that. I was thinking about how silver's going to go down.'

'Oh, what do we care if it does? Everything's just a gamble anyway.'

Bless that dope, still trying. The daughter of old Fred Springer, local high roller. Rolled himself into a satin-lined coffin. In the old days they used to bury the silver and put the corpses in slots in the wall.

'I'll walk down to the car with you,' Janice says, worried-wifely. 'I have to get my packages from that bitch as you call her. How much did you want to fuck that bitch by the way?' Trying to find a topic he'll enjoy.

'Hardly at all,' he confesses. 'It's terrifying in fact, how little. Did you get a look at her fingernails? Sccr-*ratch*.'

The week between the holidays is a low one for car sales: people feel strapped after Christmas, and with winter coming, ice and salt on the road and fenderbenders likely, they are inclined to stick with the heap they have. Ride it out to spring is the motto. At least the snowmobile's been moved around to the back where nobody can see it, instead of its sitting there like some kind of cousin of those new little front-wheel drive Tercels. Where do they get their names? Sounds like an Edsel. Even Toyota, it has too many *o*'s, makes people think of 'toy.' Datsun and Honda, you don't know where they're coming from. Datsun could be German from the sound of it, data, rat-tat-tat, rising sun. The Chuck Wagon across Route 111 isn't doing much of a business either, now that it's too cold to eat outdoors or in the car, unless you leave the motor running, people die doing that every winter, trying to screw. The build-up is terrific though of hoagie wrappers and milkshake cartons blowing around in the lot, with the dust. Different kind of dust in December, grayer and grittier than summer dust, maybe the colder air, less lift in it, like cold air holds less water, that's why the insides of the storm windows now when you wake up in the morning have all that dew. Think of all the problems. Rust. Dry rot. Engines that don't start in the morning unless you take off the distributor cap and wipe the plugs. Without condensation the world might last forever. On the moon, for example, there's no problem. Or on Mars either it turns out. New Year's, Buddy Inglefinger is throwing the blast this year, guess he was afraid of dropping out of sight with the old gang, getting the wind up about the trip to the islands they're taking without inviting him. Wonder who his hostess is going to be, that flat-chested sourpuss with straight black hair running some kind of crazy shop in Brewer or that girl before her, with the rash on the inside of her thighs and even between her breasts you could see in a bathing suit, what *was* her name? Ginger. Georgene. He and Janice just want to make an appearance to be polite, you get to a certain age you know nothing much is going to happen at parties, and leave right after midnight. Then six more days and, *powie*, the islands. Just the six of them. Little Cindy down there in all that sand. He needs a rest, things are getting him down. Sell less than a car a day in this business not counting Sundays and you're in trouble. All this tin getting dusty and rusty, the chrome developing pimples. Metal corrodes. Silver dropped two dollars an ounce the minute he bought it from that bitch.

Nelson, who has been in the shop with Manny fussing over the repairs to the Chrysler, the kid wanting a break on the full $18.50 customer rate and Manny explaining over and over like to a moron how if you shave the rate for agency employees it shows up in the books and affects everybody's end-of-the-month incentive bonus, comes over and stands by his father at the window.

Harry can't get used to the kid in a suit, it makes him seem even shorter somehow, like one of those midget emcees in a tuxedo, and with his hair shaped longer now and fluffed up by Pru's blow-drier after every shower Nellie seems a little mean-eyed dude Harry never knew. Janice used to say when the boy was little how he had Harry's ears with that crimp in the fold at the tip like one of the old-fashioned train conductors had taken his punch, but the tips of Nelson's are neatly covered by soft shingles of hair and Harry hasn't bothered to study his own since at about the age of forty he came out of that adolescent who-am-I vanity trip. He just shaves as quick as he can now and gets away from the mirror. Ruth has sweetly small tightly folded ears, he remembers. Janice's get so tan on top an arch of tiny red freckles comes out. Her father's lobes got long as a Chinaman's before he died. Nelson has a hot-looking pimple almost due to pop in the crease above his nostril, Harry notices in the light flooding through the showroom window. The slant of sun makes all the dust on the plate glass look thick as gold leaf this time of year, the arc of each day is so low. The kid is trying to be friendly. Come on. Unbend.

Harry asks him, 'You stay up to watch the 76ers finish?'

'Naa.'

'That Gervin for San Antonio was something, wasn't he? I heard on the radio this morning he finished with forty-six points.'

'Basketball is all goons, if you ask me.'

'It's changed a lot since my day,' Rabbit admits. 'The refs used to call travelling once in a while at least; now, Christ, they eat up half the floor going in for a lay-up.'

'I like hockey,' Nelson says.

'I know you do. When you have the damn Flyers on there's nowhere in the house you can go to get away from the yelling. All those apes in the crowd go for is to see a fight break out and someone's teeth got knocked out. Blood on the ice, that's the drawing card.' This isn't going right; he tries another topic. 'What do you think about those Russkis in Afghanistan? They sure gave themselves a Christmas present.'

'It's stupid,' Nelson says. 'I mean, Carter's getting all upset. It's no worse than what we did in Vietnam, it's not even as bad because at least it's right next door and they've had a puppet government there for years.'

'Puppet governments are O.K., huh?'

'Well *every*body has 'em. All of South America is our puppet governments.'

'I bet that'd be news to the spics.'

'At least the Russians, Dad, *do* it when they're going to do it.

We *try* to do it and then everything gets all bogged down in politics. We can't do *any*thing anymore.'

'Well not with people talking like you we can't,' Harry says to his son. 'How would you feel about going over and fighting in Afghanistan?'

The boy chuckles. 'Dad, I'm a married man. And way past draft age besides.'

Can this be? Harry doesn't feel too old to fight, and he's going to be forty-seven in February. He's always been sort of sorry they didn't send him to Korea when they had him in the Army, though at the time he was happy enough to hunker down in Texas. They had a funny straight-on way of looking at the world out there: money, booze, and broads, and that was it. Down to the bones. What is it Mim likes to say? God didn't go west, He died on the trail. To Nelson he says, 'You mean you got married to stay out of the next war?'

'There won't be any next war, Carter will make a lot of noise but wind up letting them have it, just like he's letting Iran have the hostages. Actually, Billy Fosnacht was saying the only way we'll get the hostages back is if Russia invades Iran. Then they'd give us the hostages and sell us the oil because they need our wheat.'

'Billy Fosnacht – that jerk around again?'

'Just for vacation.'

'No offense, Nelson, but how can you stand that pill?'

'He's my friend. But I know why you can't stand him.'

'Why can't I?' Harry asks, his heart rising to what has become a confrontation.

Turning full toward his father beside the gold-dusted pane, the boy's face seems to shrink with hate, hate and fear of being hit for what he is saying. 'Because Billy was there the night you were screwing his mother while Skeeter was burning up Jill in the house we should have been in, protecting her.'

That night. Ten years ago, and still cooking in the kid's head, alive like a maggot affecting his growth. 'That still bugs you, doesn't it?' Rabbit says mildly.

The boy doesn't hear, his eyes lost in those sockets sunk as if thumbs had gripped too deep in clay, trying to pick up a lump. 'You let Jill die.'

'I didn't, and Skeeter didn't. We don't know who burnt the house down but it wasn't us. You got to let it go, kid. Your mother and me have let it go.'

'I know you have.' The sound of Mildred Kroust's electric typewriter rattles muffled in the distance, a couple in maroon parkas is stalking around in the lot checking the price stickers taped inside the windows, the boy stares as if stunned by the sound of his father's voice trying to reach him.

'The past is the past,' Harry goes on, 'you got to live in the present. Jill was headed that way no matter what the rest of us did. The first time I saw her, she had the kiss of death on her face.'

'I know that's what you want to think.'

'It's the only way to think. When you're my age you'll see it. At my age if you carried all the misery you've seen on your back you'd never get up in the morning.' A flicker of something, a split second when he feels the boy actually listening, encourages Harry to urge his voice deeper, more warmly. 'Once that baby of yours shows up,' he tells the boy, 'you'll have your hands full. You'll have a better perspective.'

'You want to know something?' Nelson asks in a rapid dead voice, looking through him with lifted eyes the slant light has stolen color from.

'What?' Rabbit's heart skips.

'When Pru fell down those stairs. I'm not sure if I gave her a push or not. I can't remember.'

Harry laughs, scared. 'Of course you didn't push her. Why would you push her?'

'Because I'm as crazy as you.'

'We're not crazy, either of us. Just frustrated, sometimes.'

'Really?' This seems information the kid is grateful for.

'Sure. Anyway, no harm was done. When is he due? He or she.' Fear rolls off this kid so thick Harry doesn't want to keep talking to him. The way his eyes looked transparent that instant, all the brown lifted out.

Nelson lowers his eyes, surly again. 'They think about three more weeks.'

'That's great. We'll be back in plenty of time. Look, Nelson. Maybe I haven't done everything right in my life. I know I haven't. But I haven't committed the greatest sin. I haven't laid down and died.'

'Who says that's the greatest sin?'

'Everybody says it. The church, the government. It's against Nature, to give up, you've got to keep moving. That's the thing about you. You're not moving. You don't want to be here, selling old man Springer's jalopies. You want to be out *there*, learning something.' He gestures toward the west. 'How to hang glide, or run a computer, or whatever.'

He has talked too much and closed up the space that opened in Nelson's resistance for a second. Nelson accuses: 'You don't want me here.'

'I want you where you're happy and that's not here. Now I didn't want to say anything but I've been going over the figures with Mildred and they're not that hot. Since you came here and Charlie left, gross sales are down about eleven per cent over last year, this same period, November–December.'

The boy's eyes water. 'I *try*, Dad. I try to be friendly and aggressive and all that when the people come in.'

'I know you do, Nelson. I know you do.'

'I can't go out and *drag* 'em in out of the cold.'

'You're right. Forget what I said. The thing about Charlie was, he had connections. I've lived in this county all my life except those two years in the Army and I don't have that kind of connections.'

'I know a *lot* of people my age,' Nelson protests.

'Yeah,' Harry says, 'you know the kind of people who sell you their used-up convertibles for a fancy price. But Charlie knows the kind of people who actually come in and buy a car. He expects 'em to; he's not surprised, they're not surprised. Maybe it's being Greek, I don't know. No matter what they say about you and me, kid, we're not Greek.'

This joking doesn't help; the boy has been wounded, deeper than Harry wanted. 'I don't think it's me,' Nelson says. 'It's the economy.'

The traffic on Route 111 is picking up; people are heading home in the gloom. Harry too can go; Nelson is on the floor till eight. Climb into the Corona and turn on the four-speaker radio

351

and hear how silver is doing. Hi ho, Silver. Harry says, in a voice that sounds sage in his own ears, almost like Webb Murkett's, 'Yeah, well, that has its wrinkles. This oil thing is hurting the Japanese worse than it is us, and what hurts them should be doing us good. The yen is down, these cars cost less in real dollars than they did last year, and it ought to be reflected in our sales.' That look on Cindy's face in the photograph, Harry can't get it out of his mind: an anxious startled kind of joy, as if she was floating away in a balloon and had just felt the earth lurch free. 'Numbers,' he tells Nelson in stern conclusion. 'Numbers don't lie, and they don't forgive.'

New Year's Day was when Harry and Janice had decided to go to Ma Springer with their news, which they had been keeping to themselves for nearly a week. Dread of how the old lady might react had prompted the postponement, plus a groping after ceremony, a wish to show respect for the sacred bonds of family by announcing the break on a significant day, the first of a new decade. Yet now that the day is here, they feel hungover and depleted from having stayed at Buddy Inglefinger's until three in the morning. Their tardy departure had been further prolonged by an uproarious commotion over cars in the driveway – a car that wouldn't start, belonging to Thelma Harrison's Maryland cousin, who was visiting. There was a lot of boozy shouting and falling-down helpfulness in the headlights as jump cables were found and Ronnie's Volvo was jockeyed nose to nose with the cousin's Nova, everybody poking their flashlight in to make sure Ronnie was connecting positive to positive and not going to blow out the batteries. Harry has seen jump cables actually melt in circumstances like this. Some woman he hardly knew had a mouth big enough to put the head of a flashlight in it, so her cheeks glowed like a lampshade. Buddy and his new girl, a frantic skinny six-footer with frizzed-out hair and three children from a broken marriage, had made some kind of punch of pineapple juice and rum and brandy, and the taste of pineapple still at noon keeps returning. On top of Harry's headache Nelson and Pru, who stayed home with Mom-mom last night watching on television straight from Times Square Guy Lombardo's brother now that

Guy Lombardo is dead, are hogging the living room watching the Cotton Bowl Festival Parade from Texas, so he and Janice have to take Ma Springer into the kitchen to get some privacy. A deadly staleness flavors the new decade. As they sit down at the kitchen table for their interview, it seems to him that they have already done this, and are sitting down to a rerun.

Janice, her eyes ringed by weariness, turns to him in his daze and says, 'Harry, you begin.'

'Me?'

'My goodness, what can this be?' Ma asks, pretending to be cross but pleased by the formality, the two of them touching her elbows and steering her in here. 'You're acting like Janice is pregnant but I know she had her tubes tied.'

'Cauterized,' Janice says softly, pained.

Harry begins. 'Bessie, you know we've been looking at houses.'

Playfulness snaps out of the old lady's face as if pulled by a rubber band. The skin at the corners of her set lips is crossed and recrossed, Harry suddenly sees, by fine dry wrinkles. In his mind mother-in-law has stayed as when he first met her, packed into her skin; but unnoticed by him Bessie's hide has loosened and cracked like putty in a cellar window, has developed the complexity of paper crumpled and then smoothed again. He tastes pineapple. A small black spot of nausea appears and grows as if rapidly approaching down the great parched space of her severe, expectant silence.

'Now,' he must go on, swallowing, 'we think we've found one we like. A little stone two-story over in Penn Park. The realtor thinks it might have been a gardener's cottage that somebody sold off when the estates were broken up and then was enlarged to fit a better kitchen in. It's on a little turnaround off Franklin Drive behind the bigger houses; the privacy is great.'

'It's only twenty minutes away, Mother.'

Harry can't stop studying, in the cold kitchen light, the old woman's skin. The dark life of veins underneath that gave her her flushed swarthy look that Janice inherited has been overlaid with a kind of dust of fine gray threads, wrinkles etched on the light-struck flat of the cheek nearest him like rows and rows of indecipherable writing scratched on a far clay cliff. He feels himself towering, giddy, and all of his poor ashamed words strike across a great distance, a terrible widening as Ma listens motionless to her doom. 'Virtually next door,' he says to her, 'and with three bedrooms upstairs, I mean there's a little room that the kids who lived there had used as a kind of clubhouse, two bedrooms though absolutely, and we'd be happy to put you up any time if it came to that, for as long as needs be.' He feels he is blundering: already he has the old lady living with them again, her TV set muttering on the other side of the wall.

Janice breaks in: 'Really, Mother, it makes much more sense for Harry and me at this point of our lives.'

'But I had to talk her into it, Ma; it was my idea. When you and Fred very kindly took us in after we got back together I never thought of it as for forever. I thought of it as more of a stop-gap thing, until we got our feet back under us.'

What he had liked about it, he sees now, was that it would have made it easy for him to leave Janice: just walk out under the streetlights and leave her with her parents. But he hadn't left her, and now cannot. She is his fortune.

She is trying to soften her mother's silence. 'Also as an investment, Mother. Every couple we know owns their own house, even this bachelor we were with last night, and a lot of the men earn less than Harry. Property's the only place to put money if you have any, what with inflation and all.'

Ma Springer at last does speak, in a voice that keeps rising in spite of herself. 'You'll have this place when I'm gone, if you could just wait. Why can't you wait a little yet?'

'Mother, that's ghoulish when you talk like that. We don't want to wait for *your* house; Harry and I want our house *now*.' Janice lights a cigarette, and has to press her elbow onto the tabletop to hold the match steady.

Harry assures the old lady, 'Bessie, you're going to live forever.' But having seen what's happening to her skin he knows this isn't true.

Wide-eyed suddenly, she asks, 'What's going to happen to this house then?'

Rabbit nearly laughs, the old lady's expression is so childlike, taken with the pitch of her voice. 'It'll be fine,' he tells her. 'When they built places like this they built 'em to last. Not like the shacks they slap up now.'

'Fred always wanted Janice to have this house,' Ma Springer states, staring with eyes narrowed again at a place just between Harry's and Janice's heads. 'For her security.'

Janice laughs now. 'Mother, I have plenty of security. We told you about the gold and silver.'

'Playing with money like that is a good way to lose it,' Ma says. 'I don't want to leave this house to be auctioned off to some Brewer Jew. They're heading out this way, you know, now that the blacks and Puerto Ricans have come into the north side of town.'

'Come on, Bessie,' Harry says, 'what do you care? Like I said, you got a lot of life ahead of you, but when you're gone, you're gone. Let go, you got to let some things go for other people to worry about. The Bible tells you that, it says it on every page. Let go; the Lord knows best.'

Janice from her twitchy manner thinks he is saying too much. 'Mother, we might come back to the house –'

'When the old crow is dead. Why didn't you and Harry tell me my presence was such a burden? I tried to stay in my room as much as I could. I went into the kitchen only when it looked like nobody else was going to make the meal –'

'Mother, stop it. You've been lovely. We both love you.'

'Grace Stuhl would have taken me in, many's the times she offered. Though her house isn't half the size of this and has all those front steps.' She sniffs, so loudly it seems a cry for help.

Nelson shouts in from the living room, 'Mom-mom, when's lunch?'

Janice says urgently, 'See, Mother. You're forgetting Nelson. He'll be here, with his *fam*ily.'

The old lady sniffs again, less tragically, and replies with pinched lips and a level red-rimmed gaze, 'He may be or he may not be. The young can't be depended on.'

Harry tells her, 'You're right about that all right. They won't fight and they won't learn, just sit on their asses and get stoned.'

Nelson comes into the kitchen holding a newspaper, today's Brewer *Standard*. He looks cheerful for once, on his good night's sleep. He has folded the paper to a quiz on Seventies trivia and asks them all, 'How many of these people can you identify? Renée Richards, Stephen Weed, Megan Marshack, Marjoe Gortner, Greta Rideout, Spider Sabich, D. B. Cooper. I got six out of seven, Pru got only four.'

'Renée Richards was Patty Hearst's boyfriend,' Rabbit begins.

Nelson sees the state his grandmother's face is in and asks, 'What's happening here?'

Janice says, 'We'll explain later, sweetie.'

Harry tells him, 'Your mother and I have found a house we're going to move to.'

Nelson stares from one to the other of his parents and it seems he might scream, the way he goes white around the gills. But instead he pronounces quietly, 'What a copout. What a fucking pair of copout artists. Well screw you both. Mom, Dad. Screw you.'

And he returns to the living room where the rumble of drums and trombones merges with the mumble of unheard words as he and Pru confer within the tunnel of their young marriage. The kid had felt frightened. He felt left. Things are getting too big for him. Rabbit knows the feeling. For all that is wrong between them there are moments when his heart and Nelson's might be opposite ends of a single short steel bar, he knows so exactly what the kid is feeling. Still, just because people are frightened of being alone doesn't mean he has to sit still and be everybody's big fat patsy like Mim said.

Janice and her mother are holding hands, tears blurring both faces. When Janice cries, her face loses shape, dissolves to the ugly child she was. Her mother is saying, moaning as if to herself, 'Oh I knew you were looking but I guess I didn't believe you'd actually go ahead and buy one when you have this free. Isn't there any adjustment we could make here so you could change your minds or at least let me get adjusted first? I'm too old, is the thing, too old to take on responsibility. The boy means well in his way but he's all *ferhuddled* for now, and the girl, I don't know. She wants to do it all but I'm not sure she can. To be honest, I've been dreading the baby, I've been trying to remember how it was with you and Nelson, and for the life of me I can't. I remember the milk didn't come the way they thought it should, and the doctor was so rude to you about it Fred had to step in and have a word.'

Janice is nodding, nodding, tears making the side of her nose shine, the cords on her throat jumping out with every sob. 'Maybe we could wait, though we said we'd pass papers, if you feel that way at least wait until the baby comes.'

There is a rhythm the two of them are rocking to, hands clasped on the table, heads touching. 'Do what you must, for your own happiness,' Ma Springer is saying, 'the ones left behind will manage. It can't do worse than kill me, and that might be a blessing.'

She is turning Janice into a mess: face blubbery and melting, the pockets beneath her eyes liverish with guilt, Janice is leaning hard into her mother, giving in on the house, begging for forgiveness, 'Mother we thought, Harry was certain, you'd feel less alone, with –'

'With a worry like Nelson in the house?'

Tough old turkey. Harry better step in before Janice gives it all away. His throat hardens. 'Listen, Bessie. You asked for him, you got him.'

Free! Macadam falls away beneath the wheels, a tawny old fort can be glimpsed as they lift off the runway beneath the rounded riveted edge of one great wing, the gas tanks of South Philadelphia are reduced to a set of white checkers. The wheels thump, retracted, and cruel photons glitter on the aluminum motionless beside the window. The swift ascent of the plane makes their blood weighty; Janice's hand sweats in his. She had wanted him to have the window seat, so she wouldn't have to look. There is marsh below, withered and veined with saltwater. Harry marvels at the industrial buildings beyond the Delaware: flat gravel roofs vast as parking lots and parking lots all inlaid with glittering automobile roofs like bathroom floors tiled with jewels. And in junkyards of cars the effect is almost as brilliant. The NO SMOKING sign goes off. Behind the Angstroms the voices of the Murketts and the Harrisons begin to chatter. They all had a drink at an airport bar, though the hour was eleven in the morning. Harry has flown before, but to Texas with the Army and dealers' confer-

357

ences in Cleveland and Albany: never aloft on vacation like this, due east into the sun. How quickly, how silently, the 747 eats up the toy miles below! Sun glare travels with them across lakes as momentarily as across a mirror. The winter has been eerily mild thus far, to spite the Ayatollah; on golf courses the greens show as living discs and ovals amid the white beans of the traps and on the fairways he can spot moving specks, men playing. Composition tennis courts are dominoes from this height, drive-in movies have the shape of a fan, baseball diamonds seem a species of tattered money. Cars move very slowly and with an odd perfection, as if the roads hold tracks. The houses of the Camden area scatter, relenting to disclose a plowed field or an estate with its prickly mansion and eye of a swimming pool tucked in the midst of woods; and then within another minute, still climbing, Harry is above the black-red carpet of the Jersey Pines, scored with yellow roads and patches of scraping but much of it still unmarred, veins of paler unleafed trees following the slope of land and flow of water among the darker evergreens, the tints of competition on earth made clear to the eye so hugely lifted. Janice lets go of his hand and gives signs of having swallowed her terror.

'What do you see?' she asks.

'The Shore.'

It is true, in another silent stride the engines had inched them to the edge of the ocean of trees and placed underneath them a sandy strip, separated from the mainland by a band of flashing water and filled to a precarious fullness with linear summer cities, etched there by builders who could not see, as Harry can, how easily the great shining shoulder of the ocean could shrug and immerse and erase all traces of men. Where the sea impinges on the white sand a frill of surf slowly waves, a lacy snake pinned in place. Then this flight heads over the Atlantic at an altitude from which no whitecaps can be detected in the bluish hemisphere below, and immensity becomes nothingness. The plane, its earnest droning without and its party mutter and tinkle within, becomes all of the world there is.

An enamelled stewardess brings them lunch, sealed on a tray of blond plastic. Though her make-up is thickly applied Harry thinks he detects beneath it, as she bends close with a smile to ask what beverage he would prefer, shadowy traces of a hectic night. They fuck on every layover, he has read in *Club* or *Oui*, a separate boyfriend in every city, twenty or thirty men, these girls the fabulous horny sailors of our time. Ever since the airport he has been amazed by other people: the carpeted corridors seemed thronged with freaks, people in crazy sizes and clothes, girls with dead-white complexions and giant eyeglasses and hair frizzed out to fill a bushel basket, black men swaggering along in long fur coats and hip-hugging velvet suits, a tall pale boy in a turban and a down vest, a dwarf in a plaid tam-o'-shanter, a woman so obese she couldn't sit in the molded plastic chairs of the waiting areas and had to stand propping herself on a three-legged aluminum cane. Life outside Brewer was gaudy, wild. Everyone was a clown in costume. Rabbit and his five companions were in costume too, flimsy summer clothes under winter overcoats. Cindy Murkett is wearing high-heeled slides on naked ankles; Thelma Harrison pads along in woolly socks and tennis sneakers. They all keep laughing among themselves, in that betraying Diamond County way. Harry doesn't mind getting a little high, but he doesn't want to sacrifice awareness of the colors around him, of the revelation that outside Brewer there is a planet without ruts worn in it. In such moments of adventure he is impatient with his body, that its five windows aren't enough, he can't get the world all in. Joy makes his heart pound. God, having shrunk in Harry's middle years to the size of a raisin lost under the car seat, is suddenly great again, everywhere like a radiant wind. Free: the dead and the living alike have been left five miles below in the haze that has annulled the earth like breath on a mirror.

Harry turns from the little double-paned airplane window of some tinted soft substance that has been scratched again and again horizontally as by a hail of meteorites. Janice is leafing through the airline magazine. He asks her, 'How do you think they'll do?'

'Who?'

'Your mother and Nelson and Pru, who else?'

She flips a glossy page. Her mother is in her profile, that set of the lips as if they have just pronounced a mournful truth and will not take it back. 'I expect better than when we're there.'

'They say anything to you about the house?'

Harry and Janice passed papers two days ago, a Tuesday. The day before, Monday the seventh, they had sold their silver back to Fiscal Alternatives. The metal, its value driven up by panic buying in the wake of Afghanistan by heavy holders of petro-dollars, stood at $36.70 that day, making each of the silver dollars, bought for $16.50 including sales tax, worth $23.37, according to the calculations of the platinum-haired young woman. Janice, who had not worked all these years off and on at her father's lot for nothing, slid the hand computer toward herself and after some punching politely pointed out that if silver stood at $36.70 a troy ounce, then seventy-five per cent of that would give a melt value of $27.52. Well, the young woman pointed out, you couldn't expect Fiscal Alternatives to sell at less than melt value and not buy back for less too. She was less soignée than formerly; the tiny imperfection at one corner of her lips had bloomed into something that needed to be covered with a little circular Band-Aid. But after a phone call to some office deeper than hers, hidden by more than a sheet of thin Venetian blinds, she conceded that they could go to $24 even. Times 888 came to $21,312, or a profit in less than a month of $6,660. Harry wanted to keep eight of the handsome old cartwheels as souvenirs and this reduced the check to $21,120, a more magical number anyway. From the Brewer Trust safe-deposit box and the safe at Springer Motors they retrieved their cumbersome riches, taking care this time to minimize portage by double-parking the Corona on Weiser Street. The next day, while silver was dropping to $31.75 an ounce, they signed, at this same Brewer Trust, a twenty-year mortgage for $62,400 at $13\frac{1}{2}\%$, $1\frac{1}{2}\%$ below the current prime rate, with a one-point fee of $624 and a three-year renegotiation proviso. The little stone house, once a gardener's cottage, in Penn Park cost $78,000. Janice wanted to put down $25,000, but Harry pointed out to her that in inflation-ary times debt is a good thing to have, that mortgage interest is tax-deductible, and that six-month $10,000-minimum money market certificates are paying close to 12% these days. So they opted for the 20% minimum of equity, or $15,600, which the bank, considering the excellent credit standing in the community of Mr Angstrom and his family, was pleased to allow. Stepping out between the monumental pillars into the winter daylight blinking, Janice and Harry owned a house, and the day after tomorrow would fly into summer. For years nothing happens; then everything happens. Water boils, the cactus blooms, cancer declares itself.

Janice replies, 'Mother seems resigned. She told me a long story about how her parents, who were better regarded, you know, in the county than the Springers, offered to have her and Daddy come to stay with them while he was still studying accountancy and he said, No, if he couldn't put a roof over a wife he shouldn't have taken a wife.'

'She should tell that story to Nelson.'

'I wouldn't push at Nelson too hard these days. Something's working at him from inside.'

'I don't push at him, he's pushing me. He's pushed me right out of the house.'

'It may be our going off has frightened him. Made it more real, that he has these responsibilities.'

'About time the kid woke up. What do you think poor Pru makes of all this?'

Janice sighs, a sound lost in the giant whispering that upholds them. Little dull nozzles above their heads hiss oxygen. Harry wants to hear that Pru hates Nelson, that she is sorry she has married him, that the father has made the son look sick. 'Oh, I don't think she knows what to make,' Janice says. 'We have these talks sometimes and she knows Nelson is unhappy but still has this faith in him. The fact of it is Teresa was so anxious to get away from her own people in Ohio she can't afford to be too picky about the people she's gotten in with.'

'She still keeps putting away that crème de menthe.'

'She's a little heedless but that's how you are at that age. You think whatever happens, you can manage; the Devil won't touch you.'

He nudges her elbow with his comfortingly, to show he remembers. The Devil touched her twenty years ago. The guilt they share rests in their laps like these safety belts, holding them fast, chafing only when they try to move.

'Hey you two lovebirds.' Ronnie Harrison's loud shallow voice breaks upon them from above; he is looking down with his boozy breath from the backs of their seats. 'Deal us in, you can neck at home.' For the rest of the flight's three droning hours they party with the other four, swapping seats, standing in the aisle, moving around in the 747's wide body as if it were Webb Murkett's long living room. They stoke themselves with drinks and reminisce about times they have already shared as if, were silence and forgetfulness once to enter, the bubble of this venture together would pop and all six would go tumbling into the void that surrounds and upholds the shuddering skin of the plane. Cindy seems, in this confusion, amiable but remote, a younger sister, or another passenger swept up into their holiday mood. She perches forward on the edge of her reclined window seat to catch each gust of jocularity; it is hard to believe that her outer form, clothed in a prim dark suit with a floppy white cravat that reminds Harry of George Washington, has secret places, of folds and fur and moist membranes, where a diaphragm can go, and that entry into these places is the purpose of his trip and his certain destination.

The plane drops; his stomach clenches; the pilot's omnipotent Texas voice comes on and tells them to return to their seats and prepare for arrival. Harry asks Janice now that's she's loose on booze if she wouldn't like the window seat but she says No, she doesn't care to look until they land. Through his patch of scratched Plexiglas he sees a milky turquoise sea mottled with purple-green shadows cast from underneath, islands beneath the surface. A single sailboat. Then a ragged arm of rocky land in a sleeve of white beach. Small houses with red corrugated roofs rise toward him. The wheels of the plane groan and unwind down and lock in place. They are skimming a swamp. He thinks to pray but his thoughts scatter; Janice is grinding the bones of his fingers together. A house with a wind sock, an unmanned bulldozer, branchless trees that are palms flash by; there is a thud, a small swerve, a loud hiss, and a roar straining backwards, a screaming straining. It stops, they slow, they are down, and a low pink air terminal is wheeled into view as the 747 taxis close. They move, suddenly sweating, clutching their winter coats and groping for sunglasses, toward the exits. At the head of the silver stairs down to the macadam, the tropical air, so warm, moist, and forgiving, composed all of tiny little circles, strikes Rabbit's face as if gusted from an atomizer; but Ronnie Harrison ruins the moment by exclaiming distinctly, behind his ear, 'Oh boy. That's better than a blow job.' And, worse even than Ronnie's smearing his voice across so precious and fragile a moment of first encounter with a new world, the women laugh, having been meant to overhear. Janice laughs, the dumb mutt. And the stewardess, her enamel gone dewy in the warmth by the door where she poses saying goodbye, goodbye, promiscuously smiles.

Cindy's laugh skips girlishly above the others and is quickly followed by her drawled word, 'Ronnie.' Rabbit is excited amid his disgust, remembering those Polaroids tucked in a drawer.

As the days of the vacation pass, Cindy turns the same mahogany brown she wears in the summer, by the pool at the Flying Eagle, and comes up dripping from the beryl Caribbean in the same bikini of black strings, only with salt-glisten on her skin. Thelma Harrison burns badly the first day, and has some pain connected with that quiet ailment of hers. She spends the whole second day in their bungalow, while Ronnie bounces in and out of the water and supervises the fetching of drinks from the bar built on the sand entirely of straw. Old black ladies move up and down the beach offering beads and shells and sunclothes for sale, and on the morning of the third day Thelma buys from one of them a wide-brimmed straw hat and a pink ankle-length wrapper with long sleeves, and thus entirely covered, with sun block on her face and a towel across the top of her feet, she sits reading in the shade of the sea-grape trees. Her face in the shade of her hat seems sallow and thin and mischievous, when she glances toward Harry as he lies in the sun. Next to her, he tans least easily, but he is determined to keep up with the crowd. The ache of a sunburn reminds him nostalgically of the muscle aches after athletic exertion. In the sea, he doggy-paddles, secretly afraid of sharks.

The men spend each morning on the golf course that adjoins the resort, riding in canopied carts down sere fairways laid out between brambly jungles from which there is no recovery; indeed, in looking for lost balls there is a danger of stepping into a deep hole. The substance of the island is coral, pitted with caves. At night, there is entertainment, set in a rigid weekly cycle. They arrived on a Thursday, the evening of the crab races, and on the next night witnessed a limbo dance, and on the next, a Saturday, themselves danced to a steel band. Every night there is music to dance to, beside the Olympic-length pool, under stars that seem closer down here, and that hang in the sky with a certain menace, fragments of a frozen explosion. Some of the constellations are strange; Webb Murkett, who knows stars from his years in the Navy – he enlisted in '45, when he was eighteen, and crossed the Pacific on an aircraft carrier as the war was ending – points out the Southern Cross, and a ghostly blur in the sky he says is another galaxy altogether; and they can all see that the Big Dipper stands on its handle here in a way never seen in southeastern Pennsylvania.

Oh, that little Cindy, browner at every dinnertime, just begging for love. You can see it in her teeth, they are getting so white, and the way she picks an oleander blossom from the bush outside their bungalow every night to wear in her hair all fluffy from swimming so much, and the swarthiness of her toes that makes the nails look pale as petals also. She wears on her dark skin white dresses that shine from far across the swimming pool – lit from underneath at night as if it has swallowed the moon – when she is coming back from the ladies' room beyond the bamboo bar. She claims she is getting fatter, too: those piña coladas and banana daiquiris and rum punches, all those calories, shameless. Yet she never turns a drink down, none of them do; from the Bloody Marys that fortify the golfers for their morning on the course to the last round of Stingers after midnight, they keep a gentle collective buzz on. Janice wonders, 'Harry, what's the final tab going to look like? You keep signing for everybody.'

He tells her, 'Relax. Might as well spend it as have it eaten up by inflation. Did you hear Webb saying that the dollar now is worth exactly half what it was ten years ago in 1970? So these are fifty-cent dollars, relax.' The expense in his mind is part of a worthy campaign, to sleep with Cindy before their seven days are over. He feels it coming, coming upon all of them, the walls between them are wearing thin, he knows exactly when Webb will clear his throat or how he will light his cigarette, eye-glance and easy silence are hour by hour eroding constraint, under sun and under stars they stretch out their six bodies on the folding chaises, with vinyl strapping, that are everywhere. Their hands touch passing drinks and matches and suntan lotion, they barge in and out of one another's bungalows; indeed Rabbit has seen Thelma Harrison bare-assed by accident returning their Solarcaine one afternoon. She had been lying on the bed letting her burned skin breathe and hustled into the bathroom at the sound of his voice at the door, but not quick enough. He saw the crease between her cheeks, the whole lean sallow length of her fleeing, and handed the Solarcaine to Ronnie, himself naked, without comment or apology, they were half-naked with each other all day long, but for Thelma huddled under the sea-grape: Janice rubbing Copper-tone into the criss-crossing creases of Webb's red neck, Ronnie's heavy cock bulging the front of his obscene little European-style trunks, sweet Cindy untying a black string to give her back an even tan and showing the full nippled silhouette of one boob when she reached up for her Planter's Punch from the tray of them the boy had brought. These blacks down here silkier than American blacks, blacker, their bodies moving to a softer beat. Toward four o'clock, the shadows of the sea-grape coming forward like knobby fingers onto the sand, the men's faces baked red despite the canopies on the golf carts, they would move their act from the beach (the rustling of palm trees gets on Harry's nerves; at night he keeps thinking it's raining, and it never is) to the shaded area beside the Olympic pool, where young island men in white steward's jackets circle among them taking drink orders and the hard white pellet of the sun slowly lowers toward the horizon of the sea, which it meets promptly at six, in a perfunctory splash of purples and pinks. Stupefied, aching with pleasure, Harry stares at the way, when Cindy rolls her body into a new position on the chaise, the straps have bitten laterally into her delicious fat, like tire treads in mud. Thelma sits among them swaddled and watchful. Webb drones on, Ronnie is making some new friends at the bamboo bar. It's the salesman in him, he has to keep trying his pitch. His voice balloons above the rippling as a single fair child, waterlogged and bored, dives and paddles away the time to dinner. Some evenings just after sunset a green strip appears on the horizon. Janice, much as he loves her now and then, down here is a piece of static, getting between Harry and what signals Cindy may be sending; luckily Webb keeps her entertained, talking to her as one member of the lesser Brewer gentry to another, about that tireless subject of money. 'You think fourteen per cent is catastrophic, in Israel they live with a hundred eleven per cent, a color television set costs eighteen hundred dollars. In Argentina it's a hundred fifty per cent per year, believe me I kid you not. In Tokyo a pound of steak costs twenty dollars and in Saudi Arabia a pack of cigarettes goes for a fin. Five dollars a pack. You may think we're hurting but the U.S. consumer still gets the best deal to be had in any industrialized nation.' Janice hangs on his words and bums his cigarettes. Her hair since summer has grown long enough to pull back in a little stubby ponytail; she sits by his feet, dabbling her legs in the pool. The hair on Webb's long skinny legs spirals around like the stripes on a barber pole, and his face with its wise creases has tanned the color of lightly varnished pine. It occurs to Harry that she used to listen to her father bullshit this way, and likes it.

By Sunday night they are bored with the routine around the resort and hire a taxi to take them across the island to the casino. In the dark they pass through villages where black children are invisible until their eye-whites gleam beside the road. A herd of goats trotting with dragging rope halters materializes in the headlights of the taxi. Shuttered cabins up on cinder blocks reveal by an open door that they are taverns, with bottle-crammed shelves and a sheaf of standing customers. An old stone church flings candlelight from its pointed windows, which have no glass, and the moan of one phrase of a hymn, that is swiftly left behind. The taxi, a '69 Pontiac with a lot of voodoo dolls on the dashboard, drives ruthlessly, on the wrong side of the road, for this was an English colony. The truncated cone-shapes of abandoned sugar mills against the sky full of stars remember the past, all those dead slaves, while Janice and Thelma and Cindy chatter in the surging dark about people left behind in Brewer, about Buddy Inglefinger's newest awful girlfriend with all that height and all those children, Buddy's such a victim-type, and about impossible Peggy Fosnacht, whom rumor has reported to be very hurt that she and Ollie weren't asked along on this trip to the Caribbean, even though everybody knows they could never afford it.

The casino is attached to another beach resort, grander than theirs. Boardwalks extend out over the illuminated coral shelf. There are worlds within worlds, Harry thinks. Creatures like broken bags of noodles wave upward from within the golden-green slipslop. He has come out here to clear his head. He got hooked on blackjack and in an attempt to recoup his losses by doubling and redoubling his bets cashed three hundred in Travel-ler's Checks and, while his friends marvelled, lost it all. Well, that's less than half the profit on the sale of one Tercel, less than three per cent of what Nelson's pranks have cost. Still, Harry's head throbs and he feels shaky and humiliated. The black dealer didn't even glance up when, cleaned out, he pushed away from the garish felt of the table. He walks along the boards toward the black horizon, as the tropical air soothes his hot face with micro-scopic circular kisses. He imagines he could walk to South America, that has Paraguay in it; he thinks fondly of that area of tall weeds behind the asphalt of the lot, and of that farm he has always approached as a spy, through the hedgerow that grew up over the tumbled sandstone wall. The grass in the orchard will be flattened and bleached by winter now, smoke rising from the lonely house below. Another world.

Cindy is beside him suddenly, breathing in rhythm with the slipslop of the sea. He thinks their moment has come, when he is far from ready; but she says in a dry commiserating voice, 'Webb says you should always set a limit for yourself before you sit down, so you won't get carried away.'

'I wasn't carried away,' Harry tells her. 'I had a theory.' Perhaps she figures that his losses have earned a compensation and she is it. Her brown arms are set off by a crocheted white shawl; with the flower behind her ear she looks flirty. What will it be like, to press his own high heavy face down into those apple-hard roundnesses of hers, cheeks and brow and nose-tip, and her alert little life-giving slits, long-lipped mouth and dark eyes glim-mering with mischief like a child's? Slipslop. Will their faces fit? Her eyes glance upward toward his and he gazes away, at the tropical moon lying on its side at an angle you never see in Pennsylvania. As if accidentally, while gazing out to sea, he brushes his fingertips against her arm. An electric warmth seems to linger from her Sunday in the sun. Kelp slaps the pilings of the catwalk, a wave collapses its way along the beach, his moment to pounce is here. Something too firm in the protuberances of her face holds him off, though she is lightly smiling, and tips her face up, as if to make it easier for him to slip his mouth beneath her nose.

But footsteps rumble toward them and Webb and Janice, almost running, their hands in the confused mingled lights of moon and subaqueous spots and blazing casino beyond seeming linked, then released, come up to this angle of the boardwalk and announce excitedly that Ronnie Harrison is burning up the crap table inside. 'Come and see, Harry,' Janice says. 'He's at least eight hundred ahead.'

'That Ronnie,' Cindy says, in a tone of girlish dry reproach, and the casino lights glow through her long skirt as she hurries toward these lights, her ass all dark, her legs silhouetted.

They get back to their own resort after two. Ronnie stayed too long at the crap table and wound up only a few bucks better than even. He and Janice fell asleep on the long ride back, while Thelma sits tensely in Rabbit's lap and Webb and Cindy sit up front with the driver, Webb asking questions about the island that the man answers in a reluctant, bubbling language that is barely English. At the gate to their resort a uniformed guard lets them in. Everything down here is guarded, theft is rampant, thieves and even murderers pour outward from the island's dark heart to feed on its rim of rich visitors. Guest bungalows are approached along the paths of green-painted concrete laid down on the sand, under muttering palm trees, between bushes of papery flowers that attract hummingbirds in the morning. While the men confer as to what hour tomorrow's golf should be postponed to, the three women whisper at a little distance, at the point in the concrete walk where the paths to their separate bungalows diverge. Janice, Cindy, and Thelma are tittering and sending glances this way, glances flickering birdlike in the moonglazed warm night. Cindy's shawl glimmers like a splotch of foam on surging water. But in the end, making the hushed grove of palms ring with cries of 'Goodnight,' each wife walks to her own bungalow with her husband. Rabbit fucks Janice out of general irritation and falls asleep hoping that morning will be indefinitely postponed.

But it comes on schedule, in the form of bars of sunlight the window louvers cast on to the floor of hexagonal tiles, while the little yellow birds they have that song about down here follow the passage of clinking breakfast trays along the concrete paths. It is not so bad, once he stands up. The body was evolved for adversity. As has become his custom he takes a short, cautious swim off the deserted beach, where last night's plastic glasses are still propped in the sand. It is the one moment of the day or night when Harry is by himself, not counting the old couples, with the wives needing an arm to make their way down across the sand, who also like an early swim. The sea between soft breakers seems the color of a honeydew melon, that pale a green. Floating on his back he can see, on the roads along the scraggly steep hills that flank the bay, those to whom this island is no vacation, blacks in scraps of bright cloth, strolling to work, some of the women toting bundles and even buckets on their heads. They really do that. Their voices carry on fresh morning air, along with the slap and swoosh and fizz of warm salt-water sliding and receding at his feet. The white sand is spongy, and full of holes where crabs breathe. He has never seen sand this white, minced coral fine as sugar. The early sun sits lightly on his sensitive shoulders. This is it, health. Then the girl with the breakfast tray comes to their door – their bungalow number is 9 – and Janice in her terrycloth bathrobe opens the louvered door and calls 'Harry' out across the area where an old slave in khaki pants is already sweeping up seaweed and plastic glasses, and the party, the hunt, is on again.

He plays golf badly today; when he is tired he tends to overswing, and to flip his hands instead of letting the arms ride through. Keep the wrist-cock, don't waste it up at the top. Don't sway onto your toes, imagine your nose pressed against a pane of glass. Think railroad tracks. Follow through. These tips are small help today, it seems a long morning's slog between hungry wings of coral jungle, up to greens as bumpy as quilts, though he supposes it's a miracle of sorts to have greens at all under this sun. He hates Webb Murkett, who is sinking everything inside of twenty feet today. Why should this stringy old bullshitter hog that

369

fantastic little cunt and take the Nassau besides? Harry misses Buddy Inglefinger, to feel superior to. Ronnie's sparse scalp and naked high forehead look like a peeling pink egg when he stoops to his shot. Swings like an ape, all the hair off his head gone into his arms, how can Thelma stand him? Women, they'll put up with anything for the sake of a big prick evidently. Harry can't stop thinking of that three hundred dollars he blew last night, that his father would have slaved weeks for. Poor Pop, he didn't live to see money get unreal.

But things look up in the afternoon, after a couple of piña coladas and a crabmeat-salad sandwich. They all decide to rent three Sunfishes, and they pair up so that he and Cindy go out together. He has never sailed, so she stands up to her tits in the water fussing with the rudder while he sits high and dry holding the ropes that pull this striped three-cornered sail, that doesn't look to him firmly attached enough, flapping this way and that while one aluminum pipe rubs against another. The whole thing feels shaky. They have you wear a kind of black rubber pad around your middle and in hers Cindy looks pretty cute with that short otter haircut, butch, like one of those female cops on TV or a frogwoman. He has never before noticed how dark and thick her eyebrows are; they knit toward each other and almost touch until the rudder catch clicks in finally. Then she gives a grunt and up she jumps, flat on her front so her tits squeeze out sideways, the untanned parts of them white as Maalox, her legs kicking in the water to bring her ass all black and shiny aboard, she is too much woman for this little boat, it is tilting like crazy. He pulls her by the arm and the aluminum pole at the bottom of the sail swings and hits him on the back of the head. She has grabbed the rope from him while still holding on to the rudder handle and keeps shouting, 'The centerboard, the centerboard,' until he figures out what she means. This splintery long wood fin under his leg should go in that slot. He gets it out from under him and shoves it in. Instead of congratulating him, Cindy says, 'Shit.' The little Fiberglas shell is parallel to the beach, where an arc of bathers has gathered to watch, and each wave is slopping them closer in. Then the wind catches the sail and flattens it taut, so the aluminum mast creaks, and they slowly bob out over the breaking waves toward the point of land on the right where the bay ends.

Once you get going you don't feel how fast you're moving, the water having no landmarks. Harry is toward the front, crouching way over in case the boom swings at his head again. Sitting yoga-style in her stout rubber gasket, the center strip of her bikini barely covering her opened-up crotch, Cindy tends the tiller and for the first time smiles. 'Harry, you don't have to keep holding on to the top of the centerboard, it doesn't have to be pulled until we hit the beach.' The beach, the palms, the bungalows have been reduced to the size of a postcard.

'Should we be this far out?'

She smiles again. 'We're not far out.' The sailing gear tugs at her hands, the boat tips. The water out here is no longer the pale green of a honeydew melon but a green like bile, black in the troughs.

'We're not,' he repeats.

'Look over there.' A sail scarcely bigger than the flash of a wave. 'That's Webb and Thelma. They're much further out than we are.'

'Are you sure that's them?'

Cindy takes pity. 'We'll come about when we're closer to those rocks. You know what come about means, Harry?'

'Not exactly.'

'We'll change direction. The boom will swing, so watch your head.'

'Do you think there are any sharks?' Still, he tells himself, there is an intimacy to it, just the two of them, the same spray hitting his skin and hers, the wind and water sounds that drown out all others, the curve of her shoulder shining like metal in the light of that hard white sun that makes the sun he grew up under seem orange and bloated in memory.

'Did you see *Jaws II*?' she asks back.

'D'you ever get the feeling everything these days is sequels?' he asks in turn. 'Like people are running out of ideas.' He feels so full of fatigue and long-held lust as to be careless of his life, amid this tugging violence of elements. Even the sun-sparkle on the water feels cruel, a malevolence straight from heaven, like

371

those photons beating on the wings of the airplane flying down.

'Coming about,' Cindy says. 'Hard alee.'

He crouches, and the boom misses. He sees another sail out here with them, Ronnie and Janice, headed for the horizon. She seems to be at the back, steering. When did she learn? Some summer camp. You have to be rich from the start to get the full benefits. Cindy says, 'Now Harry, you take over. It's simple. That little strip of cloth at the top of the mast is called a telltale. It tells what direction the wind is coming from. Also, look at the waves. You want to keep the sail at an angle to the wind. What you don't want is to see the front edge of the sail flapping. That's called luffing. It means you're headed directly into the wind, and then you must head off. You push the tiller away from you, away from the sail. You'll feel it, I promise. The tension between the tiller and the line – it's like a scissors, sort of. It's fun. Come on, Harry, nothing can happen. Change places with me.' They manage to maneuver, while the boat swings like a hammock beneath their bulks. A little cloud covers the sun, dyeing the water dark, then releasing it back into sunshine with a pang. Harry takes hold of the tiller and gropes until the wind takes hold with him. Then, as she says, it's fun: the sail and tiller tugging, the invisible sea breeze pushing, the distances not nearly so great and hopeless once you have control. 'You're doing fine,' Cindy tells him, and from the way she sits with legs crossed facing ahead he can see the underside of all five toes of one bare foot, the thin blue skin here wrinkled, the littlest dear toe bent into the toe next to it as if trying to hide. She trusts him. She loves him. Now that he has the hang of it he dares to heel, pulling the mainsheet tighter and tighter, so the waves spank and his hand burns. The land is leaping closer, they are almost safe when, in adjusting his aim toward the spot on the beach where Janice and Ronnie have already dragged their Sunfish up, he lets out the sail a touch and the wind catches it full from behind; the prow goes under abruptly in a furious surging film; heavily the whole shell slews around and tips; he and Cindy have no choice but to slide off together, entangled with line. A veined translucence closes over his head. *Air* he thinks wildly and comes up in sudden shade, the boat looming on edge above them. Cindy is beside him in the water. Gasping, wanting to apologize, he clings briefly to her. She feels like a shark, slimy and abrasive. Their two foam-rubber belts bump underwater. Each hair in her eyebrows gleams in the strange light here, amid shadowed waves, and the silence of stilled wind, only a gentle slipslap against the hollow hull. With a grimace she pushes him off, takes a deep breath, and disappears beneath the boat. He tries to follow but his belt roughly buoys him back. He hears her grunting and splashing on the other side of the upright keel, first pulling at, then standing on the centerboard until the Sunfish comes upright, great pearls of water exploding from it as the striped sail sweeps past the sun. Harry heaves himself on and deftly she takes the boat in to shore.

The episode is inglorious, but they all laugh about it on the beach, and in his self-forgiving mind their underwater embrace has rapidly dried to something tender and promising. The slither of two skins, her legs fluttering between his. The few black hairs where her eyebrows almost meet. The hairs of her crotch she boldy displayed sitting yoga-style. It all adds up.

Lunch at the resort is served by the pool or brought by tray to the beach, but dinner is a formal affair within a vast pavilion whose rafters drip feathery fronds yards long and at whose rear, beside the doors leading into the kitchen, a great open barbecue pit sends flames roaring high, so that shadows twitch against the background design of thatch and carved masks, and highlights spark in the sweating black faces of the assistant chefs. The head chef is a scrawny Belgian always seen sitting at the bar between meals, looking sick, or else conferring in accents of grievance with one of the missionary-prim native women who run the front desk. Monday night is the barbecue buffet, with a calypso singer during the meal and dancing to electrified marimbas afterward; but all six of the holidayers from Diamond County agree they are exhausted from the night at the casino and will go to bed early. Harry after nearly drowning in Cindy's arms fell asleep on the beach and then went inside for a nap. While he was sleeping, a sudden sharp tropical rainstorm drummed for ten minutes on his tin roof; when he awoke, the rain had passed, and the sun was setting in a band of orange at the mouth of the bay, and his pals had been yukking it up in the bar ever since the shower an hour ago. Something is cooking. They seem, the three women, very soft-faced by the light of the candle set on the table in a little red netted hurricane lamp, amid papery flowers that will be wilted before the meal is over. They keep touching one another, their sisterhood strengthened and excited down here. Cindy is wearing a yellow hibiscus in her hair tonight, and that Arab thing, unbuttoned halfway down. She more than once reaches past Webb's drink and stringy brown hands as they pose on the tablecloth to touch Janice on a wrist, remembering 'that fresh colored boy behind the bar today, I told him I was down here with my husband and he shrugged like it made no difference whatsoever!' Webb looks sage, letting the currents pass around him, and Ronnie sleepy and puffy but still full of beans, in that grim playmaker way of his. Harry and Ronnie were for three years on the Mt Judge basketball varsity together and more than once Rabbit had to suppress a sensation that though he was the star Coach Tothero liked Ronnie better, because he never quit trying and was more 'physical' around the backboards. The world runs on push. Rabbit's feeling has been that if it doesn't happen by itself it's not worth making happen. Still, that Cindy. A man could kill for a piece of that. Pump it in, and die like a male spider. The calypso singer comes to their table and sings a long dirty song about the Big Bamboo. Harry doesn't understand all the allusions but the ladies titter after every verse. The singer smiles and the song smiles but his bloody eyes glitter like those of a lizard frozen on the wall and his skull when bent over the guitar shows circlets of gray. A dying art. Harry doesn't know if they are supposed to tip him or just applaud. They applaud and quick as a lizard's tongue his hand flickers out to take the bill Webb, leaning back, has offered. The old singer moves on to the next table and begins one about Back to back, and Belly to belly. Cindy giggles, touches Janice on the forearm, and says, 'I bet all the people back in Brewer will think we've swapped down here.'

'Maybe we should then,' Ronnie says, unable to suppress a belch of fatigue.

Janice, in that throaty mature woman's voice cigarettes and age have given her but that Harry is always surprised to hear she has, asks Webb, who sits beside her, gently, 'How do you feel about that sort of thing, Webb?'

The old fox knows he has the treasure to barter and takes his time, pulling himself up in his chair to release an edge of coat he's sitting on, a kind of dark blue captain's jacket with spoked brass buttons, and takes his pack of Marlboro Lights from his side pocket. Rabbit's heart races so hard he stares down at the table, where the bloody bones, ribs and vertebrae, of their barbecue wait to be cleared away. Webb drawls, 'Well, after two marriages that I'd guess you'd have to say were not fully successful, and some of the things I've seen and done before, after, and between, I must admit a little sharing among friends doesn't seem to me so bad, if it's done with affection and respect. Respect is the key term here. Every party involved, and I mean every party, has to be willing, and it should be clearly understood that whatever happens will go no further than that particular occasion. Secret affairs, that's what does a marriage in. When people get romantic.'

Nothing romantic about him, the king of the Polaroid pricks. Harry's face feels hot. Maybe it's the spices in the barbecue settling, or the length of Webb's sermon, or a blush of gratitude to the Murketts, for arranging all this. He imagines his face between Cindy's thighs, tries to picture that black pussy like a curved snug mass of eyebrow hairs, flattened and warmed to fragrance from being in underpants and framed by the white margins the bikini bottom had to cover to be decent. He will follow her slit down with his tongue, her legs parting with that same weightless slither he felt under water today, down and in, and around the corner next to his nose will be that whole great sweet ass he has a thousand times watched jiggle as she dried herself from swimming in the pool at the Flying Eagle, under the nappy green shadow of Mt Pemaquid. And her tits, the fall of them forward when she obediently bends over. Something is happening in his pants, like the stamen of one of these floppy flowers on the tablecloth jerking with shadow as the candle-flame flickers.

'Down the way,' the singer sings at yet another table, 'where the nights are gay, and the sun shines daily on the moun-tain-top.' Black hands come and smoothly clear away the dark bones and distribute dessert menus. There is a walnut cake they offer here that Harry especially likes, though there's nothing especially

Caribbean about it, it's probably flown in from Fort Lauderdale.

Thelma, who is wearing a sort of filmy top you can see her cocoa-colored bra through, is gazing into middle distance like a schoolteacher talking above the heads of her class and saying, '. . . simple female curiosity. It's something you hardly ever see discussed in all these articles on female sexuality, but I think it's what's behind these male strippers rather than any real desire on the part of the women to go to bed with the boys. They're just curious about the penises, what they look like. They *do* look a lot different from each other, I guess.'

'That how you feel?' Harry asks Janice. 'Curious?'

She lowers her eyes to the guttering hurricane lamp. 'Of course.'

'Oh I'm not,' Cindy says, 'not the shape. I don't think I am. I really am not.'

'You're very young,' Thelma says.

'I'm thirty,' she protests. 'Isn't that supposed to be my sexual prime?'

As if rejoining her in the water, Harry tries to take her side. 'They're ugly as hell. Most of the pricks I've seen are.'

'You don't see them erect,' Thelma lightly points out.

'Thank God for that,' he says, appalled, as he sometimes is, by this coarse crowd he's in.

'And yet he loves his own,' Janice says, keeping that light and cool and as it were scientific tone that has descended upon them, in the hushed dining pavilion. The singer has ceased. People at other tables are leaving, moving to the smaller tables at the edge of the dance floor by the pool.

'I don't love it,' he protests in a whisper. 'I'm stuck with it.'

'It's you,' Cindy quietly tells him.

'Not just the pricks,' Thelma clarifies, 'it has to be the whole man who turns you on. The way he carries himself. His voice, the way he laughs. But it all refers to that.'

Pricks. Can it be? They let the delicate subject rest, as dessert and coffee come. Revitalized by food and the night, they decide after all to sit with Stingers and watch the dancing a while, under the stars that on this night seem to Harry jewels of a clock that moves with maddening slowness, measuring out the minutes until he sinks himself in Cindy as if a star were to fall and sizzle into his Olympic-sized pool. Once, on some far lost summer field of childhood, someone, his mother it must have been though he cannot hear her voice, told him that if you stare up at the night sky while you count to one hundred you are bound to see a shooting star, they are in fact so common. But though he now leans back from the Stinger and the glass table and the consolatory, conspiratory murmur of his friends until his neck begins to ache, all the stars above him hang unbudging in their sockets. Webb Murkett's gravelly voice growls, 'Well, kiddies. As the oldest person here, I claim the privilege of announcing that I'm tired and want to go to bed.' And as Harry turns his face from the heavens there it is, in a corner of his vision, vivid and brief as a scratched match, a falling star, doused in the ocean of ink. The women rise and gather their skirts about them; the marimbas, after a consultation of fluttering, fading notes, break into 'Where Are the Clowns?' This plaintive pealing is lost behind them as they move along the pool, and past the front desk where the haggard, alcoholic resort manager is trying to get through long-distance to New York, and across the hotel's traffic circle with its curbs of whitewashed coral, down into the shadowy realm of concrete paths between bushes of sleeping flowers. The palms above them grow noisy as the music fades. The *shoosh* of surf draws nearer. At the moonlit point where the paths diverge into three, goodnights are nervously exchanged but no one moves; then a woman's hand reaches out softly and takes the wrist of a man not her husband. The others follow suit, with no person looking at another, a downcast and wordless tugging serving to separate the partners out to draw them down the respective paths to each woman's bungalow. Harry hears Cindy giggle, at a distance, for it is not her hand with such gentle determination pulling him along, but Thelma's.

She has felt him pull back, and tightens her grip, silently. On the beach, he sees, a group has brought down a hurricane lamp, with their drinks; the lamp and their cigarettes glow red in the shadows, while the sea beyond stretches pale as milk beyond the black silhouette of a big sailboat anchored in the bay, under the half-moon tilted onto its back. Thelma lets go of his arm to fish in her sequinned purse for the bungalow key. 'You can have Cindy tomorrow night,' she whispers. 'We discussed it.'

'O.K., great,' he says lamely, he hopes not insultingly. He is figuring, this means that Cindy wanted that pig Harrison, and Janice got Webb. He had been figuring Janice would have to take Ronnie, and felt sorry for her, except from the look of him he'd fall asleep soon, and Webb and Thelma would go together, both of them yellowy stringy types. Thelma closes the bungalow door behind them and switches on a straw globe light above the bed. He asks her, 'Well, are tonight's men the first choice for you ladies or're you just getting the second choice out of the way?'

'Don't be so competitive, Harry. This is meant to be a loving sharing sort of thing, you heard Webb. One thing we absolutely agreed on, we're not going to carry any of it back to Brewer. This is all the monkey business there's going to be, even if it kills us.' She stands there in the center of her straw rug rather defiantly, a thin-faced sallow woman he scarcely knows. Not only her nose is pink in the wake of her sunburn but patches below her eyes as well, a kind of butterfly is on her face. Harry supposes he should kiss her, but his forward step is balked by her continuing firmly, 'I'll tell you one thing though, Harry Angstrom. You're *my* first choice.'

'I am?'

'Of course. I adore you. A*dore* you.'

'Me?'

'Haven't you ever sensed it?'

Rather than admit he hasn't, he hangs there foolishly.

'Shit,' Thelma says. 'Janice did. Why else do you think we weren't invited to Nelson's wedding?' She turns her back, and starts undoing her earring before the mirror, that just like the one in his and Janice's bungalow is framed in woven strips of bamboo. The batik hanging in here is of a tropical sunset with a palm in the foreground instead of the black-mammy fruit-seller he and Janice have, but the batik manufacturer is the same. The suitcases are the Harrisons', and the clothes hanging on the painted pipe that does for a closet. Thelma asks, 'You mind using Ronnie's

378

toothbrush? I'll be a while in there, you better take the bathroom first.'

In the bathroom Harry sees that Ronnie uses shaving cream, Gillette Foamy, out of a pressure can, the kind that's eating up the ozone so our children will fry. And that new kind of razor with the narrow single-edge blade that snaps in and out with a click on the television commercials. Harry can't see the point, it's just more waste, he still uses a rusty two-edge safety razor he bought for $1.99 about seven years ago, and lathers himself with an old imitation badger-bristle on whatever bar of soap is handy. He shaved before dinner after his nap so no need now. Also the Harrisons use chlorophyll Crest in one of those giant tubes that always buckles and springs a leak when he and Janice try to save a couple pennies and buy one. He wonders whatever happened to Ipana and what was it *Consumer Reports* had to say about toothpastes a few issues back, probably came out in favor of baking soda, that's what he and Mim used to have to use, some theory Mom had about the artificial flavoring in toothpaste contributing to tartar. The trouble with consumerism is, the guy next door always seems to be doing better at it than you are. Just the Harrisons' bathroom supplies make him envious. Plain as she is, Thelma carries a hefty medicine kit, and beauty aids, plus a sun block called Eclipse, and Solarcaine. Vaseline, too, for some reason. Tampax, in a bigger box than Janice ever buys. And a lot of painkiller, aspirin in several shapes and Darvon and more pills in little prescription bottles than he would have expected. People are always a little sicker than you know. Harry debates whether he should take his leak sitting down to spare Thelma the sound of its gross splashing and rejects the idea, since she's the one wants to fuck him. It streams noisily into the bowl it seems forever, embarrassingly, all those drinks at dinner. Then he sits down on the seat anyway, to let out a little air. Too much shellfish. He imagines he can smell yesterday's crabmeat and when he stands tests with a finger down there to see if he stinks. He decides he does. Better use a washcloth. He debates which washcloth is Ronnie's, the blue or the brown. He settles on the brown and scrubs what counts. Getting ready for the ball. He erases his scent by giving the cloth a good rinsing no matter whose it is.

When he steps back into the room Thelma is down to her underwear, cocoa bra and black panties. He didn't expect this, nor to be so stirred by it. Breasts are strange: some look bigger in clothes than they are and some look smaller. Thelma's are the second kind; her bra is smartly filled. Her whole body, into her forties, has kept that trim neutral serviceability nurses and grade-school teachers surprise you with, beneath their straight faces. She laughs, and holds out her arms like a fan dancer. 'Here I am. You look shocked. You're such a sweet prude, Harry – that's one of the things I adore. I'll be out in five minutes. Try not to fall asleep.'

Clever of her. What with the sleep debt they're all running down here and the constant booze and the trauma in the water today – his head went under and a bottomless bile-green volume sucked at his legs – he was weary. He begins to undress and doesn't know where to stop. There are a lot of details a husband and wife work out over the years that with a strange woman pop up all over again. Would Thelma like to find him naked in the bed? Or on it? For him to be less naked than she when she comes out of the bathroom would be rude. At the same time, with this straw-shaded light swaying above the bed on so bright, he doesn't want her to think seeing him lying there on display that he thinks he's a *Playgirl* centerfold. He knows he could lose thirty pounds and still have a gut. In his underpants he crosses to the bamboo-trimmed bureau in the room and switches on the lamp there whose cheap wooden base is encrusted with baby seashells glued on. He takes off his underpants. The elastic waistband has lost its snap, the only brand of this type to buy is Jockey, but those cut-rate stores in Brewer don't like to carry it, quality is being driven out everywhere. He switches off the light over the bed and in shadow stretches himself out, all of him, on top of the bedspread, as he is, as he was, as he will be before the undertakers dress him for the last time, not even a wedding ring to realize his nakedness, when he and Janice got married men weren't expected to wear wedding rings. He closes his eyes to rest them for a second in the red blankness there, beneath his lids. He has to get through this, maybe all she wants to do is talk, and then somehow be really

rested for tomorrow night. Getting there . . . That slither underwater . . .

Thelma with it seems the clatter of an earthquake has come out
of the bathroom. She is holding her underclothes in front of her,
and with her back to him she sorts the underpants into the dirty
pile the Harrisons keep beside the bureau, behind the straw
wastebasket, and the bra, clean enough, back into the drawer,
folded. This is the second time in this trip, he thinks drowsily,
that he has seen her ass. Her body as she turns eclipses the bureau
lamp and the front of her gathers shadow to itself; she advances
timidly, as if wading into water. Her breasts sway forward as she
bends to turn the light he switched off back on. She sits down on
the edge of the bed.

His prick is still sleepy. She takes it into her hand. 'You're not
circumcised.'

'No, they somehow weren't doing it at the hospital that day. Or
maybe my mother had a theory, I don't know. I never asked.
Sorry.'

'It's lovely. Like a little bonnet.' Sitting on the edge of the bed,
more supple naked than he remembers her seeming with clothes
on, Thelma bends and takes his prick in her mouth. Her body in
the lamplight is a pale patchwork of faint tan and peeling pink and
the natural yellowy tint of her skin. Her belly puckers into flat
folds like stacked newspapers and the back of her hand as it holds
the base of his prick with two fingers shows a dim lightning of blue
veins. But her breath is warm and wet and the way that in
lamplight individual white hairs snake as if singed through the
mass of dull brown makes him want to reach out and stroke her
head, or touch the rhythmic hollow in her jaw. He fears, though,
interrupting the sensations she is giving him. She lifts a hand
quickly to tuck back a piece of her hair, as if to let him better see.

He murmurs, 'Beautiful.' He is growing thick and long but still
she forces her lips each time down to her fingers as they encircle
him at his base. To give herself ease she spreads her legs; between
her legs with one aslant across the bed edge he sees emerging from
a pubic bush more delicate and reddish than he would have
dreamed a short white string. Unlike Janice's or Cindy's as he

imagined it, Thelma's pussy is not opaque; it is a fuzz transparent upon the bruise-colored labia that with their tongue of white string look so lacking and defenseless Harry could cry. She too is near tears, perhaps from the effort of not gagging. She backs off and stares at the staring eye of his glans, swollen free of his foreskin. She pulls up the bonnet again and says crooningly, teasingly, 'Such a serious little face.' She kisses it lightly, once, twice, flicking her tongue, then bobs again until it seems she must come up for air. 'God,' she sighs. 'I've wanted to do that for so long. Suck you. Come. Come, Harry. Come in my mouth. Come in my mouth and all over my face.' Her voice sounds husky and mad saying this and all through her words Thelma does not stop gazing at the little slit of his where a single cloudy tear has now appeared. She licks it off.

'Have you really,' he asks timidly, 'liked me for a while?'

'Years,' she says. 'Years. And you never noticed. You shit. Always under Janice's thumb and mooning after silly Cindy. Well you know where Cindy is now. She's being screwed by my husband. He didn't want to, he said he'd rather go to bed with me.' She snorts, in some grief of self-disgust, and plunges her mouth down again, and in the pinchy rush of sensation as he feels forced against the opening of her throat he wonders if he should accept her invitation.

'Wait,' Harry says. 'Shouldn't I do something for you first? If I come, it's all over.'

'If you come, then you come again.'

'Not at my age. I don't think.'

'Your age. Always talking about your age.' Thelma rests her face on his belly and gazes up at him, for the first time playful, her eyes at right angles to his disconcertingly. He has never noticed their color before: that indeterminate color called hazel but in the strong light overhead, and brightened by all her deep-throating, given a tawny pallor, an unthinking animal trans-lucence. 'I'm too excited to come,' she tells him. 'Anyway, Harry, I'm having my period and they're really bloody, every other month. I'm scared to find out why. In the months in between, these terrible cramps and hardly any show.'

'See a doctor,' he suggests.

'I see doctors all the time, they're useless. I'm dying, you know that, don't you?'

'Dying?'

'Well, maybe that's too dramatic a way of putting it. Nobody knows how long it'll take, and a lot of it depends upon me. The one thing I'm absolutely supposed not to do is go out in the sun. I was crazy to come down here, Ronnie tried to talk me out of it.'

'Why did you?'

'Guess. I tell you, I'm crazy, Harry. I got to get you out of my system.' And it seems she might make that sob of disgusted grief again, but she has reared up her head to look at his prick. All this talk of death has put it half to sleep again.

'This is this lupus?' he asks.

'Mmm,' Thelma says. 'Look. See the rash?' She pulls back her hair on both sides. 'Isn't it pretty? That's from being so stupid in the sun Friday. I just wanted so badly to be like the rest of you, not to be an invalid. It was terrible Saturday. Your joints ache, your insides don't work. Ronnie offered to take me home for a shot of cortisone.'

'He's very nice to you.'

'He loves me.'

His prick has stiffened again and she bends to it. 'Thelma.' He has not used her name before, this night. 'Let me do something to you. I mean, equal rights and all that.'

'You're not going down into all that blood.'

'Let me suck these sweet things then.' Her nipples are not bumpy like Janice's but perfect as a baby's thumb-tips. Since it is his treat now he feels free to reach up and switch off the light over the bed. In the dark her rashes disappear and he can see her smile as she arranges herself to be served. She sits cross legged, like Cindy did on the boat, women the flexible sex, and puts a pillow in her lap for his head. She puts a finger in his mouth and plays with her nipple and his tongue together. There is a tremble running through her like a radio not quite turned off. His hand finds her ass, its warm dents; there is a kind of glassy texture to Thelma's skin where Janice's has a touch of fine, fine sandpaper. His prick, lightly teased by her fingernails, has come back nicely. 'Harry.' Her voice presses into his ear. 'I want to do something

383

for you so you won't forget me, something you've never had with anybody else. I suppose other women have sucked you off?'

He shakes his head yes, which tugs the flesh of her breast.

'How many have you fucked up the ass?'

He lets her nipple slip from his mouth. 'None. Never.'

'You and Janice?'

'Oh no. It never occurred to us.'

'Harry. You're not fooling me?'

How dear that was, her old-fashioned 'fooling.' From talking to all those third-graders. 'No, honestly. I thought only queers . . . Do you and Ronnie?'

'All the time. Well, a lot of the time. He loves it.'

'And you?'

'It has its charms.'

'Doesn't it hurt? I mean, he's big.'

'At first. You use Vaseline. I'll get ours.'

'Thelma, wait. Am I up to this?'

She laughs a syllable. 'You're up.' She slides away into the bathroom and while she is gone he stays enormous. She returns and anoints him thoroughly, with an icy expert touch. Harry shudders. Thelma lies down beside him with her back turned, curls forward as if to be shot from a cannon, and reaches behind to guide him. 'Gently.'

It seems it won't go, but suddenly it does. The medicinal odor of displaced Vaseline reaches his nostrils. The grip is tight at the base but beyond, where a cunt is all velvety suction and caress, there is no sensation: a void, a pure black box, a casket of perfect nothingness. He is in that void, past her tight ring of muscle. He asks, 'May I come?'

'Please do.' Her voice sounds faint and broken. Her spine and shoulder blades are taut.

It takes only a few thrusts, while he rubs her scalp with one hand and clamps her hip steady with the other. Where will his come go? Nowhere but mix with her shit. With sweet Thelma's sweet shit. They lie wordless and still together until his prick's slow shrivelling withdraws it. 'O.K.,' he says. 'Thank you. That I won't forget.'

'Promise?'

'I feel embarrassed. What does it do for you?'

'Makes me feel full of you. Makes me feel fucked up the ass. By lovely Harry Angstrom.'

'Thelma,' he admits, 'I can't believe you're so fond of me. What have I done to deserve it?'

'Just existed. Just shed your light. Haven't you ever noticed, at parties or at the club, how I'm always at your side?'

'Well, not really. There aren't that many sides. I mean, we see you and Ronnie –'

'Janice and Cindy noticed. They knew you were who I'd want.'

'Uh – not to, you know, milk this, but what is it about me that turns you on?'

'Oh darling. Everything. Your height and the way you move, as if you're still a skinny twenty-five. The way you never sit down anywhere without making sure there's a way out. Your little provisional smile, like a little boy at some party where the bullies might get him the next minute. Your good humor. You *believe* in people so – Webb, you hang on his words where nobody else pays any attention, and Janice, you're so proud of her it's pathetic. It's not as if she can *do* anything. Even her tennis, Doris Kaufmann was telling us, really –'

'Well it's nice to see her have fun at something, she's had a kind of dreary life.'

'See? You're just terribly generous. You're so grateful to be anywhere, you think that tacky club and that hideous house of Cindy's are heaven. It's wonderful. You're so glad to be alive.'

'Well, I mean, considering the alternative –'

'It kills me. I love you *so much* for it. And your hands. I've always loved your hands.' Having sat up on the edge of the bed, she takes his left hand, lying idle, and kisses the big white moons of each fingernail. 'And now your prick, with its little bonnet. Oh Harry I don't care if this kills me, coming down here, tonight is worth it.'

That void, inside her. He can't take his mind from what he's discovered, that nothingness seen by his single eye. In the shadows, while humid blue moonlight and the rustle of palms seep through the louvers by the bed, he thrusts himself to her as if speaking in prayer, talks to her about himself as he has talked to none other: about Nelson and the grudge he bears the kid and the grudge the boy bears him, and about his daughter, the daughter he thinks he has, grown and ignorant of him. He dares confide to Thelma, because she has let him fuck her up the ass in proof of love, his sense of miracle at being himself, himself instead of somebody else, and his old inkling, now fading in the energy crunch, that there was something that wanted him to find it, that he was here on earth on a kind of assignment.

'How lovely to think that,' Thelma says. 'It makes you' – the word is hard for her to find – 'radiant. And sad.' She gives him advice on some points. She thinks he should seek out Ruth and ask her point-blank if that is his daughter, and if so is there anything he can do to help? On the subject of Nelson, she thinks the child's problem may be an extension of Harry's; if he himself did not feel guilty about Jill's death and before that Rebecca's, he would feel less threatened by Nelson and more comfortable and kindly with him. 'Remember,' she says, 'he's just a young man like you once were, looking for his path.'

'But he's not like me!' Harry protests, having come at last into a presence where the full horror of this truth, the great falling-off, will be understood. 'He's a goddam little Springer, through and through.'

Thelma thinks he's more like Harry than he knows. Wanting to learn to hang glide – didn't he recognize himself in that? And the thing with two girls at once. Wasn't he, possibly, a bit jealous of Nelson?

'But I never had the impulse to screw Melanie,' he confesses. 'Or Pru either, much. They're both out of this world, somehow.'

Of course, Thelma says. 'You shouldn't want to fuck them. They're your daughters. Or Cindy either. You should want to fuck *me*. I'm your generation, Harry. I can *see* you. To those girls you're just an empty heap of years and money.'

And, as they drift in talk away from the constellations of his life, she describes her marriage with Ronnie, his insecurities and worries beneath that braggart manner that she knows annoys Harry. 'He was never a star like you, he never had that for a moment.' She met him fairly well along in her twenties, when she was wondering if she'd die a spinster schoolteacher. Being old as she was, with some experience of men, and with a certain gift for letting go, she was amused by the things he thought of. For their honeymoon breakfast he jerked off into the scrambled eggs and they ate his fried jism with the rest. If you go along with everything on that side of Ronnie, he's wonderfully loyal, and docile, you could say. He has no interest in other women, she knows this for a fact, a curious fact even, given the nature of men. He's been a perfect father. When he was lower down on the totem pole at Schuylkill Mutual, he lost twenty pounds, staying awake at nights worrying. Only in these last few years has the weight come back. When the first diagnosis of her lupus came through, he took it worse than she did, in a way. 'For a woman past forty, Harry, when you've had children ... If some Nazi or somebody came to me and they'd take either me or little Georgie, say – he's the one that's needed most help, so he comes to mind – it wouldn't be a hard choice. For Ronnie I think it might be. To lose me. He thinks what I do for him not every woman would. I suspect he's wrong but there it is.' And she admits she likes his cock. But what Harry might not appreciate, being a man, is that a big one like Ronnie's doesn't change size that much when it's hard, just the angle changes. It doesn't go from being a little bonneted sleeping baby to a tall fierce soldier like this. She has worked him up again, idly toying as she talks, while the night outside their louvered window has grown utterly still, the last drunken shout and snatch of music long died, nothing astir but the incessant sighing of the sea and the piping of some high-pitched cricket they have down here. Courteously he offers to fuck her through her blood, and she refuses with an almost virginal fright, so that he wonders if on the excuse of her flow she is not holding this part of herself back from him, aloof from her love and shamelessness, pure for her marriage. She has explained, 'When I realized I was falling in love with you, I was so *mad* at myself, I mean it couldn't contribute to *any*thing. But then I came to see that something must be missing between me and Ronnie, or maybe in any life, so I tried to accept it, and even quietly enjoy it, just watching you. My little hairshirt.' He has not kissed her yet on the mouth, but now guessing at her guilty withholding of herself from being fucked he does. Her lips feel cool and dry, considering. Since she will not admit him to her cunt, as compromise he masturbates her while sitting on her face, glad he thought of washing where he did. Her tongue probes there and as her fingers, as cool on top of his as if still filmed with Vaseline, guide his own as they find and then lose and find again the hooded little center that is *her*. She comes with a smothered cry and arches her back so this darkness at the center of her pale and smooth and unfamiliar form rises hungrily under his eyes, a cloud with a mouth, a fish lunging upwards out of water. Getting her breath, she returns the kindness and with him watches the white liquid lift and collapse in glutinous strings across her hand. She rubs his jism on her face, where it shines. The stillness outside is beginning to brighten, each leaf sharp in the soft air. Drunk on fatigue and self-exposure he begs her to tell him something that he can do to her that Ronnie has never done. She gets into the bathtub and has him urinate on her. 'It's hot!' she exclaims, her sallow skin drummed upon in designs such as men and boys drill in the snow. They reverse the experience, Thelma awkwardly straddling, and having to laugh at her own impotence, looking for the right release in the maze of her womanly insides. Above him as he waits her bush has a masculine jut, but when her stream comes, it dribbles sideways; women cannot *aim*, he sees. And her claim of heat seems to be exaggerated; it is more like coffee or tea one lets cool too long at the edge of the desk and then must drink in a few gulps, this side of tepid. Having tried together to shower the ammoniac scent of urine off their skins, Thelma and Harry fall asleep among the stripes of dawn now welling through the louvers as if not a few stolen hours but an entire married life of sanctioned intimacy stretches unto death before them.

A savage rattling at the door. 'Thelma. Harry. It's *us*.' Thelma puts on a robe to answer the knocking while Rabbit hides beneath the sheet and peeks. Webb and Ronnie stand there in the incandescence of another day. Webb is resplendent in grape-colored alligator shirt and powder-blue plaid golf pants. Ronnie wears last night's dinner clothes and needs to get inside. Thelma shuts the door and hides in the bathroom while Harry dresses in last night's rumpled suit, not bothering to knot the necktie. He still smells of urine, he thinks. He runs to his own bungalow to change into a golf outfit. Black girls, humming, pursued by yellow birds, are carrying tinkling breakfast trays along the cement paths. Janice is in the bathroom, running a tub.

He shouts out, 'You O.K.?'

She shouts back, 'As O.K. as you are,' and doesn't emerge.

On the way out, Harry stuffs an unbuttered croissant and some scalding sips of coffee into his mouth. The papery orange and magenta flowers beside the door hurt his head. Webb and Ronnie are waiting for him where the green cement paths meet. Among the three men, as they push through their golf, there is much banter and good humor, but little eye-contact. When they return from the course around one o'clock, Janice is sitting by the Olympic pool in the same purple gabardine suit she wore down in the airplane. 'Harry, Mother phoned. We have to go back.'

'You're kidding. Why?' He is groggy, and had pictured a long afternoon nap, to be in shape for tonight. Also his foreskin was tender after last night's workout and slightly chafed every time he swung, thinking of Cindy, hoping her vagina would be non-frictional. His golf, threaded through vivid after-images of Thelma's underside and a ticklish awareness of his two business-like partners as silently freighted with mental pictures of their own, was mysteriously good, his swing as it were emptied of impurities, until fatigue caught him on the fifteenth hole with three balls sliced along the identical heavenly groove into the lost-ball terrain of cactus and coral and scrub growth. 'What's happened? The baby?'

'No,' Janice says, and by the easy way she cries he knows she's been crying off and on all morning, here in the sun. 'It's *Nel*son. He's run off.'

'He has? I better sit down.' To the black waiter who comes to their glass table under its fringed umbrella he says, 'Piña colada, Jeff. Better make that two. Janice?' She blearily nods, though there is an empty glass already before her. Harry looks around at the faces of their friends. 'Jeff, maybe you should make that six.' He has come to know the ropes in this place. The other people sitting around the pool look pale, newly pulled from the airplane.

Cindy has just come out of the pool, her shoulders blue-black, the diaper-shape of her bikini bottom wetly adhering. She tugs the cloth to cover the pale margin of skin above, below. She is getting fatter, day by day. Better hurry, he tells himself. But it is too late. Her face when she turns, towelling her back with a contortion that nearly pops one tit out of its triangular sling, is solemn. She and Thelma have heard Janice's story already. Thelma is sitting at the table in that ankle-length wrapper, the same dusty-pink as her nose, that she bought down here along with the wide straw hat. The big brown sunglasses she brought from home, tinted darker at the top, render her expressionless. Harry takes the chair at the table next to her. His knee accidentally touches one of hers; she pulls it away at once.

Janice is telling him, through tears, 'He and Pru had a fight Saturday night, he wanted to go into Brewer for a party with that Slim person and Pru said she was too pregnant and couldn't face those stairs again, and he went by himself.' She swallows. 'And he didn't come back.' Her voice is all roughened from swallowing the saltwater of the tears. With scrapings that hurt Harry's head Webb and Ronnie pull chairs to their table in its tight circle of shade. When Jeff brings their round of drinks Janice halts her terrible tale and Ronnie negotiates for lunch menus. He, like his wife, wears sunglasses. Webb wears none, trusting to his bushy brows and the crinkles of his flinty eyes, which gaze at Janice like those of some encouraging old fart of a father.

Her cheeks are drenched with the slime of distress and Harry has to love her for her ugliness. 'I told you the kid was a rat,' he tells her. He feels vindicated. And relieved, actually.

'He didn't come back,' Janice all but cries, looking only at him, not at Webb, with that smeared lost balked expression he remembers so well from their earliest days, before she got cocky. 'But Mother didn't want to b-bother us on our vacation and P-Pru thought he just needed to blow off steam and pretended not to be worried. But Sunday after going to church with Mother she called this Slim and Nelson had never showed up!'

'Did he have a car?' Harry asks.

'Your Corona.'

'Oh boy.'

'I think just scrambled eggs for me,' Ronnie tells the waitress who has come. 'Loose. You understand? Not too well done.'

This time Rabbit deliberately seeks to touch Thelma's knee with his under the table but her knee is not there for him. Like Janice down here she has become a piece of static. The waitress is at his shoulder and he is wondering if he might dare another crabmeat-salad sandwich or should play it safe with a BLT. Janice's face, that the movement of the sun overhead is hoisting out of shadow, goes wide in eyes and mouth as she might shriek. 'Harry, you *can't* have lunch, you *must* get dressed and out of here! I packed for you, everything but the gray suit. The woman at the front desk was on the phone for me nearly an hour, trying to get us back to Philadelphia but it's impossible this time of year. There's not even anything to New York. She got us two seats on a little plane to San Juan and a room at the hotel airport so we can get a flight to the mainland first thing in the morning. Atlanta and then Philadelphia.'

'Why not just use our regular reservations Thursday? What good's an extra day going to do?'

'I cancelled them. Harry, you didn't talk to Mother. She's wild, I've never heard her like this, you know how she always makes sense. I called back to tell her the plane on Wednesday and she didn't think she could drive the Philadelphia traffic to meet us, she burst into tears and said she was too old.'

'Cancelled.' It is sinking in. 'You mean we can't stay here tonight because of something Nelson has done?'

'Finish your story, Jan,' Webb urges. Jan, is it now? Harry suddenly hates people who seem to *know*; they would keep us blind to the fact that there is nothing to know. We are each of us filled with a perfect blackness.

Janice gulps again, and snuffles, calmed by Webb's voice. 'There's nothing to finish. He didn't come back Sunday or Monday and none of these friends they have in Brewer had seen him and Mother finally couldn't stand it anymore and called this morning, even though Pru kept telling her not to bother us, it was her husband and she took the responsibility.'

'Poor kid. Like you said, she thought she could work miracles.' He tells her, 'I don't *want* to leave before tonight.'

'Stay here then,' Janice says. 'I'm going.'

Harry looks over at Webb for some kind of help, and gets

instead a sage and useless not-my-funeral grimace. He looks at Cindy but she is gazing down into her piña colada, her eyelashes in sharp focus. 'I still don't understand the rush,' he says. 'Nobody's died.'

'Not yet,' Janice says. 'Is that what you need?'

A rope inside his chest twists to make a kink. 'Son of a fucking bitch,' he says, and stands, bumping his head on the fringed edge of the umbrella. 'When'd you say this plane to San Juan is?'

Janice snuffles, guilty now. 'Not until three.'

'O.K.' He sighs. In a way this is a relief. 'I'll go change and bring the suitcases. Could one of you guys at least order me a hamburger? Cindy. Thel. See you around.' The two ladies let themselves be kissed, Thelma primly on the lips, Cindy on her apple-firm cheek, toasty from the sun.

Throughout their twenty-four-hour trip home Janice keeps crying. The taxi ride past the old sugar mills, through the goat herds and the straggling black towns and the air that seems to be blowing them kisses; the forty-minute hop in a swaying two-engine prop plane to Puerto Rico, over mild green water beneath whose sparkling film lurk buried reefs and schools of sharks; the stopover in San Juan where everybody really is a spic; the long stunned night of porous sleep in a hotel very like that motel on Route 422 where Mrs Lubell stayed so long ago; and in the morning two seats on a jet to Atlanta and then Philly: through all this Janice is beside him with her cheeks glazed, eyes staring ahead, her eyelashes tipped with tiny balls of dew. It is as if all the grief that swept through him at Nelson's wedding now at last has reached Janice's zone, and he is calm, emptied, cold as the void suspended beneath the airplane's shuddering flight like a huge fruit. He asks her, 'Is it just Nelson?'

She shakes her head so violently the fringe of bangs bobs. '*Ev*erything,' she blurts, so loud he fears the heads just glimpsable in the seats ahead might turn around.

'The swapping?' he pursues softly.

She nods, not so violently, pinching her lower lip in a kind of turtle mouth her mother sometimes makes.

'How *was* Webb?'

'Nice. He's always been nice to me. He respected Daddy.' This

392

sets the tears to flowing again. She takes a deep breath to steady herself. 'I felt so sorry for you, having Thelma when you wanted Cindy so much.' With that there is no stopping her crying.

He pats her hands, which are loosely fisted together in her lap around a damp Kleenex. 'Listen, I'm sure Nelson's all right, wherever he is.'

'He' – she seems to be choking, a stewardess glances down as she strides by, this is embarrassing – '*hates* himself, Harry.'

He tries to ponder if this is true. He snickers. 'Well he sure screwed me. Last night was my dream date.'

Janice sniffs and rubs each nostril with the Kleenex. 'Webb says she's not that wonderful. He talked a lot about his first two wives.'

Beneath them, through the scratched oval of Plexiglas, there is the South, irregular fields and dry brown woods, more woods than he would have expected. Once he had dreamed of going south, of resting his harried heart amid all that cotton, and now there it is under him, like the patchwork slope of one big hill they are slowly climbing, fields and woods and cities at the bends and mouths of rivers, streets eating into green, America disgraced and barren, mourning her hostages. They are flying too high for him to spot golf courses. They play all winter down here, swinging easy. The giant motors he is riding whine. He falls asleep. The last thing he sees is Janice staring ahead, wide awake, the bulge of tears compounding the bulge of her cornea. He dreams of Pru, who bursts while he is trying to manipulate her limbs, so there is too much water, he begins to panic. He is changing weight and this wakes him up. They are descending. He thinks back to his night with Thelma, and it seems in texture no different from the dream. Only Janice is real, the somehow catastrophic folds of her gabardine sleeve and the muddy line of her jaw, her head slumped as from a broken neck. She fell asleep, the same magazine open in her lap that she read on the way down. They are descending over Maryland and Delaware, where horses run and the Du Ponts are king. Rich women with little birdy breasts and wearing tall black boots in from the hunt. Walking past the butler into long halls past marble tables they flick with their whips. Women he will never fuck. He has risen as high as he can, the possibility of such women is falling from him, falling with so many other possibilities as he descends. No snow dusts the dry earth below, rooftops and fields and roads where cars are nosing along like windup toys on invisible grooves. Yet from within those cars they are speeding, and feel free. The river flashes its sheet of steel, the plane tilts alarmingly, the air nozzles hissing above him may be the last thing he hears, Janice is awake and bolt upright. *Forgive me.* Fort Mifflin hulks just under their wheels, their speed is titanic. *Please, God.* Janice is saying something into his ear but the thump of the wheels drowns it out. They are down, and taxiing. He gives a squeeze to Janice's damp hand, that he didn't realize he was holding. 'What did you say?' he asks her.

'That I love you.'

'Oh, really? Well, same here. That trip was fun. I feel satisfied.'

In the long slow trundle to their gate, she asks him shyly, 'Was Thelma better than me?'

He is too grateful to be down to lie. 'In ways. How about Webb?'

She nods and nods, as if to spill the last tears from her eyes.

He answers for her, 'The bastard was great.'

She leans her head against his shoulder. 'Why do you think I've been crying?'

Shocked, he admits, 'I thought about Nelson.'

Janice sniffs once more, so loudly that one man already on his feet, arranging a Russian-style fur cap upon his sunburned bald head, briefly stares. She concedes, 'It was, mostly,' and she and Harry clasp hands once more, conspirators.

At the end of miles of airport corridor Ma Springer is standing apart from the cluster of other greeters. In the futuristic perspectives of this terminal she looks shrunken and bent, wearing her second-best coat, not the mink but a black cloth trimmed with silver fox, and a little cherry-red brimless hat with folded-back net that might get by in Brewer but appears quaint here, among the cowboys and the slim kids of indeterminate sex with their cropped hair dyed punk-style in pastel feathers and the black chicks whose hair is frizzed up in structures like three-dimensional Mickey Mouse ears. Hugging her, Rabbit feels how small the old lady, once the terror of his young manhood, has become. Her former look of having been stuffed tight with Koerner pride and potential indignation has fled, leaving her skin collapsed in random folds and bloodless. Deep liverish gouges underscore her eyes, and her wattled throat seems an atrocious wreck of flesh.

She can hardly wait to speak, backing a step away to give her voice room to make its impact. 'The baby came last night. A girl, seven pounds and some. I couldn't sleep a wink, after getting her to the hospital and then waiting for the doctor to call.' Her voice is shaky with blame. The airport Musak, a tune being plucked on the strings of many coordinated violins, accompanies her announcement in such triumphant rhythm that Harry and Janice have to suppress smiles, not even daring to step closer in the jostle and shuffle, the old lady is so childishly, precariously intent on the message she means to deliver. 'And then all the way down on the Turnpike, trucks kept tooting their horns at me, tooting these big foghorns they have. As if there were someplace else I could go; I couldn't drive the Chrysler off the road,' Bessie says. 'And after Conshohocken, on the Expressway, it's really a wonder I wasn't killed. I never saw so much traffic, though I thought at noon it would be letting up, and you know the signs, they aren't at all clear even if you have good eyes. All the way along the river I kept praying to Fred and I honestly believe it was him that got me here, I couldn't have done it alone.'

And, her manner plainly implies, she will never attempt anything like it again; Janice and Harry find her at the terminus of the last great effort of her life. Henceforth, she is in their hands.

# V

Yet Ma Springer wasn't so totally thrown by events that she didn't have the wit to call up Charlie Stavros and have him come back to the lot. His own mother took a turn for the worse in December – her whole left side feels numb, so even with a cane it frightens her to walk – and as Charlie predicted his cousin Gloria went back to Norristown and her husband, though Charlie wouldn't give it a year; so he has been pretty well tied down. This time it's Harry who's come back with a tan. He gives Charlie a double-handed handclasp, he's so happy to see him at Springer Motors again. He doesn't look that hot, however: those trips to Florida were like a paint job. He looks pale. He looks as if you pricked his skin he'd bleed gray. He stands hunched over protecting his chest like he'd smoked three packs a day all his life, though Charlie like most Mediterranean types has never really had the self-destructive habits you see in northern Europeans and Negroes. Harry wouldn't have given him such an all-out handshake this way a week ago, but since fucking Thelma up the ass he's felt freer, more in love with the world again.

'The old *mastoras*. You look great,' he exuberantly lies to Charlie.

'I've felt better,' Charlie tells him. 'Thank God it hasn't been any kind of a winter so far.' Harry can see, through the plate-glass window, a snowless, leafless landscape, the dust of all seasons swirling and drifting, intermixed with paper refuse from the Chuck Wagon that has blown across Route 111. A new banner is up: THE ERA OF COROLLA. *Toyota = Total Economy.* Charlie volunteers, 'It's pretty damn depressing, watching *Manna mou* head straight downhill. She gets out of bed just to go to the bathroom and keeps telling me I ought to get married.'

'Good advice, maybe.'

'Well, I made a little move on Gloria in that direction, and it may be what scared her back to her husband. That guy, what a shit. She'll be back.'

'Wasn't she a cousin?'

'All the better. Peppy type. About four eleven, little heavy in the rumble seat, not quite classy enough for you, champ. But cute. You should see her dance. I hadn't been to those Hellenic Society Saturday nights for years, she talked me into it. I loved to watch her sweat.'

'You say she'll be back.'

'Yeah but not for me. I've missed that boat.' He adds, 'I've missed a lot of boats.'

'Who hasn't?'

Charlie rolls a toothpick in the center of his lower lip. Harry doesn't like to look at him closely; he's become one of those old Brewer geezers who go into cigar stores to put ten dollars on the numbers and hang around the magazine racks waiting for a conversation. 'You've caught a few,' he ventures to tell Harry.

'No, listen. Charlie. I'm in rotten shape. A kid who's disappeared and a new house with no furniture in it.' Yet these facts, species of emptiness and new possibility, excite and please him more than not.

'That kid'll turn up,' Charlie says. 'He's just letting off steam.'

'That's what Pru says. You never saw anybody so calm, considering. We went up to the hospital last night after getting in from the islands and, Jesus, is she happy about that baby. You'd think she was the first woman in the history of the world to pull this off. I guess she was worried about the kid being normal, after that fall she took a while ago.'

'Worried about herself, more likely. Girl like that who's been knocked around a lot by life, having a baby's the one way they can prove to themselves they're human. What're they thinking of calling it?'

'She doesn't want to call it after her mother, she wants to name it after Ma. Rebecca. But she wants to wait to hear from Nelson, because, you know, that was his sister's name. The infant that died.'

'Yeah.' Charlie understands. Inviting bad luck. The sound of Mildred Kroust's typewriter bridges their silence. In the shop one of Manny's men is pounding an uncooperative piece of metal. Charlie asks, 'What're you going to do about the house?'

'Move in, Janice says. She surprised me, the way she talked to her mother. Right in the car driving home. She told her she was welcome to move in with us but she didn't see why she couldn't have a house of her own like other women her age and since Pru and the baby were obviously going to have to stay she doesn't want her to feel crowded in her own home. Bessie, that is.'

'Huh. About time Jan stood on her own two feet. Wonder who she's been talking to?'

Webb Murkett, it occurs to Harry, through a tropical night of love; but things always work best between him and Charlie when they don't go too deep into Janice. He says, 'The trouble with having the house, is we have no furniture of our own. And everything costs a fucking fortune. A simple mattress and box spring and steel frame to set it on for six hundred dollars; if you add a headboard that's another six hundred. Carpets! Three, four thousand for a little Oriental, and they all come out of Iran and Afghanistan. The salesman was telling me they're a better investment than gold.'

'Gold's doing pretty well,' Charlie says.

'Better than we are, huh? Have you had a chance to look at the books?'

'They've looked better,' Charlie admits. 'But nothing a little more inflation won't cure. Young couple came in here Tuesday, the first day I got the call from Bessie, and bought a Corvette convertible Nelson had laid in. Said they wanted a convertible and thought the dead of winter would be a good time to buy one. No trade-in, weren't interested in financing, paid for it with a check, a regular checking account. Where do they get the money? Neither one of 'em could have been more than twenty-five. Next day, yesterday, kid came in here in a GMC pick-up and said he'd heard we had a snowmobile for sale. It took us a while to find it out back but when we did he got that light in his eyes so I began by asking twelve hundred and we settled at nine seventy-five. I said to him, There isn't any snow, and he said, That's all right, he was moving up to Vermont, to wait out the nuclear holocaust. Said Three-Mile Island really blew his mind. D'y'ever notice how Carter can't say "nuclear"? He says "nookier."'

'You really got rid of that snowmobile? I can't believe it.'

'People don't care about economizing anymore. Big Oil has sold capitalism down the river. What the czar did for the Russians, Big Oil is doing for us.'

Harry can't take the time to talk economics today. He apologizes, 'Charlie, I'm still on vacation in theory, to the end of the week, and Janice is meeting me downtown, we got a thousand things to do in connection with this damn house of hers.'

Charlie nods. 'Amscray. I got some sorting out to do myself. One thing nobody could accuse Nelson of is being a neatness freak.' He shouts after Harry as he goes into the corridor for his hat and coat, 'Say hello to Grandma for me!'

Meaning Janice, Harry slowly realizes.

He ducks into his office, where the new 1980 company calendar with its photo of Fujiyama hangs on the wall. He makes a mental note to himself, not for the first time, to do something about those old clippings that hang outside on the pressed-board partition, they're getting too yellow, there's a process he's heard about where they photograph old halftones so they look white as new, and can be blown up to any size. Might as well blow them up big, it's a business expense. He takes from old man Springer's heavy oak coatrack with its four little bow legs the sheepskin overcoat Janice got him for Christmas and the little narrow-brim suede hat that goes with it. At his age you wear a hat. He went all through last winter without a cold, because he had taken to wearing a hat. And vitamin C helps. Next it'll be Geritol. He hopes he didn't cut Charlie short but he found talking to him today a little depressing, the guy is at a dead end and turning cranky. Big Oil doesn't know any more what's up than little oil. But then from Harry's altitude at this moment anyone might look small and cranky. He has taken off; he is flying high, on his way to an island in his life. He takes a tube of Life Savers (clove flavor) from his top lefthand desk drawer, to spice his breath in case he's kissed, and lets himself out through the back of the shop. He is careful with the crash bar: a touch of grease on this sheepskin and there's no getting it off.

Nelson having stolen his Corona, Harry has allocated to himself a grape-blue Celica Supra, the 'ultimate Toyota,' with padded dash, electric tachometer, state-of-the-art four-speaker solid-state AM/FM/MPX stereo, quartz-accurate digital clock, automatic overdrive transmission, cruise control, computer-tuned suspension, ten-inch disc brakes on all four wheels, and quartz halogen hi-beam headlights. He loves this smooth machine. The Corona for all its dependable qualities was a stodgy little bug, whereas this blue buzzard has charisma. The blacks along lower Weiser really stared yesterday afternoon when he drove it home. After Janice and he had brought Ma back to 89 Joseph in the Chrysler (which in fact even Harry found not so easy to drive, after a week of being driven in taxis on the wrong side of the road), they put her to bed and came into town in the Maverick, Janice all hyper after her standing up for herself about the house, to Schaechner Furniture, where they looked at beds and ugly easy chairs and Parsons tables like the Murketts had, only not so nice as theirs, the wood grain not checkerboarded. They couldn't make any decisions; when the store was about to close she drove him over to the lot so he could have a car too. He picked this model priced in five digits. Blacks stared out from under the neon signs, JIMBO'S *friendly* LOUNGE and LIVE ENTERTAINMENT and ADULT ADULT ADULT, as he slid by in virgin blue grapeskin; he was afraid some of them lounging in the cold might come running out at a stoplight and scratch his hood with a screwdriver or smash his windshield with a hammer, taking vengeance for their lives. On a number of walls now in this part of town you can see spray-painted SKEETER LIVES, but they don't say where.

He has lied to Charlie. He doesn't have to meet Janice until one-thirty and it is now 11:17 by the Supra's quartz clock. He is driving to Galilee. He turns on the radio and its sound is even punkier, richer, more many-leaved and many-layered, than that of the radio in the old Corona. Though he moves the dial from left to right and back again he can't find Donna Summer, she went

400

out with the Seventies. Instead there is a guy singing hymns, squeezing the word 'Jesus' until it drips. And that kind of mellow mixed-voice backup he remembers from the records when he was in high school: the jukeboxes where you could see the record fall and that waxy rustling cloth, taffeta or whatever, the girls went to dances in, wearing the corsage you gave them. The corsage would get crushed as the dancing got closer and the girls' perfumes would be released from between their powdery breasts as their bodies were warmed and pressed by partner after partner, in the violet light of the darkened gym, crêpe-paper streamers drooping overhead and the basketball hoops wreathed with paper flowers, all those warm bodies softly bumping in anticipation of the cold air stored in cars outside, the little glowing dashboard lights, the body heat misting the inside of the windshield, the taffeta tugged and mussed, chilly fingers fumbling through coats and pants and underpants, clothes become a series of tunnels, Mary Ann's body nestling toward his hands, the space between her legs so different and mild and fragrant and safe, a world apart. And now, the news, on the half hour. That wise-voiced young woman is long gone from this local station, Harry wonders where she is by now, doing go-go or assistant vice-president at Sunflower Beer. The new announcer sounds like Billy Fosnacht, fat-lipped. President Carter has revealed that he personally favors a boycott of the 1980 Moscow Olympics. Reaction from athletes is mixed. Indian Prime Minister Indira Gandhi has backed off from yesterday's apparently pro-Soviet stance on Afghanistan. On the crowded campaign trail, U.S. Representative Philip Crane of Illinois has labelled as 'foolish' Massachusetts Senator Edward Kennedy's proposal that the Seabrook, New Hampshire, proposed nuclear plant be converted to coal. In Japan, former Beatle Paul McCartney was jailed on charges of possessing eight ounces of marijuana. In Switzerland, scientists have succeeded in programming bacteria to manufacture the scarce human protein interferon, an anti-viral agent whose artificial production may usher in an era as beneficial to mankind as the discovery of penicillin. Meanwhile, if the fillings in your teeth cost more, it's because the price of gold hit eight hundred dollars an ounce in New York City today. Fuck. He sold too soon. Eight hundred times thirty equals twenty-four thousand, that's up nearly ten grand from fourteen six, if he'd just held on, damn that Webb Murkett and his silver. And the 76ers continue their winning ways, 121 to 110 over the Portland Trail Blazers at the Spectrum last night. Poor old Eagles out of their misery, Jaworski went down flinging. And now, to continue our program of Nice Music for Nice Folks, the traditional melody 'Savior, Keep a Watch Over Me.' Harry turns it off, driving to the purr of the Supra.

He knows the way now. Past the giant Amishman pointing to the natural cave, through the narrow town with its Purina feed-store sign and old inn and new bank and hitching posts and tractor agency. The corn stubble of the fields sticks up pale, all the gold bleached from it. The duck pond has frozen edges but a wide center of black water, so mild has the winter been. He slows past the Blankenbiller and Muth mailboxes, and turns down the drive-way where the box says BYER. His nerves are stretched so nothing escapes his vision, the jutting stones of the two beaten reddish tracks that make the old road, the fringe of dried weeds each still bearing the form its green life assumed in the vanished summer, the peeling pumpkin-colored school bus husk, a rusting harrow, a small springhouse whitewashed years ago, and then the shabby farm buildings, corn crib and barn and stone house, approached from a new angle, for the first time from the front. He drives the Celica into the space of packed dirt where he once saw the Corolla pull in; in turning off the engine and stepping from the car he sees the ridge from which he spied, a far scratchy line of black cherry and gum trees scarcely visible through the apple trees of the orchard, farther away than it had felt, the odds were no one had ever seen him. This is crazy. Run.

But as with dying there is a moment that must be pushed through, a slice of time more transparent than plate glass; it is in front of him and he takes the step, drawing heart from that loving void Thelma had confided to him. In his sheepskin coat and silly small elf hat and three-piece suit of pinstriped wool bought just this November at that tailor of Webb's on Pine Street, he walks across the earth where silted-over flat sandstones once formed a walk. It is cold, a day that might bring snow, a day that feels hollow. Though it is near noon no sun shows through, not even a silver patch betrays its place in the sky, one long ribbed underbelly of low gray clouds. A drab tall thatch of winter woods rears up on his right. In the other direction, beyond the horizon, a chain saw sounds stuck. Even before, removing one glove, he raps with a bare hand on the door, where paint a poisonous green is coming loose in long curving flakes, the dog inside the house hears his footsteps scrape stone and sets up a commotion of barking.

Harry hopes the dog is alone, its owner out. There is no car or pick-up truck in the open, but one might be parked in the barn or the newish garage of cement-block with a roof of corrugated overlapped Fiberglas. Inside the house no light burns that he can see, but then it is near noon, though the day is dull and growing darker. He peers in the door and sees himself reflected with his pale hat in another door, much like this one, with two tall panes of glass, the thickness of a stone wall away. Beyond the old panes a hallway with a tattered striped runner recedes into unlit depths. As his eyes strain to see deeper his nose and ungloved hand sting with the cold. He is about to turn away and return to the warm car when a shape materializes within the house and rushes, puffed up with rage, toward him. The black-haired collie leaps and leaps again against the inner door, frantic, trying to bite the glass, those ugly little front teeth a dog has, inhuman, and the split black lip and lavender gums, unclean. Harry is paralyzed with fascination; he does not see the great shape materialize behind Fritzie until a hand clatters on the inner door latch.

The fat woman's other hand holds the dog by the collar; Harry helps by opening the green outer door himself. Fritzie recognizes his scent and stops barking. And Rabbit recognizes, buried under the wrinkles and fat but with those known eyes blazing out alive, Ruth. So amid a tumult of wagging and the whimpers of that desperate doggy need to reclaim a friend, the two old lovers confront one another. Twenty years ago he had lived with this woman, March to June. He saw her for a minute in Kroll's eight years later, and she had spared him a few bitter words, and now a dozen years have poured across them both, doing their damage. Her hair that used to be a kind of dirty fiery gingery color is flattened now to an iron gray and pulled back in a bun like the Mennonites wear. She wears wide denim dungarees and a man's red lumberjack shirt beneath a black sweater with unravelled elbows and dog hairs and wood chips caught in the greasy weave. Yet this is Ruth. Her upper lip still pushes out a little, as if with an incipient blister, and her flat blue eyes in their square sockets still gaze at him with a hostility that tickles him. 'What do you want?' she asks. Her voice sounds thickened, as by a cold.

'I'm Harry Angstrom.'

'I can see that. What do you want here?'

'I was wondering, could we talk a little? There's something I need to ask you.'

'No, we can't talk a little. Go away.'

But she has released the dog's collar, and Fritzie sniffs at his ankles and his crotch and writhes in her urge to jump up, to impart the scarcely bearable joy locked in her narrow skull, behind her bulging eyes. Her bad eye still looks sore. 'Good Fritzie,' Harry says. 'Down. Down.'

Ruth has to laugh, that quick ringing laugh of hers, like change tossed onto a counter. 'Rabbit, you're cute. Where'd you learn her name?'

'I heard you all calling her once. A couple times I've been here, up behind those trees, but I couldn't get up my nerve to come any closer. Stupid, huh?'

She laughs again, a touch less ringingly, as if she is truly amused. Though her voice has roughened and her bulk has doubled and there is a down including a few dark hairs along her cheeks and above the corners of her mouth, this is really Ruth, a cloud his life has passed through, solid again. She is still tall, compared to Janice, compared to any of the women of his life but Mim and his mother. She always had a weight about her, she joked the first night when he lifted her that this would put him out of action, a weight that pushed him off, along with something that held him fast, an air of being willing to play, in the little space they had, and though the time they had was short. 'So you were scared of us,' she says. She bends slightly, to address the dog. 'Fritzie, shall we let him in for a minute?' The dog's liking him, a dim spark of dog memory setting her tail wagging, has tipped the balance.

The hall inside smells decidedly of the past, the way these old farm houses do. Apples in the cellar, cinnamon in the cooking, a melding of the old plaster and wallpaper paste, he doesn't know. Muddy boots stand in a corner of the hall, on newspapers spread there, and he notices that Ruth is in stocking feet — thick gray men's work socks, but sexy nonetheless, the silence of her steps, though she is huge. She leads him to the right, into a small front parlor with an oval rug of braided rags on the floor and a folding wooden lawn chair mixed in with the other furniture. The only modern piece is the television set, its overbearing rectangular eye still. A small wood fire smolders in a sandstone fireplace. Harry checks his shoes before stepping onto the rag rug, to make sure he is not tracking in dirt. He removes his fancy little sheepskin hat.

As if regretting this already, Ruth sits on the very edge of her chair, a cane-bottomed rocker, tipping it forward so her knees nearly touch the floor and her arm can reach down easily to scratch Fritzie's neck and keep her calm. Harry guesses he is supposed to sit opposite, on a cracked black leather settee beneath two depressing sepia studio portraits, a century old at least they must be, in matching carved frames, of a bearded type and his buttoned-up wife, both long turned to dust in their coffins. But before sitting down he sees across the room, by the light of a window whose deep sill teems with potted African violets and those broad-leafed plants people give for Mother's Days, a more contemporary set of photographs, color snapshots that line one shelf of a bookcase holding rows of the paperback mysteries and romances Ruth used to read and apparently still does. That used to hurt him about her in those months, how she would withdraw into one of those trashy thrillers set in England or Los Angeles though he was right there, in the flesh. He crosses to the bookcase and sees her, younger but already stout, standing before a corner of this house within the arm of a man older, taller, and stouter than she: this must have been Byer. A big sheepish farmer in awkward Sunday clothes, squinting against the sunlight with an expression like that of the large old portraits, his mouth wistful in its attempt to satisfy the camera. Ruth looks amused, her hair up in a bouffant do and still gingery, amused that for this sheltering man she is a prize. Rabbit feels, for an instant as short and bright as the click

405

of a shutter, jealous of these lives that others led: this stout plain country couple posing by a chipped corner of brown stucco, on earth that from the greening state of the grass suggests March or April. Nature up to her tireless tricks. There are other photographs, color prints of combed and smiling adolescents, in those cardboard frames high-school pictures come in. Before he can examine them, Ruth says sharply, 'Who said you could look at those? Stop it.'

'It's your family.'

'You bet it is. Mine and not yours.'

But he cannot tear himself away from the images in flashlit color of these children. They gaze not at him but past his right ear, each posed identically by the photographer as he worked his school circuit May after May. A boy and the girl at about the same age – the senior photo – and then in smaller format a younger boy with darker hair, cut longer and parted on the other side of his head from his brother. All have blue eyes. 'Two boys and a girl,' Harry says. 'Who's the oldest?'

'What the hell do you care? God, I'd forgotten what a pushy obnoxious bastard you are. Stuck on yourself from cradle to grave.'

'My guess is, the girl is the oldest. When did you have her, and when did you marry this old guy? How can you stand it, by the way, out here in the boondocks?'

'I stand it fine. It's more than anybody else ever offered me.'

'I didn't have much to offer anybody in those days.'

'But you've done fine since. You're dressed up like a pansy.'

'And you're dressed up like a ditchdigger.'

'I've been cutting wood.'

'You operate one of those chain saws? Jesus, aren't you afraid you'll cut off a finger?'

'No, I'm not. The car you sold Jamie works fine, if that's what you came to ask.'

'How long have you known I've been at Springer Motors?'

'Oh, always. And then it was in the papers when Springer died.'

'Was that you drove past in the old station wagon the day Nelson got married?'

'It might have been,' Ruth says, sitting back in her rocking chair, so it tips the other way. Fritzie has stretched out to sleep. The wood fire spits. 'We pass through Mt Judge from time to time. It's a free country still, isn't it?'

'Why would you do a crazy thing like that?' She loves him.

'I'm not saying I did anything. How would I know Nelson was getting married at that moment?'

'You saw it in the papers.' He sees she means to torment him. 'Ruth, the girl. She's mine. She's the baby you said you couldn't stand to have the abortion for. So you had it and then found this old chump of a farmer who was glad to get a piece of young ass and had these other two kids by him before he kicked the bucket.'

'Don't be so rude. You're not proving anything to me except what a sad case I must have been ever to take you in. You are Mr Bad News, honest to God. You're nothing but me, me and gimme, gimme. When I *had* something to give you I gave it even though I knew I'd never get anything back. Now thank God I have nothing to give.' She limply gestures to indicate the raggedly furnished little room. Her voice in these years has gained that country slowness, that stubborn calm with which the country withholds what the city wants.

'Tell me the truth,' he begs.

'I just did.'

'About the girl.'

'She's younger than the older boy. Scott, Annabelle, and then Morris in '66. He was the afterthought. June 6, 1966. Four sixes.'

'Don't stall, Ruth, I got to get back to Brewer. And don't lie. Your eyes get all watery when you lie.'

'My eyes are watery because they can't stand looking at you. A regular Brewer sharpie. A dealer. The kind of person you used to hate, remember? And fat. At least when I knew you you had a body.'

He laughs, enjoying the push of this; his night with Thelma has made his body harder to insult. '*You*,' he says, 'are calling *me* fat?'

'I am. And how did you get so red in the face?'

'That's my tan. We just got back from the islands.'

'Oh Christ, the islands. I thought you were about to have a stroke.'

'When did your old guy pack it in? Whajja do, screw him to death?'

She stares at him a time. 'You better go.'

'Soon,' he promises.

'Frank passed away in August of '76, of cancer. Of the colon. He hadn't even reached retirement age. When I met him he was younger than we are now.'

'O.K., sorry. Listen, stop making me be such a prick. Tell me about our girl.'

'She's *not* our girl, Harry. I *did* have the abortion. My parents arranged it with a doctor in Pottsville. He did it right in his office and about a year later a girl died afterwards of complications and they put him in jail. Now the girls just walk into the hospital.'

'And expect the taxpayer to pay,' Harry says.

'Then I got a job as the day cook in a restaurant over toward Stogey's Quarry to the east of here and Frank's cousin was the hostess for that time and one thing led to another pretty fast. We had Scott in late 1960, he just turned nineteen last month, one of these Christmas babies that always get cheated on presents.'

'Then the girl when? Annabelle.'

'The next year. He was in a hurry for a family. His mother had never let him marry while she was alive, or anyway he blamed her.'

'You're lying. I've seen the girl; she's older than you say.'

'She's eighteen. Do you want to see birth certificates?'

This must be a bluff. But he says, 'No.'

Her voice softens. 'Why're you so hepped on the girl anyway? Why don't you pretend the boy's yours?'

'I have one boy. He's enough' – the phrase just comes – 'bad news.' He asks, brusquely, 'And where *are* they? Your boys.'

'What's it to you?'

'Nothing much. I was just wondering how come they're not around, helping you with this place.'

'Morris is at school, he gets home on the bus after three. Scott has a job in Maryland, working in a plant nursery. I told both him and Annie, Get out. This was a good place for me to come to and hide, but there's nothing here for young people. When she and Jamie Nunemacher got this scheme of going and living together in Brewer, I couldn't say No, though his people were dead set against it. We had a big conference, I told them that's how young people do now, they live together, and aren't they smart? They know I'm an old whore anyway, I don't give a fuck what they think. The neighbors always let us alone and we let them alone. Frank and old Blankenbiller hadn't talked for fifteen years, since he began to take me out.' She sees she has wandered, and says, 'Annabelle won't be with the boy forever. He's nice enough, but ...'

'I agree,' Rabbit says, as if consulted. Ruth is lonely, he sees, and willing to talk, and this makes him uneasy. He shifts his weight on the old black sofa. Its springs creak. A shift in the air outside has created a downdraft that sends smoke from the damp fire curling into the room.

She glances to the dead couple in their frames like carved coffins above his head and confides, 'Even when Frank was healthy, he had to have the buses to make ends meet. Now I rent the big fields and just try to keep the bushes down. The bushes and the oil bills.' And it is true, this room is so cold he has not thought of taking his heavy coat off.

'Yes well,' he sighs. 'It's hard.' Fritzie, wakened by some turn in the dream that had been twitching the ends of her paws, stands and skulks over to him as if to bark, and instead drops down to the rug again, coiling herself trustfully at his feet. With his long arm he reaches to the bookcase and lifts out the photograph of the daughter. Ruth does not protest. He studies the pale illumined face in its frame of maroon cardboard: backed by a strange background of streaked blue like an imitation sky, the girl gazes beyond him. Round and polished like a fruit by the slick silk finish of the print, the head, instead of revealing its secret, becomes more enigmatic, a shape as strange as those forms of sea life spotlit beneath the casino boardwalk. The mouth is Ruth's, that upper lip he noticed at the lot. And around the eyes, that squared-off look, though her brow is rounder than Ruth's and her hair, brushed to a photogenic gloss, less stubborn. He looks at the ear, for a nick in the edge like Nelson has, her hair would have to be lifted. Her nose is so delicate and small, the nostrils displayed by a slight upturn of the tip, that the lower half of her face seems heavy, still babyish. There is a candor to her skin and a frosty light to the eyes that could go back to those Swedes in their world of snow, that he glimpsed in the Murketts' bathroom mirror. His blood. Harry finds himself reliving with Annabelle that moment when her turn came in the unruly school line to enter the curtained corner of the gym and, suddenly blinded, to pose for posterity, for the yearbook, for boyfriend and mother, for time itself as it wheels on unheeding by: the opportunity come to press your face up against blankness and, by thinking right thoughts, to become a star. 'She looks like me.'

Ruth laughs now. 'You're seeing things.'

'No kidding. When she came to the lot that first time, something hit me – her legs, maybe, I don't know. Those aren't your legs.' Which had been thick, twisting like white flame as she moved naked about their room.

'Well, Frank had legs too. Until he let himself get out of shape, he was on the lanky side. Over six foot, when he straightened up. I'm a sucker for the big ones I guess. Then neither of the boys inherited his height.'

'Yeah, Nelson didn't get mine, either. A shrimp just like his mother.'

'You're still with Janice. You used to call her a mutt,' Ruth reminds him. She has settled into this situation comfortably now, leaning back in the rocker and rocking, her stocking feet going up on tiptoe, then down on the heels, then back on tiptoe. 'Why am I telling you all about my life when you don't say a thing about yours?'

'It's pretty standard,' he says. 'Don't be sore at me because I stayed with Janice.'

'Oh Christ no. I just feel sorry for her.'

'A sister,' he says, smiling.

Fat has been added to Ruth's face not in smooth scoops but in lumps, so when she lifts her head there is a scalloped look, as of extra bone. A certain mischief has lifted it. 'Annie was fascinated by you,' she volunteers. 'She several times asked me if I'd ever heard of you, this basketball hero. I said we went to different high schools. She was disappointed when you weren't there when she and Jamie went back to pick up the car finally. Jamie had been leaning to a Fiesta.'

'So you don't think Jamie is the answer for her?'

'For now. But you've seen him. He's common.'

'I hope she doesn't –'

'Go my way? No, it'll be all right. There aren't whores anymore, just healthy young women. I've raised her very innocent. I always felt *I* was very innocent, actually.'

'We all are, Ruth.'

She likes his saying her name, he should be careful about saying it. He puts the photograph back and studies it in place, Annabelle between her brothers. 'How about money?' he asks, trying to keep it light. 'Would some help her? I could give it to you so it, you know, wouldn't come out of the blue or anything. If she wants an education, for instance.' He is blushing, and Ruth's silence doesn't help. The rocker has stopped rocking.

At last she says, 'I guess this is what they call deferred payments.'

'It's not for you, it would be for her. I can't give a lot. I mean, I'm not that rich. But if a couple thousand would make a difference –'

He lets the sentence hang, expecting to be interrupted. He can't look at her, that strange expanded face. Her voice when it comes has that contemptuous confident huskiness he heard from her ages ago, in bed. 'Relax. You don't have to worry, I'm not going to take you up on it. If I ever get really hard up here I can sell off a piece of road frontage, five thousand an acre is what they've been getting locally. Anyway, Rabbit. Believe me. She's not yours.'

'O.K. If you say so.' In his surge of relief he stands.

She stands too, and having risen together their ghosts feel their inflated flesh fall away; the young man and woman who lived one flight up on Summer Street, across from a big limestone church, stand close again, sequestered from the world, and as before the room is hers. 'Listen,' she hisses up at him, radiantly is his impression, her distorted face gleaming. 'I wouldn't give you the satisfaction of that girl being yours if there was a million dollars at stake. I raised her. She and I put in a lot of time together here and where the fuck were you? You saw me in Kroll's that time and there was no follow-up, I've known where you were all these years and you didn't give a simple shit what had happened to me, or my kid, or *any*thing.'

'You were married,' he says mildly. *My kid*: something odd here.

'You bet I was,' she rushes on. 'To a better man than you'll ever be, sneer all you want. The kids have had a wonderful father and they know it. When he died we just carried on as if he was still around, he was that strong. Now I don't know what the hell is going on with you in your little life up there in Mt Judge –'

'We're moving,' he tells her. 'To Penn Park.'

'Swell. That's just where you belong, with those phonies. You should have left that mutt of yours twenty years ago for her good as well as your own, but you didn't and now you can stew in it; stew in it but *leave my Annie alone*. It's *creepy*, Harry. When I think of you thinking she's your daughter it's like rubbing her all over with shit.'

He sighs through his nose. 'You still have a sweet tongue,' he says.

She is embarrassed; her iron hair has gone straggly and she presses it flat with the heels of her hands as if trying to crush something inside her skull. 'I shouldn't say something like that but it's *fright*ening, having you show up in your fancy clothes wanting to claim my daughter. You make me think, if I hadn't had the abortion, if I hadn't let my parents have their way, it might have all worked out differently, and we could *have* a daughter now. But you –'

'I know. You did the right thing.' He feels her fighting the impulse to touch him, to cling to him, to let herself be crushed into his clumsy arms as once. He looks for a last topic. Awkwardly he asks, 'What're you going to do, when Morris grows up and leaves home?' He remembers his hat and picks it up, pinching the soft new crown in three fingers.

'I don't know. Hang on a little more. Whatever happens, land won't go down. Every year I last it out here is money in the bank.'

He sighs through his nose again. 'O.K., Ruth, if that's how it is. I'll run then. Really no soap on the girl?'

'Of course not. Think it through. Suppose she *was* yours. At this stage it'd just confuse her.'

He blinks. Is this an admission? He says, 'I never was too good at thinking things through.'

Ruth smiles at the floor. The squarish dent above her cheek-bone, seen this way from above, was one of the first things he noticed about her. Chunky and tough but kindly, somehow. Another human heart, telling him he was a big bunny, out by the parking meters in the neon light, the first time they met. Trains still ran through the center of Brewer then. 'Men don't have to be,' she says.

The dog became agitated when they both stood and Ruth's voice became louder and angry, and now Fritzie leads them from the room and waits, tail inquisitively wagging, with her nose at the crack of the door leading outside. Ruth opens it and the storm door wide enough for the dog to pass through but not Harry. 'Want a cup of coffee?' she asks.

He told Janice one o'clock at Schaechner's. 'Oh Jesus, thanks, but I ought to get back to work.'

'You came here just about Annabelle? You don't want to hear about me?'

'I *have* heard about you, haven't I?'

'Whether I have a boyfriend or not, whether I ever thought about you?'

'Yeah, well, I'm sure that'd be interesting. From the sound of it you've done terrifically. Frank and Morris and, who's the other one?'

'Scott.'

'Right. And you have all this land. Sorry, you know, to have left you in such a mess way back then.'

'Well,' Ruth says, with a considering slowness in which he imagines he can hear her late husband speaking. 'I guess we make our own messes.'

She seems now not merely fat and gray but baffled: straw on her sweater, hair on her cheeks. A shaggy monster, lonely. He longs to be out that double door into the winter air, where nothing is growing. Once he escaped by telling her, *I'll be right back*, but now there is not even that to say. Both know, what people should never know, that they will not meet again. He notices on the hand of hers that grips the doorknob a thin gold ring all but lost in the flesh of one finger. His heart races, trapped.

She has mercy on him. 'Take care, Rabbit,' she says. 'I was just kidding about the outfit, you look good.' Harry ducks his head as if to kiss her cheek but she says, 'No.' By the time he has taken a step off the concrete porch, her shadow has vanished from the double door's black glass. The gray of the day has intensified, releasing a few dry flakes of snow that will not amount to anything, that float sideways like flecks of ash. Fritzie trots beside him to the glossy grape-blue Celica, and has to be discouraged from jumping into the back seat.

Once on his way, out the driveway and past the mailboxes that say BLANKENBILLER and MUTH, Harry pops a Life Saver into his mouth and wonders if he should have called her bluff on the birth certificates. Or suppose Frank had had another wife, and Scott was his child by that marriage? If the girl was as young as Ruth said, wouldn't she still be in high school? But no. Let go. God has never wanted him to have a daughter.

Waiting in the overheated front room of Schaechner's surrounded by plush new furniture, Janice looks petite and prosperous and, with her Caribbean tan, younger than forty-four. When he kisses her, on the lips, she say, 'Mmm. Clove. What are you hiding?'

'Onions for lunch.'

She dips her nose close to his lapel. 'You smell of smoke.'

'Uh, Manny gave me a cigar.'

She hardly listens to his lies, she is breathy and electric with news of her own. 'Harry, Melanie called Mother from Ohio. Nelson is with her. Everything's all right.'

As Janice continues, he can see her mouth move, her bangs tremble, her eyes widen and narrow, and her fingers tug in excitement at the pearl strand the lapels of her coat disclose, but Rabbit is distracted from the exact sense of what she is saying by remembering, when he bent his face close to old Ruth's in the light of the door, a glitter there, on the tired skin beneath her eyes, and by the idiotic thought, which it seems he should bottle and sell, that our tears are always young, the saltwater stays the same from cradle, as she said, to grave.

The little stone house that Harry and Janice bought for $78,000, with $15,600 down, sits on a quarter-acre of bushy land tucked in off a macadamized dead end behind two larger examples of what is locally known as Penn Park Pretentious: a tall mock-Tudor with gables like spires and red-tiled roofs and clinker bricks sticking out at crazy melted angles, and a sort of neo-plantation manse of serene thin bricks the pale yellow of lemon-ade, with a glassed-in sunporch and on the other side a row of Palladian windows, where Harry guesses the dining room is. He has been out surveying his property, looking for a sunny patch where a garden might be dug in this spring. The spot behind Ma Springer's house on Joseph Street had been too shady. He finds a corner that might do, with some cutting back of oak limbs that belong to his neighbor. The earth generally in this overgrown, mature suburb is well-shaded; his lawn is half moss, which this mild winter has dried but left exposed and resilient still. He also finds a little cement fish pond with a blue-painted bottom, dry and drifted with pine needles. Someone had once sunk seashells in the wet cement of the slanting rim. The things you buy when you buy a house. Doorknobs, windowsills, radiators. All his. If he were a fish he could swim in this pond, come spring. He tries to picture that moment when whoever it was, man, woman, or child or all three, had set these shells here, in the summer shade of trees a little less tall than these above him now. The weak winter light falls everywhere in his yard, webbed by the shadows from leafless twigs. He senses standing here a silt of caring that has fallen from purchaser to purchaser. The house was built in that depressed but scrupulous decade when Harry was born. Suave gray limestone had been hauled from the quarries in the far north of Diamond County and dressed and fitted by men who took the time to do it right. At a later date, after the war, some owner broke through the wall facing away from the curb and built an addition of clapboards and white-blotched brick. Paint is peeling from the clapboards beneath the Andersen windows of what is now Janice's kitchen. Harry makes a mental note to trim back the branches that brush against the house, to cut down the dampness. Indeed there are several trees here that might be turned altogether into firewood, but until they leaf out in the spring he can't be sure which should go. The house has two fireplaces, one in the big long living room and the other, off the same flue, in the little room behind, that Harry thinks of as a den. His den.

He and Janice moved in yesterday, a Saturday. Pru was coming home from the hospital with the baby and if they were not there she could take the bedroom with its own bathroom, away from the street. Also they thought the confusion might mask for Janice's mother the pain of their escape. Webb Murkett and the others got back from the Caribbean Thursday night as planned, and Saturday morning Webb brought one of his roofer's trucks with extension ladders roped to both sides and helped them move. Ronnie Harrison, that fink, said he had to go into the office to tackle the backlog of paperwork that had built up during his vacation, he had worked Friday night to ten o'clock; but Buddy Inglefinger came over with Webb, and it didn't take the three men more than two hours to move the Angstroms. There wasn't much furniture they could call their own, mostly clothes, and Janice's mahogany bureau, and some cardboard boxes of kitchen equipment that had been salvaged when the previous house they could call their own had burned down in 1969. All of Nelson's stuff, they left. One of the butch women came out onto her porch and waved goodbye; so news travels in a neighborhood, even when the people aren't friendly. Harry had always meant to ask them what it was like, and why. He can see not liking men, he doesn't like them much himself, but why would you like women any better, if you were one? Especially women who hammer all the time, just like men.

From Schaechner's on Thursday afternoon he and Janice had bought, and got them to deliver on Friday, a new color Sony TV (Rabbit hates to put any more money into Japanese pockets but he knows from the *Consumer Reports* that in this particular line they can't be touched for quality) and a pair of big padded silvery-pink wing chairs (he has always wanted a wing chair, he hates drafts on his neck, people have died from drafts on their necks) and a Queen-size mattress and box springs on a metal frame, without headboard. This bed he and Webb and Buddy carry upstairs to the room at the back, with a partially slanted ceiling but space for a mirror if they want it on the blank wall next to the closet door, and the chairs and TV go not into the living room, which is too big to think about furnishing at first, but into the much cozier room just off it, the den. Always he has wanted a den, a room where people would have trouble getting at him. What he especially loves about this little room, besides the fireplace and the built-in shelves where you could keep either books or Ma's knickknacks and china when she dies, with liquor in the cabinets below, and even room for a little refrigerator when they get around to it, are the wall-to-wall carpeting of a kind of green-and-orange mix that reminds him of cheerleaders' tassels and the little high windows whose sashes crank open and shut and are composed of leaded lozenge-panes such as you see in books of fairy tales. He thinks in this room he might begin to read books, instead of just magazines and newspapers, and begin to learn about history, say. You have to step down into the den, one step down from the hardwood floor of the living room, and this small difference in plane hints to him of many reforms and consolidations now possible in his life, like new shoots on a tree cropped back.

Franklin Drive is the elegant street their dead-end spur cuts off of; 14½ Franklin Drive is their postal address, and the spur itself has no street name, they should call it Angstrom Way. Webb suggested Angstrom Alley, but Harry has had enough of alleys in his Mt Judge years, and resents Webb's saying this. First he tells you to sell gold too soon, then he fucks your wife, and now he puts your house down. Harry has never lived at so low a number as 14½ before. He grew up with Pop and Mom and Mim at 303 Jackson Road; the Bolgers had 301, the corner house with the light. The apartment on Wilbur Street, he can barely remember, was a high number, way up the hill, 447, Apt #5, on the third floor. The ranch house in Penn Villas was 26 Vista Crescent, Ma Springer's was 89 Joseph. Though 14½ is a good stiff chip in from Franklin Drive, the mailman in his little red, white, and blue jeep knows where they are. Already they've received mail here: flyers to RESIDENT collected while they were in the Caribbean, and Saturday around one-thirty, after Webb and Buddy were gone, while Janice and Harry were arranging spoons and pans they'd forgotten they owned in the kitchen, the letter slot clacked and a postcard and a white envelope lay on the front hall's bare floor. The envelope, one of the long plain stamped ones you buy at the post office, had no return address and was postmarked Brewer. It was addressed to just MR HARRY ANGSTROM in the same slanting block printing that had sent him last April the clipping about Skeeter. Inside this new envelope the clipping was very small, and the same precise hand that had addressed it had inscribed in ballpoint along the top edge, FROM '*Golf Magazine*' *Annual 'Roundup.'* The item read:

## A COSTLY BIRDIE

Dr Sherman Thomas cooked his own goose when he killed one of the Canadian variety at Congressional C C. The court levied a $500 fine for the act.

Janice forced a laugh, reading at his side, there in the echoing bare hallway, that led through a white arch into the long living room.

He looked over at her guiltily and agreed with her unspoken thought. 'Thelma.'

Her color had risen. A minute before, they had been in sentimental raptures over an old Mixmaster that, plugged in again after ten years in Ma Springer's attic, had whirred. Now she blurted, 'She'll never let us alone. Never.'

'Thelma? Of course she will, that was the deal. She was very definite about it. Weren't you, with Webb?'

'Oh of course, but words don't mean anything to a woman in love.'

'Who? You with Webb?'

'No, you goon. Thelma. With you.'

'She told me, she loves Ronnie. Though I don't see how she can.'

'He's her bread and butter. You're her dream man. You really turn her on.'

'You sound amazed,' he said accusingly.

'Oh, you don't *not* turn me on, I can see what she sees, it's just ...' She turned away to hide her tears. Everywhere he looked, women were crying. '... the in*tru*sion. To know that that was her that sent that other thing way back then, to think of her watching us all the time, waiting to pounce ... They're evil people, Harry. I don't want to see any of them anymore.'

'Oh come on.' He had to hug her, there in the hollow hall. He likes it now when she gets all flustered and frowny, her breath hot and somehow narrow with grief; she seems most his then, the

418

keystone of his wealth. Once when she got like this, her fear contaminated him and he ran; but in these middle years it is so clear to him that he will never run that he can laugh at her, his stubborn prize. 'They're just like us. That was a holiday. In real life they're very square.'

Janice was vehement. 'I'm *furious* with her, doing such a flirtatious thing, so soon after. They'll never let us alone, never, now that we have a house. As long as we were at Mother's we were protected.'

And it was true, the Harrisons and the Murketts and Buddy Inglefinger and the tall new girlfriend with her frizzy hair now up in corn rows and juju beads did come over last night, the Angstroms' first night in their new house, bearing bottles of champagne and brandy, and stayed until two, so Sunday feels sour and guilty. Harry has no habits yet in this house; without habits and Ma's old furniture to cushion him, his life stretches emptily on all sides, and it seems that moving in any direction he's bound to take a fall.

The other piece of mail that came Saturday, the postcard, was from Nelson.

> Hi Mom & Dad –
> Spring Semester begins the 28th so am in good shape. Need certified check for $1087 (397 instrucional fee, 90 general fee, 600 surcharge for non Ohio students) plus living expenses. $2000–2500 shd. be enuff.
> Will call when you have phone.
> Melanie says Hi. Love, Nelson

On the other side of the card was a modern brick building topped by big slatted things like hot air vents, identified as *Business Administration Building, Kent State University*. Harry asked, 'What about Pru? The kid's a father and doesn't seem to know it.'

'He knows it. He just can't do everything at once. He's told Pru over the phone he'll drive back as soon as he's registered and look at the baby and leave us the car he took. Though maybe, Harry, we could just let him use it for now.'

'That's *my* Corona!'

419

'He's doing what you wanted him to do, go back to college. Pru understands.'

'She understands she's linked up with a hopeless loser,' Harry said, but his heart wasn't in it. The kid was no threat to him for now. Harry was king of the castle.

And today is Super Sunday. Janice tries to get him up for church, she is driving Mother, but he is far too hungover and wants to return to the warm pocket of a dream he had been having, a dream involving a girl, a young woman, he has never met before, with darkish hair, they have met somehow at a party and are in a little bathroom together, not speaking but with a rapport, as if just having had sex or about to have sex, between them, sex very certain and casual between them but not exactly happening, the floor of many small square tiles at an angle beneath them, the small space of the bathroom cupped around them like the little chrome bowl around the flame of the perpetual cigar lighter at the old tobacco store downtown, the bliss of a new relationship, he wants it to go on and on but is awake and can't get back. This bedroom, its bright slanted ceiling, is strange. They must get curtains soon. Is Janice up to this? Poor mutt, she's never had to do much. He makes what breakfast he can of a single orange in the nearly empty refrigerator, plus some salted nuts left over from the party last night, plus a cup of instant coffee dissolved with hot water straight from the tap. This house too, like Webb's, has those single-lever faucets shaped like a slender prick stung on the tip by a bee. The refrigerator went with the place and, one of the things that sold him, has an automatic ice-maker that turns out crescent-shaped cubes by the bushel. Even though the old Mixmaster works he hasn't forgotten his promise to Janice to buy her a Cuisinart. Maybe the trouble she has getting meals on the table related to its being Ma Springer's old-fashioned kitchen. He roams through his house warily exulting in the cast-iron radiators, the brass window catches, the classy little octagonal bathroom tiles, and the doors with key-lock knobs; these details of what he has bought shine out in the absence of furniture and will soon sink from view as the days here clutter them over. Now they are naked and pristine.

Upstairs, in a slanting closet off of what once must have been a boys' bedroom — its walls pricked with dozens of thumbtack holes and marred with ends of Scotch tape used to hold posters — he finds stacks of *Playboys* and *Penthouses* from the early Seventies. He fetches from out beside the kitchen steps, under the slowly revolving electric meter, one of the big green plastic trash barrels he and Janice bought yesterday at Shur Valu; but before disposing of each magazine Rabbit leafs through it, searching out the center spreads month after month, year after year, as the airbrushing recedes and the pubic hair first peeks and then froths boldly forth and these young women perfect as automobile bodies let their negligees fall open frontally and revolve upon their couches of leopard skin so subscribers' eyes at last can feast upon their full shame and treasure. An invisible force month after month through each year's seasons forces gently wider open their flawless thighs until somewhere around the bicentennial issues the Constitutional triumph of open beaver is attained, and the girls from Texas and Hawaii and South Dakota yield up to the lights and lens a vertical red aperture that seems to stare back, apart from the eyes' gaze, out of a blood-flushed nether world, scarcely pretty, an ultimate which yet acts as a barrier to some secret beyond, within, still undisclosed as the winter light alters at the silent window. Outside, a squirrel is watching him, its gray back arched, its black eye alert. Nature, Harry sees, is everywhere. This tree that comes so close to the house he thinks is a cherry, its bark in rings. The squirrel, itself spied, scurries on. The full load of magazines makes the trash barrel almost too heavy to lift. He lugs it downstairs. Janice comes back after two, having had lunch with her mother and Pru and the baby.

'Everybody seemed cheerful,' she reports, 'including Baby.'

'Baby have a name yet?'

'Pru asked Nelson about Rebecca and he said absolutely not. Now she's thinking of Judith. That's her mother's name. I told them to forget Janice, I never much liked it for myself.'

'I thought she hated her mother.'

'She doesn't hate her, she doesn't much respect her. It's her father she hates. But he's been on the phone to her a couple of times and been very, what's the word, conciliatory.'

'Oh great. Maybe he can come and help run the lot. He can do our steam fitting. How does Pru feel about Nelson's running off, just on the eve?'

Janice takes off her hat, a fuzzy violet loose-knit beret she wears in winter and that makes her look with the sheepskin coat like some brown-faced boy of a little soldier off to the wars. Her hair stands up with static electricity. In the empty living room she has nowhere to drop her hat, and throws it onto a white windowsill. 'Well,' she says, 'she's interesting about it. For just now she says she's just as glad he isn't around, it would be one more thing to cope with. In general she feels it's something he had to do, to get his shit together – that's her expression. I think she knows she pushed him. Once he gets his degree, she thinks, he'll be much more comfortable with himself. She doesn't seem at all worried about losing him for good or anything.'

'Huh. Whaddeya have to do to get blamed for something these days?'

'They're very tolerant of each other,' Janice says, 'and I think that's nice.' She heads upstairs, and Harry follows her up, closely, afraid of losing her in the vast newness of their house.

He asks, 'She gonna go out there and live with him in an apartment or what?'

'She thinks her going out there with the baby would panic him right now. And of course for Mother it'd be much nicer if she stayed.'

'Isn't Pru at all miffed about Melanie?'

'No, she says Melanie will watch after him for her. They don't have this jealousy thing the way we do, if you can believe them.'

'If.'

'Speaking of which.' Janice drops her coat on the bed and bends over, ass high, to unzip her boots. 'Thelma had left a message with Mother about whether or not you and I wanted to come over to their house for a light supper and watch the Super Bowl. I guess the Murketts will be there.'

'And you said?'

'I said No. Don't worry, I was quite sweet. I said we were having Mother and Pru over here to watch the game on our brand-new Sony. It's true. I invited them.' In stocking feet she stands and puts her hands on the hips of her black church suit as if daring him to admit he would rather go out and be with that crummy crowd than stay home with his family.

'Fine,' he says. 'I haven't really seen –'

'Oh, and quite a sad thing. Mother got it from Grace Stuhl, who's good friends apparently with Peggy Fosnacht's aunt. While we were down there Peggy went into her doctor's for a check-up and by nighttime he had her in the hospital and a breast taken off.'

'My God.' Breast he had sucked. Poor old Peggy. Flicked away by God's fingernail with its big moon. Life is too big for us, in the end.

'They of course said they got it all but then they always say that.'

'She seemed lately headed for something unfortunate.'

'She's been grotesque. I should call her, but not today.'

Janice is changing into dungarees to do housecleaning. She says the people have left the place filthy but he can't see it, except for the *Playboys*. She has never been much of a neatness freak wherever they have lived before. Uncurtained winter light bouncing off the bare floors and blank walls turns her underwear to silver and gives her shoulders and arms a quick life as of darting fish before they disappear into an old shirt of his and a motheaten sweater. Behind her their new bed, unmade, hasn't been fucked on yet, they were too drunk and exhausted last night. In fact they haven't since that night on the island. He asks her irritably what about *his* lunch.

Janice asks, 'Oh, didn't you find something in the fridge?'

'There was one orange. I ate it for breakfast.'

'I know I bought eggs and sliced ham but I guess Buddy and what's-her-name –'

'Valerie.'

'Wasn't her hair wild? do you think she takes drugs? – ate it all up in that omelette they made after midnight. Isn't that a sign of drugs, an abnormal appetite for food? I know there's some cheese left, Harry. Couldn't you make do with cheese and crackers until I go out and buy something for Mother later? I don't know what's open Sundays around here, I can't keep running back to the Mt Judge Superette and using up gas.'

'No,' he agrees, and makes do with cheese and crackers and a

Schlitz that is left over from the three sixpacks Ronnie and Thelma brought over. Webb and Cindy brought the brandy and champagne. All afternoon he helps Janice clean, Windexing windows and wiping woodwork while she mops floors and even scours the kitchen and bathroom sinks. They have a downstairs bathroom here but he doesn't know where to buy toilet paper printed with comic strips. Janice has brought her mother's waxing machine in the Maverick along with some Butcher's paste and he wipes the wax on the long blond living-room floor, each whorl of wood grain and slightly popped-up nail and old scuff of a rubber heel his, his house. As he lays the wax on with circular swipes Rabbit keeps chasing the same few thoughts in his brain, stupid as brains are when you do physical work. Last night he kept wondering if the other two couples had gone ahead and swapped, Ronnie and Cindy doing it the second time, after he and Janice had left and they did act cozy, as if the four of them made the innermost circle of the party and the Angstroms and poor Buddy and that hungry Valerie were second echelon or third worlders somehow. Thelma got pretty drunk for her, her sallow skin gleaming to remind him of Vaseline, though when he thanked her for sending the clipping about the goose she stared at him and then sideways at Ronnie and then back at him as if he had rocks in his head. He guesses it'll all come out, what happened down there afterwards, people can't keep a good secret, but it pains him to think that Thelma would let Webb do to her everything the two of them did or that Cindy really wanted to go with Ronnie again and would lift up her heavy breast with a motherly hand so that loudmouthed jerk could suck and tell about it, with his scalp bare like that he's such a baby, Harrison. No point in keeping secrets, we'll all be dead soon enough, already we're survivors, the kids are everywhere, making the music, giving the news. Ever since that encounter with Ruth he's felt amputated, a whole world half-seen in the corner of his eye snuffed out. Janice and the waxing machine are whining and knocking behind him and the way his brain is going on reminds him of some article he read last year in the paper or *Time* about some professor at Princeton's theory that in ancient times the gods spoke to people directly through the left or was it the right half of their brains, they were like robots with

424

radios in their heads telling them everything to do, and then somehow around the time of the ancient Greeks or Assyrians the system broke up, the batteries too weak to hear the orders, though there are glimmers still and that is why we go to church, and what with all these jigaboos and fags roller-skating around with transistorized earmuffs on their heads we're getting back to it. How at night just before drifting off he hears Mom's voice clear as a whisper from the corner of the room saying *Hassy*, a name as dead as the boy that was called that is dead. Maybe the dead are gods, there's certainly something kind about them, the way they give you room. What you lose as you age is witnesses, the ones that watched from early on and cared, like your own little grandstand. Mom, Pop, old man Springer, baby Becky, good old Jill (maybe that dream had to do with the time he took her in so suddenly, except her hair wasn't dark, it was so intense, the dream, there's nothing like a new relationship), Skeeter, Mr Abendroth, Frank Byer, Mamie Eisenhower just recently, John Wayne, LBJ, JFK, Skylab, the goose. With Charlie's mother and Peggy Fosnacht cooking. And his daughter Annabelle Byer snuffed out with her whole world he was watching in the corner of his eye like those entire planets obliterated in *Star Wars*. The more dead you know it seems the more living there are you don't know. Ruth's tears, when he was leaving: maybe God is in the universe the way salt is in the ocean, giving it a taste. He could never understand why people can't drink saltwater, it can't be any worse than mixing Coke and potato chips.

Behind him he hears Janice knocking her waxer clumsily against the baseboards at every sweep and it comes to him why they're being so busy, they're trying not to panic here in this house, where they shouldn't be at all, so far from Joseph Street. Lost in space. Like what souls must feel when they awaken in a baby's body so far from Heaven: not only scared so they cry but guilty, guilty. A huge hole to fill up. The money it'll take to fill these rooms with furniture when they had it all free before: he's ruined himself. And the mortgage payments: $62,400 at 13½ per cent comes to nearly $8500 interest alone, $700 a month over twenty years nibbling away at the principal until he's 66. What did Ruth say about her youngest, 6/6/66? Funny about numbers, they don't lie but do play tricks. Three score and ten, all the things he'll never get to do now: to have Cindy arrange herself in the pose of one of those *Penthouse* sluts on a leopard skin and get down in front of her on all fours and just eat and eat and eat.

Last night Buddy turned to him so drunk his silver-rimmed eyeglasses were steamed and said he knew it was crazy, he knew what people would say about her being too tall and having three children and all, but Valerie really did it for him. She is the one, Harry. With tears in his eyes he said that. The big news from over at the Flying Eagle was Doris Kaufmann's planning to get married again. To a guy Rabbit used to know slightly, Don Eberhardt, who had gotten rich buying up inner-city real estate when nobody wanted it, before the gas crunch. Life is sweet, that's what they say.

Light still lingers in the windows, along the white windowsills, at five when they finish, the days this time of year lengthening against the grain. The planets keep their courses no matter what we do. In the freshly waxed hall by the foot of the stairs he touches Janice underneath her chin where the flesh is soft but not really repulsive and suggests a little nap upstairs, but she gives him a kiss warm and competent, the competence cancelling out the warmth, and tells him, 'Oh Harry, that's a sweet idea but I have no idea when they might be coming, it's all mixed up with a lie-down Mother was going to have, she really does seem frailer, and the baby's feeding time, and I haven't even shopped yet. Isn't the Super Bowl on?'

'Not till six, it's on the West Coast. There's a pre-game thing on at four-thirty but it's all hoopla, you can only take so much. I wanted to watch the Phoenix Open at two-thirty, but you were so damn frantic to clean up just because your mother's coming over.'

'You should have said something. I could have done it myself.'

While she goes off in the Maverick he goes upstairs, because there isn't any place downstairs to lie down. He hopes to see the squirrel again, but the animal is gone. He thought squirrels hibernated, but maybe the winter is too strange. He holds his hand over a radiator, his, and with pride and satisfaction feels it breathing heat. He lies down on their new bed with the Amish quilt they

426

brought from Mt Judge and almost without transition falls asleep. In his dream he and Charlie are in trouble at the agency, some crucial papers with numbers on them are lost, and where the new cars should be in the showroom there are just ragged craters, carefully painted with stripes and stars, in the concrete floor. He awakes realizing he is running scared. There has been another explosion, muffled: Janice closing the door downstairs. It is after six. 'I had to drive out almost to the ballpark before I found this MinitMart that was open. They didn't have fresh anything of course, but I got four frozen Chinese dinners that the pictures of on the box looked good.'

'Isn't crap like that loaded with chemicals? You don't want to poison Pru's milk.'

'And I bought you lots of baloney and eggs and cheese and crackers so stop your complaining.'

The nap, that at first waking had felt as if somebody had slugged him in the face with a ball of wet clothes, begins to sink into his bones and cheer him up. Darkness has erased the staring depth of day; the windows might be black photographic plates in their frames. Thelma and Nelson are out there circling, waiting to move in. Janice bought thirty dollars' worth at the MinitMart and as she fills the bright refrigerator he sees in a corner there are two more beers that escaped the vultures last night. She even brought him a jar of salted peanuts for all of $1.29 to watch the game with. The first half sways back and forth. He is rooting for the Steelers to lose, he hates what they did to the Eagles and in any case doesn't like overdogs; he pulls for the Rams the way he does for the Afghan rebels against the Soviet military machine.

At half-time a lot of girls in colored dresses and guys that look like fags in striped jerseys dance while about a thousand pieces of California brass imitate the old Big Bands with an off-key blare; these kids try to jitterbug but they don't have the swing, that one-beat wait back on your heels and then the twirl. They do a lot of disco wiggling instead. Then some little piece of sunshine with an Andrews-sisters pageboy sings 'Sentimental Journey' but it doesn't have that Doris Day wartime Forties soul, how could it? These kids were all born, can you believe it, around 1960 at the earliest and, worse yet, are sexually mature. On the 'a-all aboard' they snake together in what is supposed to be the Chattanooga Choo-choo and then produce, out there in cloudless California, flashing sheets like tinfoil that are supposed to be solar panels. 'Energy is people,' they sing. 'People are en-er-gy!' Who needs Khomeini and his oil? Who needs Afghanistan? Fuck the Russkis. Fuck the Japs, for that matter. We'll go it alone, from sea to shining sea.

Tired of sitting in his den alone with a hundred million other boobs watching, Harry goes into the kitchen for that second beer. Janice sits at a card table her mother parted with as a loan grudgingly, even though she never plays cards except in the Poconos. 'Where are our guests?' he asks.

Janice is sitting there helping the Chinese dinners warm up in the oven and reading a copy of *House Beautiful* she must have bought at the MinitMart. 'They must have fallen asleep. They're up a good deal of the night, in a way it's a mercy we're not there any more.'

He trims his lips in upon a bitter taste in the beer. Grain gone bad. Men love their poison. 'Well I guess living in this house with just you is the way for me to lose weight. I never get fed.'

'You'll get fed,' she says, turning a slick page.

Jealous of the magazine, of the love for this house he feels growing in her, he complains, 'It's like waiting for a shoe to drop.'

She darts a dark, not quite hostile look up at him. 'I'd think you've had enough shoes drop lately to last ten years.'

From her tone he suppose she means something about Thelma but that had been far from his mind, for now.

Their guests don't arrive until early in the fourth quarter, just after Bradshaw, getting desperate, has thrown a bomb to Stallworth; receiver and defender go up together and the lucky stiff makes a circus catch. Rabbit still feels the Rams are going to win it. Janice calls that Ma and Pru are here. Ma Springer is all chattery in the front hall, taking off her mink, about the drive through Brewer, where hardly any cars were moving because she supposes of the game. She is teaching Pru to drive the Chrysler and Pru did very well once they figured out how to move the seat back: she hadn't realized what long legs Pru has. Pru, pressing a pink-wrapped bundle tight to her chest out of the cold, looks worn and thin in the face but more aligned, like a bed tugged smooth. 'We would have been here earlier but I was typing a letter to Nelson and wanted to finish,' she apologizes.

'It worries me,' Ma is going on, 'they used to say it brought bad luck to take a baby out visiting before it was baptized.'

'Oh Mother,' Janice says; she is eager to show her mother the cleaned-up house and leads her upstairs, even though the only lights are some 40-watt neo-colonial wall sconces in which the previous owners had let many of the bulbs die.

As Harry resettles himself in one of his silvery-pink wing chairs in front of the game, he can hear the old lady clumping on her painful legs directly above his head, inspecting, searching out the room where she might some day have to come and stay. He assumes Pru is with them, but the footsteps mingling on the ceiling are not that many, and Teresa comes softly down the one step into his den and deposits into his lap what he has been waiting for. Oblong cocooned little visitor, the baby shows her profile blindly in the shuddering flashes of color jerking from the Sony, the tiny stitchless seam of the closed eyelid aslant, lips bubbled forward beneath the whorled nose as if in delicate disdain, she knows she's good. You can feel in the curve of the cranium she's feminine, that shows from the first day. Through all this she has pushed to be here, in his lap, his hands, a real presence hardly weighing anything but alive. Fortune's hostage, heart's desire, a granddaughter. His. Another nail in his coffin. His.

## MORE ABOUT PENGUINS
## AND PELICANS

For further information about books available from Penguins please write to Dept EP, Penguin Books Ltd, Harmondsworth, Middlesex UB7 0DA.

*In the U.S.A.*: For a complete list of books available from Penguins in the United States write to Dept CS, Penguin Books, 625 Madison Avenue, New York, New York 10022.

*In Canada*: For a complete list of books available from Penguins in Canada write to Penguin Books Canada Ltd, 2801 John Street, Markham, Ontario, L3R 1B4.

*In Australia*: For a complete list of books available from Penguins in Australia write to the Marketing Department, Penguin Books Australia Ltd, P.O. Box 257, Ringwood, Victoria 3134.

*In New Zealand*: For a complete list of books available from Penguins in New Zealand write to the Marketing Department, Penguin Books (N.Z.) Ltd, P.O. Box 4019, Auckland 10.